3 DETECTIVES:

MURDER ON THE RAILS

3 DETECTIVES:
MURDER ON THE RAILS

Stories by
Victor L. Whitechurch
Guy Thorne
Edwin D. Torgerson

COACHWHIP PUBLICATIONS
Greenville, Ohio

3 Detectives: Murder on the Rails
© 2020 Coachwhip Publications

The Investigations of Godfrey Page published 1903-1904
  Victor L. Whitechurch (1868-1933)
Sir Jasper Buckland stories published 1916-1918.
  Guy Thorne [Cyril Arthur Edward Ranger Gull] (1875-1923)
The Mystery of the Private Car published 1933 (serial).
  Edwin Dial Torgerson (1896-1938)
No claims made on public domain material.
Cover image: Locomotive © JZ Hunt

CoachwhipBooks.com

ISBN 1-61646-490-9
ISBN-13 978-1-61646-490-5

CONTENTS

The Investigations of Godfrey Page, Railwayac

Related by His Brother-in-Law,
and Here Set Forth by
Victor L. Whitechurch

1903-1904

Godfrey Page takes the most intense interest—amounting almost to madness—in anything and everything connected with railways, and for this reason I have termed him
a "railwayac," which is a shortened form
of "railway maniac." By profession he is an
architect, but being possessed of ample
means, only works occasionally, spending
his leisure in solving railway mysteries.
—V. L. W.

THE MURDER ON THE OKEHAMPTON LINE

The solution of the murder on the Okehampton line was, at best, only partial; and yet there can be no doubt whatever that Godfrey Page penetrated the mystery as deeply as it could be penetrated and that his theory was correct; in fact, though some links in the chain of evidence were missing, there was quite sufficient to prove that my brother-in-law had fathomed the leading points.

He was not pressed into the investigation, but took it up out of sheer curiosity.

I have been dining at his house one night and he had sent out for the last edition of the evening paper. I think there was a railway strike or something of the kind going on that interested him. But however that might be, his attention was caught directly he opened the paper with the following paragraph, which he handed me to read:

"Murder on the Okehampton Line!
"A Railway Mystery.
"On the arrival of the last train from Exeter to Okehampton at the latter station last night, a gruesome discovery was made. A porter on the platform noticed a gentleman

seated in the corner of a third-class compartment and, as he made no attempt to get
out of the carriage, opened the door to wake
him, thinking he might be asleep. To his
horror he discovered that the man was dead
and a subsequent examination revealed the
fact that he had been stabbed in the heart
with some sharp instrument. There were
signs of a struggle in the carriage.

"The murdered man was dressed in a
dark blue suit with a soft felt hat, but there
was absolutely nothing on him to lead to
his identification—not a scrap of paper of
any sort.

"That robbery was not the object is
proved by the fact that some five or six
pounds in gold and silver and his watch and
chain were still on him.

"Although the police were communicated
with at once nothing further has been ascertained up to going to press. The body has
been removed to the White Hart Hotel and
there awaits identification."

"Here's a mystery if you like," said Godfrey Page.
"Let me see, the last down train arrives at Okehampton
at 10.50. It's the one that leaves Waterloo at 5.50 and
Exeter, St. David's, at 10.3. Of course the great question
is—where did he get into the train and whereabouts on
the journey was he murdered?"

"And who he was?" I added.

"Exactly. Do you know, I've half a mind to run down
tomorrow and have a look at things. Would you care to
come?"

"Well," I said, "I think I could spare the day."

"It means two days. We'll go down tomorrow morning by the 10.30 express from Paddington. I've been wanting to have a run on that train for a long time."

"But Okehampton is on the L & S. W. Railway," I ventured to suggest.

"I fancy I'm aware of that," he replied snappishly. "But I tell you I want a run on the Great Western. I've got a friend at Paddington, too, who'll give me a leg up. I'll write to him tonight. Meet me at Paddington at 10.15 under the clock."

I found him waiting for me when I arrived, holding in his hand a newspaper and a letter.

"It's all right," he said; "I've got a line of introduction to the officials at St. David's in case I want information. And there's a whole column about the case in this morning's paper. We'll read it as we go down."

He spent the rest of the time before starting in noting the name of the engine, the number of the coaches, and other details of the express, and then we found ourselves in a comfortable carriage, speeding westward.

"Now," he said, when we had read the paper, "you see, there are several new points in the case. Let's try and some them up.

"First of all, the identity of the murdered man is still unknown. Secondly, you see, the crime must have been committed between Exeter and Okehampton, because the guard of the train remembers speaking to the man at Exeter.

"It appears that the guard put his head in the window just before the train started and said: 'Where are you for, sir?' To which the man made a singular reply. He answered: 'Where does this train go to?' Upon the guards saying 'Okehampton,' he simply replied, 'All right.' Now this seems to show that he was in a train *the destination of which he didn't know.*"

"And the next point evidently touches the murderer," I said.

"Yes; I think so, too. Two men got off the train at Yeoford Junction, telling the ticket-collector that there had not been time for them to get a ticket at St. David's and paying him the fare. These two men seem to have disappeared. They couldn't have got away by train, for that was the last one at the junction that night. But it's only a seven or eight miles' walk back to Exeter, and that's probably how they've eluded search.

"Now, you see, this gives us two more points.

"First, if these two men committed the crime, they did it between Exeter and Yeoford; and, secondly, the fact of their having no tickets proves our theory correct that the murdered man was in a train that was strange to him."

"How so?"

"Because *they* didn't know where they were going either. They must have been following him. They saw him get into the Okehampton train and they got in after him."

"But the guard said he was alone when he saw him at St. David's and spoke to him."

"Very likely. But the train had not quite started. There was time for them to get in—if not in his compartment in another one. And there is such a thing as walking along the footboard of a train in motion, and getting into another compartment. I've done it lots of times.

"Now," he went on, "acting on these theories, the next question is—what made the murdered man get into the Okehampton train, and where was he before he got in? Perhaps our good friend Bradshaw will help us."

He opened it and consulted its pages carefully. "I won't say what I think yet," he remarked presently, "but

I have a sort of an idea. There's an island platform at St. David's."

"What on earth's that?"

He looked at me scornfully.

"An island platform is one between two lines, so the trains run on either side of it. But now I'm going to enjoy the run."

I scarcely saw where the enjoyment came in. He was not still on for five minutes together. And every station his head went out of the window, once or twice when we slowed down he grew impatient, but brightened up when he timed a mile in fifty-seven and three-fifths seconds. He made notes of all sorts of things and generally fidgeted during the whole journey.

"It's been a glorious run," he exclaimed as we drew up at St. David's. "One hundred and ninety-four miles without a stop, and a minute ahead of schedule time in spite of that signal against us at Taunton and the slowing down for the P.W. operations."

"What's 'P.W.'?" I asked.

"Permanent way, you ignoramus. Stop a minute. I want to speak to the driver."

He was back in a few minutes.

"Our train leaves for Okehampton at 3:25," he said. "Now, we'll just have a chat with one of the officials here to begin with."

We found our way to one of the officials, and Godfrey Page presented the letter of introduction.

"Ah, I've heard of you, Mr. Page," he said. "You unearthed that strange affair at Warchester, didn't you? Well, I see you've come down to have a look at this Okehampton mystery. Can I do anything for you?"

"Not at present," said my brother-in-law, "except to tell me if the train in which the murder took place wasn't a bit late in starting from St. David's."

"Aha," laughed the other, "we Great Western men always like to get a rise out of the South-Western you know. Yes, she *was* three or four minutes late."

"That's all I want to know. It confirms me in a little theory, though. If I find out anything further at Okehampton I shall trouble you again."

"Certainly. Anything we can do for you, please ask us. But it seems to me that it is a South-Western job, Mr. Page."

"Ah! I'm not so sure that your line isn't mixed up in it!"

Arrived at Okehampton we quickly found our way to the hotel. Godfrey Page made himself known to the detective-inspector on the premises and we were ushered by him into the room where the body of the murdered man had been taken. He lay in the bed, quiet and serene, with quite a smile upon his face.

He was a man of some five and thirty years of age, with very dark mustache and beard and a bronzed countenance which even death had not been able to stamp with pallor.

"Are there no marks about him?" asked Godfrey Page of the inspector.

"Only this," and he turned down the sheet and showed the man's right arm, on which a small dragon was tattooed in black and red.

"H'm!" said my brother-in-law, "looks as if he's been in the Far East. Only a Chinese or Japanese artist could have done that."

"Yes," said the inspector, "there was a silver dollar along with his money, too, which corroborates that."

"Were there no marks on his clothes?"

"No."

"May I look at them?"

"Here they are."

The inspector narrowly watched Godfrey Page as he turned over garment after garment until he arrived at the shirt. It was an ordinary white one, but with a nasty red stain upon it that told its own tale.

"It's no use," said the inspector, "there's no name upon it."

"By George, though, there's something else. Look, have you noticed this?"

And he pointed to a faint penciling inside the starched linen cuff.

"What is it?" asked the inspector. "Looks like a penciled note. Strange we never noticed it."

"You gentlemen don't always look everywhere. But I'll just jot that down, please. It's interesting."

And he entered the following in his notebook, a copy of what had been scrawled on the dead man's shirt cuff:

"242, E. 3. Great Marlow."

"I'll wire to Great Marlow at once," said the inspector; "it looks like a clue. It may be he's known there. It might even be the number of a street he knows, or something of that kind."

"It might be," returned Godfrey Page dryly. "I'll only detain you one moment. Was anything else found on him besides money?"

"Only this knife."

It was an ordinary, rather large, clasp knife. My brother-in-law opened it.

"The big blade's broken," he said, "and freshly done, too. Ah, and see how loose it is."

"Now, sir," said the inspector impatiently, "if you've quite finished, we'll go. I hope you won't mention what you've seen."

"Not I. And you're really going to investigate at Great Marlow?"

"Certainly!"

"Ah! Perhaps a bit of blade broken off that night lies somewhere by Great Marlow."

The inspector stared at him with astonishment.

"I've heard of you as a sort of private detective where railways are concerned," he said, "but, if you excuse my saying so, you don't seem to know much about this kind of thing."

"And perhaps you are as strangely ignorant of railways," retorted Godfrey Page, "but I don't bear you any malice. If I'm ever in a position to help you, I will."

"Now," he said to me, as we regained the street, "there's just time for us to make a little purchase, and then we'll catch the 5.12 train back to Exeter."

And, taking me into an ironmonger's shop, he bought a small screwdriver and put it in his pocket.

Arrived at Exeter we sought out the friendly C.W. official, and my brother-in-law at once began:

"I'm going to ask you for some rather curious information. We shall stay the night in Exeter, and if you can get it by tomorrow I shall be much obliged."

"What is it, Mr. Page?"

"Find out on what train the third-class coach numbered 242 was running the night before last, and where it is to be found tomorrow."

The official promised to do so.

Godfrey Page refused to say another word on the subject that night. The next morning we went to St. David's station and sought out our friend.

"Well?" asked the "railwayac."

"I've got you the information, but I don't see how it will help you. Number 242 third coach is one that at present is kept at Plymouth as a spare carriage in case there is an abnormal number of passengers for the Paddington express. The night to which you refer it ran—"

"On the 8.20 p.m. from North Road, Plymouth, arriving here at 10.3."

"How on earth did you know that? for it's quite true."

"It was only my little theory," said Page with a smile; "but go on."

"It was put on to the up-corridor express at Plymouth because some passengers, arriving by a P. and O. steamer, increased the demand for room on the train. You know, perhaps, that if we have over twenty-four P. and O. passengers we run a 'boat special,' but if not we take them by ordinary express. On this occasion only sixteen traveled to London."

"And where is number 242 now?" asked Page impatiently.

"Here."

"Here?"

"Yes. It was running back to Plymouth last night, and I took the liberty of detaining it here because you seemed interested in it."

Godfrey Page was jubilant.

"Let's go and see it at once," he said, drawing the screwdriver out of his pocket.

"What do you want that for?" asked the official.

"You'll see," was the only reply he would make.

We very soon reach the siding where the third-class carriage was standing. Page counted down to the fifth compartment and climbed in. We followed.

"Now," said he to me, "what do you see? Notice that!" And he pointed above the door. There I read as follows:

"242, E."

"All the compartments are lettered, you see," went on Page, "and K, of course is the fifth compartment from the end, commencing with A. Now look at these photographs!"

As is customary in Great Western carriages there were photographs of places of interest along the line over the seats.

"Great Scott!" I exclaimed.

"'Great Marlow!' you mean," said my brother-in-law triumphantly, for there, before me, was a photograph of that picturesque Thames town.

"Now," said Godfrey Page, "I'll give you my theory, and then we'll see if it's correct.

"A man, traveling in a train the destination of which he is seemingly ignorant of, is found murdered. Not a single scrap of paper of any kind remains upon him to prove his identity. His money being left proves that robbery of that was not an object. The two men whom we assume committed the crime were following him, and he was flying from them. He was evidently acquainted with China or Japan, and his brown face suggested a recent return from abroad.

"Let us assume that he landed at Plymouth from the P. and O. boat and took the 8.20 express to Paddington, traveling alone in this compartment. Let us further assume that he discovered that his enemies were on board the same train, having waited for his arrival in Plymouth, and further that he had in his possession some very important papers or letter that it was their object to obtain.

"He knows he is watched and in danger. First, then, he hides the paper and scribbles the key to finding it again on his wristband. Then, as the train draws up at 10.3 on the left-hand side of the island platform, here he sees another train, the Okehampton one, which ought to have been starting at that very moment, standing on the other side of the platform.

"Thinking to escape, he rushes across and takes a seat in it. But he is observed by his followers, and they do the same. Then the murder takes place, and they search in vain for the hidden paper.

"But where did he hide it?

"Behind this picture of Great Marlow," said Godfrey Page, commencing to unscrew the panel of it. "He broke the blade of his knife doing what I'm doing now."

Breathlessly we waited while the four screws were withdrawn. Then the panel was removed, and out dropped a large sheet of thin tracing paper, many times folded. We undid it carefully.

"A map," exclaimed the railway official.

"Yes, but *what* a map! Look, Tom!"

"A plan of a fortress apparently," I said.

"A plan of Port Arthur!" cried Godfrey Page.

There, sure enough, was a map of a fortress, with guns and other points marked out with care, and brief explanations in French.

"I'll tell you what," said Godfrey Page as he commenced screwing up the panel, "it's my opinion that we three had better keep this little discovery to ourselves. For depend upon it, even if we handed this over to the police, the murderers would never be discovered."

"Why not?"

"Because in all probability they are police themselves."

"Russians?"

"Exactly so. He met with a spy's fate."

"But who is this map intended for?"

"My dear fellow, our Government would have paid well for it, eh?"

On further consultation we agreed to say nothing to the police. Just before we took the train back to Paddington, Godfrey Page said to our friend the official:

"By the way, they take tickets at Reading from the passengers in the 8:20 p.m. from Plymouth? You might try and find out if three less tickets than were issued at Plymouth were collected that night?"

"All right, Mr. Page, I'll drop you a line."

On our way home my brother-in-law was much puzzled how to act. He had retained the map in his possession, and was talking of destroying it when suddenly an idea occurred to him.

"Tom," he said, "do you ever come across Colonel Sylvester now?"

"Occasionally I meet him at the club."

"Ah! Isn't he something to do with the Secret Service?"

"Yes."

"Good. Let's sound him. Ask me to meet him at your place to dinner and leave the rest to me."

A few days later the dinner came off. We three men were lazily smoking our cigars afterward when Godfrey Page exclaimed:

"Mysterious affair that at Okehampton the other night."

"Very," said the Colonel, with a quick look at him.

"I was down there a day or two afterwards."

"Indeed!"

"I made an interesting discovery."

"What?"

"I found a curious thing in a railway carriage."

"May I ask what?"

"This map," reply Godfrey Page, taking it out of his pocket.

The Colonel seized it eagerly.

"Good heavens!" he said. "Have you told anyone of this?"

"Only two besides ourselves know it."

"For goodness' sake say nothing, Mr. Page. If the Russian police knew you had that map, they'd—they'd—"

"Murder me as they did the man who brought it to England, sir?"

The Colonel was pale and trembling as he laid a hand on Godfrey Page's arm.

"Tell me," he said, "the police know nothing of this?"

"Nothing."

"What do you propose doing with it?"

"I thought you might find it more useful than I should," he said significantly.

The Colonel put it in his breast pocket with the same satisfaction. "You are a wise man, Mr. Page," he said. "I am extremely obliged to you."

"I wonder," remarked my brother-in-law a day or two later, "how the inspector got on at Great Marlow? By the way, I've had a letter from Exeter. There *were* three tickets from Plymouth to London missing at the collection at Reading!"

The Robbery on the Woodhurst Branch

"I think," said my brother-in-law, Godfrey Page, "that the little affair it was my good luck to solve on the Woodhurst branch of the South Midland line might be interesting enough for you to chronicle. Though, mind you, I don't take any great credit to myself for doing it. It was simply by chance that I happened to be near the spot at the time it was able to lay my finger on one or two points that served as clues."

"Suppose you give me the details," I said.

"All right," he replied, producing a railway map and spreading it out on the table, "I'll try to put the whole thing before you."

I have thought it best, accordingly, to tell the story in his nearly his own words as possible.

If you will take the trouble to glance at the map of the South Midland system you will see that about eighty miles from its main terminus at Silkminster there is a station called Cranfield Junction.

Cranfield itself is little more than a large village, but it possesses a weekly cattle market of no small importance which attracts the farmers and butchers from many places in the neighborhood on Mondays.

From the junction a single line of some ten miles runs to Woodhurst, a country town a fair size. About midway between Woodhurst and Cranfield Junction is a station called Stoveley, and the line is worked with two staffs—the Cranfield to Stoveley, and the Stoveley to Woodhurst. Don't you understand what I mean?

Well, you know that trains running on a single line are worked by the electric staff, or tablet. The driver in this case receives a staff at Cranfield permitting him to proceed to Stoveley, where he has to give it up. Arrived there he is not allowed to go on until a similar staff, extracted from the electrical apparatus, has been given him for the next section to Woodhurst.

Why doesn't he receive one staff for the entire journey? Because Stoveley is a "crossing" place, the line running double through the station, so that he often has to wait there till a train comes in from Woodhurst before he can go on. The idea is simple. Only one train can be on either of the two sections at the same time.

I've got an old friend living at Cranfield and I had been spending a weekend with him. I started from his house to the station on Monday morning some little time before my train left, so as to have half an hour to spare in looking round—you know my hobby—and also because I knew the station-master, a most intelligent man, who is always ready to give me any information.

On my way to the station I remember that I wanted change for a five-pound note, so I stopped into a smart little building in the village "High Street" called "Woodhurst Bank—Cranfield Branch." There was a solitary clerk behind the counter.

"Very sorry, sir," he replied when I asked him for change, "but Mr. Crane, the manager, hasn't come yet and he has the keys of the safe. I don't expect he'll be here till the next train now, though he usually isn't so late."

"Oh, then he comes by train, does he?" I remarked casually.

"Yes. He has a season-ticket between this place and Woodhurst, where he lives," replied the somewhat garrulous clerk.

I got my note changed at a shop and walked on to the station. There was plenty to see there. They've got a very neat system for indicating—but there, I'm drifting into my hobby again. Suffice it to say that I hunted up my friend the station-master and had a chat with him.

Presently he said:

"There's been a robbery on the Woodhurst branch this morning."

"A robbery?"

"Yes. I haven't heard the whole details yet, but there seems to be quite a mystery about it."

"How so?" I asked.

"The news was brought us by the 9.6 train. A gentleman, one of our season-ticket holders, appears to have lost a large sum of money while traveling between Woodhurst and Stoveley. In fact, he's the manager of the local bank here, a Mr. Crane."

"How has he lost it? Where did he miss it? What—"

"I don't know yet," interrupted the station-master. "He's stayed behind at Stoveley to investigate and the guard hadn't time to tell us all about it. I expect he'll be here by the next train, though. It's due in a few minutes. By the way, Mr. Page, you're rather well known as a revealer of railway mysteries. Would you like me to introduce you to Mr. Crane?"

"I should very much," I replied. "If I can be of any use to him I shall be delighted. I'm quite willing to put off going home till this evening—in fact, there's nothing that I would enjoy better than looking into the matter."

In due time the next train from Woodhurst arrived and there stepped out of it a short, elderly man with plenty of anger and perplexities stamped on his countenance. The station-master loss no time in introducing me to him.

"Mr. Page is a railway enthusiast who has solved several strange affairs on the line," he explained.

"I'm sure I shall be very grateful to him if he can help me to recover my money," said Mr. Crane.

"Perhaps you will allow Mr. Crane and myself to go into your office for a few minutes and talk the matter over," I suggested.

The station-master readily agreed to this and we soon found ourselves in his little private room.

"Now, Mr. Crane," I said, "can you tell me exactly what has happened?"

"Why, I've lost nearly three hundred pounds in gold, sir! *That's* what's happened."

"When did you miss it?"

"I'll tell you. I come over here from Woodhurst every day, you know. I'm a first-class season-ticket holder. On Mondays I always bring a fairly large sum in notes and gold. It's the local market day and there's no knowing how much cash some of the farmers will want to paid out in a hurry. Drivers and dealers don't always care to handle checks, they like to hear the chink of coin. The notes I always carry in a pocket-book. *They* haven't disappeared. The gold I bring in a small black handbag."

"Locked, of course?"

"Certainly. Now I'm a man of the strictest habits. Banking makes one methodical. I always try to secure a compartment to myself on Mondays and get the guard to lock me in. Then I invariably put my bag on the seat farthest from the side on which one gets in and sit in the seat next to it—the middle one—with my back to the engine. This morning I came down to the station in plenty of time and took my seat as usual. The guard, who, of course, knows me well, came up and locked both doors."

"*Both* doors?"

"Yes. I always think it's safer, you know, and I always try the doors afterwards to make sure he *has* locked them. Well, presently the train started."

"Are you sure the bag was still there?"

"Positive. Then I opened my paper and began to read. In a few minutes we entered the tunnel and, of course, I put my paper down because there were no lights in the carriage. There never are in the day trains."

"And there always ought to be," I exclaimed; "no train ought to run through a tunnel at any time without lights in the carriages. It simply means catering for crimes."

"When we got out of the tunnel," resumed Mr. Crane, "I took up my paper again." "Without noticing whether the bag was there?"

"Yes. But in less than a minute we began to slow down for Stoveley station, which is just beyond the tunnel. Then I glanced at the seat by my side which, to my horror, was empty."

"Obviously the bag was taken when the train was in the tunnel. Did you hear anything extraordinary?"

"Nothing."

"Was the window on the offside open?"

"Yes."

"Oh, that's a weak point. It would have been perfectly easy for someone outside on the footboard to put his arm in and take it. Do you always have the window open?" "No, not always."

"Now tell me exactly what happened next."

"As soon as I missed the bag I rushed to the other side and put my head out the window. The train was just coming to a standstill on the platform. When the guard stepped out I shouted to him at once and he came running up. I asked him to unlock the door, and let me out. He called to a porter to do so."

"He called to a porter?"

"Yes."

"Why didn't he unlock the door himself?"

"I'm sure I don't know. In the station-master came and I told him what had happened. We first of all search the train thoroughly, but could discover nothing."

"How about the other passengers?"

"There were only eighteen altogether. Very few travel by that early train as a rule. Of course, we've taken down their names. Most of them were local people whom I know, farmers and butchers."

"You're sure you searched the train thoroughly?"

"Certain. Then we searched the line. The station-master and a policeman and myself went back to the tunnel, looking carefully along the track, and walked right through it with lanterns. There wasn't a sign of anything. At the other end of the tunnel is a signal-box and the man assured us that no one had come out of the tunnel. He must have seen them if they had. There's only one theory."

"What is it?"

"That the bag was thrown out of the train by the thief immediately it came out of the tunnel and that someone was waiting to pick it up and make off with it. The curious point is that they were not seen, for the country is quite bare, no trees or anything, and how they could have made off I don't know. The police are searching."

"I don't agree with you at all," I said. Then I turn to the station-master and asked him for a working time-table.

"I see there was another train standing in Stoveley station when Mr. Crane's train arrived," I remarked when I had consulted the book.

"Yes," said the station-master, "a goods train that waits there for passing purposes."

"Had this train gone on when you searched the tunnel?" I asked.

"No," said Mr. Crane, "they kept it back on purpose. But tell me, what do you think?"

"I've got a glimmering of an idea," I replied, "and I'll try to help you if you like."

"I shall be most grateful."

"Then please write a line or two authorizing me to take up the case as a sort of private detective you have engaged."

He did so.

"There's only one more thing I should like to know at present," I added. "Had the bag any particular mark on it?"

"No. Only my visiting-card which was tied on the handle by a bit of string."

"Thank you," I said, "I should go to Stoveley by the next train and see what I can do. There is one little point that is struck me."

Now there were several things in this robbery that were most palpable. It was obvious that the crime was a premeditated one. The thief knew Mr. Crane's habits and that he carried this large sum of gold on Monday mornings. Therefore it was a robbery that had been carefully planned out beforehand.

The chief thing that the thief had to think of, was not so much the taking of the bag as the careful getting rid of it directly afterwards, within a minute of the train's exit from the tunnel. It would not do for him to throw it out at haphazard and go and seek for it afterwards. This would have been to have risked capture.

Again, an accomplice by the side of the line would have been too clumsy in broad daylight. All these things I carefully thought over as I journeyed to Stoveley. Arrived there I showed the station-master Mr. Crane's letter and questioned him closely as to the searching of the train.

"It couldn't have been there, sir," he said. "We looked everywhere, under the seats, on the racks, in every corner of the guard's van, even, and on the engine. Yes, we went outside and searched under the train and on the roofs of the carriages. No; it certainly wasn't there."

"Well," I said, "get a couple of powerful lanterns and we'll have another walk through the tunnel."

"That's no use," he said; "we've looked through it carefully. The bag is not there."

"Very likely not," I answered, "but I have a sort of an idea we may find something else."

So we started along the line and entered the tunnel. I searched every yard most carefully, especially on the left-hand side, the side on which the bag must have been abstracted. We had gone more than half way through when the gleam of my lantern shone upon a small bright object by the side of the rail and I stooped eagerly for it.

"I've found it!" I exclaimed triumphantly.

"What?" cried the station-master.

I handed him the thing I had picked up.

"Why, it's only a railway carriage key," he said disdainfully; "that can't have anything to do with it."

"I beg to differ from you," I said, taking back the key and putting it in my pocket, "it's more than a carriage key. It's the key to this robbery."

"How?"

"I'll explain later on. We'll go back to the station now. I want to have a look round."

Arrived in the station, I was careful to find out the exact position in which the train had stood when stopping at the platform.

"Now," I went on, "there was a goods train on the other side at the time. Tell me, was there a front brake van to it?"

"No, only the rear one."

"Good! Whereabouts was the engine standing?"

He showed me. It was, of course, at the tunnel end of the platform and the passenger train from Woodhurst had run quite past it before the latter stopped.

As I stood in the six-foot way thinking out my idea, my eye rested on a little bit of card lying, half hidden, under the rail. Judge of my great joy when on picking it up I found it was a visiting card buried the name—

MR. SAMUEL CRANE,

and that it was torn!

I knew now that my suspicions were correct.

The Stoveley station-master was so dense and the local police sergeant who was investigating the case so supercilious, that I determined to go back to Cranfield Junction by the next train and set the necessary machinery in motion there. And it was fortunate that I did so, for there I found, just arrived from Silkminster, the divisional superintendent of the line, who knew me by repute.

As soon as the station-master had introduced us I told him I did not think it was necessary for him to go on to Stoveley, and proceeded to ask him a few questions.

"First," I said, "I want to know who were the driver and fireman on the engine of the goods train that was waiting at Stoveley."

He consulted an official table.

"Driver Hall and Fireman Bryant."

"Where do they live?"

"At Silkminster."

"What's the number of their engine?"

He looked again.

"Number 218," he said.

"Tell me her work for the day."

She left Silkminster early this morning to run the goods through the Woodhurst. Then she ran back here with an empty train and has gone down the main line. This afternoon she returns to Silkminster with an express goods."

"I see. Now about Guard Franklin who worked the passenger train."

"He runs the train through to Silkminster and returns to Woodhurst this afternoon."

"Does he pass engine No. 218?"

"No."

"Tell me if you know if he is friendly with either Hall or Bryant?"

"Hall is his brother-in-law, I believe."

"Oh, that's conclusive. Now I'll tell you my little theory, and then I think you'll agree with me that our best plan will be to proceed at once to Silkminster. We might ask Mr. Crane to come with us. He'll be interested."

I laid bare my ideas of the case to the divisional superintendent, who agreed with me that my plan was well worth developing. I then left him to put the telegraph to work over certain quarters of the line and went to find Mr. Crane.

The latter was nearly distracted, having spent a most unhappy morning at the bank. He at once said he would come with us to Silkminster and presently we all three started. Before we reached our destination we caught a glimpse of engine 218 and its train, drawn up on a "refuge sighting" to allow us to run by.

We had half an hour to spare at Silkminster before Number 218 was due and we at once repaired to the engine sheds and made a few arrangements. Then we took up our positions in a dark corner so as not to arouse suspicion when the engine came in to be cleaned.

After a bit in she came, stopping over a "pit" to allow the fire to be raked out. The driver took his dinner bag and tea-can from the footplate and got off.

"He's gone to the office to 'sign off'" whispered the superintendent, "and I've given orders for him to be detained there till I come."

Meanwhile the firemen had descended and stood chatting to one of the men. We emerged from our corner and went straight up to him.

"Your name's Bryant, isn't it?" asked the superintendent.

"Yes, sir," said the man, looking at us with some surprise.

"Tell me, what were you doing when you were waiting at Stoveley this morning for the 9.8 from Woodhurst to pass you?"

The man stared.

"Nothing particular," he said.

"You didn't notice anything when the train came in?"

"I was under my engine, sir," replied the man.

"Aha," I said. "Did you go there of your own accord?"

"My driver sent me to oil up."

"Evidently *he* doesn't know anything," said the superintendent. "Now we'll go and have a look at the driver."

We found him in the office looking rather uncomfortable. He was holding his dinner bag in his hand.

The superintendent looked at him sharply.

"Your bag appears to be very heavy, my man," he said.

The driver gave a gasp.

"Allow me to feel the weight of it," went on the superintendent, stretching out his hand.

"It's no concern of yours, sir."

"I'm not so sure. Give it to me."

He seized it and opened it. There was something wrapped up in paper, and when the paper was torn away there was the glitter of golden sovereigns.

"You'd better count them, Mr. Crane," he went on, handing the bag to the delighted bank manager.

Driver Hall saw the game was up.

"I'm not the only guilty one—" he began.

"No," replied the superintendent sharply, "but the receiver is worse than the thief. And the thief is your brother-in-law, Guard Franklin. I'll wire at once to have him arrested at Woodhurst, and, meanwhile, these two gentlemen will wait on you."

And there stepped forward a couple of railway detectives, one of them holding a pair of handcuffs.

As we passed out and through the cleaning sheds we discovered the last link in the chain. In raking out the fires of Number 218 a small brass lock tumbled through the grating. The driver had thrown the black bag of Mr. Crane into the furnace after transferring the cash from it, thinking to destroy all evidence.

All came out exactly as I had anticipated. Franklin and Hall had plotted together and planned the robbery very cleverly. When the train entered the tunnel, Franklin stepped out of his van, slipped along the footboard, and put his hand in at the window of the carriage containing the bag.

The only thing he could not be quite certain about was whether he should find the window shut, in which case he would have had to unlock the door.

Prepared for such an emergency he carried his key in his hand, but accidentally dropped it. It was the fact of his not unlocking the door himself at Stoveley, but calling up a porter, that gave me the idea of looking for the key in the tunnel.

Meanwhile Driver Hall was on the lookout to receive the bag as the train rushed by him, and had sent his fireman under the engine to keep him out of the way. As the train came running in Guard Franklin held the bag out of his window on the off side, and Hall clutched at it as it passed, but in doing so the card was torn off and fell unnoticed.

Then the driver calmly put the bag in his tool chest and transferred the money when the firemen was conveniently out of sight later on in the day. Needless to say Mr. Crane was very much more relieved at the end of the day than at the beginning of it.

The Case of the "Bluebell"

My brother-in-law, Godfrey Page, frequently used to boast, in connection with his railway hobby, of the keen perception of his hearing. "You know," he would say, "that every sound of the railway interests me, from the bang of a fog-signal to the whistle of a guard.

"Sound really plays a great part in the working of the line. I don't only mean whistles and detonators and the like, but every good driver or guard can tell his where-abouts on the darkest night by the sound of his train as it rushes through the country; in tunnel, or cutting, or on embankment, he knows, intuitively, by the different succession of sounds, exactly where he is.

"Then too, there are the different sounds on different lines. No one, for example, who knows anything of the matter, could mistake the sonorous puff of the Great Northern single wheel locomotives, now, alas! vanishing from our midst, or fail to pick the shrill North London engine whistle blasts out from a dozen others. Perhaps some day I may have a little story to tell you about distinctive railway sounds."

"I should like to see you put to some test," I exclaimed, with a smile.

"I daresay you would," he replied; "but that reminds me that I am expecting to be consulted concerning some mystery of the railway this very evening."

Just then a knock came at the door and a man was shown into the room.

"Mr. Page," he asked, looking from one to the other of us inquiringly.

"I am Mr. Page," answered Godfrey, "this gentleman is my brother-in-law. Perhaps your business is not such that it may require him to leave?"

"Certainly not—if he will not let it go any further. I must introduce myself as Mr. Thomas Hall, an officer of the Inland Revenue—of the Excise Department.

"I have heard of your cleverness in railway matters, Mr. Page, and I thought you might be able to help me in a little difficulty."

"Perhaps I ought to tell you at once that I don't profess to be a detective—or even a private inquiry agent. I have merely sometimes, out of pure curiosity, attempted to fathom certain mysteries connected with the line."

"I perfectly understand. At all events, you will allow me to put my case before you?"

"Certainly. I shall be most interested. And if I can I will help you."

"Thanks. Well, the case is a very slender one and there is very little to go upon in it, merely a chance word overheard in a railway carriage."

"My dear sir, many a chance word spoken too loudly in a train has been enough to arrest the perpetrator of a crime, to bring about a divorce, or to begin a romance. But go on."

"About ten days ago I was traveling on the Underground from Praed Street to Gloucester Road. I was seated in one of those third-class carriages which have partitions running nearly, but not quite, up to the roof. We stopped a very long time at High Street, Kensington; why, I don't know."

"To change engines," remarked Godfrey Page.

"Oh, is that so? Well, I overheard two men talking in the next compartment. One said to the other: 'You don't get all our stuff in London, I know, Jim,' and the man addressed as Jim replied, with a laugh: 'You're right, old pal, it comes up on the train. But nobody knows how. That's our little secret.' I wouldn't have thought very much of it but that when the two men got out at Gloucester Road I recognized one of them, the one who by his voice was Jim, as a character that had long been under suspicion."

"Who is he?"

"The landlord of a small public house in Turner Street—off Hammersmith Road—called the 'Bluebell.' It is what is known as a 'free house' that is, one not owned by a brewer, and the landlord can get his liquor where he likes. This man's name is Rogers and we've had our eye on him for a long time, though we can't discover a thing against him."

"What do you suspect?"

"Well, he certainly seems to be selling more liquor than he gets in."

"Beer?"

"No, whiskey. It's quite a famous house for it. People say they get more for their money there. We've watched him in every possible way, and the more we watch the more certain we feel that he's playing some very deep game that we can't fathom. When I overheard him mention that his stuff came up by train, its seemed to me that there was a sort of track to go upon."

"Have you found out anything?"

"No, though we've tried hard. We've watched all the railway vans running near his house; we've made inquiries of rail officials, but cannot discover that any goods are being reassigned to him—in fact, we're as much in the dark as ever."

"And that's why you've come to me?"

"Exactly so, Mr. Page, can you suggest anything that may help us?"

"Let me see," said my brother-in-law. "As you say there is not much to go upon. You simply hear a man say a train delivers stuff, which you conjecture to be spirits, and on the merit of this very slender clue you want to determine who—using the railways—it is that supplies him, how it gets to him. It's not much to go on. And you've never heard or seen anything suspicious?"

"Never."

"Nothing by which you could connect him with a railway?"

"Nothing."

"Well, Mr. Hall, I can't promise anything. But just leave your name and address and also the name and position of the public house and I'll see if I can do anything to unearth the mystery."

When the excise officer had left, Godfrey Page turned to me.

"Well," he said, "the first thing is to go and have a look at this mysterious public house and its occupant. What do you say to coming with me tomorrow morning about ten or eleven? It's a quiet time and we might find out something."

I readily agreed and met him the next morning.

"You see," he said, as we ferreted out our way to Turner Street, "it's just possible that we might gather a bit of a clue. Keep your eyes and ears well open to catch every object and every chance word. We'll go in the private bar in smoke a pipe there."

A man, evidently the landlord, was standing behind the bar as we entered, a sharp, keen-eyed fellow who took us both in with a quick glance as Godfrey Page nonchalantly ordered two glasses of bitter. There was evidently nothing about us to raise his suspicions, and he began chatting to us on the weather and kindred topics.

Presently a customer entered the public bar and he turned aside to serve him. We heard a voice calling for "three-penn'orth of the special," and by straining our necks round the partition we saw Rogers measure out a magnum of spirits with a glass—certainly more than the ordinary "three-penn'orth."

We stood, lounging in the private bar. Suddenly my brother-in-law clapped me on the shoulder.

"It's time we were off," he said.

As soon as we got outside he went on:

"I've got a curious little psychological problem to work out, Tom. You know what I was telling you last night about railway sounds, don't you?"

"Well?"

"You said you'd like to put me a test case."

"I did."

"I believe you've got your wish."

"How?"

"While we were standing in that bar I'm certain I heard a sound connected with a railway in some way."

"What was it?"

"That I can't explain yet, but I'm going to try to fathom it. But did you hear anything?"

"Only once or twice they seemed to be washing some pots and pans beyond the bar parlour—or a tea-tray fell down with a crash—or something of that kind. But what that has to do with a railway, I don't know."

"That's the sound I mean. And it *has* something to do with a line. Haven't you ever had some familiar scene unconsciously brought before your mind by something connected with it suddenly appealing to your senses? A piece of music, for example—or the smell of some scent?"

"Oh, yes. A minor, unconscious brain impression will often recall incidents and places."

"Exactly so. Well, when I heard that sound a scene flashed across my mind each time."

"What was it?"

"The main departure platform, Number 1, at Paddington."

"That's curious. What do you propose to do?"

"Well, we'll go to Paddington and see if we can make the place give us the sound. It seems fantastic, I know, but there's no harm in trying."

"The beauty of the Great Western is departing," remarked my brother-in-law a little later as we strolled down the Number 1 platform at Paddington, "look at that new engine. It may be very powerful but where is the beautiful brass dome that has always characterized the G. W. R. engines? Where is that graceful, curved line of beauty that distinguished—Hullo! By George, my boy, I've discovered the sound!"

As he spoke there came a peculiar jangling sound on the stone part of the platform where a porter was working. I looked. He was rolling some empty milk churns—those familiar cylindrical tapering cans—from one part of the platform to the other, and every time he stood them on end there was a crash of tinware.

"Clue number one!" said Godfrey Page exultantly. "Now we'll go and have some lunch and think things out. Upon the assumption that a railway milk churn was being rolled about on the premises of the 'Bluebell,' the question is, what comes next?"

"I don't quite see what you're driving at," I confessed.

"Well, I'll try and make things plainer to you presently. But let's have lunch."

After our meal he asked me if I would go back with him to the street in which the "Bluebell" was situated.

I consented and we presently found ourselves there. We strolled up and down once or twice. Suddenly he caught my arm.

"I have it," he said.

We walked around quickly to Harvey Street, a thoroughfare that lies at the back of and parallel with Turner Street.

"Here we are," he exclaimed, "I thought we should find something of the kind."

And he pointed to a little dairy establishment, beautifully neat and clean.

"Do you notice the position of the shop?" he asked.

"Why, it's just at the back of the public house."

"Exactly. Now what we want to find out is where they get their milk from."

"Ah!" I exclaimed, "I'm beginning to see daylight."

"A soda and milk is an excellent tipple, Tom. Let's go in and have one."

We entered the shop. A young girl behind the counter served us with our drinks. I saw Godfrey Page glancing carefully over the shop and marked his eye rest upon a milk churn behind the counter. Presently he said:

"Can you change me a sovereign?"

The girl took the coin and looked in the till. There was not enough silver.

"In one moment, sir," she replied going to the back of the shop.

"Good!" muttered my brother-in-law, as, unobserved, he darted behind the counter for a moment and looked at the milk churn.

Two minutes later we were in the street.

"Well?" I asked.

"It had a London and South-Western label on it," he replied, "from Witley to Addison Road. And there was something else, too. Stamped on the cover was 'Hillside Farm.' I think we're on the right track now."

"Where's Witley?" I said.

"Two stations beyond Godalming. It's a charming country. What do you say? Shall we go and enjoy its pastoral air for a few hours?"

"With all my heart. I'm anxious to see the end of this."

"All right. We'll start tomorrow morning. And we must be prepared to spend the night there."

Accordingly we took the train from Waterloo the following morning and in due time reached the little out-of-the-way station at Witley. We asked a porter there our way to Hillside Farm.

"Hillside Farm? Why it's a matter of about five or six miles. 'Tis a lonely place, that, sir."

"A dairy farm, isn't it?" asked Godfrey Page carelessly.

"Yes, sir. Leastways, it has been for the last eighteen months or so. Old Farmer Jones couldn't make much of it, but the new chap what's bought it seems to get along very well, judging by the lot-o' milk he sends up to London three or four times a week."

"What's his name?"

"O'Brien, sir. He's an Irishman. Brought all his own laborers over with him."

"Oh, *has* he?"

"Works in a reg'lar scientific way, I've heard. I know a lot of dairy machinery came down more'n a year ago."

"That settles it," remarked my brother-in-law as we went out of the station. "Now we must be very careful not to excite suspicion."

A good long walk through the lovely Surrey country at length brought us near the farm. An old man was breaking stones by the side of the road. We asked him the way, offered him a pipeful of tobacco, and drew him out.

"I suppose they keep hundreds of cows at that farm yonder?" asked Page innocently.

"Lor', bless yer, no! They ain't got more'n a dozen, I reckon. But they do get a wonnerful lot o' milk out of them. Whoy, I seed six churns go by to the station yesterday, and they churns holds eight barn gallons, as we calls 'em. It's a sight of milk!"

"All right," said Godfrey Page, as we started once more for the station. "The *finale* will soon come. We'll stay the night at Guildford and travel up with the milk in the morning. I got a special authorization from the company last night."

"What time do they send that milk up to town in the morning?" he asked the porter when we had regained the station.

"It leaves by the 7.44, sir. I believe they transfer it at Woking to a train that stops at Clapham Junction. It arrives at Kensington at 10.4."

Godfrey Page procured a pail at Guildford, which we took with us in the train next morning, his written permit allowing us to travel in the compartment with the churns.

"Quick," he said as soon as the train had started, "undo that pail. Good! Look I've opened this can. It's only fastened with a clasp. Locking would attract suspicion. Now, then, I expect that pail will hold all the milk there is in it."

It seemed filled almost to the brim, but Page was right. We tipped it over the pail and it scarcely took up two-thirds of it.

"Just what I suspected," he said, "the can's in two parts. And there's a screw stopper inside. I'll undo it. Put your nose inside and take a sniff, what do you smell?"

"Whiskey—unmistakably!"

"A clever little trick, eh? There—I've screwed up the stopper. Now we'll pour the milk back. Good! They'll never think it's been tampered with. Well, Tom, here's another railway mystery solved!"

And when we got back to town he wrote the following letter to the excise officer:

> Dear Sir—the 'Bluebell' gets its whiskey from Hillside Farm, near Witley, Surrey. It is taken in milk cans to the little dairy shop in Harvey Street and transferred through the back premises. It comes *via* Addison Road in railway milk churns with double compartments. It will be well worth your while to make a raid on Hillside Farms simultaneously with the 'Bluebell.' I think you will discover something very interesting there. I shall trouble you for out-of-pocket expenses.

Three days afterwards the excise officer called on Godfrey Page.

"I don't know how to thank you enough," he said. "We've unearthed a whole gang of scoundrels. They'd actually had the audacity to put up an elaborate distilling operation in the Farm and were turning out whiskey by the gallon. O'Brien and his so-called 'farm laborers' and the dairy shop people were all the same firm. Thanks to you we've got the lot. However did you find it out?"

Godfrey Page laughed.

"Do you know anything about psychology and the effect of mind impressions?" he asked.

"No," said the man.

"Ah! You would've found such knowledge useful in this case—that is, provided you have been a railway maniac like myself."

THE WARCHESTER MYSTERY

On asking my brother-in-law's permission to publish the facts of the Warchester mystery, which always had struck me as a very peculiar and unique incident, he readily gave his consent.

"But the only thing about it," he said, "is that it was not a mystery which I was called upon to investigate, but rather one concerning which there were strong antecedent facts to work upon, and one which I was able to watch throughout."

It is for this very reason that I claim a point of special interest for the story I am about to relate, for it is not often that a detective is able to get a clue to a mystery or crime before that mystery or crime has actually happened.

In other of the cases in which Godfrey Page was concerned it was his business to bring his technical knowledge of railways to bear on certain effects, and to deduce from such effects the causes which led to them. In the case of the Warchester mystery the exact opposite took place.

Starting on the groundwork that something peculiar was evidently about to happen on the London, Southton, and Middlepool Railway, Godfrey Page was able to be in at the start as well as in at the finish, and to be the instrument of directing justice to the track of a swindler of more than usually bold and original caliber.

It is also a great pleasure to me to be able to publish the narrative because it was due to myself the Godfrey Page was furnished with the all-important initial clue, a mere chance, I admit, but for all that I am glad to be able to take the credit of it.

To make a long story short and to commence at the very beginning, it all emanated from a copy of the *Telegraph* that greeted me with its customary regularity when I came down to my breakfast table at Acton one morning.

Before opening it I casually ran my eye over the Births, Marriages, and Deaths, and the "Agony Column" on the front page. In the latter I was brought face-to-face with the following:

"Gsv 10.25 gizrm uiln olmwim gl hlegaglm hszoo hglk zg dzixsvghvi gl mrtag."

"My dear," I said to my wife, "there's a cryptogram in the agony column."

"And you won't be happy till you've solved it," she laughed.

"I certainly shall not," I replied, "and I'll have a try at it after breakfast."

"I hope it won't put you into such an irritable temper as the last one did," she said.

She knew very well it was a weakness of mine. As a boy I had loved to puzzle over the cryptograms in the boy's papers and had gained several prizes for correct solutions.

Every now and then when one appeared in the *Telegraph* I set to work, generally to find that they were the composition of doting lovers unable to use the ordinary methods of correspondence on account of stern parents who kept an eye on the letter-box. Once there had been a whole series of them planning an elopement which, apparently, was carried out.

So I retired to my study after the meal and laid the paper before me. There are many ways of going to work in deciphering cryptograms. One may take the predominant letter and put it down as "e" or "r," the two letters most in use, or one can, in the case of divided words, take the little words and guess them as "at," "to," "the," and so on, applying the results to the larger words.

The great difficulty is when the cryptogram is not divided, but in this case it was pretty plain sailing.

As I glanced at it I had an immediate inspiration. The figures gave it to me. "10.25 *train*," I said to myself. This gave me five whole letters:

$$g = t$$
$$i = r$$
$$z = a$$
$$r = i$$
$$m = n$$

Glancing along, I saw the letters "gl" twice repeated. If "g" = "t" it was pretty safe to guess that "l" equaled "o." Thus I got a sixth letter. In the first word, "gsv," the "g" equaled "t" and it was a pretty safe guess that the other letters were "he," while the word following "train" one naturally guessed to be "from," and so one arrived at:

$$l = o$$
$$s = h$$
$$v = e$$
$$u = f$$
$$l = o$$
$$n = m$$

I now took "olmwim" and got from the letters I knew, "-on-on," evidently "London," giving me:

$$o = l$$
$$w = d$$

It was easy from this to transpose has "hszoo" into "shall" and "hglk" into "stop," and "mrtag" into "night."

In another minute the following transposition lay before me:

"The 10.25 train from London to Southton shall stop at Warchester to-night."

It was a rather weak and clumsy little cryptogram, but the result was certainly striking.

"Another elopement?" asked my wife, coming in at that moment.

"Not this time," I said, as I handed her the slip of paper on which I had written the sentence.

"Why, Tom," she went on when she had read it, "you ought to show this to Godfrey. I'm sure it would interest him."

"Happy thought," I replied, "I'll go down to Brondesbury at once."

Half an hour or so later I laid the cryptogram and its transposition before Godfrey Page. He was intensely interested.

"Let's have a look at that best of boon companions—Bradshaw," he said, opening the book in question. "Warchester is on the London, Southton, and Middlepool line."

"Here we are. Main line—London to Southton. This is the train. Departs from London at 10:25 p.m. Arrives at Southton at 12:43, doing the journey without a stop. Ah—there's a coach slipped from this train at Warchester at 11:50. Tom, my boy, this is certainly interesting.

The cryptogram seems to infer that the train itself shall stop at Warchester."

"How can it do that?" I asked.

"My dear fellow," he replied with withering scorn, "I know of about fourteen ways in which a train can be made to stop if you wanted to without damage to it. These ways resolve themselves into two means, stopping the train from without or from within."

"And you think one of these means is about to be resorted to?"

"It looks like it, doesn't it? Now just for the present, we won't bother as to *how* the train is to be stopped, but will ask *why?* Here again, the answer resolves itself into two general heads. First, for somebody or something to be got out of the train. Secondly, for ditto to be got into it. I am inclined to the latter in this case."

"Why?"

"Because there is a slip coach to set down anyone. By the way, very likely there is more in the fact of that slip coach running than we think. It would materially increase the facilities of stopping the main train. But now, what are we to do? Shall I go down to the company's offices and draw their attention to this cryptogram, or shall I travel in the train myself and see if there is a little mystery in the air?"

"If you do the latter I'll go with you," I said.

"Right! I confess it's entirely to my liking. There's a spice of adventure about it. Besides, I'm very anxious to see *how* the train is to be stopped. Suppose you pack your bag and meet me at the London terminus at ten o'clock tonight."

In due time we met at the station, purchased first-class tickets to Southton, and deposited our bags in a compartment. Then we strolled about the platform and kept our eyes open.

"You see," said my brother-in-law, "there may be an idea of tampering with the signals or greasing the rails, or something of that sort at Warchester. In that case there will be nothing to discover here. But, on the other hand, some trick may be played on the train before starting out, and if so you may depend upon it that slip coach will have something to do with it. Let's see if the coupling is all right."

He walked to the edge of the platform and looked between the slip coach and the rest of the train.

"All right," he said, "I thought perhaps they might have managed to do the very clumsy thing of linking the coupling chains together as well as the slip-bolt."

"What would happen then?"

"The coach wouldn't slip. The signalman would see the wrong tail lights and stop the train. By the way, we'll look at the tail lights. Yes, that's all right. One red light at the back of the last coach of the train, and a red and a white in rear of the slip. Now, there are still ten minutes. Let's take a seat on the platform and keep her eyes open."

No sooner had we sat down than Godfrey Page grasped my arm.

"Look," he said, "that fellow seems interested in slip coaches, too."

A man in a dark overcoat and a cap drawn down over his face was standing near the door of the guard's compartment of the slip coach. And here I ought to mention that this train was drawn up at the *left* side of the departure platform, so that the right side of the train was opposite to us.

"He certainly seems interested," I remarked, "but what is the guard doing to that cord?" I went on.

"Testing it, to see if the bells ring in the guard's van—there, he's finished."

And the guard walked away from the train. The man in the overcoat drew nearer to the open door of the guard's compartment.

"But how do they manage the cord when the train slips, and—"

But my brother-in-law grasped my arm with an iron grip.

"Look!" he said.

The man in the overcoat darted into the guard's compartment for an instant, holding something in his hand. Reaching up, he seemed to place it somewhere high up on the right-hand side of the coach.

Meanwhile Godfrey Page had darted forward. An instant afterwards and the man stepped out of the coach, looked around him carefully, while Godfrey seemed intent on hailing a newspaper boy.

Then I saw the strange man turn and walk quickly off the platform out of the station. Godfrey Page gave one quick glance inside the brake compartment and then came back to me.

"All right," he said, "the train is bound to stop at Warchester now. I'm very glad we came. Come, let us take our seats. The train's just off."

I followed him in amazement. He had tipped a porter to keep our compartment clear, and in a couple of minutes we were starting.

"What on earth—" I began, but Godfrey Page interrupted me.

"You were asking just now how they could manage the communication cord on slip coaches. I brought in my bag the regulations for working slips. Here they are."

"Dear me, what a lot of rules!" I exclaimed, as he put a little pamphlet into my hand.

He smiled.

"The general public little know of the elaborate arrangements for their safety," he said, "but read this."

And I read as follows:

"Cord Communication on Slip Coaches.—All slip coaches which have to travel twenty miles or more without stopping must be provided with a cord communication which must be arranged thus:

"1. The usual Wheel and a Bell must be provided in the Brake Compartment of the Slip-Coach.

"2. The Cord must be fixed to the rear of the Slip-Coach and carried along the Coach, the other end being attached to the wheel in the Guard's Compartment of the Slip-Coach, so the passengers in the Slip-Coach will be able to communicate with the Slip-Guard.

"3. A short Cord must be fastened to the Cord on the last vehicle of the Main Train, which must be passed through a tube provided in the Guard's compartment of the Slip-Coach, so that, if required, the Slip-Guard can pull it, and thus communicate with the Guard of the Main Train; the end of this Cord must be loosed, *so that it may run out when the Slip-Coach separates from the Train.*"

There were several more rules but my brother-in-law interrupted me when I had read this far.

"If the slip-guard pulled that cord he would stop the main train."

"Well?"

"That fellow has put a plug in the tube so that the short cord is jammed and *cannot run out* when the coach is slipped."

"What will happen?"

"Why, directly the coach is slipped and the main train runs on, that cord will tighten and give the alarm. Clever, isn't it?"

"And the train will be stopped?"

"Certainly. Just as it's running into Warchester. Now we must keep our eyes open and see what happens. We'll each look out on one side of the train as soon as we get anywhere near. The neatness of the whole thing is that it is impossible to find out who stopped the train, but we may discover why that plug was put in."

We were traveling in a carriage almost at the rear of the train. At about 11.45 we took up our positions on either side, and opened the windows.

"It's not so *very* dark," said my brother-in-law; "but we must keep a sharp lookout. Remember, if anyone gets in the train he may not be on the station platform. We must look everywhere."

It is a straight bit of line running into Warchester and looking ahead, I presently saw the station lights. A few hundred yards before we reached the station I glanced back at the slip-coach, just at the moment it separated from the train. Another instant and there was a long whistle blast from the engine, and I felt the peculiar grinding of the brakes. The cord had evidently acted, for we were slowing down.

I strained my eyes as we ran into the station to discern anything peculiar. Immediately before the station was a light iron footbridge over the line; I hardly noticed it at the time, only catching a glimpse of it as we ran slowly by it. But at the same moment I heard a thumping noise above me. Immediately afterwards Godfrey Page laid his hand on my shoulder.

"Pull your head in, Tom," he said, "it's all right. We've picked up another passenger."

"Where? How?" I exclaimed.

"I'll tell you presently. But I want to see what's happening here. Meanwhile just keep a lookout on the off side of the train while I jump on the platform and have a look."

We had come to a standstill now. I heard various shouts and explanations from the officials and presently Godfrey Page got in again, saying:

"The slip-guard put on his brakes when he saw the train stopping and his coach is standing outside the station waiting to run in. They've found out how it stopped, that the cord jammed. Ah, now we're off. Tom, my boy, there's a man on the roof of our carriage."

"On the roof?"

"Yes. Didn't you hear him drop?"

"I heard a noise. Where did he come from?"

"That little footbridge over the line. I caught sight of him clinging to the girders as we ran in. He was silhouetted against the station lights. As the train ran under I could just see him let himself down and hang by his hands. Then it was only a matter of a few inches' drop and the train was moving very slowly. But, look out! I expect he'll climb down one end of the coach. Ha! I'll pull the shade over our lamp, then he won't see us looking out. Keep your side and I'll take the other."

The train had begun to get up to speed when, on looking carefully, I presently saw a dark form emerge from between our coach and the one in front. He had climbed down the step at the end of the carriage, and had reached the footboard of the train, clinging on to the handles provided.

I rushed across the compartment and told my companion. The next moment we were both looking out of the same window watching his movements.

"He's looking for an empty compartment," said Godfrey Page. Then we saw a door flying open, a stream of light emerge for a moment, and then the man got in and closed it.

"The second compartment of the next coach," remarked my brother-in-law as we drew in our heads and he uncovered the lamp, revealing a very satisfied countenance. "The plot thickens, eh? This little affair was certainly worth coming to see."

"What do you propose to do?" I asked.

"Well, on the whole I think we'll track the man at Southton and see where he goes to."

At Southton we were out on the platform almost before the train had stopped and ran forward to find our man. He got out of the compartment, a gentlemanly fellow, evidently wearing a dress suit beneath his overcoat, and a cap. Godfrey Page managed to be close by him when we passed the ticket barrier and afterwards told me that he gave up a return half of a ticket from London to Southton.

Immediately afterwards he took a hansom, and we heard him tell the driver to take him to the "King's Arms Hotel."

"Good," said Godfrey Page, "we'll stay the night there ourselves."

So we followed. We engaged rooms of the porter, and Godfrey ask him casually:

"Who is the gentleman who came in just before us?"

"Mr. Stewart sir—an American. He's been staying here for a week."

Godfrey Page came into my room before I turned in to wish me good-night.

"Tomorrow we may find out something more of this mystery," he said; "meanwhile I've found out the number of his room and that's all."

Tomorrow certainly did bring some news. When I came down to breakfast Godfrey was there before me and triumphantly handed me the morning paper, pointing to the following lines:

"DARING ROBBERY AT WARCHESTER.

"Escape of the Thief.

"Late last night a robbery of a very daring and audacious description took place at Beverly Court, the seat of the Earl and Countess of Warchester. The occasion was the annual hunt ball and a very large number of guests were present. The Countess was wearing the famous diamond tiara and ruby necklace, the heirlooms of the Warchester family, and quite a little staff of detectives was in attendance.

"She had just entered the conservatory after one of the dances when a waiter came up with a tray of ices. Upon stretching out her hand to take one the man suddenly hurled the contents in her face, at the same time making a snatch at the tiara and necklace.

"For a moment those present were staggered at the unexpected incident and the noise of the falling tray, and the man seized the opportunity to make a bolt through the conservatory door to the lawn.

"Immediately chase was given. The man was distinctly seen running over the lawn to a group of shrubs by the carriage drive where he had evidently concealed a bicycle, for on coming up to him he mounted a machine and rode off down the carriage drive.

"Chase was made all over the country by horsemen and one or two cyclists; the police were communicated with by telegraph, but all that has been discovered was a bicycle near Warchester station, about two miles off. The railway officials, however, declare that he could not have escaped by train, and Warchester is being very closely searched. It might be mentioned that the waiter was one of several supplied for the occasion by a London agency."

"There," said Godfrey Page in a low voice; "I think we've reached the bottom of things now. The only thing remaining is to put the police on the right track, and we'll do that at once."

Half an hour later and the American's room was entered by the police. He was dressing at the moment, and as soon as he saw who his visitors were, attempted to bolt through the window. But they were too quick for him. And his portmanteau were discovered the priceless tiara and necklace—thanks to that astute "railwayac," Godfrey Page.

It all came out afterwards. Stewart was a very clever American swindler who had elaborately planned this robbery. He had arranged that his confederate in London should communicate to him through the *Telegraph,* so as not to chance discovery of correspondence.

A slight hitch had occurred in the arrangements, and, at the last moment, it was necessary for him to be sure that the train would really be stopped. Then, all he had to do was to provide a bicycle with a great coat strapped to it, and trust to his boldness and gymnastic skill.

There is no doubt that had it not been for my brother-in-law the Warchester "Mystery" would never have been solved, and the Countess would still be bewailing the loss of her jewels. As it was the Southton police got all the credit of the capture.

"But that doesn't matter," said Godfrey Page. "I told you I knew fourteen ways of stopping a train? Well, that plugged cord arrangement is the fifteenth that hadn't dawned upon me, and I wouldn't have missed it for anything."

The Case of James Underwood

I called to see my brother-in-law, Godfrey Page, one evening about some matter or other. He was out at the time, but as his servant said he would not be long, I determined to wait for him. So I went into his den and commenced gazing at the many photographs and sketches of the locomotives and railways that adorned his walls.

Presently I came to his bookshelf and I took down at a random one of a series of scrap books bearing the label "Railway Odds and Ends," and commenced turning over the leaves.

There was much variety in the pages. Old time-tables and excursion bills, special instructions, newspaper cuttings, and now and then a railway ticket pasted into the book with a note about it.

I soon came to a page that struck me at once as having some peculiar interest attached to it. Pasted in the center was the return half of a first-class ticket—from Waterloo to Winchester—and underneath it a scrap of printed matter torn out of a newspaper, apparently from the shipping intelligence, for I could see nothing relating to railways in it. At the bottom of the page was written:

"Two memories of the case of James Underwood," and the date.

Presently my brother-in-law returned. When I had finished my business with him I pointed laughingly at the page of the scrapbook which I had left laying open on the table.

"What's the meaning of this?" I asked.

"Eh? Oh, I see what you've been looking at. Haven't I ever told you about the Underwood case, Tom?"

"No, never."

"Ah! It's a curious little story. Now I come to think of it you might like to have it for the little series you're writing about me. That is, if you think it worthwhile."

"You might tell me it at all events," I exclaimed. So, lighting our pipes, we sat down, and Godfrey Page related the following strange episode which I have thought well to chronicle among his "Investigations."

I don't pretend that there is any particular credit due to me for the part I played in solving the mystery of James Underwood.

Anyone with a quick perception of certain possibilities afforded by the peculiar working of the line under which the affair took place might have grasped the same conclusions, though, possibly they might not have acted upon them so quickly. But the incident serves to illustrate a theory of mine that a man with a regular railway *habit* places himself more or less at the mercy of his enemies.

This was shown, as you remember, in the case of the robbery of Mr. Crane, the bank manager.

You see, the railway necessarily offers a theater for the commission of crime. Whether it be robbery, assault, or blackmail in the privacy of the compartment of a carriage in a long-distance train, or a dastardly attack on that train in an attempt to wreck it from without, there is a category of crimes confined to the railway and, as I say, because a theater for the commission of them is offered.

But I am digressing. Perhaps I had better begin this history by stating the circumstances under which I met James Underwood.

I had been on a little cycle tour in Wiltshire, and after a long ride over Salisbury Plain, had at length arrived in the old cathedral city.

It was at a somewhat late hour that night that I sought out a hotel and sat down to a very welcome meal. I was the only person in the coffee room, and the waiter was inclined to be communicative, especially as I asked him some ordinary questions.

He had gone downstairs to change the dishes, and appeared to me to have been absent rather an unwarrantable time when he reappeared, bursting with news.

"Very strange affair happened, sir."

"Indeed?"

"Only a quarter of an hour ago, sir."

"What is it?"

"Gentleman found in a goods truck, sir."

"Where?"

"At the station, sir."

"Getting a ride on the cheap?"

"No, sir. Dead. Leastways, he ain't expected to live. They took him to the waiting room and sent for a doctor, sir."

I laid down my knife and fork and forgot my appetite at this bit of news. The station was not five minutes' walk from the hotel, and in a very short time I was there. I handed my card to an official who was standing just within the door of the first-class waiting room. He glanced at it, and then, to my intense delight, said:

"I haven't the pleasure of knowing you personally Mr. Page, but I've heard of you often. You seem to be on the spot this time, at all events, for we've got a queer job to deal with. If you can help us we shall be only too glad."

"Tell me about it," I said, "I've only heard that a man has been found in a goods truck. Is that so?"

"Yes. Stunned, and totally unconscious. Come and look at him."

"One moment. When was he found?"

"Twenty minutes to half an hour ago, just after the goods train came in."

"Where did the goods train come from?"

"Nine Elms is the first place. But she's picked up empties at several stations."

"What's your theory?"

"We think he must've fallen into the truck from the parapet of a bridge or something of the sort, and pitched on his head."

"Well, let's have a look at him. Meanwhile, send for the brakesman of that goods train. I should like to have a word with him."

On a couch in the waiting-room lay a man of some sixty years of age, slightly built, below medium height, and well dressed. He was breathing heavily, add an ugly wound just over his temple showed pretty plainly where the chief mischief lay.

"Found anything on him?" I asked.

"His watch and five or six pounds in money, but no papers of any sort."

"That scarcely looks like an accident," said I, looking carefully at his overcoat. "Ah," I went on, "here's a little pocket in the sleeve. I've got one myself and that's why I came to look for it."

"What's the good of it?"

"*Tickets!*" I said, putting in my finger and thumb. "Ah, here we are!"

And I pulled out the "inward" half of a return ticket—"Waterloo to Winchester, 1st Class." Eagerly I turned it over to see the date.

"This ticket was issued today at Winchester. It's been clipped, too, by ticket-inspector. Now—"

But at this moment two persons came into the room, the doctor and the brakesman. Leaving the former to take the patient into his hands, he soon got an ambulance and had him conveyed to the hospital. I told the brakesman to wait a moment while I consulted a time-table hanging on the wall. A sudden idea had taken possession of me, a sort of instinctive clue given me by the half ticket.

I found what I wanted and then put some questions to the brakesman.

"Where did you pick up the empty truck in which you found him?"

"Basingstoke, sir."

"Are you sure it was empty then?"

"Certain of it."

"What time did you leave Basingstoke?"

The man consulted his journal.

"9.23, sir," he replied with the customary precision of a railway worker.

"Then you must've slowed down a bit between Basingstoke and Oakley?"

He stared at me in astonishment.

"How did you know that, sir?"

"Aha, I thought so. Soon after leaving Basingstoke, eh?"

"Yes, sir. The signal was against us and we had to run very slow. But we never stop, and—"

"Oh, that's nothing to do with it. Thank you, my man. Now," I added turning to the official who had just spoken to me; "you offered to take any suggestions from me. It's past eleven now; can you get a wire through the Bournemouth before 11.30?"

"Bournemouth?"

"Exactly. You can?"

"Yes, but I don't see how—"

"There's not a moment to be lost. Give me a telegraph form."

He gave me an official form. On it I scribbled:

"Do not allow 1st class compartments of down train arriving at 11.33 to be cleaned or in any way touched inside or out till further instructions follow."

"Well, I'm blowed!" said my companion when he had read it.

"Send it off!" I cried.

He disappeared for a few minutes. When he came back he said:

"And now for your 'further instructions,' please?"

"All right," I replied. "Suppose we call the 'further instructions' ourselves?"

"How?"

"Let *us* follow on to Bournemouth."

"There's no train. Impossible!"

"A light engine?" I suggested.

"Is it really of importance?"

"I think so. That poor old fellow bled a little. We may find traces of it."

"Where?"

"At Bournemouth."

"You're a conundrum, Mr. Page," he said, "but it if you really consider it necessary I think we can run through *via* Ringwood as you suggest."

"Good. When will you be ready?"

"In about half an hour."

"Very well. I'll go back to my hotel and tell them I shan't stay there tonight. Also an overcoat maybe useful for it's a bit chilly—and we shall find it more so on the footplate."

I think I almost forgot the case in hand at the joy of an engine ride. I thoroughly appreciated our midnight run, though, as perhaps you know, a light engine is very much more "jolty" to travel on than when coupled to a train.

In due time we reach Bournemouth, and very soon I was able to examine the train in question which had left Waterloo at 8.5.

Lantern in hand I walked along the outside of the carriages on the right hand, or "off" side of the train taking the direction in which it had come from London.

The telegram had been received and the train stood in the siding just as it had arrived. I saw nothing until I reach the first-class coach which of been running nearest to the engine.

Then, on the footboard just outside the door of one of the compartments, I pointed to one or two small dark splashes.

"Here we are!" I exclaimed triumphantly. "Ah, and look on the handle!"

We had mounted the footboard and were about to open the door when, as the light flashed on the brass handle, it revealed a distinct stain of blood.

Inside the compartment there was a little more evidence, a dark stain or two on the upholstery of the seat on the off side nearest the engine. Looking into every nook and corner of the carriage I made what turned out to be an important discovery.

On the rack was a copy of a London evening paper, the *St. John's Gazette*. I looked at the front page.

"Extra special edition," I said, "now it must have been bought in London before the train started, for they wouldn't have this edition down in the country at the hour the train ran." I opened it. "Hullo," I went on, "There's a paragraph cut out. This may prove a clue."

"I confess I don't see what you're driving at," remarked the official from Salisbury.

"You will soon—but look—what's this?"

I had stooped down and was looking under the seat.

"A left hand glove," said the official.

"And with a spot or two of blood on it—and—yes, this is remarkable."

"What?"

"I should advise you to give orders to have inquiries made concerning a man who got out of this train somewhere this side of Basingstoke and who has lost the little finger of his left hand. That's all. I can't do any more tonight. Tomorrow—or rather later on today—I'll go back to Salisbury and see the victim again. Then we may hear more. Meanwhile I want a sleep."

"But won't you tell us what your theory is?"

"I should have thought you must have guessed it. However, I'll explain. The ticket found on the injured man, which, you remember, had been clipped by an inspector, showed that he must have started from Waterloo in the night train for Winchester sometime yesterday. The question was, *how* did he get into the truck of the goods train?

"Now the brakesman distinctly said that the truck was empty on leaving Basingstoke, and that his train left Basingstoke at 9:23. Therefore, it must have been *after* Basingstoke that our friend was thrown into the truck."

"Thrown?"

"Exactly. Now what happens to the line directly this side of Basingstoke?"

"It is quadrupled."

"Quite so. And I believe I am correct in saying that the two *outer* lines formed the up and down main line to Eastleigh, while the two *inner* lines are the up and down main to Salisbury?"

"That is correct."

"These quadruple lines run parallel for several miles west of Basingstoke?"

"They do?"

"And then the Salisbury metals are carried *under* the up outer rail which is raised on a curved embankment for the purpose?"

"Yes."

"Well, the effect is that for these few miles the two up and down lines respectively run side by side, and if, for example, a down Southampton train overtook a down Salisbury train beyond Basingstoke they would run close together?"

"Yes."

"Now then. A goods train leaves Basingstoke at 9:23, is switched on to the Salisbury down line and runs slow, signals being against it. Meanwhile the 8.5 passenger from Waterloo comes into the station, stops, and departs at 9.30, running on the Eastleigh down line. It overtakes and passes the goods train some little distance beyond Basingstoke, running close to it.

"A murder has been planned. The victim is struck on the head suddenly with some heavy weapon. The murderer possibly had intended to throw him out, possibly to let him remain in the train and to escape himself.

"Meanwhile a unique opportunity suddenly presents itself, and the murderer, little thinking he has not really killed the man, opens the carriage door on the off side and, with a bit of an effort, lifts the body and throws it into an empty truck on the goods train. The easiest thing in the world to do, as they are running in the same direction.

"He has previously taken papers out of the pockets of his victim, possibly to put people off the scent, and now the only thing he has to do is to get out himself. He takes off his bloodstained gloves, but somehow or other leaves it."

"Mr. Page, you are a marvel. One thing, though, how about that little finger missing?"

"The little finger sheath of this kid gloves has never had anything in it, while the others have been well used. And now I must have some rest. By the way, get me a copy of the *St. John's Gazette* for last night, as I want to find what is been cut out."

The next day found me at Salisbury and in the presence of the victim. The doctor said he was getting on splendidly and had told them his name and address.

"But his memory's very shaky as yet. He wants a reminder of things that have happened."

"All right," I said, "I think I can supply that. Meanwhile, have you sent to his friends?"

"He has none—only his housekeeper. An old bachelor, evidently."

I went up to James Underwood's bed—that was his name. The doctor had cautioned me against exciting him too much, as he was very weak.

"Here is a gentleman," said the doctor, "who has come to give your memory a jog."

"I hope he can," replied Mr. Underwood with a slight smile; "for it sadly shaken. I remember going up to town yesterday to attend a certain board meeting on which I sit once a fortnight, and then, beyond a dim recollection of taking a hansom to Waterloo in the evening, my mind's a blank."

"Let me try and fill that blank. You got into the 8.5 train in the compartment of a first-class carriage nearest to the engine."

"Ah—yes—so I did—I generally take that train home, and always choose the front end of a train. I have a horror of another train running into the one I'm in from behind—owing to an accident I was once in. Well?"

"A gentleman—or at least *someone*—got in with you."

"Yes—yes—I have a dim sort of an idea on it. Let's see—ah, yes—with a big beard and dark glasses."

"Possibly his disguise. Now, were you reading the *St. John's Gazette?*"

"Certainly not. I can't stand the paper."

"Then he was."

"Why, yes—I believe you're right. Stop a bit and let me think—yes, I remember now. He opened a knife and cut something out of it which he put in his pocket."

"Good! Now then, try to remember more."

The sick man waited several minutes before he replied:

"I can remember hearing a porter call out 'Basingstoke,'" he said.

"And then?"

"All I can think of is that after that my fellow passenger got up suddenly—yes—I can't recollect any more."

"When he made the attack on you," I said, and went on to tell him my theory.

"But this is most extraordinary," he said; "I assure you I haven't the slightest idea why anyone should try to murder me. Is there any clue as to who he is?"

"There is. In the first place he was interested in the homecoming of the steamer *Black Swan* from Sidney.

The paragraph he cut out referred to its being signaled at Gibraltar."

The man in the bed turned a shade paler and convulsively clutched the top of the sheet.

"Go on!" he said hoarsely. "Anything else?"

"And he probably lost the little finger of his left hand."

"Good God!" he exclaimed; "this is horrible. Sir, whoever you are, I beg of you to stop all proceedings against this man—he is not caught, is he?"

"No."

"Thank God! I do not wish him to be. I withdraw all charges against him. It is too dreadful to think of. Doctor, when shall I get better?"

"You'll be all right in a few weeks if you don't excite yourself," replied the doctor.

"Very well. You, sir," he added, turning to me, "have a right to an explanation—"

"No, no," I said, "I am not a professional detective."

"Still, I say, you have a right to know. When I am better I will tell you—leave me your card."

It was a month later that Mr. James Underwood called on me. He was still rather feeble from the terrible experience he had gone through.

"Mr. Page," said he, "I promised to take you into my confidence. Will you come with me to Balham, to see an old friend of mine who is at the point of death."

Wondering greatly I went with him. The door was opened to us by a young man.

"How is your father?" asked Mr. Underwood.

"Very ill. I will go and tell him you are here."

"His son," explained Mr. Underwood, "just returned from New South Wales—hush—don't be surprised at anything—come with me."

We entered the sick man's room.

He lay evidently at the point of death.

"James!" he gasped as we entered; *"you* here!"

"Yes, Tom. You don't mind my bringing a friend and talking business."

The sick man seemed to gaze at him with terror. Suddenly I caught sight of his left hand.

The little finger was missing!

"James," he gasped again, "I've been very wicked—I've—"

"Stop, Tom, old chap. Think of me as your old friend. Do you remember how you and I went out to the gold diggings and made our pile together years ago?"

"Yes—I remember."

"And how we divided it into three parts? One for you, one for me, and a third that we invested jointly and had a trust deed drawn up by which the survivor was to inherit the whole of it?"

The sick man groaned.

"It was a very foolish arrangement, Tom. I saw it later, when you married and had a son, and I remained a bachelor."

"Well, James?"

"Tom, why didn't you tell me, your old friend, you've had money losses lately?"

"How do you know? I *daren't*—it—it was my son. I loved him so, and you were always so hard on him."

"No! I only objected to the way he was ruining his father. He *has* ruined you."

"Well?"

"But I've heard better accounts of him lately. Tom, I came up to London a month ago—not only to sit on my board, but to see a lawyer."

Beads of perspiration were rolling down the sick man's face now.

"I knew, Tom, what you have known for months—what you told me the doctor said—that you cannot live the year out. I knew that that money would be mine, but I did not want it. And on the day I came to town I went to my lawyer and commissioned him to draw up a deed that would place all of it in your son's hands instead of mine. I thought it would be a surprise to you—but—I have been ill—and not able to tell you."

"My God!" shrieked Thomas Everard, "I believe you know all—I loved my son—I wanted the money for him—I knew I was dying, and—"

"Stop, James. I do not ask anything. I have come to forgive you, old friend!"

I had stayed long enough. Noiselessly, I slipped out of the room. Who can doubt that James Underwood's sublime act of forgiveness was but an earthly shadow of the higher forgiveness of the Almighty?

The Heir of Barton Grange

"So you want a story to wind up this little series, do you?" said my brother-in-law, Godfrey Page. "Well, let's see what I have in the way of notes."

He reached down several manuscripts and scrap-books from his bookshelf, and began turning over the pages.

"Here's a little thing might do if it were not so short and simple," he said presently, "the affair of Mr. Richard Harting, collector of precious stones. But, no, you could never make a story of it."

"What is it?" I asked.

"Only this. Mr. Harting called on me one day to consult me about a mysterious railway journey. He stated that two men came to his house on Baker Street one evening and offered him a large fee if he would go with them and give his opinion on some stones. But they made the extraordinary condition that he should be blindfolded, and stuff cotton wool in his ears.

"Curiosity prompted him to go. He told me they started in a cab, and eventually drew up at a railway station. Having his ears stopped, he could catch no sound except once when he heard one of his guides telling someone, evidently an official, that he had just undergone an operation for his eyes. Then they got into the train.

"He described the journey as lasting about ten minutes, and, just before they stopped, he said, 'I fancy we ran through a tunnel, for there was a roaring noise above the rattle of the train. When we got out we went up two short flights of steps on to a boarded platform. We walked along this, and ascended another set of stairs at the end.'

"'Good,' I remarked, 'and then, did you turn to the right or left?'

"'Sharp to the right. Presently we got into another train, which seemed to travel slowly, and I noticed a peculiar bumping sensation—every second or so there were two quick, distinct bumps.'

"'And when you stopped at a station, could you distinguish a sharp succession of hissing sounds from the engine?'

"'Yes.'

"'And you got out of the carriage the opposite side to the one you got in?'

"'I did.'

"'What number of station was it?'

"'The third. Then we walked over a footbridge, down the other side, and into the street, turning sharply to the right after I had counted some hundred paces. Fifty paces more and we entered a house.

"'Then the bandage was removed, and I was shown the jewels. They were genuine, without a doubt, and, what was more, I recognized one of them. I had seen it once before in a necklace on the Countess of Singleton. Then I knew I was called upon to pronounce my opinion on stolen articles.

"'When it was over they paid me a handsome fee, we went out of the house and traveled some distance in a cab. Then we took train once more.

"'After stopping at several stations it suddenly struck me that I was alone. Not to break my promise I carefully felt over the carriage. No one was there. I tore the bandage for my eyes just as the train ran into a station, which turned out to be Bishop's Road. Can you help me in locating the house?'

"'Certainly,' I said. 'First you traveled from Euston to Willesden, through the tunnel under Kensal Green Roman Catholic Cemetery, the noisiest one anywhere near London, then you mounted the high-level "island" platform, and got into a Mansion House L. and N. W. train. The six-wheel coaches of these trains always give a double bump in passing over rail joints, and the engines are fitted with a peculiar sounding steam brake pump.

"'The third station was Addison Road, and the street was naturally Sinclair Road. They brought you there by a roundabout way to puzzle you, and then probably drove you to Hammersmith, and put you into an Aldgate train there. Very clumsy of them!'

"I was right, for Mr. Harting was able to put the police on the track of a gang of thieves who had been 'wanted' for months. But, as I say, this little affair is not enough to work into a story. Let me see— Ah! Now here are the notes of rather a peculiar case. I think I can hardly call it an investigation though.

"To tell you the truth, it's the only affair in which I ever took affairs into my own hands and played a trick myself upon a railway company. Not that I did any harm, though if I had been caught I might've found myself in hot water.

"However, I'll tell you all about it, and though, as I have already stated, it is scarcely an investigation, still, on account of peculiar circumstances connected with the case, you may see fit to incorporate it into your little series."

It was early in the evening of the 29th March, 190–, That a knock came at my door, and the servant brought me in a card bearing the name of:

Mr. John Saunders.
2, St. Philip's Chambers
Warnhurst

I directed the stranger to be shown in, and found myself confronted with a young man of some thirty years of age.

"I must introduce myself as a solicitor, of Warnhurst," he began, "and have come to ask your advice on a rather delicate and important case."

I handed him a chair.

"I have heard several times," he went on, "of your skill in detecting matters relating to railways. Now, it is not exactly a mystery that I am going to ask you to unravel, but I want to know how to accomplish something in connection with the train."

"And what is that?"

"It's rather a complicated story, but I'll tell you as briefly as possible. Warnhurst, as you probably know, is just over a hundred miles from London.

"About five miles from Warnhurst is a village called Little Barton, and until recently there lived at the only decent-sized house in the place, Barton Grange, a very eccentric old gentleman named Kempster. He was a bachelor, and very wealthy. He had two nephews, his brother's and his sister's sons respectively, one named Edward Kempster, and the other James Murray.

"For the last five or six years he forbade these nephews to go to his house or to communicate with him in any way, his reason being that they were both after his money, and he was not going to encourage them or promise anything.

"Edward Kempster went abroad—to India—and after a while James Murray also went out of the country—the fact was that he acted the part of a blackguard in a certain case, and found it advisable to leave.

"About three months ago the old gentleman died very suddenly, and it was found that his will was as eccentric as anything he ever did in his life. His butler, an old and trusted servant, is to take charge of the house and live in it for a period not exceeding six months.

"The estate is left to the nephew who within that period arrives first at the house and receives the keys from the butler. In the event of neither of them arriving to claim the property within the limit, everything goes to charities."

"What an absurd and extraordinary measure!" I exclaimed.

"Exactly so, but those are the terms, and the will is perfectly legal. As soon as I knew of it I set to work to advise Edward Kempster to return home without delay. He is a very old friend of mine besides being my client.

"My cablegram to India did not reach him at once as he was away on a shooting expedition. At length I had a reply saying he was leaving Calcutta by the *Irene*. Meanwhile, James Murray's friends have been doing all in their power to find him.

"Beyond the fact that he was last seen in Egypt nothing was known of him. Judge of my astonishment when I received this cablegram last week from Port Said."

He handed me the message, which read as follows:

"James Murray has come aboard. He knows.—Kempster."

"Why, they are both coming back together!" I exclaimed.

"Exactly so. That is the very difficulty. But, wait a minute. Here is another telegram sent off from Brindisi. Read it."

The second telegram ran:

"Coming overland. So apparently is James. Obstacles put in my way, but shall catch next express. Meet boat if possible, and arrange something."

"And," went on the lawyer, "here is a third wire, simply saying, 'Just starting—James on train.' It's a precious dilemma, isn't it? Of course they'll both arrive in England at the same moment."

I consulted my continental Bradshaw, and, comparing it with the time and date on the last telegram, easily worked out the train from Brindisi, and on across Europe.

"They'll get to Dover by the afternoon boat tomorrow and catch the 5.45 express," I said, "arriving at Victoria at 7.30. Then there's a fast train from London to Warnhurst at 8.5. They catch that if the boat train is it all punctual. But what do you want me to advise you about?"

"Why, can't you give me some hint as to how either Kempster can be hurried on ahead of Murray, or the latter delayed?"

"My dear sir," I replied, "I don't see how it could be managed. And even if, by tampering with the railway in some way could be done, I really don't feel disposed to assist you. Why should I?"

"I'll admit there is no claim, certainly. But I want to get my old friend in first."

"Naturally—and, I presume, the other fellow has friends wanting to get him in first?"

"Yes, he has. And I know they're very excited about it. In fact, I suspect Murray has wired to them, for a couple of the fastest horses in Warnhurst are engaged for tomorrow night. That I know. At any rate, tell me this: would it be any use getting a special train?"

"Not the slightest. They'd never run it in front of that boat express from Dover, and supposing you engaged one on the Warnhurst line—it would be the same case. You couldn't get your client to the station in time for them to run one before the 8.5. No, that won't do!"

"Now, Mr. Page, is it possible to get my man in first? That's a fair question."

I spread a railway map on the table, and placed my finger on Warnhurst. Then I said:

"Just take that pencil and mark the exact position of Little Barton."

He did so, touching a spot west of Warnhurst, and slightly to the north of it.

"You say it is five miles away from Warnhurst?"

"Yes."

"Then I don't see—ah!"

"What is it?"

A strange idea had suddenly struck me.

"Yes," I said, "it *is* possible."

"Without doing any harm?"

"Without doing any harm. But it would be difficult."

"How would you do it?"

"I don't find myself justified in telling you."

In vain he argued and expostulated. I was obdurate. At length he rose in rather a temper.

"Well," he said, "if you won't tell me, you won't. But if you should change your mind I am staying at the Langham tonight and shall wait in for you till ten tomorrow morning. I need hardly say that you would receive a handsome fee for your advice."

"I'm sorry," I said, bowing him out, "but I don't feel disposed to give it."

You'll laugh at me, but half an hour later I changed my mind. Another visitor was announced to see me, this time a lady—"Miss Ethel Howard."

"I've come up all the way from Warnhurst," she exclaimed. "Mr. Saunders told me he was coming to see you. You are so clever, he said. Have you seen him?"

"I have."

"Oh, and can you manage for Ed—for Mr. Kempster to get to Barton Grange first?"

"I told him there was a way, but—"

"Oh, how good of you! And—"

"But I am not prepared to disclose it."

"But you must! Oh, Mr. Page, please do. You don't know how much depends on it."

"You seem very interested?"

"I am. Oh, I should get into awful trouble if they knew why I'd come up. They think I'm going to stay with my aunt in town. So I am. But I've come to see you first. The truth is Edward—Mr. Kempster—and I are engaged. No one knows anything about it. And, oh, his cousin, James Murray, is such a wretch!"

"Why?"

"He—he—proposed to me."

"Is that why he's a wretch?"

"No, but I refused him—and—and he threatened he'd do dreadful things to Edward. Besides, he's a cheat—he cheated at cards at the Hardings—and—"

"The Hardings!" I exclaimed. "Not the Shropshire Hardings?"

"Yes. Do you know them?"

"Very well. Now I *knew* I'd heard the name of Murray before, and now I recollect all about him. Young Harding told me of the affair. No wonder he cut the country at the time. Upon my word, I feel half inclined—"

"Oh, *do!* Please Mr. Page, *do* help!"

"You go to your aunt," I replied, "and I'll do what I can."

As soon as she was gone I looked at my watch. It was only eight o'clock. Then I consulted my map once more, and marked off a point some four miles this side of Warnhurst.

In a few minutes time I had written the following letter:

> My Dear Townsend,—I am writing to ask you a great favor. I understand that you were the engineer superintending the construction of the new branch line from Rackham to Stonechurch, and that six or seven miles are already laid with temporary rails. You know my railway hobby? Will you give me a run over the line tomorrow evening? I have a particular reason for asking you, and I'm sure it is not trespassing on our old friendship too much. Wire reply on receipt of this, and if favorable, I will call at your offices at Rackham tomorrow afternoon.

This letter I addressed to:
    Charles Townsend, Esq.,
    Temporary Office,
    Rackham and Stonechurch Ry.,
    Rackham.

Then I went out, posted it, and eventually found my way to the Langham Hotel. Saunders was rejoiced to see me and to hear that I had made up my mind to help him.

"Now," I said, "you must do exactly what I tell you, and I warn you, to begin with, that it all depends upon your client catching the 8.5 p.m. to Warnhurst. Meet him at Dover and travel up with him, looking out for tricks.

"Get a first-class carriage to yourselves on the 8.5 train, and when you are well within half an hour of Warnhurst, the first stop, draw the cover over the lamp. Just about ten o'clock, four or five miles from reaching Warnhurst, the train will stop."

"How?"

"Never mind. I should have asked you to stop it with the cord, only, in that case, they would search the train, and might cause trouble. I'll see to it. All you have to do is to open the door and make Mr. Kempster get out. Tell him to lie at full length in the grass by the side of the line, and not to move till he hears his name called. You go on in the train and leave the rest to me."

"Is that all?"

"No. Do you know a little place called Mudford?"

"A mere hamlet."

"How far is it from Little Barton?"

"About two miles."

"The new railway to Stonechurch will run through it?"

"It will."

"Write tonight to someone you can trust at Warnhurst and give orders for a fast dog-cart to be waiting at Mudford as close as possible to that new line, the driver to be there sharp by ten tomorrow night, and to show a good strong light that will be seen from the direction of the new line—that's all—no, no questions, please. Will you do this?"

"I will, but—"

"Good night, then."

The next morning about ten o'clock, I received a wire from my friend Townsend. It was just a stroke of luck that he happened to be the engineer of that bit of

line, otherwise I could not have carried out my plans.
The wire said:

"All right. Pleased to see you."

Now let me explain. The new line in question was
eventually to branch off from the main Warnhurst line
some half mile beyond Rackham, a small village, and to
run some twenty miles or so to Stonechurch, passing,
as has been said, within two miles of Little Barton. The
junction with the main line was not yet effected, but the
temporary rails were laid within a hundred yards or so
of the point of eventual contact.

Well, I went down to Rackham by a slow train in the
afternoon and saw Townsend. I explained to him that
I wanted his little contractor's engine to be under full
steam and himself only on the footplate at a quarter to
ten at the temporary terminus.

At first he thought I was mad, so I explained the plot
to him. For some time he was against it, but afterwards
the novelty of the thing struck him, and he consented
to help.

"But how are you going to stop the Warnhurst train?"
he asked.

"With this," I replied, drawing a large loaded revolver from my pocket.

"Man alive! You're not going to shoot the driver, I
hope!"

"No, no," I laughed, "I'm only going to test an idea
of stopping a train that I've long wished to see done,
that's all."

At half past nine I took up my position on the main
line half a mile or so on the other side of Rackham and
close by the temporary terminus of the new line. It was
a very dark night, and well suited to my purpose.

Just about ten o'clock I heard a rumble on the down
line, and saw the headlights of the Warnhurst train

rapidly approaching. Then I lay down on the ground, just clear of the metals, and held my revolver close to the rails, pointing beneath a joint.

The instant the great engine rushed by me I drew trigger quickly three times.

Bang—bang—bang!

The best substitute for a fog signal I have ever heard!

There was a shrill whistle, and before the train had passed, the sparks began to fly from the wheels as the driver applied the vacuum brake.

She was stopping!

I rolled off the embankment and hid myself as the train came to a standstill some three hundred yards further. A pause, another whistle, the cry of "All right!" from the guard borne down faintly on the breeze, a few sonorous puffs, and she was off again.

"Some practical joker laying fog-signals on the line!"

Such as the verdict I afterwards heard.

Quickly I ran along to where the express had stopped.

"Mr. Kempster!" I called once or twice.

"Hullo!" came an answer from the grass.

"Come along! There's not an instant to be lost!"

"What's going to happen now?" as I hurried him over the fence and across the field.

"An engine ride," I said.

"I should be glad when it's over, I've been traveling day and night, and that cousin of mine doing his best to put a spoke in my wheel all the time."

"We've put a spoke in his now," I said. "Here we are! Jump up! Off you go, Townsend."

As long as I live I shall never forget that six mile ride over the hastily laid rails on the little contractor's engine. We held on like grim death while she snorted and jumped, rushing down unfinished inclines, and snorting up gradients, whirling round curves, and bumping over the unballasted way.

It was about as bad an experience as I ever have had, and I was by no means sorry when we drew near Mudford and suddenly spotted the light in the dog-cart in a road that crossed the line by a bridge.

"You'll come on?" said Kempster as he jumped off the little locomotive. "See me through it. Saunders is going to drive from Warnhurst, pretending I'm with him, and letting James have the lead. Come and see the fun!"

I yielded, said "Good-night" to Townsend, and off we whirled through the country lanes until presently we turned in at a gate and drew up at a large house. The lights were burning in the hall. We were evidently expected.

Edward Kempster jumped down and thundered at the door. It was opened immediately by a gray-haired old man.

"Mr. Edward!" he gasped. "You've got here first."

"The keys, Blanchard, the keys!"

"Here they are, sir."

He handed them over.

"You are the possessor of Barton Grange, Master Edward—and none too soon. Hark!"

For horse-hooves were heard galloping up the drive, and there emerged from the darkness a panting steed, covered with foam.

James Murray had ridden.

"First!" he yelled as he leapt from the horse.

"No!" shouted his cousin as he stood in the hall, waving the keys above his head. "I'm before you, James."

The other stood still for a moment spellbound. Then he gave utterance to a torrent of oaths. Suddenly, without warning, he drew a pistol from his pocket and fired at his cousin. I was just in time to strike his arm up, and the bullet went crashing into a picture in the hall.

Then, flinging his weapon at the heir, he turned and vanished. That was the last I ever heard of James Murray.

Whether I did right or wrong is a question, and I've had some qualms of conscience since. But on more than one occasion I've been down for a few days' shooting at Barton Grange and laughed over the affair with Edward Kempster and his charming wife. At all events he deserves what he got—and his cousin what he *didn't* get.

Railway Adventures
with
Sir Jasper Buckland

Guy Thorne

1916-1918

THE LOST SPECIAL

The following account of one of the greatest mysteries that has ever occurred in England is compiled partly from conversations with Sir Jasper Buckland, the famous railway magnate, and partly from his note-books, to which his friend Mr. Ridley, the novelist, was given every access:

Two men were sitting in the station-master's office at Llanway, which, as everyone knows, is a famous junction in North Wales.

It was about six o'clock in the evening of a cold winter's day. The station-master was seated by a glowing fire, while beside him was Mr. Buckland—as he was in those days—chief detective-inspector of the Great Union Railway.

A tray from the refreshment room was between them on the station-master's desk. The buttered toast was crisp and inviting, while a pot of tea, such as ordinary travelers do not get at refreshment rooms, bespoke a cozy and comfortable hour.

Buckland had been down from London supervising the one or two local railway detectives who worked on the Welsh section of the Great Union Company's system. His work was now done and on the following morning he was returning to the metropolis. Mr. Llewellyn, the station-master at Llanway, was an old friend of his, and both were enjoying the pleasant gossip and a quiet hour.

Neither of the two men had the slightest inkling of the fact that they were upon the very edge of a mystery that was to shake England to its foundations and prove unparalleled before or since the history of the railways of the world. At that moment there came a knock at the door. It was not the outer door leading on to the main platform, but an inner one which opened upon a short corridor ending in the telegraphist's room.

"Come in," shouted the station-master, and a young man with spectacles entered with a paper.

"Just to hand, sir," he said. "The special left Aber-Snowdon three minutes ago."

The station-master nodded, took the paper, and the telegraphist went away.

"Special?" Buckland asked,

"Yes. Direct through to Crew, Rugby and London."

Buckland whistled. "It must cost a pretty penny," he said, "who is it?"

"A man who can well afford to pay," said the station-master. "It is Prince Potemkin, the great Russian millionaire and statesman—the Tsar's friend. I was reading about him in the *Daily Wire* yesterday. He owns land of about the same area as England. Many of the greatest oil wells are on his property . . ."

"And is one of the greatest politicians going, I have heard," Buckland broke in.

"I believe you," said the station-master, helping himself to some more toast. "He is the head of a strong party consisting of many of the wealthy nobles who wish Russia to retain her old ideals. Naturally he is misunderstood by his political enemies."

"What is he doing in England?"

"Oh, he has been over here for some time—been at Court a great deal—he was shooting at Windsor last week. He passed through here three days ago—special again, of course—and went to stay with the Marquis of Snowdon, who you will recollect was at one time our ambassador at St. Petersburg. Now he is on his way to London. You'll see him, Buckland, my boy, as likely as not!"

"How do you mean?"

"Well, the special stops here for fifteen minutes—it is all arranged. It is due at eight-thirty. The engine is going to take in water and, if you please, there are men waiting now with freshly caught fish from Rhyl for his Excellency's dinner! There is a dining-car, a sleeping-car, a car for his attendants and secretaries and a fully equipped kitchen. Jolly good thing to be a Russian prince, what?"

"Wish I was," the detective answered, and the talk turned into other channels.

About seven Buckland left the stationmaster's office. He had some business to attend to in the town of Llanway.

"But you'll be back in time to see the special, won't you?" Llewellyn asked.

"I certainly shall. It is not every day one gets a chance of seeing such a famous person as Prince Potemkin. 8:30 you say?"

"Yes, it is sure to be up to time. And look here, have a bit of supper with me afterwards"—the station-master was a single man and lived in the station.

"Thank you very much, I will," said Buckland.

He went out into the little Welsh town, settled his hotel bill, for he was to catch a very early train to London in the morning, and said good-bye to the few

acquaintances he had made during his stay. He was
packing his kit-bag in his bedroom when he rang the
bell for some paper in which to wrap up a pair of boots.
The chambermaid brought him a newspaper. He looked
at it with surprise.

"Good gracious!" he said, "whatever is this?"

The paper was printed in strange characters quite
unfamiliar to the detective's eyes.

"I don't know, I'm sure, sir," the girl answered, "but
a gentleman who stayed here last week—a foreign gentleman—left a lot of them behind him."

"It is not German," Buckland said to himself, for,
though he knew no German, he could recognize the
German characters. "Greek, I suppose!" and with that
he wrapped up his boots, put them into the bag and
thought no more about the matter.

About five-and-twenty-minutes past eight he was
again in the station. The night was heavy with cold mist
and he turned into the refreshment room for a whiskey
and soda. The young lady in charge of the first-class bar
at that moment knew him. She was a bright, vivacious
girl with whom he had had several conversations.

"Are you going to have a look at the Russian prince?"
he asked.

"Rather! Mr. Buckland, if I can just get a look at him
through the doors. I have heard such a lot about Russia
lately, and especially about this Prince Potemkin. The
week before you came down there was a Russian gentleman staying at the Harp Hotel—where you've been
staying. He was a mining engineer—by the way, try one
of these, Mr. Buckland. I indulge in a cigarette occasionally when I'm certain there is no one about, and the
Russian gentleman gave me a box."

From under the counter the girl produced an ob-
long cardboard box in blue and brown, with the Russian
Imperial eagle upon it.

"Thank you," the detective answered, taking one of the slim, straw-colored cigarettes with their cardboard tubes and lighting it. Suddenly his eye caught the lettering upon the box.

"Russian!" he said, aloud.

"Yes, but I can't make head or tail of it, can you? The letters are quite different from our letters."

"It might be Chinese, Miss Roberts, for all I know about it," he replied as he returned the box, but he remembered the newspaper. The characters upon it were the same as upon the box, and, being a man who never forgot anything, he put the little piece of information away in his mind—one never knew when any incident might not prove valuable in the future. Then he turned in search of the station-master, for the long hand of the refreshment-room clock was one minute from the half-hour.

Mr. Llewellyn, in his best gold-braided cap and dark-blue frock coat, was ready.

"We had a telegram from Penmaenbala station, thirty miles away, forty minutes ago," he said; "directly after the special had gone through. She should be signaled any minute now from the Llanway Down Box, about a mile away round the curve. You see," he went on, speaking as one railway man to another, "there is no station for thirty miles between Penmaenbala and this. There is one 'halt' where goods wagons are taken for farm produce, but there is no one in charge of it. As a matter of fact the thirty miles is through wild, mountainous land, very sparsely inhabited."

For ten minutes the two men paced up and down platform Number Two which was brilliantly lit and with various porters in attendance. The fishmonger from Rhyl, with a great basket, was waiting, chatting to a couple of policemen who had made their appearance; there was a little stir and bustle. It was obvious that something slightly out of the usual was about to occur.

Llewellyn pulled out his watch. "She ought to have been here before now," he said. "I suppose the driver's going slow in that deserted part of the System," and he went on to say that the Prince was notoriously generous, and that he should not be surprised if he was not the richer by a diamond tie-pin before another half-hour had passed.

But after another quarter of an hour there was no more talk of tie-pins. The special train was now as near as might be over half an hour overdue. Considering that the run from Penmaenbala to the Down Llanway signal-box was only thirty miles, and that the train had passed through the former station a hundred and ten minutes ago, it seemed likely that something had gone wrong.

"And yet, Buckland," said the station-master, "I don't see what on earth could have happened. The engine is one of our new decapods. The driver is Ellis, a very trusted man, and his mate equally so. The guard is one of your fellows from London—Hooper, who is always put in charge of special and royal trains. I don't see they could have had an accident, because that part of the line is blocked to all other traffic by the signals, and, besides, there is no train due upon it at all from Aber-Snowdon till ten tonight, when a short train starts from here on the Down line."

"I expect it is the fog," Buckland answered. "Ellis is nervous, considering whom he is driving."

Llewellyn shook his head. "Yes, but that does not account for the fact that it is a hundred and ten minutes since the train passed through Penmaenbala. Fog might account for it being half an hour late here, but you must remember we had the Penmaenbala telegram. A hundred and ten minutes!" he said to himself, "for thirty miles— nearly two hours!" He shook his head and hurried from platform Number Two to the telegraph office. Buckland going with him. The station-master dictated his telegram straight to an operator, who clicked it out upon the keys word by word. It was to the station-master of Penmaenbala, asking for confirmation of his previous telegram. Another message was sent to Aber-Snowdon asking for confirmation there; and then a couple of other operators were set hard at work sending messages up the line, to Crewe and London, detailing the facts and asking for instructions.

Within two or three minutes the needle on the dial was clicking out an answer from Penmaenbala. There was no doubt about it. The special train, in all respects normal, had passed through that station at the time stated. The confirmation from Aber-Snowdon, which arrived a minute afterwards, was thus rendered unnecessary.

Crewe wired: "Have light engine in readiness to explore line between you and Penmaenbala. Am in communication with London. Full instructions in ten minutes."

And in ten minutes, London itself flashed a message to Llanway: "Take engine and explore line cautiously. Communicate Crewe and order break-down gang to proceed to Llanway immediately in case of emergency. Crewe will advise stations enroute to pass break-down unit in advance of general traffic. Spare no trouble whatever. Prince Potemkin friend of His Majesty and cousin Tsar. Inform London at earliest opportunity what transpires. Matter most urgent. If Buckland, chief investigator, not left Llanway, take him with you." And here followed the name of the general traffic manager of the Great Union Railway himself.

All was bustle and confusion in the junction for a minute or two and then an engine, with the station-master, Buckland and a former porter in addition to the foreman and driver, swung slowly out into the mist.

Llewellyn gave the order to proceed with the greatest caution and at not more than ten miles an hour. The whistle was constantly blown and the line scrutinized with the greatest care by means of side lamps. It would have been impossible for even an object the size of a suit-case to have escaped the notice of the watchers. Penmaenbala, the next station, was warned, and no train, of course, would be let through Llanway upon the Down line on which they were traveling.

Mile after mile slid behind them in the fog. The calling-whistle echoed drearily among the mountain passes, but it was the only sound they heard. It seemed that there was no living, moving thing in those high solitudes, veiled in the night mists, through which only the far-gleaming lines of steel hinted at the activities of man.

Buckland was conscious of a profound melancholy. A man of action always, he was not easily susceptible to the influence of moods. But he had imagination, as all men who succeed as greatly as he succeeded in after years must necessarily have. It was at work within him now. He felt as if he was probing into some great disaster, as if horror awaited him—a heavy load seemed to lie upon his brain and heart.

On and on they went, and now face turned to face questioningly, and eyes said things that lips did not vocalize. Slow as their progress was, the tension was so keen that the flight of the hours passed unnoticed.

"I don't know what to make of it," Llewellyn said at length with a groan. "There is only one possible solution. We are now within ten miles of Penmaenbala. The breakdown or accident must have occurred in the first ten miles after the special passed through that station. We must surely come upon it soon." And, obedient to a motion of the speaker's hand, the driver shut off still more steam and the engine proceeded at the pace of a farmer jogging to market in his heavy, butter-laden trap.

The whistle was kept going, but, as the powerful headlights could not penetrate more than thirty or forty yards in the mist, the utmost caution was necessary. A wreck would have strewn the Down line as well as the Up with debris. At any moment they might come upon the scene of the disaster.

"We're just upon the St. David's Hill Tunnel," the driver said suddenly.

Llewellyn nodded. "I know," he replied, "and God grant that the accident has not occurred there!"

And now they were actually at the tunnel's mouth— an immense black horseshoe of darkness surrounded by titanic masonry which cut through the great hill above for a mile or more.

All the spare lamps were raised on high. The reverberations of the screaming whistle were flung backwards and forwards from wall to wall, from roof to ground, until they might have been in some prehistoric cave of dragons, or some nightmare hell of Dante's.

They were fully eight minutes passing through the tunnel. A bat could hardly have escaped their notice. The metals, the walls, the roof were undisturbed. The tunnel was absolutely normal in every way.

And so it was until they ran into Penmaenbala station!

Before it was light all general traffic was suspended or delayed, and head officials from Crewe were pouring into North Wales. By midday the general manager of the Great Union Railway, together with the chairman and two detectives, had arrived in a special, full of detectives, from London.

By three o'clock the London evening papers had got the news and reporters were hurrying to the spot from every part of England. An hour later the whole civilized world was ringing with the most extraordinary and inexplicable mystery that had ever flashed over the deep-sea cables.

Prince Potemkin and his suite, a special train, of engine and several coaches, had vanished into thin air!

The mind of the world almost refused to grasp it. Such a thing could not be.

And yet it was!

And despite all the efforts of two great governments and the most expert investigators of England and Russia, a mystery it remained, until . . .

Prince Potemkin was a huge, blonde Russian with a great square spade beard, long, narrow eyes, in which there was something of the Tartar, and shoulders as broad as a prize-fighter.

He stood upon the platform of Aber-Snowdon station shaking hands with his host, the Marquis of Snowdon.

"I thank you for a most pleasant visit, my dear Snowdon," he said, in perfect English, "and I hope, when next you are in Russia, you will fulfill your promise of staying with me at Tromsk."

"Good-bye, Prince," said the ex-ambassador, "and I hope you will have a pleasant run to town."

"I am sure of it," the prince replied. "Your train service in England is magnificent—when one has one's own private cars"—he indicated the sumptuous special train with a wave of his hand—and two minutes afterward it slowly glided out of the lit station into the mist of the winter's evening.

It was now precisely twenty minutes past six. The Prince sat in his own private saloon. It was lit by electric light. The blinds were drawn over the long, plate-glass windows. It was upholstered in shades of red and gold.

His valet, Feodor, had divested him of his fur coat, and he sat back in a beautifully poised armchair with a sigh of comfort. This traveling room in which he found himself was the acme of luxury. Upon a table by his side was a cedar-wood box of Russian cigarettes, packed in tea to preserve and add to the flavor.

"Get me some vodka, Feodor," the prince said in purring, spitting Russian.

The valet, a pallid-faced, furtive-looking man, hastened away towards the kitchen car and returned in a moment or two with a little cut-glass decanter of the furious, colorless spirit Russians love. When the man had gone, the prince poured out a generous measure and tossed it down with a gasp of satisfaction. He sat there all alone in the miniature traveling palace of red and gold, a striking and significant figure. The breadth and bigness of him, the mighty blonde beard, the bright watchful eyes, instinct with power, and yet full of that indolence which is characteristic of the Russian in repose. The man was intensely typical of his country's extraordinary dormant force, that apparently slept, yet was never more wide-awake.

Here was a man with absolute wealth, absolute power, both as a politician and as a landowner. In the nineteenth century he was as dominant as a king in the Middle Ages. But between him and some ruler of these times there was this difference—Prince Potemkin, cousin of the Tsar, in spite of his seeming indolence, had yet a brain as keen and trained as that of any statesman in the world. He was as adequate and polished a courtier as he was a brave and courageous leader when riding at the head of his Cossacks on some Caucasian raid.

In the adjacent saloon was his secretary, Count Boris Skobeler, his aide-de-camp, Colonel Komarov, and Monsieur Bianchon, his private physician. Beyond that again

was a long compartment with servants of the Prince's
suite; the assistant valet, the courier, a couple of footmen
and a groom, also two huge Cossacks in fur caps, who
formed a sort of personal guard—Cossacks of the Don. And
among this foreign entourage sat Inspector Winterbottom
from Scotland Yard, stolid, uninterested and bored.

All Russians are great eaters, and Prince Potemkin
was no exception to the rule. His chef was even now preparing a sort of preparatory meal to the dinner which
would be served at nine or a quarter past, after the special train had left Llanway.

Feodor brought a silver samovar to his master, with
cut lemons and glasses in filagree holders. There was
caviar upon toast, and the Prince sipped the fragrant
tea and lemon juice and smoked and ate and thought of
various plans he had for tomorrow's evening in London.

And there was a silver samovar for the officers also—
more caviar, cigarettes in thin, brown-tinged paper.

In the front saloon, the servants also had their tea—
and even for them it was caravan tea which had traveled out of China on the backs of camels in compressed
blocks. Inspector Winterbottom alone refused what
many epicures in London would have paid anything for,
and intimated his desire to the kitchen attendant for "a
small Bass, please."

The train went on; luxury, pleasant absence of care,
a general sense of well-being pervaded everyone. The
guard in his van behind knew that he was certain of
a ten-pound note tomorrow morning in London. Ellis,
the driver, had much the same pleasing suspicion. From
the humblest member of the suite to the Prince himself
the hour was rosy!

Inspector Winterbottom, after he had finished his
Bass, suddenly bethought himself of Hooper, the guard.
He knew Hooper and liked him. Hooper, he thought,

would probably be very glad of a bottle of beer. Mr. Winterbottom pressed the bell of the saloon, gave his order, was given the Bass in a foaming tumbler, and, glad to be away from the chattering foreign servants, went out into the corridor and himself carried his little surprise to Hooper.

In the red and gold saloon the great blonde head of Prince Potemkin began to nod. The wrinkled eyelids fell over the bold and staring eyes. The white, jeweled hands relaxed upon his knees—the Prince began to breathe stentoriously in sleep.

The gentlemen of the suite, who had been playing cards, had now disposed themselves for a nap, and, curiously enough, the big carriage full of inferior servants was quite silent—no doubt the soothing motion of the well-hung special train contributed to drowsiness. And, if there had been anyone there to see, he would have been intensely surprised to find that Hooper, the trusted guard of special trains on the Great Union Railway, and Inspector Winterbottom, who always attended upon royalty and celebrated people in England, were actually within two feet of each other upon the floor of the van and snoring!

Somnolence seemed to have overtaken the kitchen attendants in the far part of the train. The only people awake were the driver, Ellis, and the fireman, Alexander, as the traveling palace of Prince Potemkin glided through the lonely mountain places. Penmaenbala station, all lit up, slid behind in a long blur of light. The train approached the tunnel of St. David's Hill.

It was just about a quarter of a mile away from it when the fireman, Alexander, took a flat tin case from his pocket. The driver, Ellis, had his hand upon the regulator and was looking out from the mist-blurred window to his left.

Alexander withdrew a curious-looking object from the flat tin case—it was a pad, wet and dripping, and from it came a strange, sickly smell.

The next incident happened very rapidly. Alexander was a powerful man. He leaped at Ellis, put his arms around him, and pressed the pad to the driver's face. The man struggled unavailingly in the grasp of one stronger than himself; but he did not struggle for long. In sixty seconds or less, Alexander laid him gently down upon the floor of the cab. Then the fireman clutched the regulator and turned the whistle tap. There was a loud, mournful echoing of escaping steam as it vibrated on the metal tongue of the whistle.

Then the train, going much more slowly, entered St. David's tunnel.

Six months after the total disappearance of the special train the mystery remained as impenetrable as ever. The greatest detectives of Europe had exhausted their efforts upon it in vain.

It was six months to the very day when Chief Railway Inspector Buckland called at the house of Sir William English, in Belgrave Square. He called by appointment to have a private interview with the then Chairman of the Great Union Railway.

When he was seated in the great man's study he stated his business without delay.

"I have ventured to ask for this interview, Sir William," he said, "upon a matter of the very greatest importance. It is unusual, I know, for an officer of the company to request a private interview with you."

"I am very glad to grant it, Mr. Buckland," Sir William answered kindly. "I hear of you as the very best Chief of Detective Staff the railway has ever had."

Buckland bowed and took out a bundle of papers from a small bag. "It is about the disappearance of Prince Potemkin's special train, six months ago," he began.

Sir William sighed. "A terrible affair," he said, "I often think, Mr. Buckland, but I have now given it up as a bad job. We shall never know."

"I venture to think, sir, that we shall know very shortly," the other answered in a businesslike voice. "I have been directing all my private time to the investigation. I have not neglected my other work, but I have conducted my little campaign from London until three weeks ago. Three weeks ago I started on my annual holiday. This, also, I devoted to the further elaboration of my theories."

Sir William's face grew very interested, but there was an incredulous look upon it nevertheless. He, more than any man in England, knew what an enormous amount of money had been spent upon the matter. It vitally affected him as Chairman of the Great Union. He had never been quite the same man since the impossible had happened, and a solid express engine, five or six coaches and more than a dozen people had melted into nothingness.

"Then you have something new, Mr. Buckland?" he said.

"I think I have got the solution of the whole mystery."

Sir William started violently. "Go on," he said, "please go on."

Then Buckland began. "I sat in my London rooms, Sir William, and began to reconstruct the whole of this affair, after the month of investigation was over and all hope of any clue was abandoned. First of all, I sought for a motive. It was obvious that some one or some people were deeply interested in getting rid of the Prince. The answer to that was apparent enough. It is well-known privately that by a large section of Young Russia the Prince was regarded as one of the most dangerous foes to reform that existed. The next deduction was equally simple. The only people who could possibly have engineered the mystery were that society known as the Terrorists. They alone would have the necessary funds, the necessary intelligences, to carry out their colossal scheme.

"Quite by chance I discovered that, at the time of the disappearance, a foreign mining engineer had been staying at Llanway. He was a Russian. I mentioned this to the Scotland Yard people investigating at the time, but they found that this gentleman, a Monsieur Goldberg, was a perfectly accredited engineer whose career and record were above suspicion. In fact, my information was rather poohpoohed.

"I clung to my theory, however, and made this man, Goldberg, the point of departure for my investigation. One thing seemed to me to be perfectly clear. Goldberg must have acted in concert with a party of highly skilled and desperate people. You will observe, Sir William, that I did not yet ask myself *how* the disappearance was managed. I accepted it as an indubitable fact and sought for motive first, and people who carried it out second.

"The driver of the train was, as you know, Ellis, the most trusted driver we have had—a man above suspicion. Nevertheless I made many inquiries. I interviewed the poor fellow's wife and found out everything about his life. The inevitable conclusion was that he had nothing willingly to do with the affair. It seemed to me that nothing whatever could have been done without the concurrence of either the driver or the fireman."

Buckland opened a sheaf of papers and went on: "The fireman was named Alexander. He was married. He lived in the upper part of a house quite close to the Great Union Station. I went to that house and made inquiries. It was of rather better quality than one would expect a fireman earning 25/9 a week to occupy. The people down below gave me certain information—briefly as follows: This man, Alexander, spoke French—at least the people down below thought it was French—with considerable fluency. His wife was a foreign woman, very reserved and, so my informants told me, 'a perfect lady.' On the very day on which the special train disappeared Mrs. Alexander sent for the landlord, paid an extra week's rent in advance, sent for a furniture-dealer and sold her furniture and left the house, stating that she was going to Paris.

"That was significant. My thoughts were immediately focused on Alexander as the traitor in the engine."

"But Alexander has disappeared also," Sir William said.

"Quite so, sir," the detective answered, "but we will come to that later."

"I had now decided in my own mind that Alexander and Goldberg were deeply implicated in the affair. But who else? There must have been many people involved.

"An idea struck me. I took my ordnance map of North Wales and I scrutinized it carefully for the nearest small port of harbor to Penmaenbala station. I found it in the village of Moel, some ten miles away. There is a quay there where steamers come to take slates from the quarries. There is also a small fishing fleet. I interrogated the harbor-master, looked at his books, and then found I was absolutely upon the right track."

"This is extraordinarily interesting, Mr. Buckland, please go on," said Sir William, tense and rigid now.

"It seems," the detective continued, in the same calm, business-like voice, "that a month before the disappearance of the special train a yacht arrived at Moel. She was owned by a foreign gentleman, who the harbor-master told me was a German, and manned entirely by foreign sailors. The skipper was an Englishman who made friends with the harbor-master—his name, if it was a real name, was Smith. Now the harbor-master of Moel was, and is still, a fool. I found out without any trouble at all that the crew of the yacht, which seemed very numerous, were of a distinctly Slavonic type. Jones, the harbor-master, has hardly ever been out of Moel and was quite content to believe that these people were all Germans. The apparent owner of the yacht, Count Schmoulder, stayed at the village inn and made himself very popular. It was said that he was taking a change of air. At all hours of the day and night boats would be backwards and forwards from the ship, until the inhabitants of the village got quite used to the fact that the sailors were always going ashore on leave. I have notes of many other peculiar circumstances which I will not detail here, but simply state the fact that at midday of the morning after the disappearance of Prince Potemkin, farewells were said, and the yacht steamed away. I also was able to ascertain that the mining engineer, Monsieur Goldberg, was at Moel for the week preceding the disappearance."

Buckland paused and cleared his throat.

"And then?" Sir William asked eagerly.

"And then the circle of my investigations was very much narrowed. I had established the fact that there was an organization hard at work to do what had been done; and what remained was to find out the method.

"I went up and down the line over and over again, partly on foot, partly on engines supplied by the

station-masters on the route. I could discover nothing for a long time. Then I took a little walking tour
upon the mountains with a knapsack, a compass and an
alpenstock. I stayed at lonely little crofters' farmhous-
es. I made myself acquainted with the whole locality—
and it is the wildest and most untrodden in the United
Kingdom. Then, without making any further investigations, I returned to town."

"You returned to town?"

"I returned to town, Sir William, and worked out
my further theories on paper. The special train, with
all its inmates—with the probable exception of Alexander, the fireman, and one or two members of Prince
Potemkin's suite—is, at the present moment, inside St.
David's Hill!"

Sir William jumped up from his chair, his face perfectly white and his hands trembling.

"What do you mean, sir?" he said in a quavering
voice.

"Exactly what I say, Sir William. You may not be
aware—nobody has remembered the fact or taken the
trouble to ascertain it—but a hundred and twenty years
ago extensive mining operations were carried out at the
top of the hill. It was thought that coal was to be found
in North Wales."

"And that means?"

"It means that, forgotten by everyone, there are extensive workings in the interior of the hill, right down
to, and probably below, the level of the tunnel."

"Ah! the tunnel!"

"Yes, Sir William; I saw at once that was the only
possible point of attack."

"But still, I quite fail to see."

"As everyone else has failed, unprovided with the
information that I have gathered."

The tone was very confident, but Sir William English saw that Buckland was in deadly earnest.

"'The conspirators,' I said to myself, as soon as I arrived back in London, 'have found out about these workings. They were Russian agents aboard that yacht. Now, how should I proceed in the like case?'

"And now, Sir William, it all becomes perfectly clear. I stake my position with the company and my reputation upon the result of further investigation.

"About the middle of the tunnel, as far as I have been able to calculate—though that will have to be proved— there is only a wall of mingled slate and granite between the masonry of the tunnel and some large natural or possibly artificial cavern. The thickness of the wall I do not know, but it was undiscovered and unsuspected when the tunnel was bored. Now imagine a gang of twenty or thirty men, specially trained and capable. Can't you see them making every preparation within this cave, and with unerring skill? Can't you see the wall bored through to the height of, say fifteen feet, to a width of, say eleven to twelve feet—until an aperture is made high enough and wide enough for any train to enter? There would then only remain the actual fitted stone of masonry between the cavern and the interior of the tunnel. This could have been partially loosened a considerable time before. Each stone could have been numbered from the back, ready to be fitted into its place again. I have made it my business to find out that there is a special quick-drying cement which, though not lasting and durable for more than a year or two, will harden in a few hours. Now, supposing the driver of the train was murdered or incapacitated by the fireman, just as it entered the tunnel; supposing that the train proceeded at a foot's pace until it came opposite a yawning aperture made by the removal of the stones; imagine further that the train proceeded a hundred yards beyond the aperture and that a set of temporary rails, already prepared as switch rails, was fitted to the Up line. From my own experience I know that, if everything was arranged beforehand and if the affair was in the hands of skilled experts, the special train could be packed into a cavern within twenty minutes at the outset."

"And then?" came in a whisper from Sir William.

"And then the stones would be replaced with lightning speed, and cemented with the special preparation of which I have spoken. A mixture of soot would be ready. The traces of the disturbance could be cleverly hidden by a man in the tunnel within half an hour. Moreover—I need not explain to you, Sir William, who knows every detail of railway work, how simply this could be done, and, this is an important point, there was ample time. You have only to refer to these notes to see that it must be so. What happened in the cavern, I have no idea; but I am certain that the perpetrators of this fiendish outrage were safely away over the mountains and on board their ship long before the news became general."

Sir William was walking up and down the room with a bowed head.

"This is wonderful. Mr. Buckland," he said. "It seems to me like absolute truth: but supposing—just supposing—that there is no cavern after all?"

"Then where is the special train and its occupants, Sir William?" the detective said, gathering his papers together.

They were found in a low, subterranean chamber—all dead. Fungi had grown over the paint of the carriages. The red and gold had peeled off the engine in scales. No detailed description of that place has ever been given to the world, or ever will.

Among the tale of bodies, two were missing. There was no trace of Alexander, the fireman, nor of Feodor, the Prince's confidential valet.

And though his part in the matter was never made public, from that moment Jasper Buckland's career was assured.

THE CASTLECURRY HORROR

Everybody knows Sir Jasper Buckland, the chairman of the Great Union Railway. He is a popular figure in England. Many of our most distinguished public men have risen from the lowest rung of the ladder by sheer force of merit, but few have mounted so high from so low a position as Sir Jasper Buckland, Bart. He started life as a ticket clerk in a small country station. He went through almost every department of railway life, until he attained his present great position.

It is owing to my personal friendship with him that I am enabled to write these memoirs of one of the most interesting personalities of our time. Some of the stories I have told exactly as he detailed them to me. Others I have built up from Sir Jasper's notes and diaries, which he has kindly allowed me to use. The present story I report almost exactly as it came from his lips.

It was after dinner, in Sir Jasper's house. The rain was pouring down outside in Berkeley Square. The toots of the taxicabs and motors came faintly into the rich, luxurious study, where we were sitting with our coffee.

The dinner had been excellent—Sir Jasper, bachelor though he is, has certainly one of the best chefs in town. We were sitting on either side of a great carved fireplace. The lights were discreetly shaded. The tall

distinguished figure of my host—they say everywhere
that Sir Jasper is the ideal figure of an English country
squire— was illuminated by the glow from the crackling
cedar logs in the open hearth. To look at him, no one
would have thought of all he had been through, of the
fight against fortune that he had waged—and won.

"You have your cigar, Ridley?" he asked.

I nodded.

"Then what was it you were asking me?"

"I want another railway experience."

Sir Jasper smiled and leaned back in his chair. "My
dear fellow," he said, "I am afraid you make me talk too
much. But still, as I promised to give you a faithful and
unvarnished record of my career for your book, I am
entirely at your service."

"I was so interested in the story of the lost train,"
I said, "that I should like another reminiscence of the
days when you were a railway detective. Have you anything else as interesting as that?"

Sir Jasper leaned forward, flipped the ash of his cigar
into the fender, and stared into the fire. Suddenly he
turned his face toward me. It had grown appreciably
paler.

"Something has come back to me, Ridley," he said,
"something which is no welcome guest in my memories.
Still, you shall have it."

I settled myself in my chair and waited. After a minute or so's thought, Sir Jasper began.

"During the whole of my railway career, Ridley, I
have come across every type of man and woman, from
kings to costermongers. When I was a railway detective,
much of my time was taken up in the investigation of
theft. It was only now and again that anything more
interesting or mysterious turned up. But when I say
that the Castlecurry murders afforded me the keenest

excitement of my life—as well as the keenest horror—I shall only be telling you the truth."

The baronet's voice shook a little. The great red-faced, white-haired man paused as he lifted his coffee cup to his lips, splashing a little cognac into it before he did so. "Of all the cold-hearted, devil-possessed, human fiends that I ever met or heard of, Patrick O'Neill, was the worst," he burst out.

He put down his cup with a clatter. "Now listen, Ridley," he said, "and I will tell you the whole story from first to last. The murders made a great stir and outcry at the time, but as they were in a remote part of Ireland and the press was not so well organized as it is now, little was heard of them in the papers. Indeed, the full horror of it was never published, and is only known to a very few people, of whom, I suppose, I am the chief.

"I was head investigator of the Great Union Railway at the time. When you pass through three grades as detective you become junior, and then senior, investigator. It means that you control others and do not have the watching in the goods yards and the arresting of petty thieves to do yourself. Well, I was head of the whole thing when, one morning, I was sent for to the general manager's office—it was old Sir William McKean. He had not much genius for general management and ought to have been a traffic superintendent all his life, for he was a walking time-table. "'Now, Mr. Buckland,' he said, 'I must tell you I have had a communication from the managing director of the Castlecurry Railway in the southwest of Ireland—to be precise, in the division of Connaught. There have been,' the old fellow said, his voice shaking and his hand trembling among his papers, 'there have been some most dreadful murders occurring entirely upon the Castlecurry Railway. Perhaps you will have seen something of them in the papers?'

"'Well, sir,' I replied, 'I have seen a brief account, but no details.'

"'The details are here,' he said, handing me a thick envelope, stuffed with papers.

"'And that means, Sir William?'

"'Mr. O'Brien, the general manager of the Castlecurry Railway, used to be with us some years ago. He was a trusted official of the Great Union. He now writes to me confidentially to ask for the loan of my best investigator. You are the chief of the branch, Mr. Buckland, and I am going to lend you to Mr. O'Brien to see if you can throw any light upon these dreadful happenings—that is, with your concurrence, of course.'

"I bowed. 'I shall be very pleased to go, Sir William, and thank you very much for the confidence which you have reposed in me.'

"'You will receive full first-class expenses on a liberal scale, of course,' the manager went on. 'You will draw what money you require from London and we shall arrange it with the Castlecurry Company later. I may say that, if you do your duty to the satisfaction of Mr. O'Brien—and I have no doubt you will—it has been hinted to me that you may expect to receive a very handsome present indeed. Be off at once and delegate all your work to your second.'

"I rose, distinctly pleased at the prospect before me, and more than complimented by the kind way in which Sir William had spoken of my work.

"He was a kindly old man, and he waved a tremulous hand of farewell. 'Bring them to justice, Buckland, bring them to justice, whoever they are!' in his tremulous old voice, 'for never in my life have I come across so black and sinister a mystery.'

"I left Euston for Liverpool during the afternoon, intending to catch the night boat to Dublin. I traveled first-class, of course, and was fortunate enough, by a hint to the guard of who I was, to get a carriage to myself. I had some tea brought in and, as soon as we were well upon the way, I opened the envelope Sir William had given me and plunged into the contents.

"Of course, I was deeply interested. This was a great chance to show my abilities as a railway detective. It meant not only money but fame for me as well, while the compliment itself was a great one. I was to go and investigate where the Irish police themselves had failed. I was to take charge of the whole investigation, and I confess the prospect whetted my appetite and I was as keen as a man could be.

"I am not going to inflict the whole contents of those papers upon you. I will only give you the briefest outline.

"It seemed that the Castlecurry Railway was a system of not more than a hundred miles. It covered the large area of central Connaught and was in connection with the Great Northern of Ireland, though it was a separate company. The line wound in and out among a fairly large extent of country and was the principal means of communication between Castlecurry in the east and Ballygrove in the northwest of Sligo. The last was the terminus.

"It tapped a lot of small market towns.

"During the last month, three appalling murders had occurred upon this secluded, local railway system.

"Every indication pointed to the fact that the crimes were committed by the same hand or hands.

"The first victim was Miss Cregan, a middle-aged spinster who was a capable business woman and the proprietress of a successful lace-making establishment at Ballygrove. Miss Cregan was well known and much respected in the Sligo district of Connaught. She had left

Ballygrove in the morning and taken the train to Castlecurry, a distance of some thirty miles—the main line of the system going straight between terminus and terminus, while other branch lines spread into the country on either side.

"At Castlecurry, Miss Cregan had made various personal purchases and also had arranged for a large consignment of thread to accompany her upon the return journey at night. She had gone to her bank and withdrawn a sum of fifty pounds partly in gold and partly in notes, which she carried in a reticule upon her wrist.

"She left Castlecurry upon a dark autumn night by the last train from Ballygrove, which started at eight forty-five. She was alone in a first-class carriage. There were about six stations between Castlecurry and Ballygrove. At five of them the lady was seen alone in her carriage. Porters and station masters touched their hats to her as they went by, for she was a most popular woman and had done much to encourage the lace industry in that part of Ireland. After the fifth station, Ballincen, there was a twelve-mile run up to Ballygrove. The train mounts all the way, for Ballygrove is situated on the slope of a high, mountainous moor. This last twelve miles took longer than almost all the rest of the journey.

"When the train arrived at Ballygrove, Miss Cregan was discovered, dead! Her throat had been cleanly cut from ear to ear by some sharp instrument. The reticule containing the money was gone.

"A week passed, and then the whole district was given another frightful shock, even worse than the previous one.

"This time the victim was a priest. Father O'Flaherty left Ballygrove at eight o'clock at night for Castlecurry. He had been holding a mission at Ballygrove, in aid of a new convent which was being built at Roscommon. The offertories for ten days had been devoted to this. During the afternoon the money had been exchanged for notes at the Ballygrove bank for greater convenience. Father O'Flaherty carried a very considerable sum in his pocketbook.

"The train only arrived at Ballincen—twelve miles from Ballygrove—when the Father was discovered dead; and murdered in precisely the same way as the unfortunate elderly lady only a few days before.

"His pocketbook was missing.

"The third murder was that of a horse-breeder, a Mr. O'Farrell. The details were very much the same as those of the other two, except for one sinister circumstance. O'Farrell might easily have carried money as he had sold several horses at Castlecurry. As a matter of fact he had nothing upon him but a sovereign or so, having paid all the proceeds of his sales into the bank. The unfortunate man's face was horribly gashed and cut, as if some fiend, disappointed of its prey, had taken this grisly revenge.

"Here was food for thought enough! I arrived at Liverpool, went to the Adelphi for a meal, and, on my way to the landing stage, I purchased a small but very business-like revolver. It was a thing I had never carried before in all my detective work, but as I pictured the lonely railway winding among the hills and bogs of Ireland, and brooded over the black mystery I was going to solve, I felt glad, the weapon in my hand felt like a friend.

"In the early afternoon of the next day I arrived at Castlecurry from Dublin. I drove straight to the house of Mr. O'Brien, the general manager of the railway. It was situated in the principal street of the town, a handsome, square house of brown stone.

"Acting upon advices which I had received in a letter handed me by the police at Dublin, I announced myself as Doctor Buckland, from London. I was clean-shaved, then, as now. I had changed into dark, pro-fessional-looking clothes, and a maid-servant at once showed me in to the manager.

"'He is terribly upset, doctor,' she whispered to me as I took off my coat in the hall, 'and it's glad to see you he will be, for sure master's nerves have gone entoirely since this bloody business on the line!'

"I was shown into a large library. A fire was burning upon the hearth, and in a great arm-chair, his head sunk forward, his eyes without much speculation or interest in them, sat a little, thin, elderly man with iron-gray hair. He looked the picture of nervous collapse.

"The door closed behind me and I advanced towards him. Then I was startled. The dejected face changed in an instant. The eyes grew bright and glittering. The little man almost leaped out of his chair and caught me by the hand. I never saw such a picture of energy and determination, and though I'm not easily taken aback I gasped in surprise.

"He saw it. 'It is nothing, Mr. Buckland,' he said. 'Faith! and I have had to pretend that I am struck down by these murders. It is to put people off their guard, for, faith, I don't know from one moment to another who may or may not be the black devil that has done these things. I'm glad to have you, I'm glad to have you! Sir William McKean has written of you to me. I hear you are the best investigator in all the railways of England, and I tell you this, without any further preamble, that if you can discover what is behind these horrors on our line, you are a made man.'

"After that, Mr. O'Brien offered me a cigar, and we sat talking earnestly for nearly an hour. He placed me in full possession of all the facts, answered my questions with great lucidity and directness and then inquired exactly what I proposed to do.

"'I want full authority from you, sir,' I said, 'to do exactly as I like on the line.'

"'You shall have it,' he said, taking from his waistcoat pocket a gold token rather larger than a five shillings piece. 'There is the key of the line,' he continued. 'With this you can do anything and everything. But I implore you to be careful. It must not get out in the town who you are. Of course, some of the railway officials must know, but don't put any unknown people upon their guard by the slightest indiscretion.'

"I took the token—two or three of the higher officials of all railways have such a talisman—and then I outlined my campaign.

"'I want you, sir,' I said, 'to remain as you are supposed to be at present—overcome and stricken down by these events. We must not be seen together in the investigation. In Castlecurry and in Ballygrove I can still be the English doctor who is visiting you, and in the intervals of attending upon his patient is making a little tour of the country. What is the principal hotel in this town?'

"'The "Saint Patrick," Mr. Buckland. Indeed, it is the only hotel of any merit whatever.'

"'I shall take up my quarters there. I shall come and see you again tonight, probably quite late. Meanwhile, I will go about my investigation in my own way, if you will allow me.'

"'Good luck to you, Mr. Buckland,' he said, 'you are entering upon as dark and desperate a business as well could be.'

"With that I left the library and the house. The outside car which had brought me from the station was still waiting with my luggage, and I drove up to the 'Saint Patrick' hotel, which was situated in the big market square of the town.

"I engaged rooms in the name of Doctor Buckland. At four o'clock it was already beginning to be dusk. I had some tea and then, about half-past five, when it was quite dark, I slipped over to the station.

"The station was a fairly large one, roofed over with glass, but at this moment there were few people about as no train was due to start for at least another hour. I was, of course, very well acquainted with the topography of stations, and, without inquiring of any porter, I made my way at once, without difficulty, to the station master's office.

"Knocking at the door, without waiting for an answer, I went straight in.

"The station master was sitting at his writing table, and by a glowing fire of peat and coal was sitting an inspector of police. Both men looked up quickly as I entered.

"'I should like to look at your official time-table, if you please,' I said, bowing to the station master.

"His face grew red. 'This is not the place—' he began, when I pulled out Mr. O'Brien's token and showed it to him. Without a word he searched among the papers on his table and handed me a draft time-table, written in ink upon a sheet of card.

"'We have modified things a little, sir,' he said, glancing at me curiously.

"I looked over the time-table. 'Have you a light engine in the yard, with steam up?' I asked.

"'There is an engine in the yard,' he answered, 'and she can get up steam in twenty minutes.'

"'Then I am going right over the line from here to Ballygrove. I want the most reliable driver at present in the yard, and one who can be trusted to keep his mouth shut. The same applies to the fireman.'

"Without a further word, the station master lifted up his desk telephone and gave a few brief orders.

"After that I introduced myself. The inspector, whose name was Connor, shook me warmly by the hand. 'I knew you were coming, sir,' he said, 'and, indade, it's myself that is glad to see you. We're all at fault here, and that's the truth. We want another mind on the problem.'

"'Have you any photographs?' I asked.

"The station master unlocked a drawer and pulled out a little bundle of proofs. There were the carriages in which the murders had been committed. There were careful photographs of the victims—not pleasant things, my dear Ridley, but the police and detectives are accustomed to them.

"I scrutinized them with extreme attention and put them in my pocket. 'Now,' I said, 'you have doubtless got the coach or coaches intact in which the three murders were committed?'

"'We have, sor,' said the inspector, 'they are in the yard.'

"'I will go and look at them,' I replied. The three of us left the warm and comfortable office, crossed the three lines, and went into the big goods yard and locomotive depot. Here and there a steely-cold arc light threw its radiance upon the trucks and goods, the locomotive turn-tables and the long gaunt sheds silhouetted against the dark evening sky.

"The coaches in which the murders had been committed, two in number, were in a locked shed. As we entered, the place was in darkness, but the station master switched on the electrics. The first thing I noticed was that both the coaches consisted of four compartments. They were of an old-fashioned type—the Castlecurry

Railway was by no means up-to-date—and had the high 'clerestory' roofs.

"'All first-class, I see,' I remarked.

"'All the murders were committed in first-class carriages,' said the inspector.

"'And, I understand, that in each case the victim was traveling alone.'

"The inspector took a key from his pocket and unlocked a door. Then he handed me a lantern.

"'Go in and see for yourself, sir,' he said. 'This is the compartment in which Mr. O'Farrell, the horse-farmer, was killed.'

"I took the lantern, climbed into the compartment and made a thorough investigation.

"The compartment had not been touched since the body was removed. I don't want to horrify you with gruesome details, Ridley, but I discovered one or two strange things while my companions waited outside in the shed. A first-class compartment is cushioned rather higher than a man's head. The dark brown stains seemed to me rather curiously disposed upon the cushions and upon the floor. I had always been a student of railway murders from the time of that of Mr. Briggs, by Franz Muller, in 1864, or when Lefroy murdered Mr. Gold on the Brighton line, right down to the Miss Camp's tragedy between Hounslow and Waterloo, to say nothing of the Merstham Tunnel mystery of 1905.

"Then I made another discovery. There were one or two faint splashes of brown upon the white paint above the cushions and below the luggage rack and there was one tiny splash right up in the higher part of the carriage roof—that in which the lamp hung. I think I have explained that these carriages were what were known as being of the clerestory type; that is to say, in the center the roof rose up for two feet or so into a kind of inverted

alcove. You may still see carriages like this on some railways, but they are almost abandoned now as the ordinary first-class coaches are built so much higher than
they were in the past.

"I straddled on the two seats of the compartment. I
lifted the lantern high and took a little lens from my
pocket and magnified this splash. What I saw almost
caused me to lose my balance. A whole rush of wild surmise flooded into my mind.

"I finished my examination and came down into the
yard. Looking at my watch, I found that only ten minutes had elapsed. The station master had said it would
take twenty minutes for the light engine I had requisi-
tioned to get up steam.

"'We have a little more time before I need start,' I
said as we left the shed. "Ah, they are making up a train
there?'

"'It is the 8:45,' the station master answered, 'the
identical train in which all the murders have been done.
They are getting it ready quite early for the run to Ballygrove. You see we have to take every precaution now, sir.
They are lighting the coaches already. There is a constable superintending everything. Before it comes to the
platform everything will be thoroughly searched—under the seats and everywhere. Then, when it starts, the
inspector here will travel in the guard's van and there
will be another constable on the engine.'

"'Let us stroll over, I should like to see the train
made up,' I said, and accordingly we did so.

"The train consisted of three coaches. The first one
was a coach of 'thirds' with five compartments of the
old, crude and cramped design. In the middle was a
coach similar to the one I had just examined in the
shed, consisting entirely of first-class compartments.
There was another third-class coach, a couple of trucks

already piled high with bales and packages and then a
guard's van.

"A porter was running along the roofs of the carriages,
while another handed him up the already lighted oil
lamps which were to illuminate the compartments.

"Just as the man was jerking up one of the lamps
upon his hooked pole, I stopped him.

"'I should like to have a look at this lamp,' I said.

"With a stare of astonishment he lowered the pole
and gave it to me. The lamp was of a very early type. It
gave a fair illumination—that I could see at once—but
out of all proportion to its cumbrousness and size. The
circumference was almost equal to that of a small wash-
ing-basin.

"'I will just come up on the roof of this coach,' I
said, stepping on to a buffer at the end and climbing up
the rigid iron ladder. As I did so, I saw the police inspector wink at the station master solemnly. The porter
helped me up and I stood beside him while he dropped
the lamp into the round hole in the roof.

"When he had done so, I bent down and lifted up
the lamp again by its handle above the chimney. For its
size it was not very heavy. It came out easily enough and
without the slightest noise or jar. I fitted it once more
into its place and descended.

"Then we walked to the locomotive side of the yard,
where my iron steed was waiting.

"Already I had a theory. It was only the very faintest
glimmering of an idea—the very seed of a thought. And
yet it persisted in my mind, incredible as it seemed. I
would not have mentioned it to either of my companions for a hundred pounds, but nevertheless it was there!

"'This is a gentleman who comes from the general
manager,' the station master said to the engine driver,
as I climbed into the cab. 'You will do exactly what he

tells you. He wants to make a run to Ballygrove. I have telegraphed to Long and the line will be clear.'

"An instant afterwards the driver had cautiously jerked the throttle to the right and we were gliding out of the yard into the darkness of the night.

"'I will tell you exactly what I want to do,' I said. 'I want you to run this engine as if you were running the ordinary 8:45 train. Go no faster and no slower.'

"And the man touched his cap.

"'Right, sir,' he said, briefly—he was a Scotchman from Belfast—and off we went.

"We stopped at each one of the four stations for exactly the time that the ordinary train would have stopped. I let nothing escape me. I descended from the engine and spoke a few words to the station master in each case. I watched the faces of the porters.

"We arrived at Ballincen.

"And here, at last, I began to concentrate all my forces.

"It was between Ballincen and Ballygrove that all the murders had been committed. I suppose we were about two minutes in this station which was rather larger than the others. The driver had just turned to me and was saying 'we had better get on, sir,' when a porter came up with a market basket.

"'This stuff for Coster,' he said. 'I was going to send it on by the 8:45, but if you are running through to Ballygrove, you might drop it at the signal.' Then the man caught sight of me and touched his cap. 'Beg your pardon, your honor,' he said, 'I didn't know there was a gentleman upon the engine!'

"'What is it?' I asked the driver.

"'It's some stuff for the signalman four miles from here on the run, sir,' he said. 'We have to slow down and we generally—'

"'By all means,' I replied, 'and now let us get on.'

"Erskine—that was the driver's name—tooted upon the whistle, and we ran slowly out into the night.

"I began to question him.

"'I understand,' I said, 'that we are now entering what we might call the murder area?'

"He shivered. 'It is, sir,' he said. 'I have been driving the train when the murders happened. This bit of road haunts me, and that's the truth. I was in charge when poor Miss Cregan was killed, and Father O'Flaherty, too, and yet I saw nothing, knew nothing, and know nothing now, no more than a new-born babe.'

"I had been standing peering out through the great round windows ahead. Now I sat down on the oily, steel seat by the side of the furnace door. There was nothing to disturb my thoughts but the rhythmical pulsing of the connecting rods, the roar and rattle in the air above, the occasional scrape and crackling fall of coal, as the fireman labored in the tender.

"At last, I felt that we were slowing up. Glancing at Erskine, I saw that he had pressed up the throttle. We were not moving at more than five miles an hour.

"'What is this?' I asked.

"'Company's regulations, sir. We are now eight miles from Ballygrove. We have got to mount right up into the moors on a gradient of one in ninety. We have no engines of the newest patterns, and the railway was made before modern scientific methods came in.'

"He snapped the lever to the level, and the engine stopped.

"To the right was a low signal box, set in the embankment of the line, and almost on a level with the carriages.

"The fireman lifted up the basket which had been put in at Ballincen.

"'Here's Coster's nuts and bananas,' he said, and jumping off the engine, he hurried to the lighted box. I peered out of the cab and saw a short, dark-haired man come down the low steps and snatch at the basket. A moment or two afterwards the fireman climbed up again to the engine.

"'A dirty rogue,' he muttered to himself as Erskine opened the throttle and we went on at a snail's pace. 'Never so much as said thank you—never does, damn him!'

"'Who is he?' I asked the driver.

"'He has been a sailor, sir,' Erskine answered. 'He is in charge of this signal box, the last before we get to Ballygrove. He's half foreign and lives with a brother of his a mile away upon the bog. They're queer people, and nasty tempered. That stuff Shamus has just dropped— it's bags of nuts and bananas and such-like stuff. They don't even eat like Christians!'

"I said nothing at all, and the engine went on mounting the steep gradient at a snail's pace.

"'Ye'll recollect, sir, that ye asked me to drive this engine as if I had three coaches and some trucks behind it,' Erskine said.

"I nodded.

"'Otherwise, he continued, 'I could run ye in to Ballygrove in a verra few minutes.'

"The lighted signal box faded out of sight behind, and we groaned onwards. About four hundred yards from the box we passed under a bridge. The embankment on either side of the line was not very high and the bridge was only a flying structure of wood which hardly cleared the chimney of the engine by two feet.

"'And what is this for?' I asked, as we gradually accelerated our speed.

"'Tis just a way from one part of these trackless bogs to another. Right away on the other side of the line there are a few pasture lands and a scattered farm or two. The bridge is for the convenience of the peasants.'

"At this point, I took out my case and lit a cigar. Strange things were weaving and interweaving in my mind.

"We were now traveling at the rate of about fifteen miles an hour until—another steep gradient intervening some three miles from the signal box—again we made almost a halt. Surmounting this, we arrived upon a high level and ran into Ballygrove almost at top speed, the engine clanking joyfully and even on the face of the driver and the fireman a sense of relief showing visible.

"At the terminus, the engine needed some water. I ordered Erskine to let it run into the tank in charge of the fireman. I took him into the fussy little refreshment room and stood him a whiskey.

"I could see the man was an honest, decent fellow. 'D'you know, Erskine,' I said, 'I think I'm getting rather to the solution of this mystery?'

"He started. 'Sir,' he said, 'I would to God ye were! After the first two murders they lockit the doors; and train traveled with an armed guard, and yet Mr. O'Farrell arrived at Ballygrove slit from ear to ear. Who could be the murderer? How could he get out when he had done his bloody work? It's far-r beyond me sir, but if you have got even an inkling—'

"'I've more than that,' I replied. 'Now tell me about this man, Coster.'

"The Scotchman laughed as he sipped his whiskey. 'Sir,' he said, 'he couldna have been concer-r-ned in these affairs. He must be at his post in the signal box.'

"'Does he often have boxes of bananas and nuts?'

"Erskine started. 'Once or twice a week,' he answered.

"I put my hand upon his shoulder and turned him round. 'Now, you get back on the engine at once,' I said, 'and run me through to Castlecurry as fast as you can go.' The man's face was a mask of amazement, but I don't suppose a light engine ever ran and racked over the lines so fast before as his did when he took me back to Castlecurry. I was shaken about like a pea in a tin!

"A week later, my dear Ridley," Sir Jasper continued, "I got into the 8:45 train at Castlecurry."

He pushed over the cigar box and I took another weed. I was tremendously interested in the narrative. Sir Jasper had led up to the climax with the skill of a practiced writer. His shrewd old eyes had been watching me—I felt all the thrill and sense of horror that he had felt thirty years ago.

"Now, Sir Jasper, go on please—"

"It was just a week after my journey on the light engine. During that time, I had successfully sustained my reputation as a wealthy doctor from London attending upon Mr. O'Brien, while at the same time I had been zealous in prosecuting private investigations all round the country side.

"There was a lull in the reign of terror. There had been no more murders, but, on the night that I started alone in a first-class carriage from Castlecurry to Ballygrove, I had a rather shrewd idea that I might provoke one!

"My method had been as follows. After a long conference with the general manager, it had been arranged that a sister of his, Miss O'Brien, who lived at Ballygrove, should apparently fall ill. I removed my belongings to Ballygrove and visited the old lady, who was no more ill than I am and who was a charming and witty Irishwoman with whom it was a pleasure to talk—regularly every day.

"In the afternoons I went to Castlecurry to attend upon Mr. O'Brien, and I began to make it a practice to return to Ballygrove every night by the 8:45, always alone and always in a first-class carriage.

"By this time, my suspicions were crystallized almost into a certainty, and a very dreadful certainty it was. At the same time, it was necessary to catch the fiends actually at work, and to that end I made myself a decoy.

"I now come to the actual night upon which I made the ghastly discovery.

"Seated in the first-class carriage, I passed the first five stations without any incident. The doors of the carriage were locked and I possessed the key.

"Directly the train glided out of Ballincen I opened a small black bag I carried and lit a dark lantern, placing it on the seat beside me. Then I hurriedly unfastened my collar and strapped round my neck a thick leather band, which I had had made at a local saddler's and which effectually protected the throat. Then, drawing my loaded revolver from my pocket, I sat in a corner of the carriage and watched.

"If things were as I thought, then the attack would come from above. My eyes were fixed upon the roof of the carriage. I am a fairly courageous man, Ridley, but I can still remember the horror of those minutes of waiting. My life depended upon my coolness, but though my hand was steady and my pulse normal, there was fear about my heart!

"Moment after moment passed by. Each one seemed as long as an hour until the train gradually slowed to a walking pace and almost stopped in front of the lonely signal box to the right of the line.

"Just before we came to it, I sat upright in the middle of the carriage, with my head sunk forward, in the attitude of a sleeping man. Out of the corner of my eye,

I saw the dark, saturnine face of the signalman peering at the train as it moved slowly by, and something told me that the moment had come.

"I hurried back to my corner, lifted my revolver, and waited. The lantern was in my left hand.

"I calculated that it took exactly forty-five seconds from the time we left the signal box, and at the pace we were going, to reach the light flying bridge over the line. Either my calculations were wrong or, in the terrible strain of the moment, I had made a mistake in my counting, but it was only half a minute before my strained attention caught the sound of a faint thud above the noise of the groaning wheels and the panting of the engine ahead. Nine people out of ten would not have heard it.

"But I was watching for it—it was what I expected to hear.

"Then it came.

"Without a sound, the great oil lamp in the roof went upwards and disappeared. The rush of cold wind—it was a stormy night—came into the compartment.

"In an instant, I turned the full beam of my lantern upwards towards the black circle in the roof.

"As I did so, two things happened simultaneously. The japanned tin of the lantern had grown almost red hot—I had turned the wick too high. The contact with my fingers was unbearable. I let the thing drop involuntarily and it rolled under the seat. There was a slight scuffling sound above me and, raising my revolver, I fired into the dark.

"There was a horrible sound, half snarl, half shriek, and something huge, warm and terribly alive leaped down upon me. There was a hot and fetid breath in my face. An arm like steel curved round my neck and I felt a knife hacking at the leather band around my throat.

"It is quite useless to try to express the horror that I experienced. I had half expected some such thing as this and even at that hideous moment I remember how I thought of the three poor people who had been done to death in the dark by that which was upon me.

"I was then, as now, a very strong man. I used to be able to tear a pack of cards in two. My left hand shot out and I grasped a tight, vibrating, leather thong. In a flash, my hand ran down it and I clutched a living column of muscles which rippled horribly under the fierceness of my grasp. Once, twice, my grip slipped, but I got my fingers well inside the leather collar round the neck.

"A horrible, snarling gurgle filled the compartment. With my right hand I grasped a wrist, supple as an eel, and felt the handle of the knife that had been hacking at my throat.

"It was done quickly enough. With all the strength of my right arm, I bent the wrist back—the hair upon it slipped in my fingers as I did so—there was a quick snap, a frightful agitation at the throat of the thing from which I was slowly choking the life, and then the arm fell useless while the one around my neck whipped away suddenly.

"The train began to slow again. We had run three miles from the signal box, and the frightful struggle which I have described to you in a few words must have taken several minutes. Obviously my shots had not been heard above the noise of the engine and the roaring of the wind. The air of the carriage was full of a horrible, musty smell and the lower part of my body and my legs began to be beaten and scratched by the legs of the thing that I was holding, when, without a moment's warning, the lamp above dropped into its place with a thud, flooding the carriage with light.

"Within an inch or two of my face, there was another face!

"My right hand was free. The revolver lay upon the seat by my side. I snatched it up, pressed it close, close to the writhing brown mass with which I fought, and fired the remaining three shots.

"The heavy horror fell away from me. I heard my own loud, almost agonized sob of relief. I stared down at something writhing slowly upon the floor, and then I fell over it myself and all was dark.

"I came to life again in the little refreshment room at Ballygrove. Cold water had been dashed in my face. A glass containing something pungent and stinging was held to my lips and I swallowed it as best I might.

"Then my eyes cleared.

"There was a little group of people around me—the guard of the train, the police inspector, the station master and two uniformed constables.

"I began to laugh hysterically. I shrieked with mirth—I can remember it to this day. They gave me some more brandy and I grew calmer.

"Somebody was shaking me warmly by the hand. It was Connor.

"'There won't be any more murders now, sir,' he said, 'thanks to your courage. Faith, but you've the seeing eye, Mr. Buckland, and our wits are slow—can you bear to look at him?'

"I was my own man now and I rose from the chair and went to the further corner of the refreshment room. Upon a horsehair sofa, stretched out in grotesque imitation of a human being, was the body of the horrid beast with which I had fought in the dark train.

"I shuddered as I saw and leaned back upon my friends—and if you've ever seen the body of a thing which is not human, but which has been taught by

human fiends the most devilish part of humanity, then
Ridley, you would have staggered back as I did. I was
sick at heart for the moment. All that I had gone through
was as nothing to this and for a moment my whole belief
in God and goodness seemed slipping from me.

"Upon the sofa, blood-stained, malevolent and stiff,
lay a long and sinuous ape. As it transpired afterwards,
it was a combination of the docile and clever chimpan-
zee with the ferocious baboon. The two Costers had
brought the creature with them from Africa when it was
a pup—no, I won't insult good, honest dogs by calling it
that—when it was a potential instrument of hell. They
had trained it to all kinds of hideous and intelligent
behavior.

"It all came out at the trial of the older Coster—the
signalman. He confessed everything.

"The ape knew its business well enough. The elder
Coster scrutinized the train as it stopped in front of his
box. Then he signaled by a flash lantern to his young
brother who was waiting with the ape by the side of the
embankment by the bridge. The brother, a sailor like
the signalman, would drop lightly on the roof of the
carriage indicated by the signal, withdraw the lamp and
fling the monkey upon the head of the victim. A collar
was round its neck, attached to a cord which was held
by the fiend upon the roof. It slit the throats of the
three poor people, it searched their pockets for pocket-
books and purses. When the train slowed down again,
three miles nearer Ballygrove, it was easy for the man
upon the roof to clamber down the end of the coach and
make off homeward over the bog."

"And what happened to them, Sir Jasper?" I asked.

"Coster the elder was hanged, after making a full
confession and showing exactly how he and his brother
had trained the brute that nearly killed me."

"And the younger?"

"Never seen again. He got clear away. He was then thirty years of age. This all happened thirty years ago. I like to think that such a monstrous criminal, and such a brilliant and perverted brain has long since gone out into the unknown."

"And the throat-slitting beast?"

"Oh, they burned his body in the public square of Ballygrove, and I have no feeling of animosity whatever. He simply did what he was told and trained to do, to the very best of his ability. And how few of us can say the same!" Sir Jasper concluded with a smile as he rose from his chair and bade me a kindly good-night.

Speed! Speed! Speed!

It was when I was invited to Craig Loch, Sir Jasper's Scottish seat, that I obtained the particulars of the extraordinary events which I give in this story.

There was a big house party, and we had been out after the grouse all day. It was wonderful to see how Sir Jasper, who had only learned to shoot late in life, acquitted himself at the butts. It was only another instance of how easily the supreme mind can adapt itself to any circumstances, and how genius for success persists even in so comparatively small a matter as shooting grouse upon a moor. The man who had started life as a clerk in the ticket office of an obscure station and was now millionaire and railway king, held his own with men of the house party who had done nothing else but shoot from their youth upwards.

I had acquitted myself fairly well. Keenly as I love shooting, I have no claim to be called a crack shot. Still, I had not missed too flagrantly.

About half-past ten, most of the men left the smoking-room to go to bed, tired by their exertions. Personally, I felt extremely fresh and Sir Jasper seemed the same. He was smoking a big, old-fashioned meerschaum pipe—why is it that nobody smokes meerschaum any more?—and he seemed good for an hour's talk at least.

This was my chance. One has to catch Sir Jasper when and how one can; but I thought I saw another story in his eye to add to these memoirs of the strongest personality, of the most genial host, I have ever known.

We were left alone, sitting together on either side of an elaborate smoking-table of ebony. All round the room, which was lighted by lamps, huge antlered stags' heads stared down upon us from the frieze. Sporting pictures by celebrated artists hung upon the walls, and the aroma of Havana cigars lingered fragrantly in the big, luxurious place.

"I wonder you have never married, Sir Jasper!" I said. "With this beautiful house, your place in Berkeley Square and your maisonette at Brighton, I wonder you have never felt the want of a chatelaine."

He blew a spiral of smoke from his lips.

"My dear Ridley," he said, "I have excellent servants and housekeepers. My every wish is anticipated almost before I can formulate it. I have never been in any sense a 'lover of ladies.' I admire women tremendously. I have the most true and faithful women friends. But a bachelor I am, and a bachelor I shall remain, to the end of my life."

I said nothing in reply, but leaned back in my chair and gazed up at the wagon-roof ceiling.

I knew that the old man was in a communicative mood. I felt certain that he was going to tell me something or other of supreme interest. I did nothing to break the current of his reminiscence.

"I was in love once, Ridley," he said at length, "and only once. She would not have anything to do with me. She afterwards married the proprietor of a public house in Birmingham and grew very fat. Only the other day I put her two sons in subordinate positions upon the Great Union Railway—for the sake of old times. She wrote to me and I saw her in London—Ridley, fate saved me from an irrevocable mistake! At the same time, what I have told you reminds me of an episode in my railway career which I suppose is without precedent."

It was coming at last! I tried not to appear too keen and interested, but my ears were very wide open indeed.

"Without precedent," I said, "that is rather a large order, Sir Jasper!"

"And yet, when you've heard the story, I believe you will agree with me," the dear old fellow said. "At any rate, in my life it was a very definite incident. When I told you the story of the Castlecurry horrors I explained to you how I knew utter horror, black fear, for the first and last time in my life. What I am going to tell you now, if you are not too tired to listen to me, is the story of how I knew the maddest and most reckless exhilaration of my whole career. There come times to all of us, Ridley, when ordinary considerations go by the board and for a few wild minutes we know the fierce joy that the knights of the past must have felt as they clanged into the tournament, or perhaps these modern boys, when they loop the loop in aeroplanes, experience today."

"I am all attention."

"Very well, then. At the time of which I speak, I was district manager of the Great Union at Plymtown—that great port in the West. It was a long time since my days as a railway detective. I had been promoted and promoted. I was then marked out as one of the rising men in our great system.

"Plymtown, as you know, is in Devon, and stands at the gate of Cornwall and the farthest west. It was not so in the days of which I speak, but since then the longest non-stop run of any train in England takes place between London and Plymtown, on our system. Since the new line was made, we have beaten the G. W. R. by twenty minutes.

"My salary was at that time seven hundred a year. A bachelor, without ties, and liable at any moment to be called for duty, I thought it best not to take a house or live in rooms but to make my home in a hotel. My head-quarters, accordingly, were at the 'Rodney,' upon that famous terrace which overlooks the bay. From my bed-room windows I could see the famous breakwater a mile and a half long, with Raleigh Island, bristling with forts, in the foreground. The great liners from South America moved in and out of the harbor. Bugles sounded all day long from the barracks and cruisers, battleships and snake-like destroyers moved ceaselessly up and down the estuary to Evonport.

"I enjoyed my life at Plymtown, but there came a time when—as I have told you—there seemed to be nothing more left in life for me. I had been refused, definitely refused, and without Fanny—girls had strange names in those days, my dear Ridley—my career and my ambition seemed worthless.

"There was a young fellow staying in the hotel with whom I had made friends. He was unhappy also, though he made no confidences to me; but I saw that life to him was by no means a radiant business, and we became great friends within the space of a week or so. His name was Henry Gilbert, and he was a clerk in a big London firm of financiers—I forget the name at the moment. He was obviously a trusted clerk, for he had told me that he was in the West upon an important negotiation, the successful result of which would mean a fortune for his employers, promotion and a substantial commission for himself.

"The 'Rodney' was not a large hotel. It was old-fash-ioned and very comfortable. They made everyone feel at home there. At the time of which I am speaking—to be precise, upon a certain memorable Sunday morning—the only three people staying in the hotel were myself, my friend Henry Gilbert, and an elderly, quiet-mannered Jew, whose name was registered as Moses Mayerstein.

"Henry Gilbert was a man of thirty-two. He had crisp, curling, brown hair, clean-cut face, and the manner of an athlete. I found, indeed, that in his spare time he was one of the mainstays of the 'Old London Running Club' and was also a lieutenant in the Volunteers—there were no territorials at that time, Ridley.

"Mr. Mayerstein, on the contrary, had what the tailors call a very marked 'lower chest.' He was short and inordinately fat. His hair was iron-gray, his nose and lips typically Jewish, and he had three, or perhaps four, chins. He dressed very quietly. He was the ideal person to wear a diamond as large as a sixpence in a ring on his little finger—according to popular ideas. However, he did nothing of the sort, was reticent, well-mannered and had a certain air of power and reserve force which was very noticeable. He seemed to like Henry Gilbert very much, though the compliment was not returned.

"'Many times,' Gilbert said to me, 'I wish I could get rid of this Jew, Mayerstein. He insists on being friendly. He follows me about everywhere and I can't shunt him off without absolute rudeness. I don't want to be rude to him because he has given me no possible opening, and he seems an extremely able man. Besides, he is one of the partners in Mayerstein & Mayerstein, of Fenchurch Street, in London. They are a rising financial house and I can't afford to quarrel with anybody so important in the city.'

"'Then what have you got to complain of?' I asked.

"'Only that I want to be alone,' he replied, briefly. 'I have private troubles which don't make me feel very sociable.'

"That was the situation of affairs when, one Sunday morning, I went down to breakfast in the coffee-room. As district manager, I had practically nothing to do the whole of the day. My cold bath had not invigorated me. The grilled sole they brought me tasted like ashes, I could have thrown the coffee at the waiter's head; I was absolutely and utterly miserable—for the reason of which I have told you.

"Henry Gilbert generally breakfasted at my table during his stay at the hotel. I was down first, and half-way through my breakfast when he appeared.

"There is, of course, a Sunday delivery in Plymtown and two letters were waiting by my friend's plate as he came up and nodded a good-morning. His face was gray and haggard. He had obviously had a bad night, and as he sat down and opened his letters I had a curious sense of companionship, though neither of us spoke.

"Here was another unhappy man!

"Gilbert opened one letter—a small envelope addressed in a woman's hand. I am not naturally curious about the affairs of others, but my training as a railway detective had made me very observant and I could hardly help seeing what I did. He opened the other—a square envelope, addressed in curious old-fashioned handwriting—rather listlessly. He took out the sheet of paper and read it carefully.

"Then I saw his whole face change. A little color came into his cheeks. His lips quivered as if with excitement. His eyes lit up and became keen.

"At that moment, Mr. Moses Mayerstein entered the coffee-room and went to his table—only a couple of yards away from ours. Gilbert had said nothing to me and I remained silent, thinking over my troubles, and idly watching Mayerstein.

"I saw the Jew shuffle the packet of letters waiting for him and then withdraw one of them. The envelope of Gilbert's second letter lay face downward on the table and there was a red crest in the angle of the flap.

"I could not help seeing that Mayerstein's envelope was exactly the same shape as Gilbert's, and that, as he turned it about, the writing was identical, and the same crest was on the back.

"I went on eating my breakfast, and I saw that Mayerstein hurriedly opened the rest of his letters, drank a cup of coffee, nibbled at a roll, and rose from his place, refusing anything further. He left the room with quick, noiseless footsteps. I was idly wondering what this might mean when a newcomer came into the coffee-room—a thick-set, bearded man, who, directly he caught sight of Gilbert, came up to him with a loud word of greeting.

"'Good gracious, who'd have thought of seeing you here—Gilbert, by all that's wonderful!'

"My young friend started, and took the proffered hand of the newcomer. 'I might as well say the same to you,' he said. 'What are you doing in Plymtown?'

"'I came down by the morning train—left London at three, and here I am hungry as a hunter. I have come down for my firm. We're going to put up the machinery at a new mine near Cambourne, and tomorrow I am going over there to make the preliminary survey. I thought I'd get a clear day off down here first. And you?'

"'Well, I'm here for my firm, too,' Gilbert replied, introducing the newcomer to me as Mr. Edwards, manager for the big London firm of mining engineers, Wellington & Son.

"The two men appeared to know each other well and to be friends. Asking permission, Mr. Edwards drew a chair up to our table and ordered breakfast. He seemed a cheery sort of fellow, the kind of man one took to at sight.

"'I say,' he said, helping himself to sausages and bacon, 'I met that fellow Mayerstein in the hall just as I was coming in.'

"'I know," Gilbert replied. "He has been here almost as long as I have, and that is some little time. He is a very civil, quiet-spoken fellow, but wants to be rather too friendly for my taste."

"'When Mr. Moses Mayerstein wants to be friendly, my dear Henry, then look out! That firm is one of the most unscrupulous in London, though I should think it is pretty near its end.'

"'How do you mean, Edwards?'

"The other's voice dropped. 'Well, there is no harm in telling you,' he said, 'because it will soon become generally known; but I have very good inside information that unless the Mayersteins can bring off some big coup within the next few weeks they are done, absolutely, and will go into bankruptcy. I have heard'—his voice became still lower—'that there may be some very astonishing revelations! Shareholders getting most uneasy and if I were a betting man I'd lay you a fiver that our friend out there will be enjoying His Majesty's hospitality before six months are out—unless,' he concluded, 'the miracle happens and they can get hold of money or credit. And it often does happen, you know, so let's change the subject.'

"We chatted for half an hour or so—or rather Mr. Edwards did the talking, for I was in no mood to make conversation and I could see that Gilbert was restive and impatient. Eventually, we rose from the table and Gilbert made an appointment with Edwards for the evening, saying that he had work to do and would not be free till then.

"We passed out. As we went by the table lately vacated by Mayerstein—Gilbert was in front—I saw the envelope of the letter I had noticed was lying empty on the floor. Some instinct, I do not know what it was, moved me and I picked it up and slipped it into my pocket. I suppose it was not a right thing to do—anyhow, I did it.

"As soon as we got into the hall Gilbert turned to me.

"'Look here, Buckland,' he said, 'you have been a very good friend to me. We have not known each other very long, but you are a man I like and a man I know I can trust. Will you allow me to make a further claim upon your friendship, and that is to ask your advice upon certain subjects which have an almost life and death importance for me at the moment?'

"'Of course, my dear fellow,' I said. 'Come up to my room.'

"I had a sitting room upstairs looking out over the harbor, and we went there together.

"Gilbert came to the point as soon as he had filled and lit his pipe. 'I have got my chance at last,' he said—'by this morning's post, if nothing spoils it at the last moment. If I lose this chance, I lose everything that makes life worth living to me,'—his voice trembled, he was terribly in earnest.

"'I must tell you,' he said, 'that I am the sole support of my family. My mother is a widow and I have two sisters, young girls at school. My mother's health is in a very grave condition indeed. She is suffering from an obscure complaint. If her life is to be saved this necessitates an almost immediate operation, and there is only one surgeon in London—Sir Felix Sayer—who can be trusted to perform it with absolute safety. He has made this branch of surgery his life study. His fee is a hundred guineas. After this operation it is essential that my mother should go to a certain place abroad, there to

complete her cure under the direction of German doctors who are in touch with Sir Felix. The whole affair—
if my mother's life is to be saved—can't cost less than
from four to five hundred pounds.'

"I nodded sympathetically, and he went on.

"'My salary is three hundred pounds a year. Out of
that I have to keep us all and pay my sisters' school fees.
My father left us all utterly unprovided for.'

"'And now,' I said, 'you have your chance, isn't it so?'

"'I have,' he replied, 'if nothing goes wrong. Have
you ever heard of old Squire Pentreith of West Cornwall?'

"'Who has not!' I said. 'Why he's famous all over
the West Country. At eighty he still rides to hounds and
boasts that he has never been in a railway train in his
life, and never will. He is one of the few survivals of
the old squires of the last century. I have even seen him
at the Cattle Show here when he has driven the whole
hundred miles from Trezance in three days on his own
coach. But what about him, Gilbert?'

"'I have had a letter from him this morning,' the
young man replied. "I am acting down here as agent
for my firm, whose business consists of floating mining
companies, with a special relation to tin and copper.
Now it has been discovered that Mr. Pentreith's estate
is very rich in tin. It is an unexplored field of many
thousand acres in the heart of the richest tin district in
Cornwall. For months my people have been negotiating
with him. At last he has come to grips, though he held
out for a long time. I received the confirming letter
this morning. It does not matter what terms we have
arranged with him, but I may tell you that an initial
payment of ten thousand pounds in cash was one of
the old fellow's stipulations. Well, I have that sum here
with me in my pocket at the present moment. If I pull

off this deal, my commission will be at least a thousand pounds and I shall receive substantial promotion in my firm. It means my dear mother's life, Buckland,' he concluded, and there was a break in his voice which did him credit.

"'I congratulate you,' I said, 'it is to be plain sailing then?'

"'I hope so,' he answered, 'but there is something that worries me.'

"He handed me Mr. Pentreith's letter. 'Sir,' it ran, 'I will accept your terms as representative of the firm of Bland & Whitaker. You are to bring me the necessary papers and the sum of ten thousand pounds in notes, when the matter can be concluded.

"'I have, though, to tell you that I have been in negotiation with another firm whose name it is not necessary to mention. Exactly the same terms have been offered to me by this firm as yours. It is perfectly immaterial to me with whom I deal provided I receive my money. I therefore say that I will conclude the business with the first representative of the two firms—yours and the other—who reaches me. In order to be perfectly fair, I have to tell you that an exactly similar letter to this, in which the name of your firm will not be mentioned, will be received by the representative of the other firm at precisely the same time you receive this. Yours faithfully, Walter Moseley Pentreith.'

"Gilbert had been watching me with some anxiety. 'Now,' he asked, 'what do you suppose this means?'

"'I *know* what it means,' I replied, 'You may be an excellent business man, my dear Gilbert, and I am sure you are, but you are not always on your guard—look here!'

"With that I withdrew Mayerstein's envelope from my pocket and handed it to him. "He looked at it, read the address, and grew white as linen. I was sorry for him. I had been too abrupt.

"His pipe fell from his hand on to the floor. 'Good God!' he said, 'what an utter ass I have been! Of course!'

"'Yes,' I replied, 'and if what your friend, Edwards, told you just now at breakfast is true, Mayerstein is as desperate to conclude this business as you yourself are, though for very different reasons.'

"I do not think I ever saw such pain upon a face, but it only lasted for a moment.

"'I have been a fool, a confounded fool,' he said, 'but still, I told him nothing and it was difficult to foresee this. The point is, I must get to Trezance before Mayerstein. How?'

"'There is no train whatever until six o'clock this evening,' I said. 'All through Cornwall traffic is suspended until that time—you must remember this is Sunday, and nobody travels in the Duchy on Sunday. The six o'clock train takes three and a half hours from here to Trezance, so you would be there at half-past nine.'

"'Pentreith House is only two miles out of the town,' he answered, 'but Mayerstein will be on that train, too.'

"'I don't think so,' I replied, for already a scheme had come into my mind. 'You rather underestimate your adversary, Gilbert, if you think that. My own impression is that, in dealing with people like Mr. Mayerstein, one has to be very wide awake indeed.'

"And that I was a prophet was proved just thirty seconds afterwards. The waiter knocked at the door and announced that Mr. Peters, the sub-station-master of Plymtown Town Station, wished to see me.

"As I went down stairs into the hall of the hotel, I knew instinctively why—as I remarked before, I had not been a railway detective for nothing.

"'A gentleman wants a special train to Trezance, sir,' said Peters. 'The money is all right, he showed me the notes, and, of course, the line's clear until tonight.'

"'Then why didn't you give it to him?' I asked, though I knew very well.

"'Well, sir, we've never had an inquiry of this sort before. And what is more, there are only two engines ready in the shed. They're both heavy express engines. One of them is 404, and the other the new 1A. The fireman and driver of 1A are in the shed now looking after her—she takes the mails to London tonight; and there are no coaches available at all that I can see. The carriage shed is locked, and will be till four o'clock—until Mr. Penhalligan comes back—though to be sure the gentleman did say that he would be quite content to ride on an engine.'

"'Well, go back and tell him that he can't have it,' I said. 'Let there be no mistake about it. As soon as he is well off the station premises, you tell the driver and fireman of 1A—who are they, by the way?'

"'Stokes and Taylor, sir.'

"'Good men, both. Very well, tell them to get up steam as fast as they possibly can. As a matter of fact, I am taking an engine down to Trezance myself within an hour and a half. You quite understand?'

"'Yes, sir.'

"'Very well. Go back to the station at once and be quite certain that this gentleman—it is a Jewish gentleman, I think, Mayerstein by name?' Peters nodded, rather surprised. 'I thought so. Well, be sure he knows nothing about the orders I have given you. Now be off.'

"Peters hurried away and I went upstairs again.

"Gilbert was pacing up and down the room. It was a bright autumn day and not too warm, but his face was covered with perspiration. 'Mayerstein has just ordered a special train,' I said.

"He jumped. 'Good God!" he cried.

"'He is not going to have it,' I answered, hurriedly, rather ashamed of myself when I remembered what life and death issues hung upon the young man's success in his business.

"'You won't let him?'

"'No. But you can have one—in fact I have already given orders, and in an hour and a half we will start. I'll get you to Trezance without using too much coal by two o'clock. I have nothing to do today till evening, and I will come with you. I have my own troubles and per- haps—' he was wringing my hand vigorously, his whole face changed.

"'Of course, you will have to pay the usual rates,' I said. 'The engine and the coal belong to the Great Union and not to me.'

"'Of course, of course,' he shouted, 'I have carte blanche in that respect.'

"'And you will have to travel on an engine. There are no coaches available at this time in the day.'

"'Jolly,' he answered, 'that will be an experience to remember.'

"'I suppose it will,' I said, little knowing how both he and I were to remember it to the end of our days.

"An hour afterwards, wearing old suits, we were walk- ing towards Plymtown Town Station—only five minutes away from the hotel.

"We crossed the Goods and Mineral Yard, with its interminable shunting sidings, and came into the Mar- shalling Yard, as it is called, where the engine houses are and the turntables.

"Just as we were coming up to the shed, I saw two men sitting at the end of the turntable bridge. I was passing without any particular notice when one of them swore foully to the other, coupling my name with the oath.

"I turned round and saw a driver, Rogers, and his fireman, Tilson. They had no right to be in the yard at all. I had discharged them both at the end of the week. They were drunken and insolent scoundrels, though good enough railway men in their way.

"'Get out of this yard in ten seconds,' I said, going up to them.

"They laughed impudently and I could see that, though not drunk, they had been drinking.

"I caught hold of Rogers by the arm, pulled him off the turntable and sent him spinning over a series of reception sidings, where he stumbled and fell heavily. Tilson, a big, powerful Cornishman, came for me with a run. I stepped aside and hit him full on the side of the jaw, and he also dropped like a stone. He scrambled up again, however, having had quite enough, and following the driver disappeared out of the yard.

"Then, as I was explaining the incident to Gilbert, we entered the shed.

"1A was there, and a beauty she was! She was the very newest and most powerful engine then invented, made to haul the London express, with three pairs of coupled wheels, single slide cylinder valves each worked by a separate link motion, and, what was then quite fresh, the leading end of the engine carried on a four-wheeled bogie swiveling on a central pivot so as to adapt itself to the curve of the road.

"She was painted a deep claret color, picked out with gold. Her brass shone like fire. From the copper rim of her funnel to the rear buffers of forged steel, she was as fresh and dainty as a bride.

"'By Jove, what a monster!' Gilbert said—his head hardly reached to the top of one great driving wheel as he stood on the floor of the shed.

"'She will bring you good luck,' I answered, and called to Stokes, the driver, who was up in the cab with an oil can in his hand.

"He skipped down at once, and touched his hat.

"'Of course,' I said, 'this will be extra pay for you, Stokes. This gentleman wants to run into Trezance and I am going with him. We will see him safely there and then run back. It will make no difference to your taking the mails to town tonight, I suppose?'

"'None whatever, sir,' Stokes answered; he was a pleasant-faced man of fifty, and one of the most trusted drivers on the system.

"'It will mean five pounds each to you and your mate,' Gilbert said, and the grin upon Stokes' face was almost worth the money to see.

"Steam was nearly up. We climbed into the cab and watched the needle of the gauge mounting steadily. The doors of the shed were opened and, when Peters had come to tell me that the line was warned to Trezance, we were almost ready to start. I remember it was just 11:30 when Stokes tugged gently at the lever of the throttle.

"Without the slightest jerk the mighty engine began to move, almost to steal out of the shed, with a gentle purring noise.

"'It's wonderful,' Gilbert whispered to me—yes, I remember quite well that he whispered as if he was in a church— 'what does the thing weigh?'

"'A hundred and ten tons,' I answered, 'with the tender,' and he gave a low whistle of astonishment.

"Easily, slowly, we glided through the environs of Plymtown, with a movement so light, 'graceful,' Gilbert called it, that it astounded a man who had hitherto only traveled in a train.

"He began to talk to Stokes who stood with his hand upon the lever, while Taylor was at one of the huge round windows of plate glass at the side of the cab. 'This is the first time I have ever ridden on an engine,' he said, 'and, do you know, I have the sort of feeling that she is tugging at the leash as it were—like a big dog on a lead that it is difficult to hold back.'

"Stokes smiled delightedly—he was a very intelligent fellow. 'I can tell you, sir,' he replied, 'you've got it. That is just what she's doing.' He pointed to the steam gauge with its trembling needle. 'She's longing to be off, as you may say, and when we are a little farther on I can let her out.'

"He turned to me. 'I suppose you know the line, sir,' he said. 'I've never driven farther west than Plymtown, as you are aware.' Stokes always drove the express from Plymtown to London and was not concerned with Cornish traffic.

"'Oh, yes, I know the line well enough,' I answered, 'but it does not matter; there are no gradients that can trouble you without any coaches at all. And there is no traffic on the line for several hours. The line is warned that a special train is coming down and all signals will be "open." Indeed, except at certain points, all the signalmen will be off duty until the middle of the afternoon.'

"'And are you in any hurry, sir?'

"I shook my head, looking at Gilbert as I did so. 'No, make an easy run of it,' I said; 'as long as you get us to Trezance between two and three, that will answer this gentleman's purpose, I imagine.'

"'Quite,' Gilbert replied as we passed through a short tunnel, with a rattle and a roar, and came gliding out into the open country.

"Taylor pulled the balancing weights and the doors of the furnace swung open, an awe-inspiring cavern of pulsing white and rose pink heat. A long shovel threw its load scientifically into the glow five times before the steel doors swung back.

"The noise of the shoveling coal hardly died away when I heard a rhythmic throbbing in the air. It seemed to come from behind and I turned.

"Quick as I was, the keen ears of the driver were quicker. He was leaning out on the right-hand side of the cab, looking backwards.

"Withdrawing his head, he turned to me with a puzzled look.

"'There is an engine on the line,' he said, 'coming along at a fair rate, too. Do you know anything about it, sir?'

"'Impossible,' I said.

"'Look for yourself, sir,' he answered, and as he did so the throbbing sound became more distinct.

"Taylor sprang to the brass handle which controlled the whistle. 'She'll be on us,' he cried.

"'Don't blow,' Stokes replied briefly. 'Sir, it's very strange, but she's on the up line!'

"His face was shocked, positively shocked at such an unheard of breach of all rules and regulations.

"'Then it's the chairman of the Great Union himself,' I answered, 'for no one else would dare to do it, even on a Sunday when the line is clear.'

"All this took but an instant, and I was looking out of the side of the cab almost before the words were out of my mouth. It was as Stokes had said. We were on a straight run of line and I could see, I suppose, at least a mile behind us, to where the four gleaming lines all merged together into nothingness.

"Two-thirds of the way down this long perspective, I saw the front of a big engine growing larger and larger every second as it raced towards us. Taylor was up on the coal in the tender. 'Good Lord!' he shouted, 'it's "404" out of the shed. I'd know her anywhere.'

"We were running at about thirty-five miles an hour, but as a certain thought came into my mind, I shouted to Stokes: 'Let her out at once. Get on speed as quickly as you can.'

"He pulled the lever, slowly at first, or the wheels would have slipped upon the metals, and then with ever longer tugs, we could feel 1A giving, as it were, little preliminary bounds, until the monotonous hum of our progress grew louder and deeper and it was less easy to stand upon the footplates.

"And now '404' was on us. It was as I thought—but worse than I had thought.

"The Jew, Mayerstein, stood grinning on the footplates. His face was perfectly white. His lips were curled away from his teeth, his eyes were blazing like a madman's.

"The engines became absolutely level. The noise was terrific. The tearing fury of the two great machines sent blasts of air from one to the other which hit us in the face like blows from some unseen hand.

"Gilbert gripped my arm, clinging on to the rail by the reverse gear. He was shouting in my ear, but I doubt if I heard him. The driver of '404' was the drunken scoundrel, Rogers. The fireman was the great brute, Tilson, whom I had knocked down in the yard of the Town Station an hour or two ago.

"And Tilson was working, working hard! The furnace doors of '404' were open and the brute was stoking at furious speed.

"I had just time to gather in all these details, and to see the driver lift a bottle to his lips, and, turning, hurl a curse at us, when '404' forged ahead, and the cab was lost to view. The tender, with its piled coal, passed in a flash.

"I think I kept pretty calm, though I was terribly excited. 'Stokes,' I said, 'you've got to beat that engine. They've stolen it. They're on the up line. If it wasn't all clear, there would be some frightful disaster. You've got to beat it.'

"Stokes nodded. It seemed as if it had not been necessary for me to give the order, for now our furnace doors were open and Taylor was working like a machine. It was wonderful to see how the man pressed the handle bar of the long shovel against his breast and forced it into the coal, withdrew it with an easy swing of his muscular arms, curved, balanced it, and shot it with unerring certainty into the heart of the fire.

"Stokes had his hand upon the lever of the throttle, his eyes upon the steam gauge. Almost every ten seconds he turned a tap or a wheel, coaxing the steam, regulating it with expert care from high pressure to low pressure cylinders, watching the radial gear with extraordinary intensity.

"'It's a race, Stokes,' I said. 'If that Jew man you saw on "404" gets to Trezance before us—'

"'You need not tell me, sir,' the driver shouted. 'I've got eyes in my head. I promised to get this young gentleman through to Trezance, and, by heaven, I'll do it!' He was standing aside by the seat in the cab where Gilbert was sitting, leaving the center free for the herculean efforts of Taylor.

"'He'd kill himself rather than be beat by that drunken swab, Rogers,' Stokes said, nodding towards the fireman. 'Question of his wife, sir. He's hammered him once already.'

"And now there began in my ears a tremendous and gigantic sound. It was as though titanic hammers were beating upon the anvils of fate. If the great machine which hurled us through the afternoon had seemed like a straining dog at Plymtown, it was a race horse now. And now again—time seemed to be standing still and we to be flying through it—it was some fierce and ravening dragon screeching through the air of the primeval world.

"With what little coherent thought remained to me I could see that we were all in the grip of some madness. We were lifted out of ourselves. The real motives for our race through the West Country were blotted from our minds. The madness of speed, speed, speed, speed! was rioting in our veins, and we would have flung ourselves against death and all his legions to win this race.

"In four minutes we passed them, passed them easily. I suppose in that yard to yard fight for supremacy it took us nearly a minute to show them the buffers of our tender. Although I knew this was a still and quiet afternoon, our raging progress had created a furious, shrieking gale around us—as evil thoughts, Ridley, may create a hellish tempest in the mind of a man lying at full length upon a couch.

"While we were passing them I saw the Jew clinging to the steel stay which supported the forward roof of the cab. His face was hardly human. There was an expression of deadly fear on it, but there was a grim determination, too—and when I turned and looked at Gilbert, I saw the same clenched teeth and rigid jaw, though there was no fear upon the young man's face.

"I saw, also, that the herculean stoker of '404' was working like some devil in the pit. Sweat gleamed in red beads upon his black, oil-stained face. His teeth grinned in a rictus.

"Once the driver passed him a bottle—I could even see the label—and the fellow tossed down nearly a tumblerful of raw whiskey.

"I knew what had happened. The Jew had bribed these men. He had caught them in their blackest hour; by some means or other he had loaded the cab with whiskey.

"We thundered on, clinging to stay and stanchion, grim, intent and purposeful. For my part, I knew that Stokes and Taylor would drive to the edge of the world rather than be beaten. Gilbert's face was glowing with internal excitement, and I—well, Ridley, I threw all scruples to the winds. I had made my first, and only, failure in love—I laughed aloud as our pursuers again drew up to us, and, by some extra trick of speed, gradually drew in front.

"We did eighty miles out of the hundred. We tore through tunnels like yelling fiends. Quiet Sunday stations fled behind us like frightened birds—the whole mellow landscape under the mellow autumn sun must surely have reverberated and thundered with our passage for miles on either side of the iron road.

"Still the Jew and his crew of drunken maniacs seemed able to show us their heels.

"Constantly we overhauled them; as constantly again they came up with us and shot ahead.

"We were rushing through Exton station like two projectiles from a gun—I saw white, upturned faces and little, ant-like figures emerging from office doors as we went by—when something came into my mind.

"Five miles away, the down line and the up line converged into one for the distance of half a mile, with waiting places above and below the single line area. At that moment we must have been going at fully eighty miles an hour."

Sir Jasper's face quivered.

"I have always been a good mathematician, Ridley," he said, "and, at that moment, my faculty for mental calculation served me very well. I realized that in three and three-quarter minutes our two engines would converge upon the point which meant absolute death to all concerned.

"Three and three-quarter minutes! And then, annihilation—unless—

"I went mad. I went mad. I pulled Stokes by the arm and yelled the coming horror in his ear. He looked at me with a blank, set face. He could not hear me—perhaps—more probably, he could not understand me.

"I tried to grip Taylor, but the man was working like a demon, and the heat from the furnace doors pressed me upon one side and sent me staggering on to Gilbert's knees, just as we drew level again with '404.'

"At least a minute and a half must have elapsed—so I thought. For a few seconds I closed my eyes and resigned myself to death. What saved me, what probably saved us all, was the fact that a hot spark from the funnel blew over the cab roof and burned me on the cheek. That seemed to make me alive again, and in a second my decision was taken. The two engines were absolutely side by side. The driver and fireman of '404' were lolling about the cab like dolls—but they were working still. "I was a pretty good cricketer, Ridley; a poor bat, a fair bowler, but a first-class fielder. I had saved more than one match for Plymtown by a strong shy in from long leg.

"A minute and a half.

"It must have been done in a second, but it seemed to me it was done with great deliberation. I selected two round, hard lumps of coal, each the size of a large orange. I judged my distance. I flung the first lump with all the strength of my arm. I did not aim it directly at Rogers. Something clicked in my brain, mathematics came to my aid in a flash of thought. Somehow or other I calculated the speed, the air resistance—the whole thing—and aiming far in advance of the cab shelter, I hit the drunken scoundrel full upon the side of the head. He went down like a log.

"As he fell, he clutched the handle of the throttle and pulled it to the left.

"There was a great roar of steam from the safety valve of '404.'

"We went past her, and then, in a few seconds more, we were on the half-mile of single line.

"Then I think nobody spoke at all until we glided into Trezance. We had all been too near death to want to talk about it!

"We arrived at Trezance about half-past two. I forced the station master to make a burglarious entrance into the closed refreshment room and administered brandy to everyone.

"A porter, who had been enjoying a nap, was dispatched to find a carriage for Gilbert, who drove away towards Squire Pentreith's house without a word."

Sir Jasper flung the end of his cigar in the fire and rose.

"We ought to have been in bed long ago, Ridley," he said.

"I know," I answered, "but what happened—the end of the story, I mean?"

"Oh, well," my host answered, with a yawn, "we sent an engine up the line from Trezance and found '404' stationary, with Mr. Mayerstein sitting fuming in the tender, the driver stunned and the fireman dead drunk. The Jew got six months for stealing rolling stock. The firm went smash—of course—and I am happy to say my friend, Mr. Gilbert, pulled off his business with the Cornish squire. He received his commission and Sir Felix Sayer went to operate upon his mother, when that celebrated surgeon discovered that all the other doctors had been quite wrong and that it was only an aggravated form of indigestion after all.

"So, you see, my dear Ridley, how apt the young are to exaggerate the importance of events. I myself, at that period, was ready to fling myself into the river for the sake of a woman—but I think I have already told you that part of the story."

An Engine in Egypt—And After!

I always liked traveling with Sir Jasper Buckland. It amused me; it was like a Royal Progress to be with the Chairman of the greatest railway in England, in a train.

He had invited me, one summer's day, to run up to York for the night, where he had some business, I casually having mentioned that I had never seen the famous minster. It was after the superexcellent lunch that was provided for us that our conversation began to turn upon the supernatural.

There was a paragraph in one of the London papers we had brought with us which stated that a certain old manor house in Essex was haunted, and that there had been several appearances of a ghost to the inmates.

"Of course it is all nonsense," I said. "One is always reading this sort of thing in the papers. People wake up in the middle of the night with indigestion and think they see a man in armor, while rats in the wainscoting provide the appropriate clanking of chains."

From such a hard-headed man of business I expected nothing less than an unqualified consent; but, to my surprise, he shook his head.

"This particular case," he said, "may, no doubt, have no foundation. Many cases prove to be so when they are investigated. But I should be very sorry indeed to say that the supernatural does not exist, very sorry."

As I watched him I saw that his mind was working upon something—how well I knew that reminiscent look!

He caught my eye and smiled. "Well, yes," he said, "I can see what you are thinking, and if you care to hear a story unparalleled in the history of the supernatural, I will tell it you. Although it did not happen to me personally, it happened to a dear friend of mine, a railway official like myself, and who married a girl cousin of my own. I can vouch for the truth of every particular, and, as it is distinctly a 'railway' mystery, it may not be out of place in the book of my experiences which you are preparing."

Of course I was all attention, and the story which follows is compiled from Sir Jasper's narrative, assisted by some notes in his diary which he subsequently handed to me.

Bob Bland simply fell upon the wooden case. He was a big, clean-shaved boy of five and twenty, fair-haired, bold-eyed, heavy-lipped, and with the manner of an exuberant but highly intelligent bulldog.

The case contained things more precious than gold to a pioneer in the desert. He wrenched the cover off with a spanner and there were revealed two dozen of Schweppes soda water and three bottles of gin in packing of straw.

The tents of the railway pioneers stood among the scrub some fifty yards from the line which ran from Sidfa el-Kebir towards Fawashir. Dalga was a junction— or at least the headquarters—of the railway, which was slowly advancing through the desert. A few wilted palms surrounded the brackish wells. There were tents for the engineers and native workmen, and there was a hideous structure of corrugated iron which served as an engine shed. Dalga was, in fact, a depot.

Robert Bland's voice rang through the quivering, heated air of the late afternoon.

"Phillips! Phillips! They've sent up gin and soda from the base. We can have a drink at last!"

A lean, brown-faced man in khaki, wearing a solar topee and smoking a long cheroot, lounged towards his colleague.

"All right, Bob," he said, "let's have it in the mess tent. I want a civilized drink as much as you do, but I've not enough energy to bellow about it."

Two active little Egyptians carried the case into the mess tent. The engine and the train of trucks containing railway material shunted on to a siding. The sun approached the horizon of the desert, flaming like a blood-red eye—and then suddenly came long indigo shadows and a slight breath of coolness.

Bland and Phillips sat together and took great draughts of the precious liquids sent up to them. The soda was lukewarm, the gin had never seen Plymouth, but, to them, it was nectar.

"Washes the sand out of one's throat, doesn't it, Bob?"

"I should rather think it did—after this filthy, brackish water from the wells and the bitter taste of permanganate which we have to put in to prevent ourselves being poisoned."

They smoked and drank—two young engineers who, under military organization, were flinging the steel road towards the Sahara. Phillips was engineer of the road itself—though Bob Bland knew a good deal about that, too—and Bland himself was the locomotive and mechanical expert sent out to sweat and toil to bring the desert places of the world within the map of commerce.

But they were very different men. The civil engineer was a dreamy, reticent man, to whom the wide places of the desert had a strange appeal. His colleague, a hearty, good-natured, downright boy, was as matter-of-fact as one of his own engines, hard as nails, happy as a sand-boy, seeing only the material things of life.

An Anglo-Egyptian put his head through the door of the mess tent. It was little Abbas, the telegraphist.

"Sorry interrupt," he said, "but wire come from Sidfa el-Kebir. You got to go Fawashir tonight, Mistah Bland. Big breakdown there. Sorry, I am shore."

The little man in the fez smirked and went away. The dispatch lay between Phillips and Bland upon the table. It was quite efficiently clear. One or other of the junction engineers—and the wire clearly pointed to Bob Bland—must be at Fawashir by dawn. The line was already laid for sixty miles beyond the junction, but its further progress depended upon experts, and the man at the far end had obviously come to grief.

Phillips was the senior officer. "They want you, old chap," he said nevertheless.

"Oh no, I don't think—"

"Don't be a young ass. There is a deadlock there, and you'll pull things through. It will all be reported and you'll get a rise. You are to go."

"It's awfully good of you Phillips, and I should like to, but—"

"But what?"

Bob Bland grinned. "Simply this," he said; "there is not enough coal or wood in the depot to get up steam and take the engine more than thirty miles out. Supplies have not come from the base. The train that brought up this gin and soda and construction material also brought a letter for me from that lazy scamp, Teufik. There won't be any fuel till tomorrow's train, and that won't arrive here till long after mid-day."

"Are you quite sure?" Phillips asked.

"Quite, and there is nothing about here to burn"—the engines on the pioneer line were constructed to burn coal or wood—"but we'll go over to the sheds and see if you like."

The two men got up and went out of the tent. The sun was now almost gone, hurling great spears and javelins of red and gold at approaching night. Already a great moon globed herself low in the opposite sky— soon to wash the desert with silver, for, in the land of the Pharaohs, twilight is unknown. The air was deliciously invigorating and cool, the breeze had blown over thousands of miles uninhabited by living things, uninfected by village or by town. It was like wine to the Englishmen, tired with the heat and fatigue of the long, sweltering day.

In the immediate foreground were the supply and engine sheds; behind them, where the barren ground rose to form a low hill, the last rays of the sun touched the great pylons and architrave of a ruined temple set in the red rock. Calm and inscrutable, the great guardian figure of stone gazed out over the desert with serene majesty; and behind it was the fifty-foot wedge-shaped opening to the tombs within the hill.

The two men went into the fuel shed. Said, the foreman of the fellaheen laborers who worked at Dalga and whose encampment was some two hundred yards away to the left, was sitting upon some empty coal sacks, meditatively smoking cigarettes. In grey burnoose and with his distinguished clear-cut face—he was of Arab extraction—he seemed like a ghost in the waning light.

He shook his head when they explained their mission. "Thirty miles you can go, Messieurs," he said in excellent French—he was an Arab from Tunisia—"but not a mile more; unless—" a strange and enigmatic smile came upon his face, and there was a flash of white teeth.

"Unless what?" Bob Bland said quickly.

Said shrugged his shoulders. He had acquired European gestures from the Frenchmen of Tunis. "There *is* a way," he answered, "but—" again an expressive shrug.

"Well, let's have it then." Phillips broke in with a slight irritation in his voice.

The Arab went to the door of the shed. The sun had quite gone now, and the moonlight was already strong. He made a gesture of his arm towards the temple tomb.

"Plenty of fuel there," he said laconically.

"What do you mean?" both men exclaimed.

"I have seen it done before, Effendi. There are hundreds of dead people in there, dead people who will burn well."

"Mummies, by Jove!" shouted Bob Bland. "Just the very thing! It is quite true; I've heard of them being used to stoke a locomotive before. You see," he went on, turning excitedly to Phillips, "mummy is a word derived from the Arabic for 'bitumen.' They are chock-full of pitch and resinous substances. They'll burn like billy-oh—Said, you are a trump. I'll give you a chit for twenty piasters next pay-day. Now then, how shall we get them out?—I've never taken the trouble to go inside that bally old tomb, but I suppose there will be no difficulty?"

"I have," Phillips said in a slow voice, "and don't you have anything to do with such a proposal. It is far better to wait."

"Rot! Wait? Why should I wait? We'll have a tender full of those old mummies within a couple of hours."

"Please don't, Bob. I'm sure no good can come of it. It is a desecration."

"Desecration be blowed! Those old chaps have been lying there doing no good for three thousand years. If they could possibly know anything about it they ought to be pleased to think of assisting in a good action. Now, Said, how are we to get them out?"

The Arab smiled. He had no superstition at all about the still, swathed figures in the tomb. He was not an Egyptian, and the cynical French spirit of mockery was in his veins.

"There are the mule carts, Monsieur," he said. "I, also, have been into the tomb. It is not a large one—as these things go in Egypt—but it contains plenty for our purpose."

"But it is the tomb of a Princess of the sixth dynasty," Phillips said, with great agitation in his voice. "You know, Bob, I am a bit of an Egyptologist, and take an interest in these things. It is a tomb of the Princess Meryra. She lies there in a sarcophagus of painted wood in a great coffin of stone surrounded by her retinue, who were put to death when she died, and embalmed with her, so that even in death she should hold Royal state."

Bob Bland laughed aloud. "Why, you're a regular poet, Phillips," he said. "I should never have thought it of you. Well, we'll have the old girl out within a very short time, and I'll get up to Fawashir by midnight."

He was hurrying away with Said to give the necessary orders when Phillips caught him by the arm.

"I beg you, I implore you, Bob, to leave those bodies alone. Harm will come to you if you disturb them. Surely that is an argument you can understand if you are not touched by any other feeling."

"I can understand it all right, old chap, but I don't believe it, see? We're in the nineteenth century—we're

modern men. We have got rid of, or we ought to have
got rid of, all such superstitious tommyrot. I believe in
what I can touch and see and nothing else at all. Now, let
me go. This is an important matter—I have got to settle
that breakdown at Fawashir, and I am going to do it."

He broke away from Phillips and Said followed him.
But when they went to the native camp not a man of the
fifty there would budge. Bob Bland cursed and swore,
asserted himself in every way. But it was all no use. The
natives, who obeyed his slightest word under ordinary
circumstances, now cowered sullenly in their huts.

It seemed that there were other people who did not
agree with young Bob Bland in his material estimate of
life.

"Well, what are we to do?" Bland said to Said when
they had left the compound.

"Make them harness two mule carts, Monsieur; they
can't refuse to do that. Then we'll take the lamps and
we'll go and get the things ourselves."

"Good for you," said Bob, big-shouldered, British
bulldog, in the moonlight—and in half an hour two light
carts, harnessed with three mules apiece, were waiting
outside the immemorial gateway of the tomb.

Inside, the Arab and the Englishman had traversed
hot and narrow passages, until they stood at last in the
vast, hollowed-out chamber of the sarcophagus. In their
progress they had disturbed innumerable bats that had
fluttered past them with flapping, leathery wings and
little, toy-like squeaks of alarm. They stood now in the
central room of the tomb, and the air was warm. There
was a faint but very perceptible odor of spices.

Upon sides in carved stone niches lay the long,
swathed figures of the dead. Wrapped in layer upon layer of linen bands, they waited there as they had waited
for three thousand years.

In the center of the place was a sort of altar or stone table with a large stone coffin upon it.

"Well, come on, Said," Bob Bland called out. "We'll take one of these beggars apiece until we have filled the first cart."

With a genial laugh he lifted a mummy from its shelf, shouldered it with ease and tramped through the passages behind the Arab, who carried a lamp.

For nearly three-quarters of an hour this progress continued. Now Bland carried the corpse upon his back, now Said, while each held the lamp in turn. In the brilliant moonlight one of the carts was loaded up with the silent figures. There was no sound save the whining of the distant jackals and, once, the hideous, mocking laugh of a hyena. But huge, leathery bats flickered through the honey-colored air as if they were the very spirits of those old Egyptians stolen from their last resting place.

One cart was heaped with dead. Another grew until, with a light jest, the strong young Englishman placed the last mummy upon the apex of a ghastly pyramid.

"Now we'll go back for the lamp in the tomb," he said, and, followed by Said, he traversed the dark, sour-smelling corridors until, for the last time, he was in the hall of the dead.

The second lamp was standing upon a central table. Bland lifted it and then a thought seemed to strike him.

"Look here, Said," he said, "here's the old lady herself. We'll have her in, too! She'd be lonely without her pals."

He went to the sarcophagus and gazed down upon the coffin lid of gilded, painted wood. "Why, she can't be more than a little thing," he said, but, as he did so, he saw that Said's face had changed.

"Leave the Princess alone, Monsieur; that is my advice," the Arab muttered.

The strong, coarse-natured engineer was put upon his mettle. Very possible, though by no means certain, bravado alone had kept him keyed up to his ghastly business. One may suppose that it was to reanimate his own courage that he drew a marline-spike from his pocket and pressed upon the hitherto inviolate tomb of the Princess Meryra.

With a shaking hand Said held up the lamp. Immediately the sweetest odors filled the air, smells of nard and cassia—the perfumes of all Arabia.

With strong, red hands—hands which trembled a little, nevertheless—Bob Bland withdrew a slim, female figure.

"Come on, Polly!" he said, and even in his own ears his tone rang false while in his heart he was afraid.

He carried that which had once been the beautiful Princess Meryra through the tortuous passages. As he held the mummy he felt his pulses beat. His heart was disturbed. It was as if he was carrying a living girl.

The engine left Dalga at ten o'clock. Phillips absolutely refused to have anything to do with the matter. His farewell to Bland was icy cold.

The whole encampment was asleep as Said and Bland slid out upon the upward way. They could not get driver or fireman, and had to work their way themselves.

Down poured the brilliant white moonlight over the desert. It flooded the long, low-funneled Egyptian engine—and showed a cargo in the tender at which any man might well have trembled.

Bob Bland stood with his hand upon the regulator while Said stoked the furnaces with the remainder of the coal. Neither of them gave a thought to the grim, moving catafalque behind. But there, piled up, long, motionless, and splendid in death, were the mummies of the old Egyptians of three thousand years before.

In three-quarters of an hour the needle of the steam gauge began to point backwards.

"Come on, Said," Bland said—it seemed as if he wanted some help in what he was about to do. The furnace door was opened. The two men dragged a swathed figure from the tender. They swung it between them for a moment and then it shot into the heart of the fire. Immediately they saw how the glow whitened and the flames leaped up to lick the boiler tubes. Four more rigid, linen-swathed forms disappeared before the furnace door clanged into place again and the needle of the steam gauge trembled upwards towards a decent pressure.

Clank, clank, clank, went the engine over the rough line. To right and left, ahead and behind, were vast spaces of the desert covered with scrub, all silver under the moon. Bob Bland stamped once or twice upon the footplates of the cab. He blew his nose. "Queer sort of gummy smell these mummies have," he said, as vapor streamed from the funnel of the engine and seemed to linger around him.

He pulled a corkscrew from his pocket and opened a bottle of gin. His big. red hand was shaking a little as he did so Temperate enough in the ordinary way, he now put the neck of the bottle to his lips and drank the raw spirit. It seemed to animate him. He turned upon the Arab with a curse.

"Steam!" he said—"Damn you! pitch those brutes into the furnace; we shall never get to Fawashir unless you do."

The pile upon the tender was growing less and less as the sinewy Arab heaved body after body into the pulsing flames. Only a few mummies now remained, looking upward, as it were, into the moon-flooded sky.

For some reason or other, Bland's usually ruddy countenance was pale. His jaw was grimly set, his hands clenched. It was as though he was fighting with himself. As they sped onwards he crossed the cab and went to the tender. Instead of the usual piles of coal, the great iron box now contained but a few motionless figures; it was like a mortuary on wheels, and, despite himself, Bland shuddered.

Close to him, upon the right-hand side of the tender, was the body of what had once been Princess Meryra Seti. Bob drank some more gin.

"Now, my dear," he said, "we'll have a look at you before you go to join your friends. Never been so near a princess before!"—the man was drunk with rising terror and the gin he had taken to drive it away. He took his clasp knife from his pocket and cut furiously at the linen wrappings about the head—cut straight through the yards and yards of diaphanous material—and pulled it aside.

Over the face itself lay a gilded mask of some thin metal. The hands were crossed upon her breast and they were clear to view. They were the color of old ivory, very small and beautiful, after all the innumerable centuries. Upon one finger gleamed a gold ring set with a brilliant green beetle—the scarabaeus of the Egyptians.

It caught the eye of the maddened man. "A curiosity, this," he muttered to himself, and with a few powerful cuts he severed the little hand at the wrist and put it in his pocket He hardly knew why he did it, but directly it was done he turned away, sick at heart, bitterly ashamed of himself. He had no courage left now to lift the gilded mask and see the face beneath.

He called to Said. The Arab came and lifted the mummy. The balance weight of the furnace door sank down and the huge, red glow lit up the whole interior of the cab as the Princess Meryra Seti of the sixth dynasty vanished in the heart of the flames.

Bland did not wish to see it done. He went to the side of the engine and leaned out, gazing moodily over the desert.

Suddenly, he heard a loud shriek—an almost inhuman cry of horror. He wheeled round and saw the Arab, Said, leap from the engine upon the other side—leap out into the night, and then he saw, or thought he saw, something else.

For a single instant the clanking engine seemed surrounded by a company of people rushing onward with it through the moonlight. One second only, but hawk-faced, shadowy forms, whose eyes glowed darkly, encompassed him.

And then, just as the vision flashed away, he saw another face.

It was the face of a young girl. The nose was aquiline, the lips calm and of deep, dusky crimson. Great masses of black hair fell on either side, and in the hair were the brilliant yellow and purple flowers of the lotus.

It came, it was gone. The whole ghastly company had vanished as the solitary engineer reeled upon the footplates and clutched the wheel of the reversing gear to save himself from falling.

He felt as though his heart had been stabbed straight through by a spear. He was no longer afraid, but pain so bitter that he almost wondered at it took possession of his very soul. The big, kindly, coarse-natured man had seen a vision of the Ideal. He had had a glimpse of the love that moves the sun and stars and gives her light to the moon. He had tempted unseen powers, and this had been his answer—hopeless, irremedial love.

Two years afterwards, Robert Bland was sitting alone in his rooms in London. The Egyptian Service knew him no more. He had left it almost immediately after his strange experiences in the Fawashir Desert. He was now one of the assistant locomotive engineers in the service of the Great Union Railway.

Everyone said of him that he was bound to rise to the very top of his profession. Already, several of his patents had been adopted by the company. He put into his work a furious passion of energy unequaled in the department.

But there were other things that people said about him also. They said he was a man with one idea—a monomaniac, who thought locomotive, dreamed locomotive, and was interested in nothing else. He was big, blond and handsome still, but certainly the most unsociable man one could possibly meet. When he was not actually at work in the designing rooms, or carrying out experiments with engines on the line, his eyes were haunted, his lips set rigidly.

"He looks as if he might have murdered his mother," said one of the young engineers of the company; and though no one suspected Bob Bland of any crime, it was generally agreed that he was the most impossible person to have anything to do with apart from the "Shop."

Bland's only friend at this time was Jasper Buckland, the Chief Detective Inspector of the Great Union Railway. Colleagues wondered why the two men apparently got on together, but they soon ceased to inquire, and the friendship became a settled fact.

Bland was staring at the fire in his comfortable lodgings. The pipe in his mouth had gone out; he was startled when, with a preliminary knock, the door opened, and Buckland came in.

"Now look here, my dear Bob," Buckland said, "I've come to take you out to a party—at my uncle's, not more than twenty minutes from here in a taxi; Chiswick, in fact."

Bland shook his head. "Thanks awfully, Buckland, but you know I don't go out."

"I do know, but that is just the reason why I am here. There is something the matter with you, Bob. There has been something the matter with you ever since you came back from Egypt. I don't know what it is but for Heaven's sake, pull yourself together and be a little more sociable. Now, look here, if I can't persuade you by words, perhaps this will."

Buckland put his hand into his breast pocket and withdrew a photograph. "That is my cousin," he said, as he handed it to Bland. "Mary Seton. She's one of the most charming girls going—what?"

Buckland was astounded. The big man in the chair had risen and was holding the photograph in front of him. His eyes were dilated; his lips parted; he was breathing heavily. Once, he swayed a little, as if about to fall.

"What on earth is the matter, Robert?"

Bland made no answer—his eyes were fixed upon the photograph with burning intensity. It was that of a girl, slightly aquiline in feature and with great masses of dark hair on either side of her face. In her hair were broad-leaved flowers.

"I'll come with you, Jasper," the engineer said at length, and Buckland, greatly marveling, but too wise to say anything, went out and whistled for a taxi.

It was exactly a fortnight after Jasper Buckland had dragged his morose friend out to the evening party at Chiswick that he received a telegram from him.

"Come dine with me tonight if you possibly can. Important news. Bland."

Buckland arrived in due course. He found Bland, whom he had not seen since the night of the Chiswick entertainment, a different man. Buckland had noticed that his cousin, Mary, and the young engineer had taken a mutual liking to each other, but he had not speculated further upon the matter. He had not been in the room now for more than half a minute before he was listening to the most extraordinary news.

"Mary has accepted me, Jasper! I am the happiest man that ever lived. I—" Words seemed to fail him.

Buckland tendered the appropriate congratulations. Indeed he was very pleased. He liked his dark, enigmatic cousin very much. Not a marrying man himself, engaged always upon ambition and the furthering of his career, he could yet sympathize with those to whom the softer side of life meant so much. He was very fond of Robert Bland—more especially so because he had set himself the task of weaning the engineer from his moody outlook upon ordinary affairs; had long wished to see him more sociable and human.

But Buckland was puzzled—distinctly puzzled.

"Well, you don't waste time at any rate, old chap," he said. "Why it's only a fortnight today since I took you to my uncle's house, and now you have fixed up everything."

Bland's face changed in expression. "Yes," he said, "I know it has been very rapid, but from the very moment I saw Mary's photograph I knew that I loved her, that she was the one and only girl in the world for me."

"Yes," the other answered, "now I come to think of it, you were rather odd when I showed you the photograph. I wondered at it at the time."

"You are the best pal I have at all," Bland replied. "I know that I can confide in you. Now I'm going to tell you a story that will strain your capability of belief to the very limit. Do you care to hear it?"

His voice had become very serious, and Jasper Buckland fell in with his mood.

"Of course, I care to hear it," he said gravely, "and, as far as I am concerned, it will be as secret as the grave."

"Then wait a minute." Bland left the room and went upstairs. In a few seconds he reappeared carrying a small leather dispatch box. He took a bundle of keys from his pocket and opened it.

"What have you got there?" Buckland asked, his curiosity strangely stimulated.

"My engagement ring," the other answered, in a solemn voice.

From wrappings of cotton wool he withdrew something and laid it on the table. Buckland gasped.

"Good God!" he said, "it's a hand, it's a withered hand!"

Upon the table lay a girl's hand. It was the color of old ivory, a little wrinkled, a little withered, but beautiful still. Upon the first finger was an antique ring of reddish gold, and set in the back was a brilliant scarabaeus, a beetle that glowed in the lamplight like an emerald.

There was a silence in the sitting-room for a moment or two. Then Robert Bland withdrew the ring from the dead finger. "It's for Mary," he said—"and now I will tell you everything."

As Jasper Buckland left his friend's house that night, his brain was full of pictures. He walked through the lighted London streets unseeing and oblivious of all his surroundings.

He was upon an engine that clanked through the far desert in the moonlight. He saw the swathed bodies of the old Egyptians flung into the cavern of flame. He saw a man staggering as from a mortal wound as a haunting face of unutterable beauty loomed mysteriously upon the vision of his soul.

He could not sleep that night. How strange the world really was! How curious the hidden springs of human

action! His cousin, Mary Seton, was a reincarnation
in face and figure of the little dead Princess whom his
friend had treated with the callous brutality of youth and
health. When, at last, sleep came to Buckland, he sank
into dreams with a famous phrase ringing in his ears—
he had recently been to see *Hamlet* performed—"There
are more things in Heaven and Earth, Horatio, than are
dreamt of in your philosophy."

It was what the newspapers call "a pretty wedding."
It was not, of course, in a fashionable West End church.
It took place at Chiswick, but the dark-haired, dark-
eyed bride was beautiful, and the ladies attending the
function were loud in praise of the stalwart, beaming
groom. Everyone was in the highest spirits at the breakfast; but, as the young couple left for Eastbourne, where
the honeymoon was to be spent, Jasper Buckland left his
uncle's house with a distinct sense of unrest.

He had been in bad spirits all the day. He had tried
not to be, but it was useless. The afternoon had clouded
over and in Buckland's heart there was a sense of fatal-
ity, of something ominous. He took a taxi back to his
rooms, or, rather, not to his own rooms, but to Robert
Bland's. Buckland's apartments were being repapered,
and Robert Bland—he had not yet removed all his personal belongings to the little house in North-West London which he had taken—had suggested that Buckland
should occupy them until his own place was renovated.

The Chief Detective of the Great Union dined comfortably enough in his friend's rooms. It was about ten
o'clock, and a strange restlessness came over him; he
began to pace up and down the sitting-room. If he had
been asked he could not possibly have analyzed his sen-
sations yet, nevertheless, he had a vivid sense that something was wrong.

As he walked up and down the room his eye fell upon Bland's leather dispatch box, which was on a shelf by the side of the fireplace. Something drew him to it. He fidgeted with the lock for a moment and found the box was open. He lifted the lid and looked inside.

There was a pile of cotton wadding, but the little, withered hand was not there.

"I am almost certain," Buckland said to himself, "that Bob said he was going to leave the thing behind him, and get rid of it altogether when he came back from his honeymoon. What on earth can he have taken it for, I don't know."

Shortly afterwards, Buckland, very depressed, went upstairs to bed. It was exactly half-past ten as he turned in, thinking of his friends.

At that moment, Robert Bland was smoking a cigarette in the almost deserted lounge of the "Rex Hotel" at Eastbourne.

It was twenty minutes ago that his wife left him. He looked at his watch and then entered the lift and was shot up to the second floor. His dressing-room was next to the bedroom, and communicated with it by a door; it was also reached by a door in the corridor. He undressed, put on his pajamas, and then knocked at the communicating door.

There was no answer.

He knocked again, still meeting with no response. Then he gently turned the handle of the door and went into his wife's room.

The electric lights were turned full on and he saw the black mass of her unbound hair upon the pillow.

He went up to the bed, bent over the polished brass rail for a second, and then, with a hideous shout, fell motionless upon the floor.

This is what he had seen. A yellow, old ivory hand was clutched into the throat of the lovely girl who lay there—dead. Back on the first finger of the hand was the gleaming beetle ring.

The mummied hand had to be broken up with pincers before it could be taken from Mary's throat.

The Prison Train

"It's astonishing," said Sir Jasper, "how little the general public knows of the inner working of our great railways."

"They will know a great deal more," I replied, "when I have finished this book dealing with your extraordinary career."

"Perhaps so, Ridley," he answered absently. I was dining with him in Berkeley Square, and we were sitting over dessert. "Now, for instance, did you know that on our railways today there are special vans to prevent bananas from catching cold?"

I stared at him. "What do you mean, Sir Jasper?" I asked.

"Simply that bananas are shipped from the West Indies in a green state, and if the temperature is low during their journey to England they will not ripen. On the Great Union we have had to build special vans heated by steam to convey the bananas from the ship to the ripening-houses. Traveling aquariums are quite common. The Great Union has, I suppose, fifty traveling railway tanks for conveying live trout and salmon from the fish hatcheries to the river or loch, the interior arranged so that the tanks are kept in the greatest possible state of agitation so as to areate the water; and, especially, I suppose you are quite unaware of a necessary and useful adjunct to our system called the Prison Train?"

"The Prison Train?"

"Yes. There is a special convict train, belonging to the Prison Commissioners, which runs on our line."

I saw meaning in my old friend's eye, and I said, "You have something to tell me about one of these 'Prison Trains'?"

He smiled. "You were remarking just now," he said, "upon the beauty of these enameled fruit dishes from Japan."

"I was," I replied, "and I have never seen such exquisite modern Satsuma ware."

"They are a present," he said, "from an Englishman of great wealth who resides permanently in Japan and who is the hero—if you like to put it that way—of one of the most extraordinary adventures of my life, intimately connected, my dear Ridley, with the Prison Train."

I slipped my notebook from my pocket and took a pencil in my hand. Sir Jasper passed the port to me and then, leaning back in his chair, began to talk.

"It was long after my railway detective days," he said. "After my adventure of the racing trains, of which I have already told you, I was promoted from being district manager at Plymtown in Devon to London itself. I was now right up at the top, earning fifteen hundred a year and with prospects which might lead me anywhere—to where I have arrived, in fact, as Chairman of the Great Union," he said modestly.

"The Scottish railways had inaugurated a Prison Train for conveying convicts from one place to another. The Prison Commissioners in England approached the Great Union, because our system, with all its ramifications, is within easy access of all the pricipal convict and most of the local prisons. Accordingly, we had a train built—not in our own yards, but elsewhere. The work was done by tender and given to a celebrated engineering firm. One day, in my new capacity of Chief Traveling Inspector of the line, I was instructed to proceed to Princemoor in the West, and to accompany the newly built Prison Train on its first run. My functions were to look into every detail and to report upon the efficiency or otherwise of the experiment.

"I arrived at Princemoor late one evening, and I stayed at the hotel in the village. The convict prison is a mile and a half away up in the moor. Early in the morning I went to the station, where the new Prison Train stood upon a siding, and examined it thoroughly.

"It certainly seemed a marvelous piece of work and I will describe it to you in detail. Please take particular note of what I say, Ridley, because the interest of this part of the story depends a good deal upon your thoroughly understanding what the Prison Train was like. There was a guard's van of the ordinary pattern. Then came a long coach. The only entrance to the coach was by a platform and door at one end. This door, of steel, slid in grooves and locked itself automatically when pushed to. Entering, one came into a small but comfortably furnished compartment for the chief warder. Passing through this, there was another steel door which led into the convict portion of the coach.

"All along the right-hand side were little cells. Each was just big enough to accommodate a man, each had a steel-plated door which closed upon the inmate.

"These cells were only lighted by a barred aperture in the doors—a little above the height that the convict's head would be when sitting down. There were ten of these cells in all, going right up one side of the coach. In front of them, just as the corridor of an ordinary train runs in front of the compartments, was the space for the guards. As the cells were so small, however, the corridor portion was much wider than that on an ordinary train. The floor was covered with matting. There was a fixed armchair at each end and plenty of room for a warder to promenade up and down in front of the cells and look into each one through the aperture as he passed. Light came from large plate-glass windows in the corridor, which were also heavily barred. As there was no light in the cells themselves, over each doorway, but outside, there was an electric bulb which could be turned on at night and which would throw its radiance through the barred slit. Escape was utterly impossible. The station master at Princemoor showed me everything.

"'You see, sir,' he said, rapping with his knuckles upon the side of the coach, 'it's all steel plates.' The convicts were constantly in view of the warder patrolling the passage, while another with loaded rifle sat at the door leading into the head warder's compartment.

"At one end of the row of cells—the end farthest away from the only door leading into the corridor—there was a slightly larger cell, though in all other respects it was as secure as the other cells; the inmate would not be quite so like a 'finger in a glove,' as the station master put it. Also, the seat itself was padded.

"'What is this for?' I asked.

"'For any convict who is not in good health, sir,' the station master answered. 'It is just a little easier than the others, though I should not care to travel for any great distance even in this.'

"'Nor I,' I replied with perfect sincerity, and shortly afterwards we went back to the hotel and took breakfast.

"At half-past ten I was at the station again and saw two wagonettes drive up. There were five convicts in each, chained together and guarded by warders with loaded carbines. It was a morning in late autumn. There was a haze upon the moorlands like the bloom upon a plum. The air was fresh and sweet as these poor, fantastic creatures were marshaled out of their conveyances and tramped onto the platform.

"There they stood, hideous and cowed, the very clowns of sin and sorrow. The close-cropped hair under the yellow Glengarry caps gave each head a curious, bulletlike appearance. The faces, not clean-shaved, but disfigured with several days' growth of hair, gave them all a singular likeness and coarseness. The huge black arrows on their yellow clothes mocked God's pleasant morning.

"I was glad when I saw these poor men—whatever they might have done—marshaled hurriedly into their moving prison. They seemed a blot upon the fair landscape and they seemed to know it, too.

"The engine backed in after a few minutes and I mounted the train and went into the chief warder's compartment. He saluted me and we began to glide out of the station.

"The warder-in-charge was a pleasant, middle-aged man with a grizzled beard. He was a Scotsman, had been sergeant-major of a Highland regiment, and was in every way an intelligent and humane man. We lunched together—the Governor of the prison had very kindly sent down a special repast for me—and after the meal we pulled out our pipes and had a chat.

"I told him that, in the past, I had been a railway detective. Then, as now, I never made any attempt at disguising the fact that I had risen from the ranks.

"He was intensely interested, though no less respectful for that, and we swapped yarns.

"'Now, sir,' he said at length, 'would you like to come along the corridor with me and have a look at my birds? There are some desperate characters among them

and they are all criminals of the first water. And yet,'
he concluded with a sigh, 'I believe that one or two of
them are as good men as you or I. Because a man does
one bad thing—perhaps in a moment when he can't control himself—he has to pay the penalty. But it does not
always mean that he is an absolute scoundrel.'

"'Thank you very much, Mr. MacAlister,' I said; 'I
should like to make a little tour.'

"The warder-in-charge opened the steel door leading out of his compartment, pushed it into its groove
and we passed through. Then, mechanically, he pulled it
back and locked it again.

"Looking right up the broad space of the corridor,
we could see the two warders, both sitting in their arm-
chairs. Their carbines were resting against the wall; one
was eating a packet of sandwiches, the other was smoking a pipe.

"Mr. MacAlister made a motion of his hand to prevent them getting up. This was their luncheon hour and
he did not wish to disturb them.

"Immediately to our right was the barred slit of a
cell.

"'They're eating their lunches now,' MacAlister whispered to me, 'prison bread and cheese. We couldn't very
well give them a hot meal as there is no kitchen provided
on this experimental train, but they have got a double
allowance and they'll like it better—look in here, sir.'

"I looked in through the barred slit and saw a dim
gray figure seated within a foot or two of the grating
and eating voraciously. '14 B,' said the warder; 'nice,
quiet prisoner, too. Industrious and clever burglar when
he's out. He has never drunk in his life and keeps a little family in Camden Town in the most respectable way.
He's got another year to run, and then we shan't hear
of him again for three years, when, I expect, he will be

back. Curious thing about 14 B,' said Mr. MacAlister as we passed to the next cell, 'but he won't steal anything but diamonds. That has been the cause of his downfall. In his profession he is known as Cullinan Charlie.'

"In the next cell was a little wizened creature, munching at his bread like an ape.

"'Now that,' said Mr. MacAlister, 'though you wouldn't think it, is as violent a little swine and as bad a prisoner as you could possibly meet with. His little game is forgery—a nice, gentlemanly occupation, so to speak, and yet while he is in, we can do nothing with him.'

"We passed onwards. At the eighth cell I was told that the inmate—from what I could see of him, a tall, sickly looking youth—had been convicted for terrorizing a whole countryside as a highway robber, with violence. He had served two sentences before and twice had suffered the extreme punishment of the Cat—'and you'd think butter would not melt in his mouth, wouldn't you, sir?' said Mr. MacAlister.

"Then we came to the end cell of all—the slightly larger one which I have already mentioned.

"The man within was leaning his head against the side of the wall. His bread and cheese remained beside him. His eyes were closed and his face was pale.

"'I haven't been able to show you anything very much out of the ordinary up till now,' MacAlister whispered, 'but here's a celebrity, sir. That is'—he drew me away from the observation slit—'that is a baronet, and a murderer, serving a life sentence.'

"I started violently, and well I might. 'A baronet and a murderer,' I whispered.

"'I'll tell you all about it,' he replied. 'Martin, you can have half an hour off in my compartment: I will take your guard.'

"The man went away and we seated ourselves in the corridor, about the middle, while the remaining warder was stationed outside the door of the compartment which his fellow had just entered and locked the door behind him.

"'It is the Charliewood case,' said MacAlister, 'you remember that surely, sir.'

"'I have not much time to read the papers. The name is familiar, but that is all.'

"'Two years ago the prisoner was Captain John Charliewood of the Hundredth Hussars. He was the eldest son of Sir Richard Charliewood, M.P., head of the great engineering firm of Charliewood's, Limited. Captain Charliewood was arrested for the murder of a brother officer—Maynard, I believe his name was. The evidence was circumstantial, but it was very complete, while the motive, some love affair, was fully established. There was no way out of it and he was sentenced to death. He held the D. S. O. for service in India, and that counted towards the commutation of his sentence to penal servitude for life; and I expect the high position of his father, who was a strong supporter of the government, had something to do with it, too.'

"'Good heavens! what an end!' I said.

"'You may well say so, sir,' the warder answered. 'You never know what a man will do in a moment of passion, but he is a gentleman if ever there was one. His father died after his first year in prison, and he is the baronet. It is his younger brother who controls the big business and who comes to see him whenever visitors are allowed. It is very sad, but we can make no difference in such a case.'

"I sat chatting with MacAlister I should say for some twenty minutes. During that time nothing out of the way occurred. We were going at a good pace, and the only thing I noticed was that once, when we were passing through a tunnel, the warder at the far end switched on the electric lights in front of each cell, turning them off again when we emerged into daylight. At last MacAlister got up, the keys jingling on a steel chain fastened to his belt. 'I think we'll go back into the more comfortable carriage.' He went along, beginning at the end nearest his compartment, speaking to each man through the grid asking if he wanted anything.

"I stood waiting for the door into the private compartment to be unlocked when, just as he arrived at the far end of the corridor, at the invalid cell, in fact, I observed him stagger back from the door.

"'Turn on the lights,' he shouted.

"The warder by me did so.

"Seeing that something was wrong, I ran along the corridor to MacAlister. 'What is it?' I said.

"The big man was trembling violently. He made a motion towards the grid and I stared in. The little cell was flooded with light. It was perfectly undisturbed, and it was absolutely empty. 14 B, ex-Captain Sir John Charliewood, had disappeared, vanished into thin air without the slightest trace or clue."

The Red House, in the little Devonshire village of Carne, was a rambling, tumble-down old place which very few of the villagers ever cared to go near. It was situated in a small pine wood, gloomy and remote, and was in the possession of Major Morrison, late of the Hundredth Hussars.

At one time the whole of the village and the surrounding farms had belonged to Squire Morrison, the father of the retired soldier. But, during the Squire's lifetime, farm after farm had been sold, and it was known that this was done owing to the extravagant debts of his son, whose reputation as a racing man and gamester was notorious. The Squire had died. Major Morrison had not been near his dwindling property for a long time until just two years ago. Then he had retired from the army and come to settle in the Red House. Of all the big property only one farm remained to him, together with the house of his fathers and an acre or two of grounds. His income was not more than two hundred and fifty a year.

From the very first he had avoided any social intercourse. He lived the life of a recluse in the Red House. An old housekeeper and her daughter attended him. A boy groom looked after the only horse in the stables. It was known that the Major was a man of gloomy, disappointed and saturnine temperament. He drank heavily, and villagers would tell each other in hushed voices of how sounds of loud and bitter laughter were heard at night as the Major was carousing—carousing with himself, or, as the superstitious rustics said, with Someone or Something neither good for honest folk to hear nor to see.

Legends grew up about the house and its occupant. The simple country folk passed it with averted faces. Children whispered of it to each other in their play. It was reputed haunted by an evil spirit—shunned and barred by all.

One afternoon in late autumn a gentleman in a victoria drove into Carne from the neighboring town of Biddicombe. He stopped at the Raleigh Arms, put up his carriage, and walked to the Red House, which was some quarter of a mile from the village.

He was a man of about thirty to thirty-five, well-dressed in tweeds, clean-shaved, and with a commanding personality.

Arrived at the high wall which ran around the house, he was confronted with big wooden gates which were locked. In one of the stone gate-posts there was a rusty bell-handle. He pulled it vigorously and, some distance away, he heard a jangling bell. For five minutes there was no answer to his summons, but he pulled again and continued pulling so vigorously that eventually he heard shuffling footsteps upon gravel, and the gate was unlocked from the other side.

An old woman of sixty, very fat and with a sly expression on her face, stood waiting.

"I want to see your master, Major Morrison," said the newcomer.

"He sees no one, sir, and he is very far from well to-day."

"That may be so, but my business is of the utmost importance. I bring him news which he must hear at any cost. You must take me to him. I am Mr. Alfred Charliewood."

The old woman started—that was quite perceptible. "You know my name?"

She hesitated and shuffled with her feet. Mr. Charliewood withdrew his fingers from his waistcoat pocket. Between them there was something white that crackled.

"Here," he said, "is a five-pound note— you know my name then?"

"Indeed, sir, and I have heard it," said the old woman, her shifty eyes fixed on the money. "Master mentions it sometimes when he is—well, sir, I expect you've heard master is not quite a temperate man."

Mr. Charliewood nodded. "Take me straight to where he is," he said, "and as you open the door and announce me, I will give you this five-pound note."

"This way, sir," said the old lady.

The two crossed the moss green gravel sweep in front of an old, fine-looking house of the Tudor period, now falling into irremediable decay. She took him around by a side door, led him along a stone passage into a small paneled hall, in the far corner of which was a door.

She rapped upon it sharply, opened it, held out her hand for the five-pound note, snatched it eagerly and then scuttled away as if in mortal fear.

In a leather armchair, by the side of a dying fire, sat a pale, haggard man in a suit of tweeds. The room was furnished as a library, but there was mildew on the books and the carpet was ragged. By the side of the man in the armchair was a table and upon it were a bottle of whiskey, a jug of water and glasses.

Charliewood entered and closed the door behind him, as Major Morrison rose to his feet, shaking, unshaven, with bloodshot, questioning eyes.

"Who the devil are you?" he said in a hoarse voice.

"My name is Alfred Charliewood."

The words tolled deeply like a bell in the room, and Charliewood's eyes were fixed with fierce attention upon his involuntary host.

Major Morrison sank back into his seat. His jaw dropped a little and his face became rigid. "John's brother!" he muttered to himself.

"Yes, the brother of the man you have murdered!"

The Major stretched out his shaking hand, filled a tumbler half full with whiskey, and tossed it off as if it had been water. It quieted him instantly.

"What do you mean, sir," he said, "by coming here and talking to me of murder? It is your brother, my old friend in the regiment, who is a murderer and who is expiating his crime in prison."

Alfred Charliewood withdrew an envelope from his pocket. He took out a sheet of note-paper and held it to the other.

"Read that," he said.

The sheet of paper was headed, in printed characters, H. M. S. Prison, Princemoor, and addressed to Alfred Charliewood, Esquire, 28A Grosvenor Place, London. It ran as follows:

> "Sir—I regret to inform you that Convict 14 B, in private life Sir John Charliewood, expired last evening in the hospital of this prison. For some time he had been suffering from an infection of the lungs and though every care was given him, consistent with the regulations, he died on Wednesday evening at 8 o'clock. Inquest will be held tomorrow, and I shall be pleased to afford you facilities for attendance if you so wish.
> "I beg to be, Sir,
> > "J. B. Herres-Browne,
> > "H. M. Prison."

The paper fluttered from the lean hand of the man who held it. His eyes became suffused with horror.

Charliewood spoke. "For two years, ever since my brother was thrown into prison for his life, I have been making investigations. You had to leave the army owing to your debts. You are a ruined man with only a pittance to live upon. I am a man of great wealth and I know"— he spoke each word slowly and distinctly—"I know as surely as I know that I am standing here that you are the murderer of Captain Maynard; that you, with devilish cunning, wove a web of circumstantial evidence about my poor brother which sent him to his doom. You are a double murderer, Major Morrison! My brother lies stark and dead in his prison cell, and his blood is on your hands, like the blood of your first victim."

The face of the man in the chair was horrible to see. "You can't prove it," he gasped convulsively.

"I cannot. But beware lest the wrath of God fall upon you, even though you have escaped man's justice. Dead men, Major Morrison, are not really dead. It is only their bodies that are dead. It may still be." He made a strange gesture with his hand and turning on his heel left the room. Half an hour afterwards the victoria, with Alfred Charliewood in it, was returning to Biddicombe.

It was rumored in the village during the whole of the next day that the Major, "up at the Red House," was in a very bad way.

Mrs. Penberthy, the fat old housekeeper, had been down to the inn to order half a dozen bottles of whiskey to be sent up, and she had shaken her head ominously when questioned.

"Gentleman came to see 'im," she said, "and a nice, pleasant-spoken gentleman, too. What passed, not knowing, I can't say, but master's taken it hard. He doesn't say much, but he won't touch his food and he sits regularly glaring at the wall."

The village, collectively, shook its head, and Mrs. Penberthy returned to the Red House.

At eleven o'clock on the night after Alfred Charlie wood's visit, Major Morrison was sitting in his library. The housekeeper and her daughter had gone to bed. The lamp upon the table was burning low and the ex-soldier was nodding in his chair, half-drunk and half-asleep—it was the first hour of relief that he had known since the afternoon of the day before.

As he nodded there, he became drowsily aware of a slight hissing noise. In his confused brain, he put it down to the dying fire or the night wind upon the window panes.

Then he heard it again rather louder.

He lifted his head, sprang from his chair like some corpse galvanized into life, as an awful shriek of horror rang through the room.

Standing by the door of the library was a figure. It was clothed in some white material that glowed and smoked with greenish light. One arm was outstretched towards him. And the face of the figure was the face of the dead man, John Charliewood.

There was a dead silence for several seconds and then Major Morrison began to groan and jabber, pressing against the farthest wall from that awful accusing figure.

"Forgive! Forgive!" he muttered. "Yes, it was I who killed Maynard. I arranged it all so that you should be accused, it was because of money. I owed Maynard two thousand pounds which I could not pay—a gambling debt. There were no proofs save my I. O. U." The voice died away into inarticulate babblings. Then another voice, cold, and seemingly not of his world, spoke.

"Repent, confess! Before it is too late!"

Then an extraordinary thing happened Morrison advanced slowly from the wall against which he had been crouching. He went up to a writing-table, opened a drawer with a quiet and almost business-like movement and withdrew some sheets of foolscap. Dipping a pen in the ink, he began to write with great deliberation. For nearly half an hour he never looked up.

Scratch, scratch, scratch, went the swiftly moving pen. The paper was covered with names, dates, statements, clearly put.

At last, he signed his name with a deep groan.

Then he turned.

The figure was still there, but the accusing arm was dropped. There seemed even pity upon the set white face of the apparition.

"Oh, John, dear old John—it is all down here. I have made a complete confession. I killed Maynard! Coward that I have been! If only I had dared to say this before it was too late. You're dead now, old John, and you've come to haunt me. But I've done what I can, and so, farewell."

The nervous tension relaxed. Major Morrison fell back in his chair and neither moved nor spoke.

It was an hour afterwards when he came to his senses. The room was bitter cold. The apparition of the old friend he had betrayed was gone. Upon the table in front of him was the long, written confession. He took an envelope, folded the papers, and sealed the flap of the envelope with his ring.

Then he opened another drawer and stood upright in the middle of the room. The lamp was just expiring as he raised the gleaming revolver to his brow.

"It was some years later," said Sir Jasper Buckland. "that I made a voyage round the world, and stopped for some weeks in Japan.

"One afternoon, in Kobe, I went into the club—a famous international place, as you doubtless know, Ridley. The head waiter, an elderly, clean-shaved Englishman, was passing me when he stopped short and looked me very earnestly in the face. I returned his gaze and then I rose from my chair. 'I think,' I said in a quiet voice, 'that you must be Mr. MacAlister, once chief warder at Princemoor.'

"'Come this way, sir,' he said quickly, and took me into a sort of pantry behind the bar. 'Surely you are the gentleman that was on the convict train with me when Sir John Charliewood disappeared. You are Sir Jasper Buckland now, I believe, sir.'

"'An odd meeting, Mr. MacAlister,' I said; 'but how on earth are you here.'

"'Well, Sir Jasper,' MacAlister replied, 'you know all about the inquiry. You appeared before the Commissioners as well as myself and the other two warders. We could discover nothing.'

"'No,' I answered, 'and then came the startling confession of Major Morrison and the King's pardon to Sir John Charliewood—'

"'Who, by that time, was safely in Japan,' said MacAlister with a quiet smile.

"'Were you in it, then?' I asked. 'Do you know how the escape was managed?'

"He put his hand upon my arm. 'Sir Jasper,' he said, 'I have no more idea of it than I had then. My good faith and that of the other two warders—assisted by your kind evidence—proved that we could have had nothing to do with it. Nevertheless, we were all three dismissed from the prison service.'

"'You, at any rate, seem to be doing rather well,' I said.

"'I have nothing to complain of, Sir Jasper,' he answered with a faint smile. 'Sir John is in the club now. If you will allow me, I should like to introduce you to him.'

"The worthy steward did so, and it ended by my going to Sir John's charming bungalow and spending several days with him. We became great friends.

"He got out of the convict train when it was passing through a tunnel. The whole thing had been most carefully rehearsed. No money was wanting.

"In the tunnel, Charliewood was immediately seized and his convict clothes taken off him in three or four seconds. A carefully prepared wig, moustache and beard were put upon his face. He was dressed as a clergyman. The conspirators hurried out of the tunnel and scrambled up the embankment where a carriage was waiting. They drove quickly away from the railway to a house which had been taken for the occasion and which was not far from Carne. Everything was done with the greatest expedition and adroitness.

"The day before, Alfred Charliewood had terrified Major Morrison with a forged letter from the prison governor of Princemoor, saying that Sir John was dead.

"It was a fairly easy thing the next night to bring the real Sir John, dressed in a gown covered with luminous paint, into Morrison's library. It was a desperate chance—the most desperate chance of all—but it succeeded, and Sir John was cleared of the foul murder for which he had been unjustly condemned. The King's pardon was granted him, but he absolutely refused—though much pressure was put upon him—to explain how he left the convict train."

"It's a wonderful story, Sir Jasper," I said, "and it shows how only the highest ingenuity, aided by great means, can possibly hope to clear a condemned man for whom circumstantial evidence has been too strong."

Sir Jasper nodded. "It is so," he said gravely.

"But there is one thing I want to know. Can't you tell me how on earth the whole scheme became possible? Can't you tell me how Sir John Charliewood escaped from that steel train—vanished into air, like smoke?"

Sir Jasper smiled. "Until this very day, Ridley," he replied, "I could not possibly have told you, because I did not know. Sir John has always refused to give me the least clue to this mystery. But this morning I have received a letter from Japan. The faithful brother, Alfred Charliewood, died some two months ago, and now my curiosity is satisfied; as yours can be. I have the letter here, and I think you will agree with me that the mysterious happenings upon our railways, of which the public never hears, have never been more thoroughly illustrated than by this strange and confidential communication."

He handed me the letter:

My Dear Buckland:

You will have seen by the newspapers that my dear brother, Alfred, is dead. I owe everything to him, as you know, and my grief is profound. His death removes the last reason for concealment in the matter of my escape from the Convict Train. I am forwarding an explanation to the Home Office which, of course, will never be made public. As far as the world is concerned, the mystery will remain a mystery still.

But you, my friend, who were so intimately mixed up with the business, and whom I have so strangely met years afterwards, are entitled to know the truth.

It is this:—

The contract for designing and building the Prison Train was given to my father's firm, Charliewood's, Ltd., by your railway, the Great Union. My poor father was dead—killed by my unmerited disgrace—and Alfred was head of the firm. It was he who designed the train and supervised its construction.

He ascertained that the first use of the train was to convey prisoners from Princemoor to Parkton Prison, in the Isle of Wight. He learned also that, by a strange freak of fate, I was to be transferred to Parkton for the sake of my health—you are already aware that he had never ceased working for me from the first day of my sentence.

He saw his opportunity. Alfred was one of the greatest mechanical geniuses of the age. His patents are world-known. The end

cell of the train, from which I so mysteriously disappeared, was the result of the most
careful and most brilliant piece of work, in
conjunction with two trusted mechanics.

The back of this cell—the whole panel,
from where it met the roof to just behind
the padded back of the seat—was movable.
It swung upon two pivots. Call to your mind
one of those round windows you see in the
upper parts of a house, or a certain type
of porthole in a ship, and you will understand exactly what I mean. In such windows
or portholes, if you press the bottom half
it swings outward, and the top half swings
inward.

The whole of the panel at my back—you
must remember it was in the blind side of the
train where there were no windows at all—
was arranged to move in this way. But that
is not all. The method of my escape would
have been readily discovered had it not been
for my brother's genius. By pressing two of
the leather buttons upon the cushions—
one was upon the seat and the other in the
back—and by pressing them simultaneously,
an electric current was generated from a tiny
battery concealed in the walls. This current
acted upon the locks of the pivots and left
the panel free. I had only to press the two
buttons, to push the lower portion of the wall
behind me with my hand, and it swung open.
I was through it in a minute and, clinging to
the rail above the footboard, closed it again.
The final beauty of my brother's invention
was that this opening of the panel could only

occur once. Afterwards, it became as rigid as all the rest of the train. Indeed, unless the whole carriage had been taken to pieces bit by bit by experts, there was no possible way of the method of my exit being discovered.

There are one or two other points which will immediately arise. You will wonder how I was aware of all these preparations made by my brother. Well, that is simple enough. Even the poorer prisoners in a great convict establishment are able to get letters smuggled through to them by venal warders who are paid, I believe, a sovereign or so for each letter. For my brother, with his vast resources and knowledge of human nature, it was simply child's play. I was informed of everything. Letters came to me written in a minute handwriting upon tissue paper. I read them; and I swallowed them. The actual journey from Princemoor was mapped out with the greatest care. For a whole fortnight before I was transferred, I learned the route by heart—of course I could see nothing from my cell. It was all a question of time. As I and the other convicts were being driven down to the station, one of the warders, who did not accompany us on the train, passed a tiny watch, no bigger than a shilling, into my hand. It was touch and go, of course. The whole thing might never have come off, but I knew that when we entered upon the only long tunnel of the first stage of the train's journey, that was to be my time to set the mechanism in motion. I knew that we were entering that tunnel from

the fact that the electric lights in front of
the cells were turned up—though the sound
itself would have been enough to tell me.
Directly that happened I pressed the button,
pushed open the panel and got out upon the
footboard, clinging to the rail. In the middle
of the tunnel an electric flashlight showed
me that my friends were waiting. The train
was going about twenty miles an hour, but I
obeyed instructions and leaped. I was caught
in a net held by my brother's agents—the
rest you know.

I am sending you a painted ivory fan
which has been executed by one of the greatest artists in Japan. Sometimes, my dear Sir
Jasper, think of your friend who is perfectly happy in the East, but who has been too
deeply wounded ever to care to return to
England.

> Yours ever sincerely,
> John Charliewood.

For several minutes I held the letter in my hand.
Then I looked up.

"It's a wonderful story," I said quietly, for I had been
much moved.

"My dear Ridley," Sir Jasper replied, "you are beginning to learn that, when you want the true romance,
the most thrilling episodes, you need not search your
imagination, but you must come to an old man like me!
It is in the secret history of the railways," he continued,
"that I fervently believe can be found the strangest and
most poignant stories of modern life."

The Kidnappers

"I am going to tell you something," said Sir Jasper Buckland, "which has never transpired publicly—another story of the days when I was chief detective-inspector of the Great Union Railway.

"In the days of which I am speaking the Great Union saw an opportunity of enormously increasing its importance and its revenue. After the expenditure of a huge amount of money, a bill was passed authorizing the construction of three hundred miles of new line—a colossal enterprise, as you know. Construction was to be begun within a certain definite period, as is always the case in such affairs, or else the parliamentary concession is withdrawn. Now for some reason or other the public did not take kindly to the new scheme. Our rival was the powerful Great Southern Line.

"They did everything humanly possible to oppose our bill in Parliament. Our success would mean a tremendous loss to them, but they did not keep pace with modern requirements, and in such cases Parliament, with certain restrictions, always grants a concession. Now the Great Southern not only fought legitimately, but used methods the reverse of fair. There is no doubt whatever that in many cases the press was bribed and cold water thrown upon our scheme. This became so acute that, while the concession was granted by the experts in Parliament, the directors felt that when they went to the public for the money there was a good probability that the necessary amount would not be subscribed.

"The situation was most serious, when an offer was received privately from Cyrus P. Willstack, the famous American Railway King, to finance the undertaking himself. He would put down two-thirds of the enormous sum required, public confidence would be restored, and the rest would be easily got.

"It was in November, a particularly unpleasant month, that Mr. Willstack with his secretary arrived in England. He made his headquarters at the Great Union Railway Hotel, which, as you know, forms part of the Great Union Station and is the largest and most luxurious railway hotel in the world.

"My work at that time was mostly in the company's offices at the station. It was more supervision of the other investigators than anything else. One day the chairman of the company, Sir William English—whom I have had occasion to mention before in these stories of my life—sent for me to the board room.

"He was sitting with a small, insignificant-looking, grey-haired gentleman with a yellow face, unobtrusive clothes and no feature of distinction about him that I could see.

"'This is Mr. Cyrus Willstack, Mr. Buckland,' said Sir William, and as I bowed I was never more surprised in my life. So this was the famous multimillionaire, the keenest monopolist among the railway magnates of the world.

"Still, I was pleased to see him. An enigmatic personality with which the press of England and America was constantly busy, it was not often my lot in those days to meet so celebrated a person. When royalty traveled on the Great Union Railway, of course I had charge of the detective arrangements in conjunction with Scotland Yard, and I had more than one jeweled scarf-pin to my credit from traveling princes. But this was different, and I looked at the little man, more powerful than many kings, with great interest.

"I noticed that he wore a round black button in the lapel of his coat made of some shining black material. A pair of heavy, steel-rimmed glasses hung from it. He pulled the glasses, and there was a little clicking noise. A thin chain was attached to them which unwound from the button, just like a spring measuring-tape comes out of its case. Then Mr. Willstack put the pince-nez on his nose and looked at me. I was divided between the novelty of the spring-chain—which I had never seen before, though they are common enough now—and the fact that the glasses were not even gold-rimmed—a fact to which I was to owe five thousand solid English sovereigns in the future.

"'Please sit down, Mr. Buckland,' said Sir William.

"I did so. 'You are a very trusted servant of the company, Mr. Buckland,' the chairman went on. 'You have already done us great service, and perhaps I may tell you it has been resolved that in the immediate future you are to receive very high promotion. A man of your intellect must not be wasted as chief detective-inspector. In fact, what I have now to ask you will probably be the last business of this sort we shall require you to do for us.'

"I murmured some suitable reply. I do not deny that my pulses were beating furiously, for I have always been an ambitious man. But even in this welcome news I was conscious of the steady scrutiny of the multimillionaire. Somehow or other, I could not say why, he seemed no longer insignificant. When he spoke, I was certain he was not so.

"His voice was very quiet, yet very penetrating. Curiously enough it had hardly any trace of the American accent. It thrilled one. It was the voice of a ruler of men.

"'I have asked Sir William to lend you to me, Mr. Buckland,' he said, 'for ten days or so. I want you to guard me as if you expected I might be assassinated at any moment.'

"I started.

"'Perhaps, Sir William, you will explain,' the millionaire concluded.

"'You have heard rumors, of course,' said Sir William to me. 'The press has been busy enough of late about the possibility of Mr. Willstack taking a large interest in the affairs of the Great Union, especially in regard to the great extension of our system.'

"'Yes, Sir William,' I said. 'And you want?'

"'You are to do exactly as Mr. Willstack has said.'

"'Then you fear, Sir William?'

"'We fear nothing,' interrupted the American. 'But we want to be prepared for everything.'

"And forthwith, under promise of utter secrecy, Sir William told me exactly how matters lay.

"The time allowed by Parliament for commencing the extension was nearly up. Negotiations with Mr. Willstack had been prolonged. The transfer of such a huge amount of money was not a thing that could be done in five minutes. Nevertheless, there was plenty of time if—

"And that was the whole point. Such vast interests were involved that unscrupulous people—the Great Southern Railway was never mentioned, but it was in the minds of all of us—might well attempt some measures to prevent the final signing of agreements between Mr. Willstack and the directors of the Great Union.

"It was the possibility of this that I was to forestall.

"Within half an hour I was accompanying the millionaire to his suite of rooms in the Great Union Hotel. I expected, of course, that he would have the most gorgeous apartments possible upon the first floor. Nothing of the sort. We got into the lift, and went up, up, up, until even the attics were passed, and I realized that we were ascending the great central tower to the very top.

"'I like a high tree, Mr. Buckland,' the little man said with a chuckle, reading me like a book; 'but, as a matter of fact, the truth is that I suffer from asthma, and it is essential that I should live as high as possible when in London. Ah!'

"The lift stopped and we came out on to a carpeted landing. Mr. Willstack opened a door immediately opposite, and we entered a small room in which a secretary was writing at a table. Without a word the millionaire crossed the room, opened another door, and showed me into a place of much the same size as the last. It was furnished with considerable luxury, but it was a curious combination of a sitting-room and bedroom combined.

"'This is where you will stay, if you please, Mr. Buckland,' he said. 'These three small rooms adjoin each other. Mine is here.'

"He led me into it. It was more simply furnished than my own.

"'These are your instructions,' he said. 'At eight o'clock each night you will enter this little tower-suite with this pass-key. You will telephone for anything you desire to be sent to you, but you will remain in the anteroom to my own the whole night. My secretary sleeps down below in the hotel and so does my valet. In the daytime I am being looked after in another way. Your business will be to see that I am not molested at night.'

"He went to a drawer in his writing-table and took out a shining, silver-plated revolver. 'Put that in your pocket.' he said. 'I have another here.'

"I did so with an inward smile. We were not in the wilds of America now. Even detectives did not carry revolvers in sober, matter-of-fact London.

"Again the uncanny little man read my thoughts. 'You think I am unduly nervous and don't know London,' he said. 'You are wrong in both thoughts, Mr. Buckland. You don't realize things as I do, and perhaps I have information which you have not got. Well, I'll just say this: that you won't suffer for the four or five days you will have to sleep up here, and you have a beautiful view over London from your window.'

"'Much the best view, sir,' I replied, for my window looked out over a great part of the northwest district of London. The window of the millionaire's room was only a few feet above the huge glass dome of the Great Union Station.

"There it stretched away for nearly five hundred yards, a great curved glass shell, beneath which lay the largest station in Europe. Even on this foggy day and with the glass coated with soot it was just like looking down upon the main aisle of the Crystal Palace.

"'I have never seen that before, sir,' I said. 'It takes nearly five minutes to walk from one end of the Great Union Station to the other, and now one can see how big it really is.'

"'Well, there are two reasons for my having this room,' Mr. Willstack replied—he seemed to have taken a liking to me. 'First of all, it is the inner room of the three; secondly, to look down and hear the trains pull in and out and see the arc lights shining up at night kind of heartens me. I am a railway man, Mr. Buckland, and I guess I've no other interests in life.'

"At seven o'clock that evening I was enjoying one of the best dinners I had ever had in my life. It was brought to me in my bed-sitting-room by a couple of the hotel waiters.

"Mr. Willstack was within, and once he strolled in to me with an odd little smile. 'Champagne all right?' he asked. 'Curried oysters really fine. I am enjoying it immensely. I have just had four oatmeal biscuits and a glass of peptonized milk, which is all I shall take till tomorrow morning.' He concluded with a little sigh, 'A good digestion is a great thing.'

"He lit a cigarette and looked wistfully upon my well-spread table. 'Now then,' he said, 'at about ten o'clock I am to receive a private visit from the manager of one of the great London financial houses. My secretary will show him up. Our conversation may be protracted, but don't let anyone else enter the room under any circumstances. If I should want you, I'll call you.'

"It was just about ten o'clock that night when I was sitting in my room reading a late edition of an evening paper that there was a knock at the outer door and the secretary entered. He was followed by a tall, broad-shouldered man carrying a heavy dispatch-box and wearing a fur coat. He gave a quick glance at me as he passed and was then shown into Mr. Willstack's apartment.

"'Odd-looking bird, Mr. Buckland,' said the secretary to me. 'Well, good night, I'm off to bed.'

"The secretary was right. The newcomer had struck me at once as a rather odd-looking person. The detective is trained to take in many details at a glance. I had done so. Now I began to analyze my impressions. The 'manager of a great financial house' wore a pointed black beard and a heavy moustache. His hair was black, too, but it seemed unusually long and mingled with the astrachan of his coat-collar. Moreover the face was distinctly dark, while the eyes that had glanced at me were of a keen light blue. Of course, I thought it must be all right, but I got up from my seat and began to pace up and down quietly before the door which led into Willstack's room. For three minutes I heard the murmur of conversation, and then there was a silence. I did not take particular notice of this until I heard the key on the other side of the door being turned and withdrawn from the hole.

"Almost immediately afterwards I distinctly heard the words: 'Thank you, Mr. Willstack. As you say, the room is a little hot. I will open the window.' There was a little rattle as the window was pushed up.

"Then the conversation began again in a lower tone.

"I was a little hurt. I thought that Mr. Willstack trusted me. But I was more especially puzzled. There was something strange about that visitor. It was stranger still that the door should have been locked. Supposing Mr. Willstack were to call for me? I smiled to myself and went to the door leading into the secretary's room and removed the key from it. I had found out earlier in the evening that the keys of all three doors were identical.

"'It might be as well,' I said to myself as I slipped the key into my pocket, where it fell with a little chink against the loaded revolver that the millionaire had given me. Somehow I felt rather glad of the feel of that revolver now.

"I listened, walking up and down the heavy carpet.

"Still the conversation went on, rising and falling. As I have said, Mr. Willstack had a very quiet but penetrating voice. But he seemed excited now, for though I could hear no words, that curious metallic intonation which the Americans seem to have was much more distinct.

"After about five minutes this conversation ceased abruptly and there was a dead silence.

"Now there are all sort of silences. Silence is relative. What we call silence is very rarely so. but when I say that this was 'dead' silence. I meant that I could hear nothing whatever. Some instinct must have come to me, for I knocked gently at the door.

"There was no answer.

"I knocked again more loudly, calling out at the same time to know if Mr. Willstack desired my presence. The dead silence continued.

"Then I put my hand into my pocket, withdrew the key, pushed it into the lock, opened the door and stepped into the room.

"It was brilliantly lit by electric lights. A heavy curtain was drawn over the window and a fur coat lay upon an armchair.

"But the room was absolutely empty!

"Then I swore aloud. Upon the table standing by the side of an empty leather dispatch-box was a phonograph, the disc was still faintly moving and the small aluminum trumpet seemed to shout out to me: 'Fool! Fool! Fool!'

"I leaped to the window. I tore aside the curtain. I looked down upon the huge turtleback roof a few feet below.

"The window was closed, but I threw it up in a second. For a moment the dazzling light from the hundreds of great arc lamps which were burning to illuminate the station below blinded my vision. But it was not for long.

"The window was just above the great central iron girder which ran from one end of the roof to the other—a perilous pathway of five hundred yards in length and perhaps a yard and a half in width—a dizzy route upon which only the workmen who repair the roof ever dare venture.

"And far away down that black goat-track, from which the blue-green light streamed up into the fog on either side, I saw a dark, moving mass. The fog came cold and bitter in my throat, my eyes smarted, but if ever a man willed vision to come to him, I did then.

"I saw two men slowly, carefully, walking with death on either side and carrying a long burden between them.

"One must think quickly in such moments as this.

"I knew that I could not follow. I do not think I was afraid—I had been in tight corners too often to know real fear—but I was sure that to venture on that dizzy height would be death for me. My head swims on the slightest eminence. This would have been madness.

"There was a faint, sweet smell in the room which I recognized in a flash: it was chloroform. That meant that Mr. Willstack had been drugged and not killed. He was being kidnapped to prevent his concluding nego-tiations. I thought I saw the villains' plan. At the far end of the roof were the steel ladders which rise up to it from a little platform on the bridge that spans the station right across and beneath which every out go-ing train must pass. Somehow or other they were going to get their burden down to this platform under cover of the fog. What they were going to do next I did not know, but there might yet be time to catch them in the very act. The job was frightfully perilous and must take some time, surely I could reach the far end of the sta-tion and confront them.

"I ran through those three tower-rooms like a man possessed. There was no time to wait for the lift. I hurled myself down stairway after stairway, passing frightened chambermaids and staring visitors. I bounded into the great lounge amid a chorus of shouts from the well-dressed people sitting round the fires there smoking their cigarettes and taking their coffee. In a flash I had wheeled to the right and was running over the wide carpeted corridor which led to the doors leading out into the station. The commissionaire, burly and stolid, gave a gasp as I darted past him, but I was through the double swing-doors before he could move and out upon the bridge-platform at the end of the station from which the broad flights of stairs led down to the platform level.

"I saw the whole of the station under the dome in a bird's-eye view. Far away to the right a suburban train was coming slowly in like a caterpillar, and just before it to the main down-line platform the Bristol express, with its long coaches and its great green engine, was curving majestically in.

"At number one, the departure platform to the extreme left of the station where the main entrances to the departure platforms are, the ten-thirty mail was standing at rest, people looking like rabbits scuttled about, and there was a far-off roar of escaping steam.

"I shall never forget that sudden panoramic picture in the brilliant steel-blue light. It is etched into my brain forever.

"I was down the stairs in a second. Hardly knowing what I did, I drew out the revolver from my pocket and dashed to the left. A porter was' wheeling a truck of luggage; I leaped over it like a hurdle-racer. I distinctly remember seeing the white faces of the bookstall clerks as I sped past the counter. Then I turned. To my right was the night mail, the doors of the long post-office vans were open, the red-capped officials hurling in the great canvas bags. The platform was crowded with people. The doors of the brilliantly lit refreshment-rooms opened and shut every minute. Fur-coated men and women stood outside the doors of first-class carriages.

"I dashed by them all, running like a hare, on and on to the end of the station, which seemed a mile away. There were shouts, here and there shrieks of alarm from women; and then the inevitable—the foolish thing happened.

"There was a tall young gentleman standing by the door of one of the sleeping-cars. He saw me when I was about three yards away, bent forward with a quick, instinctive action, and I was sprawling, bruised and stunned, upon the platform within a second.

"It was Philpott, the famous international Rugby three-quarter, and, naturally enough, he supposed he had to do with a madman.

"By the time explanations were over and I was helped to my feet by officials who recognized me five minutes had elapsed.

"And, to cut this part of my adventure short, when, assisted by all the staff available, we got outside the station on to the bridges and searched the surrounding dark, there was absolutely no sign of that extraordinary procession on the roof above.

"As I went back, sick and dizzy, to the hotel, I looked upwards. The roof, a hundred and seventy-five feet above my head, was filled with light, and in the very center I saw the long band traversing it from end to end, no thicker than a tape measure. You can imagine what I felt.

"The police of the whole of London and the provinces were engaged upon the search. Nothing whatever was heard of Mr. Willstack or his captors.

"My own position was peculiar. I was not blamed, I had done all I could, superior cunning had been too much for me, though I was only a few seconds too late.

But I felt myself the sting of defeat, and even now I did not despair.

"A few additional details came to light. The real financial manager turned up at eleven. The kidnappers must have calculated their plans with the utmost nicety. The gramophone, which had been brought in the dispatch-box, and which had so deceived me, was of no regular make. It had been specially constructed for the occasion. The fur coat, left behind by the black-bearded man, could not be identified at all, it was obviously of foreign make.

"I went to the chairman and said that I would yet discover Mr. Willstack before it was too late.

"'You've only three days to do it in, Buckland,' he replied, 'and I fear it is an impossible task. The papers will never now be signed and the Great Union will lose the finest chance it ever had of becoming the paramount railway in the United Kingdom.'

"I went back to the hotel and engaged a bedroom there, spending most of my time in the tower-rooms from which Mr. Willstack had been abducted.

"I sat down to think steadily. First I came to the certain conclusion that the engineers of the abduction— the prime movers—were the Great Southern Railway. It alone could have had any interest in the matter. Very well, then, how would it set about the work?

"Eliminating this or that, it was obvious that only criminals of the highest skill and utmost daring could be employed. Yet even the most unscrupulous agent of the Great Southern could hardly approach a professional criminal without incurring risks too great to be contemplated.

"In that case what would such an agent do? My experience answered: he would approach one of those few people in London or Paris who occupy some position, who are known to be of infinite daring and resource— who are, in fact, the princes of blood and crime, but who have never been convicted and probably never will.

"On the afternoon of the second day I was sitting in the big lounge of the hotel. I had shaved off my moustache, quite sufficient disguise for anything that might turn up. I do not quite know what I expected, but some vague unformed suspicion—a mere inkling of a thought—had come to me.

"As I was sitting there a tall, handsome man, rather bald, with iron-grey hair and fair complexion, came down in the lift. He sent a page to the cloakroom for his hat and overcoat and lit a cigarette while he was wait- ing, glancing casually round while he did so. His eyes met mine and passed over me as he idly surveyed the people. Then his coat was brought and he left the hotel.

"My heart was beating so furiously and I was in such a state of mental agitation that I feared I should betray myself to the assembled guests. I walked as steadily as I could into the smoke-room and had a stiff whiskey and soda. Then I felt better.

"There was something about the tall man's keen blue eyes that gave me food for thought. I went and inquired from one of the reception clerks who he was.

"'Oh, that is Major Lothian,' the man answered. 'He has been staying here for three weeks. Suite of rooms on the third floor.'

"'And who is he?'

"'Well, I believe he is a fairly well-known man about town—a racing man and all that. Also he is a well- known Alpine explorer. He is writing a book on his last exploits now, I am told, and in the hotel. A great stu- dent, though he does not look like it. Has great cases of books nearly every day.'

"That was all I wanted.

"Within three-quarters of an hour I was at Scotland Yard talking confidentially to a very high official.

"'Oh, yes, we know him,' was that gentleman's reply. 'There has never been a shadow of evidence against him for anything. He is never seen consorting with any of the big crooks. And yet not only I, but several other people in this department, would stake their life on it that he is a dead wrong 'un. Yet he goes into society and outwardly there is not a stain against his name.'

"As I drove back in the taxicab I was certain I was hot upon the trail.

"Major Lothian was precisely the man whom the Great Southern Railway could employ without any risk to themselves, owing to his position. He was the sort of man who would do anything for ten thousand pounds, and—this was the most significant thing of all—he was a daring Alpine climber. The roof of the Great Union Station would present no difficulty whatever to a man like that.

"So far so good. I was morally certain that Major Lothian was the black-bearded man who had impersonated the financier, but how did that bring me any nearer to discovering the whereabouts of Cyrus P. Willstack? There was the rub.

"Where was Cyrus P. Willstack?

"The alarm had been given so quickly half the detectives in London had been on the scene within so very few minutes of the disappearance that it seemed almost incredible that the millionaire had not yet been discovered.

"When I returned to the hotel—it was now about four o'clock—I went upstairs to the tower again. I sat in Mr. Willstack's private room, turned on all the electric lights and had some strong tea brought to me. On my right was the window and I could look down upon the great echoing glass turtle of the station. I sipped my tea and reconstructed the whole thing in my mind—with the visible scene before me. Then it flashed upon me. Of course! What an utter idiot I had been not to see it before. The Great Southern people had had an engine waiting close by on one of our sidings, an engine with a guard's brake, no doubt—an engine of theirs painted like one of ours. For expert railway people it was easy to get that engine out of the intricate system of points and stations and run it down some suburban line, shunting for the regular trains to pass, until it came to some distant goods yard, where under cover of night the millionaire could be easily removed. A motorcar might easily be waiting in some lane near a goods yard in the country—and then?

"Again I paused.

"After about half an hour's steady thinking, I telephoned down to the reception-office and ordered that a bedroom should be got ready for me as near as possible to that of Major Lothian upon the third floor. I was to be registered on the hotel list as Mr. Smith, from Derby. Then I telephoned to one of my assistants to send some luggage into the hotel under that name and have it taken to my new room.

"Now, upon the third floor of the Great Union Railway Hotel, there were several chambermaids. One of them—the one especially attached to the suite taken by Major Lothian—was a distinctly good-looking girl.

"As I think has been apparent during these stories, I am by no means a 'ladies' man,' and I blush to think that upon the very next evening I was seated with Mary Porter—that was the girl's name—in the upper circle of Drury Lane Theater. It was her evening out. She had never been so flattered in her life before. She thoroughly enjoyed herself—and over a simple supper she told me about herself and a good deal about another person of whom I was anxious to hear something.

"'Kind gentleman, Major Lothian,' she said, 'and most free-handed. Particular, mind you, and wants everything done his own way, but as free with half-crowns as I have ever seen anyone.'

"'I have seen him once or twice. Handsome man, don't you think, Miss Porter?'

"'Indeed I do, but so retired. My theory is,' Miss Porter continued, 'that he is a gentleman that is crossed in love,' and she heaved a sigh.

"'What makes you think that?'

"'He seems anxious and so retiring always. Now there are some people that say when you are crossed in love you can't touch your food, but I have never believed it myself. It seems to me only natural that when one is like that one should eat more than usual to keep one's spirits up, don't you think so, Mr. Smith?'

"'Well, I've never been crossed in love,' I replied; 'but still, I have no doubt there is a good deal in what you say.'

"She nodded wisely. 'Yes, and Major Lothian is an instance of it, I feel sure. He never goes down to the public rooms for his meals, but has them all sent up. They're put on the table outside in the corridor and his valet takes them in. The funny thing is—it is my duty to remove the trays and send them down by the service lift—that Major Lothian seems to have a queer taste in food.'

"'Dear me, how is that?'

"'Well, he has the ordinary things that a gentleman does have, but in addition there is always some queer mess or other that he orders through his room telephone. Rice puddings, once or twice tins of meat jelly, stewed prunes and milk.'

"'A lot of milk?'

"'Yes, a good deal; though how he can take milk and a bottle of wine with his meals at the same time I can't think. And it is no ordinary milk either, Mr. Smith. It comes from Bayswater in sealed bottles. Invalid people take it who are staying in the hotel. I've often seen it, it is goat's milk.'

"'Very strange,' I replied. 'I think you must be right, Miss Porter, the major is crossed in love. And what about his valet?'

"'He would make you laugh to see him, Mr. Smith. A nice fellow and wonderfully quick and strong. He was laughing and joking with some of us in the servants' room the other day, and he picked up a basket full of linen which three of us could not lift and put it on his head and stood on one leg. Then he stood in front of the big table and jumped over it from where he stood, just like a bird, he was.'

"'Or like an acrobat?' I suggested.

"'You've got it, Mr. Smith,' replied Miss Porter, pleased at my understanding; and shortly afterwards we drove back to the hotel.

"I passed Major Lothian's suite on the way to my own bedroom. Obviously the major had been having supper, for there was a tray with dishes and plated covers standing upon the table outside his rooms.

"It occurred to me that I might just as well investigate a little, and I lifted one of the covers gently. All I saw was a dozen oyster-shells. But in another part of the tray was a plated bowl, also covered. I lifted the lid and saw the remains of what was obviously bread and milk.

"And I saw something else.

"Lying in the middle at the bottom of the basin was a pair of steel-rimmed pince-nez and a little black japanned button from which a few inches of thin chain were dimly seen through the milk. Without making a sound I lifted this object out, placed it in my pocket, and went into my bedroom.

"Mr. Cyrus P. Willstack was found.

"I sat down in front of the fire for ten minutes and calmed my nerves. The whole thing was as clear as a pikestaff. They had driven the poor little millionaire about all night. They had drugged him. They had put him in a padded case supposed to contain books. He had been taken up to Major Lothian's apartments, the last place in the world where the detectives of England would have thought of looking for him, and he was imprisoned there now. He was being fed on the special diet which he was forced to take.

"The peculiar object, the pince-nez in the basin, was his one means of endeavoring to communicate with the outside world.

"I changed quickly into evening-dress and a dinner-jacket. It may have been vanity, but I was determined to do what had to be done without any assistance.

"I slipped my revolver into my pocket and went out into the corridor. And then came a piece of stupendous luck.

"Major Lothian himself came out of his sitting-room and closed the door behind him. He went to the lift and pressed the button. I sauntered up, too, as if I was also waiting for it.

"The lift came up, and Major Lothian entered. With a quick movement of my hand I pulled the gate into place. 'Sims,' I said sharply to the commissionaire, who, of course, knew me perfectly well, 'keep this man under lock and key till I tell you. Never mind what he says. He is a criminal whom I am about to arrest.'

"I will do Major Lothian the justice to say that he attempted no explosion of oaths or protests, he merely shrugged his shoulders.

"'I do not know how you have done it,' he said, 'but you are pretty smart. You will find the little chap locked up in the bathroom. My valet is sitting outside the door. You had better be careful, because he is an ugly customer to tackle.'

"I stepped across the corridor, passed into a richly furnished sitting-room, and opened the door leading into the bathroom corridor. There I saw a broad-shoul-dered, clean-shaven young man sitting on a camp-stool reading the sporting news.

"'The game is up, my man,' I said, just letting him see my revolver. 'Open that door.'

"It was perfectly simple, as simple as the capture of the Major had been. I found poor Mr. Willstack actually asleep upon a mattress placed in the bottom of the bath. He was covered with a traveling-rug, and a pathetic, haggard little figure he looked.

"The hotel was alarmed in two minutes. The million-aire was safely bestowed elsewhere under the care of a doctor. Major Lothian and his valet—afterward discov-ered to be a gentleman called Alf Swindon—a member of an acrobatic troupe performing at the smaller halls—were locked up for the night in the hotel strong-room.

"Next morning Sir William English, two other direc-tors, Mr. Willstack—a wonderfully tough little gentle-man he was—and myself interviewed the chairman of the Great Southern Railway.

"There was no public scandal. Major Lothian is earning fresh laurels in Alpine climbing and has not yet broken his wicked old neck. Alf is now the trusted valet of Cyrus P. Willstack. And I myself," concluded Sir Jasper, "am chairman of the Great Union Railway and a baronet."

The Mystery of the Private Car

Edwin D. Torgerson

1933

J. P. Milburn Murdered in His Own Private Car!

Who--

Was the Man on the Platform?

Had he committed this baffling crime and escaped into the night— never to return?

Or, had one of the millionaire railroad magnate's own week-end guests fired the fatal shot?

Who--

Committed the Second Murder?

Were the two killings connected?
Was the crime committed to
cover up the identity of the murderer
of J. P. Milburn? — —

Follow the piecing together of clues, the discovering of motives, and the establishing of connections between these two mysterious murders by the shrewd French-Canadian detective sergeant, Pierre Montigny in Edwin D. Torgerson's

J. P. Milburn's private car had an elusive and sinister visitor at St. Johns . . . but the train pulled from the station without him! No one saw him . . . no one suspected his presence. Who was he? Why had he come? What was it he had wanted?

Helen Eastwick, "J. P. M.'s" private secretary felt a vague nausea of terror upon entering the darkened room—she was positive of a presence there — but she could not see and the light switch was on the opposite wall! . . .

"The Mystery of the Private Car"

ILLUSTRATIONS BY PAUL FREHM

I

J. Proctor Milburn's private car, the Dorothea, had three staterooms, whereas most other private cars in this world have only two.

That was J. P. M. all over, as his friends put it. He always demanded something a little better than the next best. It pleased him to have people call him J. P. M. because those were the initials of J. P. Morgan as well, and if there had been any initials just a little more suggestive of prestige he probably would have arranged to have them, instead.

He had a secretary who was just a little abler than the ablest he had had heretofore. Also a little prettier. Her name was Helen Eastwick and she did not like her job.

She reflected upon this wholly explicable repugnance as the lights of a Vermont town dashed past the windows of the Dorothea. A renewed fortissimo in the carousal at the other end of the car had reawakened her distaste for J. Proctor Milburn and all his guests—well, with one exception, possibly—as she sat at her desk in the dining room typing two or three letters that presumably had to be mailed that night.

The dining room was at the front end of the car, and Helen's extemporized office was in a corner of it. There

"J. P. M."
J. Proctor Milburn, Millionaire
Railroad Magnate and Host to a
Group of Gay Young People at a
Wild Week-End Party on His
Private Car.

was an observation lounge at the rear end, which terminated in an observation platform, and in the lounge Mr. Milburn and his noisy company were now disporting themselves in a manner which ill became the chairman of the board of a great railway system and director of—well, Mr. Milburn's industrial and financial connections took up a lot of valuable space in the Directory of Directors.

There had been a wreck on the line that had delayed them for hours at Rutland, and Mr. Milburn's friends, deciding to make a night of it, did not seem to mind at all. They would be lucky now, the conductor had said, if they got to Montreal at 2 o'clock in the morning.

The possible exception to Helen's moodily expressed distaste found her staring out of the window in the vicinity of Middlebury. His name was Robert Aitken and he was a young and rising lawyer, almost too young, people thought, to have risen to the post of attorney-in-waiting to J. Proctor Milburn. Yes, sir; when J. P. M. went on a trip he took not only his secretary and his personal bodyguard but also his lawyer.

"Take a letter!" boomed Robert Aitken, his very correct imitation of Mr. Milburn startling her from her reverie.

"Oh, you dog," exclaimed Helen. But it was evident that if she meant a dog at all she meant a roguish and very likable dog. "Why you don't ring-a da bell, when you bust in on a lady?"

"This is too urgent for a bell," chaffed Aitken. "The Royal Presence commands you to appear in the lounge for target practice."

"Target practice? Merciful patience! Is that what the party has come to now?"

"It has. The party has exhausted all other possibilities of coherent entertainment and is now—wow!" Aitken gritted his teeth and hunched his shoulders as crash of glass from the rear added itself to the consistent uproar of the train. "They're shooting out the lights, as I live!"

The porter's bell, forward, jangled its alarm.

"Heavens, somebody will be hurt," gasped Helen.

"We'll hope not—or so, as the case may be," said Aitken. "They're not shooting with real guns. Air pistols—somebody gave Mr. Milburn a set of half a dozen, for indoor target practice. They're powerful things, though."

The porter passed through to the rear. He favored Helen and Bob with a furtive glance.

"Pretty wild party, at that," added Aitken.

"I'm glad you've got sense enough to stay sober," said Helen. "All I know is that if I get as far as Montreal in one piece I'm buying a one-way ticket back to Grand Central Staish."

"You're going to miss the boat trip?" queried Bob, with disappointment in his voice and eyes as well.

"No yachts for this meek and I modest P. W. G.," said Helen fervently. "They'll be having target practice with cannons once they get on the Dottie—say, isn't that an atrocious name for a beautiful boat like that?"

"He used up Dorothea," said the lawyer amusedly, "on the car. Do you know, I'm rather sorry for the poor old boy—this Dottie business."

"Dottie is good. Practically batty. And the little vixen, hussy, demi—"

"Hush! You were going to say demi-blondaine or something, and you mustn't. Dot's all right. A little hard, but they often get that way after they've climbed to a lot of quick eminence on Broadway. Dot can't help it if millionaires find her irresistible, can she? Maybe it's not as bad as we think."

"It's worse," said Helen tartly. "Sit down, won't you, or will you, or why don't you, or whatever it is one says to one's boss' private lawyer at midnight?" He did, gazing at her brusquely. "Take a letter, he said, with his sweet brown eyes warming up.

"I know," he accused, grinning "You're a moral and model woman, one of the extinct species. You haven't taken a drink. You have laughing blue eyes and cornflower hair—no, no; corn silk is what I mean—and a skin I would love to touch and fully intend to. But— you are jealous of this lovely little danseuxe or soubrette or whatever they call 'em—you're jealous because your boss names private cars and yachts for her—"

"Grrr! Raging with jealousy," Helen broke in. "Hear my teeth go g-nash!"

Helen checked herself. The white-coated porter and cook of the expedition came back through with a dustpan in which he balanced many fragments of glass.

"Accident, George?" inquired Aitken.

The porter, whose name was Homer Wilks, did not like the appellation of George, but his grinning array of teeth belied his resentment.

"No, suh. One of the ladies missed what she was shootin' at and broke a window."

"Ah. It must have been Miss Dustin. Atrocious shot, Miss Dustin."

"No, suh. I heard Miss Decker say it was her."

Helen waited until the porter had gone and observed caustically: "Your friend."

"My friend?" protested Aitken. "Why do you say that?"

"Why does a cat say 'Meow'? Because she's a cat. I beat you to it. But the lovely Lotus has been your friend conspicuously, my dear Mr. Aitken, all evening and most of the day. Why? Not because you're the only un- attached male—there's the dapper Mr. Perry Laith, but she hasn't looked at him. I don't blame her. Or you. I'm just kidding you. Can't you see I'm just kidding you?"

"You hurt when you talk like that."

"When she hasn't been pawing you she's been high-hatting me. I'm one of the hired help, and she's a guest. But why not? I signed on as hired help."

"Hush," commanded Bob, capturing her hand. "You're as much a guest as anybody. Milburn didn't need you on this trip; he said he didn't. But I did. I thought you'd have a good time, and I knew I would. I asked him to take you."

"Of course. You're a dear, and I'm an idiot. I'm sorry, Bob. But these show girls who get to think they're society queens—"

A small and gypsy-looking show girl with curvilinear contours, sloe-black eyes and an unruly mop of black curls lurched in from the rear door. She steadied herself with a lovely jeweled hand on Helen's desk. Of course it might have been the swaying of the train—but she managed a small supplementary lurch that brought her very close to Aitken. The perfume of her presence was subtly disturbing to most men, but Bob remained put. Her soft knee pressed against his.

"What you go leave me for, Mr. Achin'?" complained the girl, with just the right touch of puerility in her pout and in her soft voice. "What you go leave me for, and let me shoot out expensive windows, when you promised to stay with me and protect me from the crool world, and teach me how to shoot? What's he been talking to you about, Miss Whoosit—business?"

"My name is Eastwick," said Helen, quite unruffled, "and I am very busy. Won't you children go farther down the car to play. There are two lovely sections adjoining us, unoccupied, and you may close the door after you when you go out. Thank you, Miss Decker."

Helen banged back the carriage of her typewriter and began copying expertly.

"C'mon," urged Lotus Decker, tugging playfully at Aitken. "Let's go. I don't like these 'ficiency experts, anyhow. She'll have us punching a clock every time we take a drink, if we don't watch her. Won't you, Miss Whoosit?"

Helen said nothing and did not take her eyes off her letter, but a mild pinkness suffused her cheeks and her forehead became suddenly a bit shiny.

Aitken caught her eye as he rose to go, and the purport of his glance was to say, "I'll take her away because I know she gets on your nerves; but you know I'd rather stay here with you."

What he said was: "Miss Eastwick is going, too. In fact. I came here specifically to get her. We need her in the shooting festival."

"Not now, please," countered Helen. "It's so late. And I've got to get these letters off for Mr. Milburn at the next stop—what is it?"

"Burlington, about 11 o'clock, if the train makes up a little. We're hours behind. It's a shame you've got to peg away like this after union quitting time."

"Come on, Achin' Heart," begged Lotus. "She's making dirty cracks at me."

Bob Aitken and Lotus started to the rear, the girl hugging his arm.

"I want to ask you something, Judge," she cooed, "and we jus' mus' have privacy."

She flashed a triumphant glance at Helen Eastwick as her prey nodded assent. Helen smiled at them sweetly and resumed her typing.

There was no privacy to be had, however, in the two standard sections between the dining room and the

staterooms. Wilks the porter was busy making down one
section, that on the left side of the car, looking forward,
and in the other sat Mr. Moode, the hefty gentleman
who all day had made pretense of not being a private
detective, but who had private detective written all over
him. Mr. Moode was solemnly reading "Zippy Stories."
He looked up at Bob Aitken and Lotus, achieved an
awkward sign of recognition and then deliberately went
back to his literature.

Finding her plan for a private conference balked,
Lotus coaxed her companion back through the dining
room. Helen Eastwick smiled absently as they passed.

"It's the vestibule for us," said Lotus, then stopped
in the side passageway that led past the galley to the
front platform. "Or can't we go into your stateroom and
talk?"

"Oh, the platform will do, won't it?" preferred Bob,
grinning.

He swung open the heavy door and held it as she
passed. The door rushed to with a click behind them.

The noise of the trucks beneath made conversation difficult, but it gave Lotus a reasonable excuse for
standing very close to him, as the lurching of the train
condoned her clinging to him for support.

"What was it you wanted to ask me, Miss Decker?"

The girl had dropped her carefree attitude now. "Gee,
but I'm nervous," she whispered, and he could feel her
trembling genuinely. "I don't know just what to ask you.
I don't know what to tell you. I just know it's all a hell
of a mess back there, and I wish I'd stayed home. I'm
scared."

"Scared of what?"

"I don't know. That's what's got me creepy. Maybe
it's that Black Hand letter, or whatever it was Mr. Milburn got."

"Who told you about that?" he asked her searchingly.

"Dot told me. She said J. P. M. wasn't worried about it—it was just a crank letter like the ones he's always getting. But why, if he's not worried, did he bring that detective along?"

"Oh, Moode's just the regular bodyguard," said Bob. "His presence on the car has nothing to do with that crank letter. Mr. Milburn just has him along as a gesture, I think. Likes to feel he needs secret service protection, as the President does. But I'm surprised he mentioned the letter. He told me he intended saying nothing about it."

"He tells Dot everything. The poor nut. She's got him wrapped around her little finger. What gets me is why the heck she won't go and marry him. Gee, I wish I had the chance."

"Is that what he wants?"

"Sure. That's what Dot says. She says he's begged her to, time and again, but she's not quite sure she wants to be hampered."

The lawyer grinned. "Mr. Milburn already has a wife—and two grown sons," he ventured.

"But he's divorced," exclaimed Lotus. "Isn't he?"

"He is and he isn't, Miss Decker. Divorced in Paris, but the validity of the decree, it seems now, is to be contested in the New York courts. Those Paris decrees are binding enough if both parties act nicely about the collusion. But in this case Mrs. Milburn isn't acting nicely."

"Well, that explains a lot, doesn't it? They can't get married, can they—Dot and Mr. Milburn?"

Aitken shrugged. "They can call themselves married, if they like, but if the courts are asked to settle disputes about property, for instance, that will be something else again. The first Mrs. Milburn might not feel kindly disposed toward a second and concurrent Mrs. Milburn."

"Poor devil. It's hell to be rich, isn't it?"

"Hadn't we better go back, Miss Decker?"

"But that letter. Tell me again, please, Achey—tell me there's nothing to it."

"Why does a silly anonymous letter bother you?"

"Did you see it?" importuned Lotus. "Do you know just what's

"Yes, I saw it. From some fanatic, evidently; threatening him with hell fire and damnation for luring little girls on the road to destruction."

"Meaning who?" pressed Lotus. "Me, you suppose? Or Dot?"

"Oh, meaning nobody, I think. Just some crank who had read in the papers about Mr. Milburn's domestic troubles. There are thousands of these crack-brained letter writers, and it's a mania with them to write to everybody in the public eye."

"Was it written on a typewriter, or hand-written?"

"It was typewritten. But what the dickens do you care? What are you getting so upset about it for?"

"Listen, Mr. Aitken." Lotus played with his coat lapels. She was just tall enough so that her wind-blown hair tickled his cheek. "I know I've been flip and fly, and you think I'm just a scatter-brained little wise-cracker, and you don't give a hoot in h-hades about me. But you're the only human being, the only square shooter in this gang, and I got to talk to you."

"Well, you're doing nothing else, as the saying goes," said Aitken amusedly. He was a tolerant man. and he found Lotus not unlikable.

"I'm—I'm worried. Do you think there's any chance that that letter was from—from my brother?"

"Your brother! I didn't know you had a brother."

"Warren, his name is. He's a peach of a fellow. I'm not worth the nail of his little finger. He's always bossed me a little, and he raised the devil when I left home and went to New York to be a show girl."

"Home? Where is that?"

"Baltimore. I'm not going to tell you the story of my life. Don't run. I just want to explain about Warren. He's a traveling man and he's in New York a lot, and he's made it a point to keep an eye on me. Well, we had a knock-down-and-drag-out—I had to call for Schmel-ing-salts—when he heard I was going with Dot Dustin, and that I had been at Mr. Milburn's house for two or three parties. He said Dot wasn't any good, and it was an open scandal about Mr. Milburn putting up for her, and he wasn't going to let me get mixed with any such crowd. I told him he was crazy with the heat, that Dot Dustin had been a real friend to me and had helped me get in the Hilarities, and if he'd let me alone and 'tend to his own business I'd show him I could get my name in lights, too, like Dot's, some of these days."

"And did you convince him?"

"I did not. He went off sore as a boil, and I didn't see him or hear anything more from him until the day before yesterday, when he turned up at my apartment and said he'd heard all about this private car joyride to Canada and the yacht trip to follow, and if I went along he'd make trouble and plenty of it."

"What kind of trouble?"

"I don't know. He said I was under age and if he couldn't do it any other way he'd have Mr. Milburn prosecuted for 'impairing the morals of a minor.' Can he do that?"

"Is your father living?"

"No. My mother is."

"Then you must do as she says. She is your guardian."

"She'll side with Warren," mourned the girl. "She'll do anything he says. Gee, I wish I hadn't come. I wish

I'd gone back home with the fool. I told him this was a perfectly proper party, with chaperons and everything. But golly, what chaperons! This Mr. and Mrs. Heston pair. I don't believe they're even married."

"How did Mr. Milburn happen to invite them?"

"Dot's friends. I guess they're all right. But it looks to me, if you ask me, like this Heston woman is trying to cut out Dot with Mr. Milburn. The nerve! Have you noticed?"

"I can't say that I have, but last time I was in the lounge everybody seemed highly cordial toward everybody else. Hard for an observer to say just who belonged to whom."

"And this boy friend of Dot's—Perry Laith—seems to me he's jealous of Mr. Milburn. The slick-haired kid is supposed to be paired up with me. And has he looked at me? Ask me a hard one, like what did the hen lay in three letters."

"I think we had better go back in, Miss Decker."

Aitken tried the knob of the car door, but it was latched fast. He rang the porter's bell, pressing the button long and hard.

"Oh, goody-goody-joy!" cried Lotus, cutting a caper behind him. "We're locked out. We're compromised! Now what'll you tell your taffy-haired friend, Miss Whoosit!"

Joy never reigned but it poured at J. Proctor Milburn's parties. A temperate man himself—doctors had advised a watchful and affectionate care of the Milburnian stomach—J. P. M. merely tasted a cocktail now and then for the sake of appearance. But he enjoyed seeing his guest indulge themselves without stint, particularly because in that unstinted condition they were easy to amuse, and found everything he said uproariously funny or terribly cute or exceedingly clever.

Mr. Milburn was a stoutish, middle-aged executive with ruddy-gray cheeks, a well-groomed mustache, whitening temples and a girl on either arm of his chair. On the right arm of his chair tonight was Dorothea Dustin, known to her millions of admirers as Dot Dustin, whose brilliant season with the Hilarities had closed last week, and in whose honor the merry excursion to Canada had been conceived.

On the left arm of his chair was Clara Heston, married, but not so you would notice it, to George Heston, who at this moment was tipsily pinging away at a steel-backed pasteboard target with one of Mr. Milburn's air pistols. The target stood near the broken window at the end of the car, the right-hand corner as one looked to the rear. It was directly opposite the curtained door to the passage which led forward from the lounge, past the three staterooms, so that by putting aside the curtains and standing in this corridor the marksman could get a longer range than the twelve-foot depth of the lounge afforded. Heston however, stood quite near the target, and others of the party, grouped on the opposite side of the lounge, were not endangered by his inaccuracy.

Mr. and Mrs. Heston were chaperons only in a manner of speaking. Mrs. Heston at this moment was chaperoning Mr. Milburn's left ear, into which she was cooing things that evidently did not go out of the other ear for the benefit of Dot; for Dot did not seem to like it. Mr. Milburn had an arm around each of them—privilege of age or of wealth—but Dot suddenly disengaged herself and left it all to Clara.

"Come on, Perry, let's dance," trilled Dot, in that cute little sawed-off voice for which she infamous. "Cut out that shooting, George Heston, you ossified bum!"

She reached the radio with a bound and a flourish and snapped it on. The young gentleman addressed as

Perry rose gracefully from the chair on which he had been debonairly draped and joined Dot at her dialing. Laith had been a dancer, at times a lightweight actor, more profitably a gigolo and playboy giving service to wealthy and neglected wives. Whatever he worked at he did it gracefully—you had to admit that. He was smugly good-looking; a suave face that might or might not mask much knavery. Milburn tolerated him because he was a friend of Dot's.

But the millionaire stirred uneasily under the minor caresses of Clara. He was watching Dot, the red-headed cut-up, as she danced with that disgustingly lithe and graceful Perry Laith. They were rich in youth. He was poor, a few steps removed from senility. His chest rose and sank in a sigh, and a fleeting glance from Dot Dustin caught his expression.

"Don't let her know you feel that way—hug me tighter," commanded the murmurous Clara. "That's the only way to handle her; make her jealous."

Perhaps Mr. Milburn wondered why Clara's husband was not jealous. Mr. Heston, having abandoned his shooting for a glum inspection of the target sheet, had now repaired to a fixed table on the other side the lounge where a tray of drinks had been left by the porter. The party was getting dull, in Mr. Heston's obvious opinion.

Clara Heston, the antithesis of Dot in type, professed an abiding friendship for the musical comedy star, but like most human beings in the profession—Clara herself had been an actress before her marriage—she was not above an occasional oh-quite-friendly nip in the back, directed at one who had been more successful. For of course everybody admitted that Dot Dustin had just had lucky breaks; the friendship of Mr. Milburn, for instance, of whom it was whispered that he was the

silent and secret angel behind the producer of the Hilarities. Clara was of the svelte and languid, dreamy-eyed
persuasion—really too good for musical comedy, if you
knew what she meant. She playfully smoothed the Milburnian brow.

"Oh, Dot's a good friend of mine, always has been,"
she continued. "But I don't think she treats you right,
J. P. I've told her so herself. She's too sure of you. You've
been awfully good to her. But she thinks she can get
by with anything, now that she's got them offering her
twelve hundred a week."

Milburn smiled bleakly, a bit disparagingly.

"What is she trying to 'get by' with?"

"Oh . . . Like Perry Laith. Look at the way he holds
her. Look at the look she gives him."

Milburn stirred uneasily. "It's the look she gives
everybody," he growled. "She uses it in the show, for
that matter."

Clara sighed theatrically. "Poor blind, adoring, trust-
ing creature. You're just a kid, after all, J. P. You let a
two-timing little devil like Dot run you ragged. And
there's no need for it. You're too faithful, that's all. Pay
her back in her own coin, that's the way to handle her."

"Be faithless?" he suggested sardonically. "With you?"

Clara laughed loudly and merrily, pretending that in
her mirth she had been threatened with a tumble from
her perch. The others would think it was just one of
J. P.'s clever cracks. Above the rumble of the train and
the oom-pa, oom-pa of the radio nobody could hear
what they were saying.

"There's bite in the gay dog after all," chaffed Clara.
"But don't be so outspoken, J. P. This is merely a suggestion, not a proposal. You needn't use me, though
I'm perfectly willing and able, and a swell actress, and
my husband knows all about it and will just think it's

funny. But it doesn't matter who it is. You just want to make Dot jealous, that's all. Show her she's not the only woman in the world. Show her tonight, when she's throwing Perry Laith in your teeth. Let her catch you kissing somebody—in private—not me, necessarily, anybody—that up-stage little baby-faced steno of yours, for instance."

"You should not judge all women by yourself," said Milburn ill-naturedly. "Nor all men by me," he added placatingly.

"That's right, too. Your blonde Venus might slap your face, mightn't she? Where is she, by the way? Where's Bob Aitken?"

"I sent Bob to get her."

"And where's the luscious little Gypsy—the Decker kid?"

"I sent her to get him."

"Oho! A play within a play. Now who'll you send to get her?"

"I'll ring for Wilks. The party is going flat."

"Flat, stale and unprofitable. No, it isn't. Look! He's kissing her!"

It obviously was true, for Perry Laith, backing his smiling partner into a corner, inclined his sleek head toward her face, and when they swung around there was a renewed and different smile on Dot's lips, the post-canary smile of the cat.

Milburn got up in repressed rage.

"You go join the others," he demanded of Clara. "Take your husband. I've something to say to this pair."

He squelched the radio.

"Come. Georgie," said Clara with a wink for her husband. "The party's moving to the other end of the car."

She grasped his arm and tugged him out grumblingly.

Dot and Perry Laith, who had stopped dancing, were the picture of manufactured astonishment.

"Why, what's the matter, J. P.?" demanded Dot cross-ly. "Are you sick again or something?"

"I'm sick. Yes. I'm sick of you and your lying, fawn-ing, parasitical friends. Now you get out, Laith, you snide, sniveling, night-cub table-crumber! I want to talk to your woman."

J. P. Milburn's anger was crisp and biting. He spoke very swiftly, in the tone of one long accustomed to be-ing obeyed. He had endured much, in sly innuendo, in gnawing suspicion, in taunts from his two sons, in insolence from such as these. Had anyone told him that the inexpert Iagoisms of Clara Heston were responsible for his outburst, he would have laughed it harshly down as ridiculous. He had come to his own cold conclusions through his own carefully ordered reasoning, he would have asserted. Of course the openly insulting and de-fiant conduct of Dot and Perry Laith had provoked it, but that was merely the final straw. He had seen this coming.

Milburn strode to the door in the left forward corner of the lounge, swung back the heavy portieres that cut off the corridor and barked again at Laith.

"Get out! Or do you prefer to be thrown out?"

Laith called up his coolest and most supercilious brand of dignity. "I do not know what has prompted your ill-mannered outburst, sir," he said. "I am your guest in this car, the equivalent of your home. If you choose to be insulting it is your own reputation as a gentleman that is imperiled, not mine."

"You have none to imperil, you stage-door scum. Get out!"

"Assuredly I will." Laith advanced to the exit with steps that were not precisely mincing but gave that im-pression faintly. "What is more, sir, I shall get out of your miserable car. You forget there is quite an ample train ahead of us, and I am not compelled to remain here and accept your insults."

"I don't care whether you leave the car now or in the morning. Get out of my sight, that's all."

Laith passed out with a confidential gesture of contempt for Dot's benefit, which seemed to convey, "Well, what else can we expect of the rotter!"

When Milburn let fall the portieres he faced a red-headed fury. The three or four freckles which Dot had sought vainly to eradicate from her fair countenance glowed reddish brown against the shifting pink and paleness of her cheeks. Her eyes, which had a tint of green in them, seemed to phosphoresce like those of a cat caught by a motor lamp in the dark.

At times, with an herculean effort abetted by her memory of lines from many a drawing room farce, Dot could be a lady, but the lady business was out tonight. She was mad, and she was going to give this man what was coming to him. Dot was privately celebrated, backstage, for the diverting foulness of her language when aroused. J. Proctor Milburn had never sampled its utmost picturesqueness. He had heard rumors that Dot could swear oaths that would put to double shame the obscenities of an East Side truckman, but he had dismissed them as the lying canards that are ever aimed at notables and notoriables. Tonight he learned his error.

"I'm through," said Milburn grimly. "I mean I have carted you and your wagonload of human garbage far enough."

"You're through, are you?" sneered Dot. "You mean you've been through. But you're not through paying. Get that. You'll make it up to me for this."

"Save the Billingsgate for your friends," bade Milburn with a bitter weariness. "Your threats mean nothing to me. You've done all the harm to me that you could possibly accomplish. And you've had all the money out of me that I intend for you to have."

"The courts will see to that," Dot replied venomously. "I've got letters—don't forget that—and witnesses."

"Sue as you please. You will gain nothing. I intend to fix it so that you will never get anything from me again; alive," he added coldly, "or dead."

"I'll drag your name through the tabloids till you're sick of it, you dirty piker. You'll be glad to settle before I'm through with you."

"Oh, no," he contradicted. "I don't think you will go into the courts at all. You will wreck your own name, not mine. The public is not fond of loose women for its stage favorites."

"You'll crawl for saying that."

"I have done my crawling. I could not debase myself lower than I have by association with you and your pals and lovers."

Dot began to cry, whether out of rage or guile it would have been difficult to guess.

"I didn't think you would treat me like this, J. P.," she sobbed. "I didn't mean any harm kissing Perry. It was just part of the dance we were doing—stage business. Perry means nothing to me."

"Don't shift your tactics so suddenly," advised Milburn. "You're not fooling me. You have never fooled me. I have known of your double-dealing conduct all along."

"Just what have I done?" demanded Dot, flaring up.

"Never mind; I have been advised. I have had daily —nightly, I had better say—reports of you and your dancing friend, Mr. Laith."

Dot glared at him with fresh hatred. "You have had me shadowed? You mean that lying hulk Moode—"

"Never mind what I mean. You have played me for a chump, as you express it, long enough. It's all right. I have deserved it. There is no fool like an old fool—except an old fool with more money."

"Damn your money," hissed Dot. "I've got money of my own. I earn enough not to have to be dependent on you and your ten-cent generosity."

"You have had a fortune out of my ten-cent generosity. But never mind that. There is nothing more I wish to discuss with you. Get out. My secretary will have return tickets for you and your crawling baggage tomorrow."

"You dirty cur," snarled Dot. "You planned this trip just to do this to me, didn't you? To belittle me before my friends, eh? Well, I'll belittle you before your friends, understand? I'll even up with you for this insult if it takes the last breath of life out of me. Do you get that?"

"Get out," repeated Milburn sternly, "or I will ring for Moode and the porter and have you put out."

"You rotten piker," shrilled Dot. "That's what you are, rotten—inside and out. Oh, I know what that doctor from Baltimore told you last week—he told you to crawl off in a hole somewhere and die, like the mangy dog you are!"

Milburn winced, maintained his poise with an effort. He strode to the bell button on his desk and pretended to press it hard. Then, with an air of grim finality, he lighted a cigar.

"Oh, you needn't ring for your bouncers," sneered Dot. "I'm going. But I'm not getting out of this car. I wouldn't give you that much satisfaction. You dirty cheap-skate."

With that Dot Dustin, the darling of Broadway, was gone.

Milburn sighed heavily. He crushed his unsmoked cigar into an ash tray and slumped into a seat by a window. There was nothing outside but the wailing blackness, against the dim and shallow reflections, caught in the glass, of things inside the car.

He arose uneasily, pressed his hand to his stomach with a grimace of pain. Slowly, as though drawn by a force opposed to his will, he approached the desk placed against the forward wall of the room. He sank into a chair in front of it and with fumbling hand drew open a drawer. His fingers closed about the butt of a thirty-eight automatic. He glanced around furtively.

He paused thoughtfully, removed his hand. From a pocket he produced his keys. He knelt beside the desk where a small lock in the steel wall of the car indicated a door. He swung open the door and fumbled with the dial of a small safe, securely built into the wall. His efforts were unavailing and he knitted his brow in perplexity.

The portieres of the door at the left of the desk swelled and moved, as though bellied out by a draft. Milburn hurriedly closed the outer door of the wall vault, though he did not lock it, and resumed his seat in the chair.

The heavy curtains moved again and Clara Heston peered mischievously into the room.

"Oh, it you." Milburn relapsed into a posture of dejection.

"Yes, just little me," said Clara entering. "Everybody's mad and gone to bed, and I haven't got anybody to play with. What on earth did you say to them, J. P.?"

"I said enough."

She settled on an arm of his chair, straightened his coat collar, rested an insouciant arm about his shoulders. He was indifferent to her presence.

"Dot's locked herself up in her stateroom and won't open the door," she went on. "Perry Laith isn't speaking to anybody. He's back there glaring at Moode. We've just rescued Mr. Aitken and Gypsy Decker off the front plat form—locked out, they said they were—the Eastwick girl found them there, and now I think she's all sored up, too. What's the matter, J. P.? In the dumps?"

She caressed his hair with light fingers. Milburn said nothing,

"Has that mean old Dot been mistreating you again?" Her free hand, which rested on the desk, crept unseen by Milburn toward the pearl button which would summon the porter. She kept the ball of her thumb pressed against it while she talked. "You didn't handle her right, J. P. I told you how to do it. You should have made her jealous. Like this!'

She sank into his unwilling arms and kissed him.

"Get away," ordered Milburn gruffly. "You're one of the gang. I want nothing to do with any of you."

With her eyes cut suddenly toward the curtained door Clara began to scream:

"Help! Oh, don't, don't, J. P.! Oh, somebody help me! Oh, don't, don't! Help!"

Her hand had ripped loose a shoulder strap of her evening gown and had rent the ribbon of her brassiere. Her nude shoulder pressed sharply against Milburn's mouth. She screamed again:

"Oh, help! Help! Oh, don't, J. P.! Don't, don't! Oh, somebody make him stop!"

He struggled to his feet with the half-nude and disheveled form of the girl still clinging to him. He cast her from him as the portieres parted and her husband rushed in. Wilks the porter was directly back of Heston, white-eyed and frightened. Rob Aitken pressed past the negro.

"Oh, oh, oh!" sobbed Clara, crumpled on the floor.

"What is the meaning of this?" shrieked Clara's husband, his fingers flexed as for Milburn's throat.

Trouble Starts When Dot and Perry Are Caught Kissing and Mrs. Heston Attempts to Carry Out Her Own Little Scheme

"Oh, help! Help! Oh, don't, J. P.! Don't! DON'T! Oh, somebody make him stop!" screamed Clara. Her hand had ripped loose a shoulder strap of her evening gown and had rent the ribbon of her brassiere

"He insulted me; he attacked me!" moaned Clara hysterically. "Look, oh, look—at the marks on my shoulder! Oooh! The brute, the brute!"

"I'll kill you for this, Milburn!" screamed George Heston, lunging toward him and finding himself checked, fortunately, by the interference of Bob Aitken.

Moode the detective shouldered in ponderously and fixed all parties with a cold and official glare. There was a garbled chatter of voice behind the curtain.

"What is it, Mr. Milburn?" asked Bob Aitken coolly. "What happened?"

"Sweep all this offal out of the car," ordered Milburn in red-faced rage. "By heaven! I no sooner cast off one of the carrion crows than another alights on me."

"What is it—a frame-up?" demanded Detective Moode hoarsely.

"Yes, the dirty little blackmailer!" roared Milburn, "if she thinks she can bleed me with any such trashy trick as this—"

"Oh, George, George," screamed Clara, getting up none too gracefully from the floor, "are you going to let that fiend in human form talk about me like that? He insulted me, he attacked me! Oh, George, kill him! Kill him!"

"I'll kill him, but I'll kill him the way it hurts," sneered George Heston. "He thinks because he's got money he can get away with this sort of stuff, does he? I'll show him!"

"Quit your kidding," admonished Detective Moode coldly. "How much did you figure to shake him down for? Ten grand? Twenty grand? Huh? Pretty crude methods you use, ain't they? Huh?"

"Come, Clara, let's get off the scoundrel's car," said Heston, ignoring the detective. "We can't do anything against his hired thugs. But just wait till we get to Montreal!"

"You don't get off this car," announced Moode grimly. "You're my prisoners, you darned cheap blackmailers, and you just think you're going to get away with it. I've got the goods on you, and I'm going to send you up!"

"Yes, you are!" taunted Heston. "You'll get yourself in trouble with all that lip, if you don't look sharp."

"Get out of here and go to your berths," ordered Bob Aitken. "We'll deal with you tomorrow."

"You mean you'll deal with my lawyer," sneered Heston. "Come on, Clara."

J. P. Milburn was leaning heavily against his desk. He looked haggard and ill.

"You'd better lie down, Mr. Milburn," said Aitken solicitously. "You're not feeling well, are you?"

Milburn passed a hand wearily over his brow. "Oh, I'm all right. You wait, Bob. I want to talk to you. You may go, Moode. Send in Miss Eastwick. We'll talk over all this mess with you later, Moode."

"Yes, sir," said Moode. "I won't let these crooks get away. I'll lock the car door."

Murder!—The Party Becomes a Panic; Detective Moode Takes Charge as the Train Enters Canada

Moode swept aside the portieres. There was an interval of voiceless awe as they surveyed the scene in the lounge. J. Proctor Milburn sat slumped in an armchair—dead!

2

At eight minutes past one o'clock—the time was definitely established because the train had just left the Canadian town of St. Johns—Detective Moode was aroused from his berth by a terrified negro porter.

"Good heavens, Captain!" breathed Wilks hoarsely. "Come with us quick. Mr. Milburn's been killed!"

Robert Aitken, garbed in his pajamas and lounging robe, was with the porter.

Moode uttered something between a sleepy moan and a growl of incredulity. The porter repeated his appeal, tugging at the mattress. Moode's giant frame emerged slowly from the lower berth. He toed his way into a pair of leather slippers and hauled out a dark green bathrobe, which he donned scowlingly. He regarded Aitken with uncertain inquiry. Then:

"Where, Wilks?" he demanded with a labored wheeze.

"In the lounge," whispered Wilks, his teeth audibly chattering. "The bell rang two, three times—I must have been dozin'—that's how come I found him."

"Hush, not so loud," muttered Moode commandingly. "Lemme take a look before you wake anybody else up."

The trio lurched soundlessly down the car, through the corridor past the three staterooms to the curtained entrance to the observation lounge.

Moode swept aside the portieres. There was an interval of voiceless awe as they surveyed the scene in the lounge.

J. Proctor Milburn sat slumped in an armchair, dead. The chair faced a window of the car diagonally, and Milburn's right temple, turned to the door, displayed a trickle of blood from a tiny wound. His collar and stiff shirt bosom—he was still dressed in his Tuxedo of the evening past—bore jagged crimson stains. On the floor, some three feet from the chair, lay one of the heavy air pistols, ominously like an automatic, which Milburn and his guests had used at target practice. Moode did not pick it up.

"Don't touch anything," he warned, turning to stare briefly at Aitken and the porter. "This looks like a job for the Province. What time is it?" He peered at a small clock on the late Mr. Milburn's desk and answered himself: "Ten minutes after one. Be in Montreal around two. Any more stops, Wilks?"

"N-no, suh," trembled the porter.

"When did you find him?"

"J-jus' now, c-couldn't a-been ten minutes," stammered Wilks. "Jus' before I woke you up, suh. I was still up on account the inspectors that come on at Rouse's Point. Bell rung and I come in here and found him, suh. Then I run told Mr. Aitken—"

"Bell rang two or three times before you answered it?" demanded Moode sternly.

"Yes, suh, yes, suh—that is, it must've, I only heard it once I was sure of, but it seems like when I did hear it I must've been dozin'—I must've heard it before."

"What are you trying to tell me?" Moode assumed his ugliest bulldozing tone. "That you were asleep, and somebody rang the bell—what bell—from where?"

"I said there was two bells," replied Wilks, fidgeting nervously, "because—well, I didn't exactly hear 'em—I looked at the 'nunciator after I heard the bell and there was two calls rung up—one from the lounge here—that desk button, sur, and—"

"What other one?" snapped Moode.

"Mister—Mister—" Wilks rolled his eyes apprehensively toward Aitken—"Stateroom B—Mr. Aitken's stateroom."

Moode turned to the lawyer bluntly.

"Well, what of it?" he demanded, when Aitken met his gaze levelly. "What did you ring for?"

"I did not ring," said Bob calmly. "The porter must be mistaken."

"No, suh, I ain't mistaken," insisted Wilks. "You can tell by the 'nunciator, right now."

"He came to my door ten or twelve minutes ago and woke me up," continued Aitken. "I had not rung the bell—unless I did it by accident, in my sleep. Had trouble waking me, didn't you, Wilks?"

"Y-yes, suh, seemed like I couldn't hardly, at all. I started to see what Mr. Milburn wanted first, but I says to myself, 'Mr. Milburn's busy—somebody talking with him in there—'"

"You heard somebody talking?" cut in Moode quickly. "Somebody in here with Mr. Milburn—not Mr. Aitken?"

"No, suh. Mr. Aitken sleep—somebody else."

"Well, who was it—did you see him when you went in?"

The negro's jaw trembled violently. "No, suh. That's it—he was gone!"

"A man's voice you heard, huh?"

"Y-yes, suh, seems like—man and Mr. Milburn talkin'."

Moode turned to Aitken. "Did you hear voices in here, too?"

"Yes. It seems to me that I did. I didn't pay much attention to the fact. I was half asleep."

Moode advanced heavily toward the cringing negro. "Who was this man?" he growled threateningly. "This man you saw when you came in here?"

"I didn't see n-nobody, suh," chattered Wilks. "All I saw was—" He walled his eyes fearfully toward the corpse—"all I saw was him, like he is now!"

Moode's eyes swept the room. "Any place in here this man could have hidden?"

"N-no, suh. Not hardly."

"There was only one way he could have got out—to come by you through that doorway and past the state-rooms?"

"Y-yes, suh. Less'n he jumped off the back, suh."

"Did you look on the back platform?" demanded Moode sharply.

"Yes, suh, yes, suh. I did."

"And there was nobody there?"

"No, suh. The door was shut, but I could see plain through the windows—lots of light in here."

"The door was locked?"

"No, suh, no, suh. It wasn't. But I latched it."

Moode glowered at him. "You latched it! What did you do that for?"

The negro quailed. "I don't know, suh. Swear I don't. Reckon I was jus' sort of skeered, seems like!"

Moode and Aitken went to the rear door of the car.

"Don't touch that knob," said Moode sourly. "Finger-prints. I know well enough the door was latched, to begin with. Mr. Milburn kept it locked for fear some of these drunks would fall off the car. Thumb bolt. Latched on the inside. And this 'man' Wilks heard let himself in—through a locked door."

"This broken window," suggested Aitken. "A man on the platform could put his arm through here and reach that thumb bolt."

"Ah," Moode considered. The door opened inward and the knob was on the right-hand side, nearest the broken window, but the break in the glass was nearly three feet from the door-knob. "Mighty long arm he'd have to have. We'll test it out when we get to Montreal."

"Why wait? Why not now?"

Moode turned on him with a gruff reply: "You heard me say I didn't want that knob touched."

"Why don't you look for fingerprints yourself?"

"I haven't got the outfit, that's why. And I know these Canadian bulls—had experience with them before. It's their murder. This job was done in Canadian territory."

"How do you know that?" questioned the lawyer coolly.

For answer Moode crossed over to the body of Milburn. He felt the inert hand that dangled on the right side of the chair. "This man hasn't been dead fifteen minutes," said Moode. "What time was it when we stopped at St. Johns, Wilks?"

"About quarter to one, suh. Stayed there fifteen minutes; got held up by the customs and immigration fellows."

"And you found him—heard voices in this room—after we left St. Johns, didn't you?"

"Y-yes, suh."

"All right," grumbled Moode. "If that don't fix the time it was done, I don't know what would."

"Somebody," suggested Aitken slowly, "got on the back platform at St. Johns, unbolted the door by putting his arm through the broken window—"

"Yeh," cut in Moode sarcastically. "Then he had a few loud words with the man he was gonna kill, so you and this porter could hear him—then he picks up one of these toy target pistols so you wouldn't hear him—shot him with that—"

"It seems to be exactly what happened," asserted Aitken, peering again at the wound in Milburn's forehead. "Neither Wilks nor I heard a shot fired. A pellet from one of these air pistols—don't you agree, Mr. Moode?"

"You couldn't kill a sparrow with one of those things," said Moode disdainfully.

"Oh, you're wrong!" Aitken crossed to the back of the lounge where the target stood. He picked up two heavy volumes of the New York telephone directory. "Look at this, Mr. Moode. We tried it. One of the bullets went all the way through one of these three-inch directories, and half-way through another."

"You know all about it, don't you?" observed Moode significantly, examining the path through which the leaden pellet had passed.

"I know that much about it," said Aitken sharply. "And I know another thing, Mr. Moode. I know this train ought to be stopped at the next town we reach, and you ought to notify the police. The man who killed Mr. Milburn may have got off the train at St. Johns, or between here and St. Johns. I suggest you see the conductor at once, Mr. Moode."

"Bright idea," sneered the big detective. "It's just the thing I been trying to get a chance to do, but instead I've got to stand here and argue with you and try to keep you from messing things up before the cops can get a chance."

"All right, get busy," snapped Aitken. "I'm not going to touch anything or interfere with you in any way."

"Much obliged. Wilks, step forward on the train and find the conductor. Tell him we got to stop at the next town and telephone Montreal."

"Yes, suh."

"And Wilks—" The porter paused. "Just a minute. I want to go with you to the front of the car. I want a look at that annunciator before any more buttons are pressed. What's more, I want a picture of it, soon as I can get it. You come along, Mr. Aitken."

They found the annunciator as Wilks had described it. It displayed two calls—one from the desk button in the lounge. Wilks said he had "jigged the jigger-thing" beneath the annunciator not fifteen minutes before, so he was sure the calls were recent ones, made at the time he heard the bell.

"Where are the batteries?" asked Moode tersely.

"Transformer in here, suh," said Wilks, indicating a metal box fixed to the wall of his linen closet nearby. "Don't use batteries. Plugs into the AC circuit."

"Well, disconnect it," ordered Moode. "Pull out the plug. I don't want nobody monkeyin' with this thing."

"If I were you," suggested Bob Aitken thoughtfully, "I would cut the wires, too."

Moode eyed him stonily. "You would, hey? And why would you?"

"Somebody might plug in that transformer again, then if anybody rang—"

"'Somebody' better not," rasped Moode. "The porter's the only man knows about the transformer. Say!" Mr. Moode was a very tactless detective. "Just why is it you are so interested in those wires, Mr. Aitken?"

The lawyer shrugged. "Oh, I'm not particularly interested. We just want to be sure that everything stays just as it is."

"Hm!" Moode turned to Wilks. "Go get that conductor."

The dining room door, behind them, opened and Perry Laith appeared in the passageway. His hair was tousled and his tan silk pajamas wrinkled out of shape. He spoke crossly, with a sneer.

"Say, what's the idea of all the loud chin music, when a fellow's trying to get some sleep?"

"Disturbed you, did we?" returned Moode ironically. "Well, now, that's too bad, ain't it? Come along to the back of the car, brother. I want to show you something."

Aitken winced at this sample of the man's crudeness, but he said nothing as Moode led the way to the rear.

"Wait till I get my robe," protested Laith sourly, "if we got to run around all over the car."

He climbed to his berth, the upper in the section of which Moode had had the lower. He rummaged there a moment as his companions waited, and stepped back into the aisle with an impatient oath. "Not here. Must have left it in your stateroom, Aitken."

"Come on," said Moode gruffly. "You won't need it. Nobody gonna criticize your beauty."

Laith found his dressing gown, a garment of figured blue silk with white cuffs and lapels, on the floor of Stateroom B.

"Guess I left it hanging in here," he muttered. "Somebody knocked it down."

Moode kept his eyes steadily on Perry Laith's face as they approached the curtained entrance of the lounge. He drew back the portieres with a jerk.

"Good heavens!" gasped Laith, staggering back at the sight as though he had been struck. "What's happened?"

"If you can't figure it out for yourself, brother," said Moode grimly, "I can't help you."

"How did this—who—when did they—find him?" stammered Laith, fearfully stepping closer to the body.

"Fifteen or twenty minutes ago. He's still warm. Feel him."

Laith drew back with a grimace of horror. His hands, in the pocket of his dressing gown, clutched convulsively.

"Somebody shot him," said Laith in an awed whisper, "with one of the target pistols."

He suddenly drew his right hand from his pocket, and stared at his cupped palm. A muted scream escaped him.

"Who put these in my pocket? he jabbered shrilly.

Aitken and Moode, coming closer, saw that he held in his hand six or seven of the small leaden pellets, about the size of a .22 bullet, which were intended for use in the air pistols.

"I never put these in here, I never put these in here!" cried Laith excitedly.

"And you didn't shoot Mr. Milburn, either, did you," demanded Moode harshly; "and sneak your bathrobe back in Mr. Aitken's compartment afterwards?"

"What are you saying!" gasped Laith. "I thought my robe was in my berth, where I was asleep."

"Ye-eh?" drawled Moode, "when did you have it on last?"

"Why, when I went to bed, it seemed to me."

"You undressed in Mr. Aitken's stateroom and put it on in there, did you?"

"Ye-es," said Laith uncertainly. "Oh, no, I didn't. I intended to do that—that was it—I left the robe in Mr. Aitken's room because I intended to undress in there, but I didn't. I undressed in the berth— oh, I don't re-member," he ended irritably. "I had a lot to drink—I wasn't the only one."

"What about it, Mr. Aitken?" questioned the detective. "Do you remember seeing the bathrobe hanging in your room?"

"I don't recall."

"All right, Mr. Laith. Give it to me. We'll have to hang on to this robe for evidence. You'd better go get some clothes on. We'll be in Montreal pretty soon, and there'll be no more sleeping on this car tonight."

When Laith had gone the detective inquired of Bob: "Did you have the door of your stateroom locked?"

"Yes. No. Wait a minute. I'm inclined to think I did not."

"Oh. You didn't?"

"No. I am sure it was unlocked. I recall now that the thought occurred to me that some of the other men in the car might want to get in. There's no smoker or men's room on the car, you know, and I happened to be the only man occupying a stateroom. That was the main reason I did not absolutely insist on one of the ladies taking it—we had to have a men's room of some sort."

"Hm! Funny situation this. Looks like somebody sneaked in your stateroom, don't it? And got the robe, or planted those bullets in the pocket; and rang the bell from your room? And then shot Mr. Milburn, maybe? Suppose anybody could do all that without open skepticism?"

"I'm sure I don't know. I suppose it is possible. There is so much noise on a moving train."

"Slept good, did you?"

"I must have."

"Hm! Do you know of anybody, Mr. Aitken, who might have wanted to kill Mr. Milburn?"

Aitken frowned.

"A rather broad field of inquiry there, I should say. I should rather not discuss it."

"You wouldn't, eh? Hm!"

The train drew into St. Lambert, six miles from Montreal, and stopped just as Wilks returned with the conductor.

That official, vastly upset by the tragic circumstances, urged Detective Moode to make his telephone calls brief.

The stop at St. Lambert, with the sound of many voices and the tread of many feet passing through the car, awakened the remainder of the passengers of the Dorothea with the exception of George Heston, who cursed, turned over and snored again heavily.

Dot Dustin, upon viewing the body of her late protector, despite the urgent appeals of Perry Laith that she deny herself that ordeal, went promptly into hysterics. She screamed, laughed, moaned and jabbered, and it seemed that her clenching teeth would break the glass when someone attempted to give her a bromide. A call for a physician went through the train and a chance passenger of that profession came to minister to her.

Clara Heston, though frightened and awed by the tragedy, accepted it more calmly. She devoted her major efforts, between St. Lambert and Montreal, to the seemingly impossible task of arousing her husband. Even with the aid of Bob Aitken and Detective Moode, this was a difficult endeavor. Mr. Heston, it seemed, obviously unstrung after the excited colloquy with Mr. Milburn, had continued to imbibe intoxicants from a private bottle in his luggage, even after he had retired to his berth.

Nor would George forego the privilege of these quarters until Detective Moode had all but dragged him bodily from the berth.

"Wake up, you fool," shouted Moode. "There's been a murder—a killing!"

"Hell of a time," muttered George thickly, "to kill anybody—jus' when I'm beginnin' to get a little res'."

Helen Eastwick, pale and distraught, sought a word in private with her late employer's lawyer. They sat at her desk in the dining room, conversing in lowered tones when anybody passed.

"Do they know—have they any idea who did this dreadful thing?" she asked him tremulously.

"Not the slightest, so far as I have been able to learn," said Bob gravely.

"Is it definitely—I mean are they sure—is there is a possibility, you think, that Mr. Milburn might have—killed himself?"

Bob nodded slowly. "I think, personally, there is. Except that the porter says he heard voices, and I believe I did, too—a man, talking to Mr. Milburn just before Wilks found him dead. I couldn't absolutely swear to it—I was half asleep and I opened the door just a crack. I could not say definitely from which direction the voices came."

"But who could have rung your bell?"

"That seems odd. It must have been an accident."

"Or Wilks lying?" suggested Helen.

"Oh, no. I saw the annunciator directly afterward. It was just as it is now. It has been disconnected so that nobody else can ring up a call."

Helen shivered. "And we—you and I—must have been the last persons to see poor Mr. Milburn alive."

"What did you do," asked Aitken abruptly, "with that memorandum you showed Mr. Milburn?"

"You mean the combination of the safe?" Her fingers fluttered into a drawer of her desk. "Oh, here it is. Why? Do you want it?" She drew out a pale blue slip and proffered it.

He took it quickly and did not answer, for Detective Moode lumbered past.

"Talking it over, are you?" said Moode gruffly. "Better save your voices. You're liable to be talking for the next twenty-four hours, in Montreal."

"I hope not," replied Aitken cheerfully. He added in a lower voice when Moode had gone: "I want to get a look into that wall safe, Helen—or can I say Helen again? You're not angry still?"

"There isn't any reason why you should not look in the safe, is there?" she returned, ignoring his question. "Aren't you—weren't you—Mr. Milburn's lawyer?"

"Yes. But you'll forgive me if I seem a bit mysterious, if I keep a secret from you?"

She answered somewhat primly: "Why, certainly."

"I want to get into that safe," he continued, "without anyone else knowing that I have done so. And I want to ask you to say nothing to anybody about having given me the memorandum."

"Not oven the police?" There was surprise in her tone.

"Not even Mr. Moode. It is simply a matter in which Mr. Milburn pledged me to absolute silence—it was the subject of my last talk with him. Some day I can explain it to you, Helen—a not very distant day—but in the meantime, whatever happens, will you try to—believe in me?"

"Why, Bob! It isn't anything that will—I mean you're not—"

"Oh, there's nothing to be worried about," he assured her. "It's just that I must handle this matter in my own way, without interference from the ponderous Mr. Moode or any other policeman. I am afraid Moode will get things in an awful mess, as it is."

They were interrupted by the approach of Lotus Decker, whose eyes, puffed from crying, gave her an oddly Oriental appearance.

"Oh, gosh, oh, double-damn-gosh!" moaned Lotus, pausing close to Bob Aitken. "I wish I could take it as calm and businesslike as you two do!"

Aitken proffered his chair, but she declined it,

"We're almost in Montreal," she said, "and I've just got to speak to you for a minute, Mr. Aitken."

Helen departed with a cheerful indifference,

"What is it, Miss Decker? asked Bob soberly.

The girl's face twisted with an anxiety which her banter had concealed. "Who do they think—" she implored tensely—"who do they think killed Mr. Milburn?"

The lawyer shook his head sorrowfully. "It's a terrible mix-up. Nobody has had time to think anything, yet."

"Did they—was it—could it have been anybody from outside that did it?" She clutched his hand awaiting an answer.

"We'll have to wait for the police to tell us that. Now don't start imagining things, Miss Decker "

"That broken window," she went on nervously; "couldn't somebody have got in that way—does the detective think anything like that?"

Bob laughed shortly. "This detective doesn't think. And don't you go to him with any voluntary ideas." He patted her hand reassuringly. "Say nothing until you are asked to."

"You mean about—my brother?" She drew a quick breath. "Should I tell them anything about him?"

"No. No, indeed. Your brother is hundreds of miles away. What could he have had to do with it?"

"That letter—I'm afraid—I'm almost sure it came from Warren."

"I disagree," said the lawyer smilingly. "It doesn't sound like a traveling salesman—it sounds like a religious crank."

"Where is it, Mr. Aitken? Who's got it? Do you know?"

"It is among Mr. Milburn's effects; or perhaps Moode has it. He was 'investigating' it. But don't worry. Say nothing until you are asked—remember that. Let's run along now. We'd better get ready for Montreal."

Lotus went to her compartment, Stateroom C, and Aitken was entering his, the adjoining one, when Detective Moode came out of the lounge. He beckoned to Bob.

"Stand watch in here for a minute, will you?" he requested. "I've got something to do, and I don't like to leave things unguarded."

"You mean you think somebody might—"

"I'm not taking any chances. I hate to ask you to do it, Mr. Aitken."

"Oh, I don't mind," said Bob, but with apparent reluctance.

The lounge was unoccupied, save for the grim dead monitor in the chair. Aitken glanced about, paused a moment. He peered through the curtains in the corridor, whence Moode had disappeared. Then he moved swiftly to the forward wall of the car, alongside the desk. The outer steel door of the safe compartment was unlocked, he referred eagerly to a blue slip of paper in his hand and whirled the dial of the small safe back and forth. He exerted pressure on the lever and the door swung open.

From one of the pigeonholes of the safe he extracted a long envelope, glanced at the red wax seal on its flap, slipped it into his inside pocket and closed the safe. Then he stepped quickly across to the rear of the car.

Detective Moode, returning, found the lawyer examining the target which the more or less crack marksmen of Mr. Milburn's company of guests had used.

"I'm not disturbing anything, or touching anything," Bob assured him. "I am merely looking over the ground. Something just occurred to me."

"What's that?" asked Moode, not encouragingly.

"These target sheets—have you noticed how they were used? There's a steel backstop here, with the pasteboard target sheets hold in a frame a little in front of it."

"Yeh. I've noticed."

"Well, each of us used an individual target sheet, so that we could compare results afterwards. Our names are scribbled on the various placards."

"Well, what does that prove?" asked Moode, displaying a little more interest.

"It proves," said Bob with a grim smile, "that I was the best shot in the bunch. I got seven bull's eyes out of a possible twelve."

"You mean it proves you was the only sober bird in the bunch," mumbled Moode, taking up the target sheets. "Who was it shot out the window?"

"Why I wasn't in here at the time, but I understand it was Miss Decker. What does her sheet show?"

Moode fumbled out the target placard bearing Lotus' name. "Only hit the sheet three times. How many times did she shoot?"

"Twelve," said Aitken. "I suspect her bullets are scattered all over the end of the car."

Moode shook his head. "Wild boys and girls. Poor old bird came to a wild end, too, didn't he? I'm sorry! This thing is an awful black eye for me, Mr. Aitken."

"Oh, I don't know. You couldn't help it."

"A fine bodyguard I turned out to be! I oughta stayed right in here with him, all night. But I didn't know there was anybody out sure enough to get the old boy. I thought it was just a bum steer he was giving himself, that somebody was out on the heavy after him."

"Well, here we are at the station," observed Bob. "It will soon be out of our hands. Did they say they would meet the train?"

Investigation by the
Canadian Police
Gets Under Way
at Montreal
Station

"How do you load it?" Asked Berthier. Laval, Who Was Examining the Pistol Found on the Floor, Demonstrated by Releasing the Barrel, Sliding Back With His Thumb a Small Check on a Spring.

3

"Oh, sure. The provincial cops and the wise boys of the city force, too, with the medical examiner. They said the Montreal coroner would probably hold the inquest, since we couldn't tell 'em exactly where the murder occurred. Say, what's the law on that, Mr. Aitken? Suppose he was killed before we crossed the line? Would they ship the whole works back across the border for New York State to take it over?

Bob shook his head. "He was killed in Canada. That seems assured, judging by the voices heard in here before the porter found Mr. Milburn's body."

"Maybe," said Moode, scowling at the window. "There's a lot you can't prove by me."

When the train came to a stop the Canadian authorities took charge with characteristic efficiency.

Seven men boarded the Dorothea, two of whom were uniformed constables who were placed on guard at the front platform and back platform, respectively. The investigation was already under way when the car was detached from the train and shunted to a siding.

Captain Berthier of the Quebec provincial police seemed to be in general command, though he deferred politely to the suggestions of Inspector Laval of the Montreal Detective Bureau. They were middle-aged men

of differing types. Berthier was tall and staunch, gray-
ing mustache, close-cropped, keen gray eyes, heavily
impassive as to countenance. He was uniformed, a man
of military bearing. Inspector Laval was small and wiry,
clean-shaven, his cheeks sallow and lean-muscled, his
eyes blank and brooding, inscrutable. He was in citi-
zen's clothing.

They stood by silently as a morgue detective and the
medical examiner, Doctor Phillips, examined the body
of J. Proctor Milburn. In the forward end of the car
Sergeant Detective Thwaite of the Montreal police, aided
by Detective Moode, was preparing a roll of the passengers and advising them that no one would be permitted
to leave the car, save under escort possibly, until the
investigation was completed. They were permitted, however, to send out mail and telegrams to be dispatched.

"Hello!" he called.

Three additional representatives of the police department arrived after the car had been sidetracked. They
were Sergeant Detective Montigny, an operative of the
bureau of identification, and a photographer.

Montigny was a personage of individual mien. Like
his superior the Inspector he was dark-complexioned
and had black hair and eyes, but he was taller and possessed also a distinctive black mustache, quite long and
quite pointed at the ends. He suggested vaguely the
stage magician of a bygone era. He was lithe and markedly graceful, and whatever he touched he touched with
long and careful fingers.

Montigny made a tentative inspection of the car from
end to end and sketched a rough plan of it. Then with
the identification man he went to the lounge to begin
a more detailed investigation there. He examined first
the pistol on the floor, which was entirely free of finger-prints.

Doctor Phillips had finished his preliminary examination.

"This man," said the examiner, "has been dead about an hour."

"It is now four minutes past two," observed the morgue detective, who was making notes for the guidance of the coroner. "Cause of death?"

"The wound was made by a bullet of very small calibre, evidently a twenty-two. I think we shall find it in the brain."

"Fired at close range?"

"That is to be determined. There are no powder burns. It is possible, though we have not yet demonstrated it, that the wound was inflicted with one of the target pistols. I am not familiar with this type of weapon—if you could call it that. Are you, Captain Berthier? Inspector Laval?"

Laval, who was examining the pistol found on the floor, answered him: "Yes, Doctor. This type of air pistol is not a weapon, nor is it precisely a toy. It is powerful and extremely accurate, and is used a good deal by marksmen, I understand, for indoor practice. It is made by a firearms manufacturer, in England. I believe there are two calibres, twenty-two and one-seventy-seven. This seems to be a twenty-two."

He passed the pistol to Captain Berthier, who tested its mechanism interestedly, inquiring, "And it shoots these little corset-shaped bullets, eh?"

There was a supply of the latter, together with several additional pistols, in a case on Milburn's desk. The pellets were approximately the size of a twenty- two short.

"How do you load it?" asked Berthier.

Laval demonstrated by releasing the barrel, sliding back with his thumb a small chock on a spring.

"To cock it," said the Inspector, "you swing the barrel up and forward, so, on its pivot near the sight. Below the barrel, here, is the air-compressing chamber. Swing the barrel far enough, so . . . you hear a faint click, and the gun is cocked. You bring the barrel back and insert the bullet just before locking. It shoots only once, of course, for each time it is cocked."

"Let me try it," proposed Berthier.

He aimed the gun steadily at the target backstop in the rear of the lounge and pulled the trigger. Nothing happened.

"Safety catch," suggested Laval. "I must have snapped it on. That pistol is put together like an automatic, and it looks like one, too."

Berthier released the safety catch and aimed the pistol again. Save for the dull "ping" against the backstop there had been virtually no noise. The report was no more emphatic than the sound of a mild sneeze.

"Silent enough," commented Berthier. "You'd never hear it, particularly on a moving train."

"You would scarcely hear it even at a distance of a few feet," agreed Laval.

The morgue detective, in turn, examined the pistol and passed it to Doctor Phillips.

"When we have made the proper tests," said Doctor Phillips, "we should be able to tell you the approximate distance at which this pistol was fired—if it is the one that was used."

"The autopsy will tell us more about that, too," suggested the morgue detective. "Nothing further we can do now, is there?"

"Nothing."

"No marks of violence, other than the bullet wound?" inquired Captain Berthier.

"None whatever," replied the examiner. "The, man evidently was sitting here quite placidly—perhaps asleep."

"Or the person who killed him," suggested Berthier, "was some one he trusted, some one whose purpose he did not in the least suspect, who seemed to be toying harmlessly with one of these target pistols; who, at a distance close enough for accuracy, allowed it 'accidentally' to go off—"

"Or who," amended Inspector Laval, stepping toward the door, "concealed himself behind these curtains and took careful and deliberate aim, so—" He stood in the passage and demonstrated.

The doctor nodded. "The course taken by the bullet and its present position may help us on that. Will you have your men make the usual measurements, Inspector—the height of the head from the floor, for instance, in a normal posture when seated? The distance to the door—angles are important."

"Yes, indeed. Montigny will see to that." He called: "Pierre."

Sergeant Detective Montigny, who was outside on the observation platform, answered through the broken window: "Yes, Inspector. At once."

The Sergeant had picked up something yellow and white and interesting—a Pullman cash fare receipt, dated the day just past, August 18th.

Save for the additional steps necessary before the body of Mr. Milburn could be removed from the car, Laval and Berthier did not prolong their inquiry for the night. They announced that they would return at nine o'clock in the morning, and that passengers on the car meanwhile must remain in detention. Those who felt in the mood for it were urged to go back to sleep, but none availed themselves of this invitation save George Heston and the porter. Wilks, thanks to his training, could catch a nap anywhere under any circumstances, and the crabbed Mr. Heston still suffered, seemingly, from an overpowering toxic fatigue. The others remained awake and dressed, discussing interminably the events of the night.

Sergeant Montigny and his assistants desired to take no recess for slumber, but Laval ordered them to defer the rest of their Investigation until the morrow. They were back at seven, however, and, assisted occasionally by suggestions from Detective Moode, they proceeded methodically to examine the car inch by inch from platform to platform, with camera, flashlight, magnifying glass and the apparatus for developing fingerprints. They were still at it when Captain Berthier and Inspector Laval returned at nine.

The coroner of the Montreal District had agreed, as was often customary, to defer the formal inquest into Mr. Milburn's death until the police had collected and collated further information for the guidance of a jury. Laval and Berthier, establishing headquarters in the lounge of the car with a uniformed clerk to make a stenographic record of the proceedings, began to ask questions.

Detective Moode, by virtue of his semi-official capacity of bodyguard to the late Mr. Milburn, was interrogated first. He was a willing, if blunt, witness, but not too willing. He offered no gratuitous suggestions and betrayed no taint of imagination. Having served in the New York police department some years as patrolman and detective before taking a job with a private detective agency, he was inured to discipline and respected authority.

He had been employed by Mr. Milburn "off and on," he said, for the past twelve months, or rather had been assigned to Mr. Milburn by his agency. Prior to the award of Mr. Milburn's divorce decree by a French court—this had been last December—Mr. Milburn had had reason to suspect that his wife was having him shadowed. He had hired Moode, originally, to find out whether this was true. Mr. Milburn had suspected that his wife's lawyers desired to "get all they could" on Mr. Milburn during this ticklish interim.

"And did it prove to be true?" Captain Berthier asked Moode.

"Yes, sir. I found out who they were—what agency they worked for—and Mr. Milburn got 'em called off."

"'Called off?' How do you mean?"

"Why, Mr. Milburn's got a fine bunch of lips—lawyers, I mean, sir—in New York, and it turned out that these lawyers had been giving this agency a lot of business. So they raised the devil with the agency, and the agency promised to send a report to Mrs. Milburn that Mr. Milburn was all okay—they couldn't get a thing on him."

"Oh," said Captain Berthier.

Inspector Laval smiled thinly. "You mean that Mr. Milburn's lawyers bought off the rival detective agency?"

"I don't know a thing about that, sir."

"Is that Mr. Robert Aitken one of these lawyers?"

"Why, he's one of the junior members of the firm, I understand, sir, but he's not in the firm name—it's Donwood, Colton & Donwood. I don't know so much about that arrangement. I don't think he's had anything at all to do with Mr. Milburn's divorce case. He was just a sort of personal lawyer, sir. taking care of Mr. Milburn's property matters and such."

"I see. Now let us get back to the crime. I understood you to say that the porter on this car discovered the body of Mr. Milburn shortly after the hour of one o'clock?"

"Yes, sir."

Moode reviewed the events of the night. He said he had gone to bed shortly after twelve o'clock, and that virtually everybody in the car had done the same, the excitement having died down following the Clara Heston episode in the lounge. The train was very late owing to the freight wreck or whatever it was—they had been held up several hours at Rutland—and while everybody knew they would arrive in Montreal around two or three o'clock, it had been decided best to spend the night in the car.

"You say everybody had gone to bed?" interrupted Captain Berthier. "Did this include Mr. Milburn?"

"Everybody but Mr. Milburn and Mr. Aitken. I think Mr. Aitken was busy with him in the lounge here some time, talking over something."

"Do you know what they were talking about?"

"No, sir. Just some business of Mr. Milburn's, I suppose."

"What time was this?"

"A little after twelve, they started talking. That was just before we reached Rouses Point, across the border; I remember I checked up the time when we got there because I wanted to figure when we'd be in Montreal."

"And this—er—misunderstanding between Mr. Milburn and Mrs. Heston had occurred just prior to that?"

"Yes, sir. I remember because right after that Mr. Milburn says to me, 'You go on out, Moode, and send Miss Eastwick to me. You stay here, Mr. Aitken,' he says, 'I want to talk to you.'"

"And you sent Miss Eastwick in?"

"Yes, sir."

"How long did she stay?"

"She came out pretty soon and went to her desk in the dining room for something—batted off a line or two on her typewriter—but she wasn't in there with Mr. Milburn and Mr. Aitken more than five, ten minutes afterwards. I saw her go back to the dining room."

"How long did Mr. Aitken remain with Mr. Milburn?"

"I couldn't tell you, sir, from what I know to be sure of, personally. Mr. Aitken said till about twelve-forty. I had gone to bed. I stayed in my berth reading for maybe fifteen, twenty minutes. Then everything seemed to be quiet, and it looked like 'most everybody had gone to bed. I put on my bathrobe and walked around in the car a little to see that everything was okay, and there was nobody stirring, so I says to myself, 'Thank heaven, this whoopee-making seems to be over, and they've quieted down.' Except for Mr. Aitken and Mr. Milburn in the lounge, everybody seemed to be asleep but Wilks. He was waiting up for the immigration and customs inspectors who came on the train at the border, so he could explain to them there was no immigrants on the car—just a pleasure trip—and nobody had nothing to declare."

"Where was Wilks?"

"Up in the galley. He's got a cubby-hole there where he sleeps."

"And Mr. Aitken was still conferring with Mr. Milburn?"

"Yes, sir. I didn't come in here, of course, because I didn't want to disturb 'em, but I came up the aisle outside far enough to hear somebody still in here talking."

"You went to bed, finally, about what time?"

"About twelve-thirty."

"And you heard and saw nothing further until the porter awakened you half an hour or so later to tell you Mr. Milburn was dead?"

"No, sir. Not a thing."

"What time was it when Wilks and Mr. Aitken came to your berth?"

"A little after one. We checked it up by the time, the train left St. Johns—eight minutes past one, they woke me up."

"Then the crime was committed, to your certain knowledge, between the hours of twelve-thirty and eight minutes past one?"

"Yes, sir. Of course I didn't see Mr. Milburn as late as twelve-thirty. I just heard somebody in here talking, and figured it was Mr. Milburn and Mr. Aitken, which Mr. Aitken says it was."

They questioned Moode at length concerning the porter's testimony as to the annunciator calls and the voices he had heard in the lounge just before he had discovered the body of Mr. Milburn.

"With all due regard for the porter's reliability," said Inspector Laval, "do you think it possible that, while applying at the door of Stateroom B, about ten feet down the corridor from this door, he could have heard voices in the lounge—with all the noise of a fast-running train?"

"That's just it," replied Moode. "We wasn't going fast. We had just pulled out of St. John's. And he could have heard the voices anyway, I think, because I heard Mr. Aitken and Mr. Milburn talking even when the train was running fast, the time I walked halfway up the aisle to see if everything was quiet. These are pretty heavy curtains, but they don't cover the whole door."

"In which case," put in Captain Berthier, "it would appear that there was an intruder in this room just prior to the time Mr. Milburn was found dead—that he killed Mr. Milburn and escaped by means of the back door and platform, before the porter could arrive and just as the train was leaving St. Johns, at slow speed."

"But the door was thumb-bolted on the inside," objected Moode. "Of course a fellow might have reached the bolt from outside, through that broken window."

"Have you tested that possibility?"

"No, sir. I didn't allow nobody to go on that back platform or touch that door-knob, till you gentlemen took charge."

"You were creditably cautious," murmured Inspector Laval. "If you approve, Captain Berthier, I suggest we stop to ask Montigny what he has learned about the door and platform."

Montigny and his assistant had carefully removed the brass knobs of the door, inside and out, and put them aside for safe keeping. They had thrown the bolt without touching save with the point of a small tool, the brass thumb catch, and had propped the door open. They had placed footboards on the back platform so that they need not step upon its surface, which they had found to contain a thin but valuable (for their purpose) coating of fine cinders and soot.

"Pardon, Pierre," said Inspector Laval. "I dislike to interrupt you. I know you would prefer to finish your work before making a report, but there are certain things we should like to ask now, while we are talking to Mr. Moode."

Sergeant Montigny came into the room, skinning off his rubber gloves. "Yes, Inspector," he said quietly.

"You are familiar in general, I believe, with the story told by the porter and Mr. Aitken—that they heard voices in here just before the porter entered and found Mr. Milburn dead?"

"Yes, sir."

"Do you find any indication that such a person could or did escape by means of the back door and platform?"

Montigny smiled, a fact barely made noticeable by the fact that his eyes twinkled and his mustache quivered. "It is possible, Inspector," he replied. "A tall man with a long arm could—and did, I think—reach the knob and thumb latch by means of this broken window."

"He left finger-prints?"

"No, Inspector. But palm-prints—something new for our system of identification. He turned the knobs by means of his palms only, reserving his finger-tips carefully. He left beautiful head, heart and life lines, on the inside knob, the outside knob and the brass rail of the observation platform. He is a tall, athletic person who wears a number eight shoe. One who believes in palmistry might say he is a nervous individual given to excessive worry—moody, introspective, highly imaginative, but not, perhaps, poetic or partial to the other arts. May I ask Detective Moode a question, Inspector? He seems astonished."

Detective Moode's face wore a grin of embarrassment—whether for himself or Montigny's sake he did not specify. "Did you find all that on the level, Sergeant, or are you kidding?"

"I am guessing, Mr. Moode," replied Montigny, a shade mischievously. "Perhaps my guesses will be nullified by your answer to my question: Are you informed whether any members of the party on this car went out upon the observation platform last night or yesterday afternoon?"

"No, sir. They all say they didn't. I asked about that. Mr. Milburn bolted the door himself, because he didn't want anybody to go out on that platform and get hurt, maybe fall off. They were all pretty—you know, feeling pretty good—and Mr. Milburn said there was plenty of room in here, they didn't have to go out there. When the porter cleaned up the glass after they broke the window last night, Mr. Milburn told him not to bother about going outside on the platform, because the door was locked; just to clean up inside."

"That is helpful," conceded Montigny. "The footprints and handprints, Inspector, seem to be the legacy of some person who climbed on the back platform some time last night, presumably at one of the stops the train made."

"We only stopped twice after dark," said Moode. "Rouses Point, across the border, and St. Johns."

"That narrows it. He would scarcely have been on the platform during the daytime."

"No, sir; and how can you tell so much about the fellow?" ventured Moode.

"Why, I judge that he is tall and athletic because of the fact that he climbed to the platform and threw his foot over the brass railing without touching the railing at any point with his leg; also, a man who wears a number eight shoe is likely to be a little more than of average height, if he is normally proportioned. As to his imagination and nervous disposition—guesswork. I am merely following the stock rules of palmistry. Sometimes the lines of the hand do really indicate the characteristics of its owner. But the gentleman left something more concrete."

Montigny fished out the white and yellow Pullman receipt slip which he had picked up on the platform. He presented it to Inspector Laval.

"This relic of our visitor," he said, "may or may not be helpful. It may have been dropped by accident, or by design—out of defiance. It is a receipt for cash payment of Pullman fare between Rutland, Vermont, and

Montreal. The date punched is yesterday, August 18th. The conductor no doubt issued a great many like that, and it may be very difficult to trace. I suppose many could be picked up in the aisles of the train."

"At least," commented Captain Berthier, examining it with interest, "it tells us that some one was on this platform who was a passenger on the train yesterday. No outsider passed through the private car, that you know of, Mr. Moode?"

"Positively not," grunted Moode, as though mildly resenting the suggestion.

"We shall try to trace it through the conductor," said Laval. "What else, Pierre?"

"The person who climbed to the platform, leaving his palm-prints on the brass railing, also tried the door-knobs." Montigny paused to smile again. "He is perhaps a person who reads detective stories or at least the popular crime news in the papers; for he seems to be aware that while the police can trace finger-prints through an international system of recording, they are not so clever in the matter of palm-prints. We catalogue finger records and we know that no two finger-tips in the world are alike, but as to palms we have not yet become record-keeping fortune tellers."

"And you think this person, as a gesture of defiance to the police, might have left his palm-prints purposely?"

"Perhaps, Inspector. Perhaps it was an accident. Many of us open doors in this manner. The knobs on train doors, too, are often very hard to turn, they require more strength than our fingers alone possess. Now this gentleman, trying the outside knob with his right hand, found the door locked. Then, passing his left arm through the broken window, evidently he tried the inside knob, on the chance that perhaps the door was latched to outsiders but could be opened from the inside. He found, however, that the door was bolted."

"And the thumb catch?" inquired Captain Berthier. "Did you try that—did he unbolt the door?"

Montigny shrugged. '"Somebody did, evidently. There are no intelligible marks of finger-prints. The porter admits rebolting the door after finding Milburn's body, the bolt had been thrown previously during the day by Milburn himself, so the result it a maze of marks that means nothing." Montigny glanced toward his assistant, still intently at work on the platform. "Is there anything else, Inspector?"

"Not for the present, Pierre. You are working with your usual thoroughness. Go back to it—and thanks."

The Inspector and Berthier resumed their discussion with Moode.

"We seem to have the fact pretty well established," opined Berthier, "that the man who killed Milburn boarded the train at Rutland and climbed on the back platform of this car either at Rouses Point or St. Johns, evidently leaving it at St. Johns after finishing his work."

"No report from your men there?" suggested Laval.

"Nothing as yet. We telephoned immediately after hearing from Mr. Moode last night, and I sent two men down there. All suspicious characters are to be detained."

"Now, the letter you were telling us about. Mr. Moode?"

"Oh, yes. I got it here."

Moode fumbled in his inside pocket and drew forth a batch of soiled and worn papers from which he selected and unfolded a single typewritten sheet.

"Just a nut letter," added the detective. "I don't know whether it means anything or not. Mr. Milburn got it last week. He was always getting something or other like it, though."

Laval and Berthier read the missive frowningly.

"MILBURN YOU ARE WARNED

"The God of Vengeance that destroyed So-
dom and Gomorrah will destroy you also,
with your strumpets and sycophants, if you
do not depart from ways that are licentious.

"The ruin of innocent girls is a challenge
to your conscience and is marked as a red
debit against your blackened soul.

"Take warning before you are repaid in
the coinage of destruction."

"Have you the envelope?" inquired Laval.

"No, sir. It was opened by Mr. Milburn's secretary
along with a lot of other letters, and all the envelopes
thrown away. I thought maybe we could trace the typewriter."

Laval shook his head. "It's a Glickenswerfer, or one
of that type."

"A what, sir?"

"A Glickenswerfer—or one of the other old-fashioned
writing machines that have no type-bars."

"What do you mean, Inspector?"

"I mean the type on a machine of this kind does
not consist of steel letters at the end of so many bars
or type-arms, but of raised letters on a hard rubber or
composition cylinder, called the typewheel, which re-
volves to the proper letter as each letter on the keyboard
is struck. There are peculiarities of type by means of
which the ordinary typewriter might be traced or identified; but the person using this kind of machine can
throw away or destroy his type entirely—dispose of his
type wheel and substitute another. You can buy such
type wheels, I think, for a dollar."

"But you could trace an odd typewriter like this quite easily, couldn't you, Inspector?"

"It is not odd. The mail order houses sell them by the thousands. They are popular with physicians and pharmacists. Many drug stores have them for the writing of prescription labels, since special type wheels are to be had with pharmacy symbols. How many drug stores are there in New York? Ten thousand?"

"Guess you're right, sir," admitted Moode. "We'd never trace that typewriter."

Captain Berthier, having read the threatening letter again, announced a discovery:

"A person of education—this crank."

"Or a person of education," amended Laval significantly, "who wished to pose as a crank."

*Passengers Are Questioned and Fingerprints Sought
But There Is No Clue
in the Clever Crime*

Sergeant Montigny
came into the room
skinning off his rub-
ber gloves. He
smiled faintly, a fact
made barely noticeable by the twinkling of his eyes and a slight
twitching of his mustachios. "Inspector," he said, "It is possible
that a tall man with a long arm could, and did, I think, reach the
thumb latch by means of the broken window"

4

The Canadian officers questioned Moode fully an hour longer. They reviewed, with a thoroughness which obviously grew tedious to him, every circumstance, every stray bit of evidence that offered the remotest promise of relevance to the subject.

"You have not discussed any of these matters with any passengers in the car?" suggested Laval. "The details, for instance, of the porter's story about the annunciator bell and the voices he heard?"

"No, sir," said Moode emphatically. "Just with Mr. Aitken—I asked him if he'd rung his bell like the porter said he did; and I asked Mr. Laith about his dressing gown That's all."

"And Mr. Aitken—has he spoken of these matters to the others?"

"He's a lawyer," replied Moode with a grin. "He knows how to talk, but he knows how not to talk, too. Like for me to get him for you?"

Laval consulted Captain Berthier's wishes on that point.

"I am more interested," said Berthier, "in the lady with the seeming grievance—Mrs. Heston. Let us talk to her first."

They sent Moode to get her.

"I think it would be well, Inspector," proposed Captain Berthier, "to ask this man Moode to sit in with us while we question the others. He is of course very familiar with the situation."

"Yes," murmured Laval without enthusiasm. "He is not a man of delicate perceptions, but he will do less damage—here."

Moode brought back Mrs. Heston. She was no longer the languid Clara of the dreaming eyes, but a truly tired and frightened Clara. She was nervous and unstrung, and her patent endeavor to act a part was slightly pathetic.

Berthier's glance invited Laval to begin the questioning.

"Did you sleep well last night?" asked the Inspector, not discourteously.

"I did not close my eyes," said Clara tragically.

"I mean before the—" Laval gestured significantly toward the chair which but lately had relinquished the lifeless form of J. P. Milburn. There was a dark blot on the carpeted floor beside it.

Clara shuddered. "No, sir, I had been unable to sleep even before they—found him. I was too worried and upset."

"Worried? About what?"

"About the way Mr. Milburn had treated me. I had always thought that he was such a gentleman!"

They drew from her, step by step, her lurid version of Mr. Milburn's alleged misconduct. It was her story and she stuck to it. But she had forgiven Mr. Milburn now. All that was over. Clara was magnanimous in the shadow of tragedy. Fate had exacted payment. Virtue, she seemed about to add, was it own reward.

"And the reason you could not sleep," suggested Berthier, "was that your husband had threatened to kill Mr. Milburn?"

"Oh, no, no, no!" cried Clara with desperate earnestness. "George didn't mean that. He was not in his right mind. He was—he had been drinking."

"And did you mean it when you told your husband, in the presence of several witnesses, that, he ought to kill Mr. Milburn?"

"Oh, of course not, sir! I was excited, overwrought. Oh, surely you don't suspect—" she paused for a little gasp—"Poor George?"

"You say you did not sleep," continued Berthier, ignoring her question, "from the time you went to bed to the time you were aroused by the news of Mr. Milburn's death?"

"No, sir. I did not."

"Did you hear anything out of the ordinary? Did you hear a shot fired?"

"No, sir. I heard the porter's bell ring two or three times, that was all—and people talking."

"Were you awake when the train stopped at St. Johns, shortly before one o'clock?"

"Was that the place we stopped at so long—the next to the last place we stopped at before we got to Montreal. . . . Yes, sir. I was awake. I remember I started to put up my shade and peep out—but I couldn't because I was in an upper berth."

"And it was after the train left this place that you heard the porter's bell ring?"

"Yes, sir. We were just pulling out. That's why I could hear it so plain. I peeped out in the aisle—for some reason, I don't know why—and saw the porter passing."

"Which way was he going?"

"Toward the rear of the car. He passed down the corridor toward the lounge here. I heard somebody talking in here with Mr. Milburn."

"Pardon, Captain," cut in Laval quickly. "This was—rather loud talking you heard, Mrs. Heston?"

"I suppose it must have been, for me to hear it. It sounded more like a man with a rather deep voice talking—than Mr. Milburn: his voice was sort of high pitched, you know."

"Did you hear what was said?"

"No, sir. I heard only the sound of the voices."

"Was it Mr. Aitken you heard talking?"

"No, sir. I heard him, too, right afterward. The porter must have stopped at his door, because I heard Wilks knocking and then I heard him say, 'Did you ring. Mr. Aitken?' And then I heard Mr. Aitken say, as though he didn't like it much, 'No, I did not. What's the matter with you, Wilks?'"

"And somebody was in the lounge talking with Mr. Milburn at the tame time?"

"Yes, sir. Or at least they seemed to stop talking about then. I didn't hear anything more at all—the train was going fast, by then, and making a lot of noise."

"You tried to go to sleep then?"

"Yes, sir. I hadn't heard anything alarming, you see. I thought I heard voices in the aisle afterward, but I didn't dream anything so terrible had happened—" Clara shuddered with emphasis—"until the train stopped at that other place, St. Lambert, and I heard Mr. Milburn had been killed."

"Your husband, all this time, was sound asleep in the lower berth?"

"Yes, sir, snoring so loud I started to reach down and pinch him. I never could sleep with anybody snoring—can you, Inspector?"

Her somewhat coy query fell on preoccupied ears. The Inspector leaned back in thought, his heavy-lidded eyes half closed. "That is all I wish to ask her, Captain," said Laval.

Berthier went into details of Clara's dramatic experience with Mr. Milburn, and could shake her on no salient point of her story.

"In other words," summed up Berthier bluntly, "you were more interested in having Mr. Milburn continue to live than in having him murdered?"

"What do you mean, sir?" demanded Clara, tautening.

"I mean," said the Captain coolly, "that your purpose was to shake him down, to blackmail him—that you and your husband proposed to demand hush money, to threaten suit or action on some trumped-up charge or other, if he did not 'come across.'"

Clara drew up stiffly. "Be careful of what you are saying, sir," she warned, her eyes flashing theatrically.

"I am being careful. How long had you known Mr. Milburn?"

"About a year," said Clara sullenly.

"Where did you meet him?"

"At a party he gave at his house in New York."

"Who introduced you?"

"Miss Dustin."

"Where did she meet him?"

"I am sure I don't know. You might ask my husband."

"What does your husband know about it?"

"He runs a theatrical agency in New York. It was he who interested Mr. Milburn in Miss Dustin. If it hadn't been for George," she added a trifle bitterly, "you'd never have heard of Dot Dustin, or the Hilarities, either."

"Ah, I begin to see the connection," observed Berthier. "Now, where does Mr. Perry Laith fit into the picture? How did he crash the gate at Mr. Milburn's?"

"He is a friend of Miss Dustin's," said Clara haughtily.

"Your friend, too—and your husband's?"

"Y-yes. My husband knew him professionally."

"And Miss Lotus Decker," continued Berthier, referring to his notes; "whose friend was she?"

"My husband knew her, through the agency, if that's what you mean," snapped Clara. "She is a friend of Miss Dustin's, too."

"It was part of your husband's duties, I would infer," said Berthier unfeelingly, "to refer likely 'talent' to Mr. Milburn—beautiful girls in whose—ah—future he was interested?"

"I don't know what you mean," countered Clara defiantly.

"Oh, yes you do," imperturbably. "Is that all you know about this case, Mrs. Heston?"

"I have answered your questions," she retorted. "If you have any more to ask, ask them."

"They may be asked later—in court," promised Berthier. "Send your husband in, Mrs. Heston."

Laval, who had stepped to the rear of the lounge where the target stood, checked her departure. He fingered the target sheets that lay on the floor and selected one, which he examined briefly.

"This," he said, approaching Clara, "appears to have your name on it. You are a pretty good shot with an air pistol, aren't you, Mrs. Heston?"

Clara's expression changed and it seemed that she paled slightly when she peered at the concentric circles. "Why, that isn't mine," she exclaimed. "That isn't mine at all!"

"It is plainly inscribed 'Clara;' and it indicates that out of twelve shots you hit the bull's-eye four times and put five in the inner circle."

"Why. I didn't hit the bull's-eye even once," protested Clara. "There's some mistake—they must have marked it wrong."

"Who marked them?"

*Clara Heston Is Questioned at Length, Inspector
Laval's Selection of Targets
Proves Embarrassing*

"This," said
Laval, ap-
proaching
Clara, "appears
to have your
name on it
You are a
good shot with an air pistol, aren't you, Mrs.
Heston?"

"Why, I don't know. Everybody was supposed to mark his own, I think. I didn't put my name on mine. I didn't care that much about it."

"You don't recognize this writing—or printing, rather?"

"N-no, sir." Clara examined it, plainly puzzled and not a bit frightened. "Why, it looks like somebody deliberately tried—" She stopped to search the Inspector, face with anxious inquiry.

Laval shrugged. "Perhaps a mistake. Do you think you could pick out your target sheet, Mrs. Heston?"

Clara went through them hastily. "I could pick out the worst one," she said nervously, "because I am a terrible shot. But the worst one is marked Lotus—she was the one who shot out the window."

"Never mind," said Laval dispiritedly. "It doesn't matter. You may go now, and send your husband in."

When she had made her exit Berthier turned to Detective Moode, who had been a silent sneering listener.

"What do you make of her?" asked Berthier.

"Same as you," returned Moode sourly. "She and that crooked husband of hers tried to frame poor old Milburn for a pushover—thought he'd be easy. I told him to lay off these Broadway grafters, but he wouldn't listen; told me to mind my business—said I was his bodyguard, not his Sunday school teacher. Hot little bodyguard," he added ruefully, "I turned out to be!"

"Were you present here in the lounge," asked Laval, "when the target shooting was going on?"

"Looked in once or twice, that's all. I wasn't invited to the tea party," Moode grinned simperingly. "So I stayed in my section and read. Far as that target sheet's concerned, though, any of those stewed prunes coulda done that, by mistake. They was all pie-eyed except Mr. Aitken. He was the best shot in the crowd, because he was sober."

George Heston came in, looking much the worse for his night-life activities. Deep moats of dissipation half-ringed his bloodshot eyes. He was thin and of unhealthy appearance, his face drawn and pasty. His head jerked when he looked from one to the other of his inquisitors.

It was early apparent to Laval and Berthier that they would extract little information from Heston. Concerning the events of the previous evening he was distressingly hazy. There were blank spaces which he tried to fill in by obvious guesswork, and the effort involved him in odd contradictions. Finally he admitted that he remembered little, and of that little he was not sure. He could not recall who helped him to bed.

Regarding his previous contacts with Mr. Milburn and others of the party he was more lucid. He had first become acquainted with Mr. Milburn some two years ago when he had furnished entertainers for a rather elaborate party at the Milburn place on Long Island. Yes; Miss Dorothea Dustin, it happened, was one of them. That was before Mr. Milburn's separation from his wife. Of further details of the Milburns' marital infelicities Heston professed to know nothing. Milburn had seemed quite friendly toward George and his wife. Following his separation from Mrs. Milburn he had entertained quite frequently at his home in the East Sixties, and had often invited the Hestons. George had become a sort of unofficial stage manager for the Milburn parties.

As for Mr. Milburn's misconduct of the previous evening, why, Mr. Heston would let that pass—it was all over now anyhow.

"I didn't kill him," summed up Heston irascibly, "if that's what you're driving at. I don't know who's killed him, but I guess he had it coming to him."

"Ah, no," said Laval suavely, stepping closer to him. "We are not suggesting that you killed Mr. Milburn.

May I borrow your handkerchief?" he asked suddenly, and when Heston had complied with automatic assent the Inspector murmured: "A bit of soot on your check, Mr. Heston," rubbed swiftly at a spot under Heston's right eye. "On the other side, too," he supplemented. "Quite gone now, however. I shall return your handkerchief later, Mr. Heston."

"What's the racket?" cried Heston angrily.

"No racket," said the Inspector calmly. "You used a bit too much of your wife's eyebrow pencil, that is all. Poor make-up. I am inclined to think you were not so thoroughly intoxicated last night as you would lead us to believe."

"Horsefeathers!" sneered Heston. "You'd have dirt on your face, too, if you'd ridden seventeen hours on a train and a couple of hick policemen wouldn't let you get away to get a bath."

"I think you may get away soon," said Laval, unruffled. "In the meantime we have no further questions for you."

Moode eyed the departing figure incredulously. "Think he was trying to fox us on the hang-over, Inspector? I don't believe he was. That man was boiled last night, if ever I saw one that was!"

"Perhaps merely overcautious," murmured Laval. "He added a few finishing touches of make-up, perhaps, to be more certain of impressing us."

"He wasted his time if he did," observed Captain Berthier. "It seems to me that Heston and everybody else on this car has a pretty clean alibi, if what the porter says is true—and he seems to be borne out fully by Mrs. Heston and Aitken, too."

Laval nodded slowly. "You mean as to the man they heard talking in the lounge?"

"Why, yes," said Berthier. "The man who killed Milburn obviously got away through the rear door and platform—and that eliminates everybody who was a passenger on the car. The porter heard him talking, Mrs. Heston heard him—Aitken is pretty sure he heard him—just as Wilks was applying at the door of Aitken's stateroom. The porter shortly afterward went in and found Mr. Milburn dead. He immediately went back down the corridor, aroused Aitken again and awakened Mr. Moode."

"Then the murder must have been committed," said Laval reflectively, "just as the porter was in the act of awakening Mr. Aitken. It follows, then, that the murderer must have pressed the bell button in the lounge here before he killed Mr. Milburn. Does that sound probable?"

Berthier lighted a cigar and puffed at it savagely. "It looks that way," he grunted. "And it doesn't make sense."

"Unless," suggested Moode, with the air of having made an important discovery, "unless he had killed Mr. Milburn before that, and was standing there talking about it?"

Berthier looked at him pityingly, but suppressed the retort he had framed, merely smoking more furiously. "I've run across killers," he observed dryly, "but I never ran across one polite enough to ring for a witness and then stand there talking about it till just before the witness arrived."

"Unless he was an awful nut," amended Moode solemnly.

Berthier glanced at him keenly.

"Say," exploded the Captain. "Maybe you've got the answer, right there. The fellow that wrote that note—" he turned quickly to Inspector Laval—"was a crank, a fanatic—nut enough to do that very thing!"

Laval smiled sardonically. "A clever nut, a supernatural nut," he agreed. "For how and when did he make his way to Mr. Aitken's compartment, press that bell button there and leave incriminating bullets in the pocket of Mr. Perry Laith's dressing gown—without disturbing Mr. Aitken?"

Berthier stared at him blankly. "I think," said the Captain after a curious pause, "there are some things we haven't found out yet!"

Dorothea Dustin, famed comedienne of the Hilarities, seemed overwrought
and frightened to the point of nervous collapse, and could add little to the inquiring officers' store of information. Nor could her friend and protegee, Lotus Decker, who was slightly more composed under questioning.

Dot declared that, following her last interview with Mr. Milburn—a mere lovers' quarrel, she called it, weepingly—she had retired to her stateroom, Compartment A, and locked the door, beyond which no sound had penetrated from the corridor until the commotion following the stop at St. Lambert told her something was wrong.

Lotus Decker likewise had taken refuge in Compartment C, for the general air of hostility which prevailed was not to her liking. Helen Eastwick and Mrs. Heston had made use of the compartment for dressing room purposes, she said, but there had been little discussion of the evening's events. Everybody, in her opinion, "had a grouch on." She had not gone promptly to sleep, she averred, but she had heard nothing until aroused by the dreadful news that there had been a murder.

Perry Laith, after a brief period of brooding over his wrongs, had gone defiantly to bed in his upper berth.

He would have left the car when Mr. Milburn offended him, he explained to Laval and Berthier, but he saw nothing to be gained, after all, by putting himself to that trouble and discomfort. The last thing of which he had been aware was the somewhat troublesome putting-to-bed of George Heston, whom Wilks had helped into the berth across the aisle. Laith had gone promptly to sleep, he said, but had awakened from some cause unknown to him when Detective Moode, Aitken and Wilks the porter were moving about in the aisle following the discovery of Mr. Milburn's body. Possibly the visit of the porter when awakening Moode in the berth below had disturbed him; he could not be sure.

Captain Berthier seemed interested in only one point of Laith's story.

"Just when," questioned the officer, "did you hang your dressing gown in Mr. Aitken's stateroom?"

"Early in the evening," responded Laith promptly, "when I dressed for dinner. I opened one of my bags in there and hung up the robe mainly to get it out of the way; and so that, of course, it would be conveniently at hand when I needed it."

"The garment, then, was there all evening?"

"Yes, sir," said Laith nervously, "and Mr. Aitken's door was unlocked at all times, so you see it would have been easy for anyone who wanted to get me in trouble to put those bullets—"

"Exactly. But you need draw no conclusions for us, Mr. Laith. That will be all."

Wilks the porter, who was next called for questioning, remembered seeing the dressing gown hanging on a wall hook in Stateroom B when he entered early in the evening for the purpose of putting Mr. Aitken's berth in order. He remembered distinctly that it was a blue silk dressing gown with white cuffs and lapels. Laval and

Berthier made him repeat in minutest detail his story of
the discovery of his employer's dead body, questioning
him with particular care in reference to the annunciator
calls.

"Are you absolutely sure," demanded Laval, "that the
two calls now showing on the annunciator—from the
lounge here and from Stateroom B were both rung up
at the same time; I mean after everybody had retired?"

"Yes, suh. Positive."

"Do you remember the last call previous to these
two?"

"Well, suh, there was the one from the front platform, about eleven-thirty, when Mr. Aitken and Miss
Decker got locked out; then there was one more, from
Mr. Aitken's stateroom, right after, that—the time the
lady started hollerin' 'Help, help,' from the lounge here,
and everybody in the car come runnin' here."

"A call from Stateroom B?" asked Berthier sharply.

"Yes, suh, that's right. I was startin' to answer it when
all the excitement broke out and people come runnin'
back here to see what was the matter with Mrs. Heston.
I didn't think about it, then, but when I went back later
and jigged the jiggerthing under the 'nunciator box, I
noticed the two calls rung up were from the front platform and Stateroom B."

"Was Mr. Aitken in his state room at the time that
call came?"

"No, suh. In the dining room, talking to Miss Decker
and Miss Eastwick."

"He was not the one who rang for you, then?"

"No, suh. I figured it was one of the gentlemen using
Stateroom B for a dressing room."

"And was there anybody in there'"

"Why, I can't say for sure, suh," Wilks hesitated
doubtfully. "We was all so excited over Mrs. Heston

screamin' that way. There was somebody ahead of me when I came to the lounge here—Mr. Heston, I believe it was—he might have come from Stateroom B."

Laval and Berthier exchanged glances. Detective Moode, who had been a respectful and silent listener during most of the questioning, growled approvingly when the porter had been dismissed.

"He's right about it, I was sitting in the dining room, reading, just about the time we heard this woman scream, and I remember Aitken was in there, and Heston wasn't. Just about what he was doing—waiting in Mr. Aitken's stateroom for his wife to cut loose with the yells. He had it all framed up with her, of course, he was to be somewhere in easy hearing distance when she yelled bloody murder, and rush in to rescue her."

"You seem to have small regard," said Laval drily, "for the integrity of Mr. and Mrs. Heston"

"You thunk a hatful, Inspector. Whole nest of crooks in this car, if you ask me. The Hestons wasn't the only ones on the take, either, when it comes to a matter of separatin' poor old Milburn from his dough."

"Others, for instance?"

Moode shrugged. "Well, I guess I better not say anything I can't prove, but I wouldn't trust the lot of 'em far as an ant could carry a hippopotamus up-hill. Like I told you, I warned Mr. Milburn about these Broadway grafters. They was all out to get him, one way or the other."

Captain Berthier interrupted briskly.

"Miss Eastwick and Mr. Aitken," he observed, "are the only two persons we have yet to hear. I suggest we call the lady."

Helen told them what she knew, in a direct and lucid manner, but that proved to be of little significance.

She had retired somewhat earlier than the others, she
believed, and though her convertible berth in the dining room was partitioned off only by curtains, she had
heard nothing beyond the usual incessant rumbling of
the train.

She had last seen Mr. Milburn alive, she said, when
following the Clara Heston interlude in the lounge, he
had sent for her.

"What did he want?" inquired Laval.

"Why, er—" Miss Eastwick's memory seemed a bit
faulty on this point. "Why, it was some matter of rou-
tine. He was in here talking to Mr. Aitken, and there
was something he wanted—some trivial matter—"

"Think hard. Miss Eastwick."

"Why, I addressed an envelope for him, and—oh, yes,
I know what it was. It was the combination of the wall
safe." She pointed to the door. "He had forgotten it."

"Did you give it to him?"

"Yes, sir. I had it in my desk. I had a memorandum
of it in my notebook."

"Can you find it now, please?"

"Why, yes, sir." Helen paused. "But the safe is not
locked now. I opened it early this morning for one of
the detectives who were searching the car."

"Which one?"

"The gentleman with the black mustache."

"Oh, Montigny," said Laval. "Very well, perhaps we
had better have a look at the contents while you are here
with us; there may be things you can explain to us."

There was little to be found in the wall safe, for
Milburn had not made use of his private car for many
months prior to the Canadian trip. The few documents
which the safe contained were examined cursorily by

Laval and Berthier, with the aid of Miss Eastwick's comments. There was nothing that could be regarded as having even a remote bearing on Milburn's death.

"What was it Mr. Milburn wanted to get out of the safe?" Captain Berthier asked her.

"I do not know. He did not tell me."

"What was the subject of Mr. Aitken's last conversation with Mr. Milburn?"

"I do not know, sir."

"Very well, Miss Eastwick. When you go out, please ask Mr. Aitken to step in here."

Bob Aitken, the last of the passengers of the Dorothea to be questioned, proved the most productive of information.

When he had seated himself, at Captain Berthier's invitation, he drew from his pocket a pistol, a thirty-eight automatic, and handed it to the Captain.

"That," he said, "was Mr. Milburn's pistol. I took charge of it last night."

"You took charge of it?" exclaimed Detective Moode angrily. "Where did you find it? You didn't say anything to me about it."

Bob Aitken Explains
His Possession of
Milburn's Gun
and Suggests
a Possible
Suicide
Motive

"That," Said Aitken, "was Mr.
Milburn's pistol. I took charge
of it last night." Capt. Berthier
Examined the Weapon. "Where
did you get it?" He Demanded.

5

"Didn't I?" questioned Aitken suavely. "I must have forgotten it. I had it in my stateroom."

"Where did you get it?" demanded Captain Berthier, examining the weapon.

"It was in the drawer of that desk. Mr. Milburn was sitting there when he and I were talking last night. He was very much depressed, and I was afraid that he intended to make use of it. I put it in my pocket."

"Make use of it?" repeated Berthier. "How?"

"I think he intended to take his own life," said Bob quietly. "In fact, he as much as told me so. I am not so sure, as a matter of fact, that he did not kill himself—with one of the target pistols."

"Say!" exploded Detective Moode. "This don't look so good to me, Captain—this fellow coming in at the eleventh hour with this sort of yarn. He didn't say anything like that to me last night. He was all for breakin' his neck to catch the killer. He's thought it up since, that's what happened!"

"Yes, yes, Mr. Moode," murmured Laval deprecatorily. "We shall discuss that angle of the subject with you later. Mr. Aitken no doubt had his reasons for withholding information about the pistol."

"I considered it best," explained Aitken, "to discuss this matter with none but the authorities investigating the case. Mr. Moode was here in an entirely unofficial capacity."

"I think you acted wisely," said Laval. "Now tell us, Mr. Aitken, what leads you to the assumption that Mr. Milburn might have taken his life."

"As I said before, he virtually told me that was his intention. He had many things to grieve and depress him. His domestic affairs, of course, had been a source of much unhappiness to him. He was, I think, genuinely fond of Miss Dustin—Mr. Moode will bear me out when I say that he was extremely generous to her—but I suspect he had come to the conclusion of late that Miss Dustin had been merely playing him, as the saying goes, for a good thing; that it was her purpose to get everything possible out of him, and then drop him. He told me last night that he had learned quite definitely that this was the case. Recently, too, to make matters worse, there was the condition of his health."

"He was ill?"

"He was a very sick man. Doctor Bartlow, the specialist, came up from Baltimore to visit him a week ago. Doctor Bartlow discussed with me privately the question of whether or not it would be wise to tell Mr. Milburn frankly of his condition. Mr. Milburn demanded the truth, and Doctor Bartlow told him—Mr. Milburn had developed cancer of the stomach."

Moode half rose, pushed his chair back with a bellicose grunt and sat down again abruptly. "Say, listen, Captain!" he snorted. "This is bunk—pure bunk. Whoever heard of a man committin' suicide with an air pistol that he didn't even know would do the trick? Bunk—horsefeathers—that's what I call it!"

Laval calmed him with a gesture. "We are not certain as yet that a slug from the air pistol killed the man. We shall hear more about that from Doctor Mitchell this afternoon. Meanwhile let us hear what Mr. Aitken has to say. Please do not interrupt him again, Mr. Moode."

Aitken seemed little disturbed by the detective's outburst. "That is about all I have to tell you," he said. "I am simply relating what passed between me and Mr. Milburn. When I left him he seemed calmer. He had no objection to make when I took charge of his pistol. He merely said, 'Well, Bob, I suppose you're right; but I can't see much sense in keeping on with it.'"

They questioned Aitken closely regarding this and other phases of Milburn's trip to Canada.

"Had he put his affairs in order?" asked Captain Berthier. "Was that perhaps the purpose of this last interview he had with you?"

"His affairs were quite in order," said Aitken guardedly.

There was a pause. "In what respect? Cannot you amplify that statement, Mr. Aitken? Had you prepared a will, for instance, for Mr. Milburn?"

Aitken reflected. "That is a question," he replied slowly, "which I cannot answer."

"You mean you will not answer?" demanded Berthier testily.

"I mean I cannot answer."

"You refuse, do you, to give the police the benefit of the full facts that are in your possession?"

"I merely remind you," said Aitken calmly, "that I am a lawyer; that I was retained by the deceased as his personal counsel; that he placed me subject to certain stipulations that it would be a breach of trust for me to violate. I will add that I am withholding nothing which, to my knowledge, can have any possible bearing on your investigation."

"That," declared Berthier with rising heat, "is for me to decide, not you. I don't care whether you are Milburn's lawyer or Chief Justice of the United States Supreme Court, you are going to answer my questions or I'll know the reason why."

"What are your questions, Captain?" suggested Aitken.

"Here's one of them: What are the 'certain stipulations' you are talking about, which it would be a 'breach of trust' for you to violate?"

"That question I cannot answer."

Captain Berthier's ample body seemed to swell, and his ruddy cheeks burned a darker red. He turned to Inspector Laval.

"I am inclined to agree with Mr. Moode," he said, with repressed malice. "This man is holding back something to protect himself. This ready-built theory of 'suicide' he brings to us looks to me like a weak attempt to cover up. What," he demanded, bellowing at Aitken, "did Milburn want to get in this safe for—when you were in here talking to him last night?"

"That, I regret," said the lawyer, unabashed, "is another question which I cannot answer at this time."

"Oh, it is, eh? Well, try this one on your breach-of-trust piano: Just why did you put those air-pistol bullets in this fellow Perry Laith's dressing gown, hanging in your stateroom?"

Aitken smiled quizzically. "That is a question which I can answer with absolute candor. I know nothing whatsoever about the bullets in Mr. Perry Laith's dressing gown. I was not even aware that that garment was hanging in my stateroom."

"You weren't, eh? Well, answer this one: Why did you press the button in your stateroom, to call the porter just about the time Milburn was being murdered?"

"I pressed no button, to my knowledge. I have told you before that if a call came from my stateroom it was entirely an accident. I must have rolled over against the button in my sleep."

"Yea," said the Captain with thick sarcasm; "and there's another reason why you could have pressed the button 'accidentally.' Do you want me to tell you why?"

"Yes."

"Alibi! The porter, coming to your stateroom, finds you 'sound asleep'—has to make a lot of noise to wake you up, eh? And, oh, no, of course you couldn't know anything about a murder taking place just about the same time—could you?"

Aitken took out a cigarette and lighted it meditatively. "Do you know. I hadn't thought of it in that light, Captain. If I needed an alibi, it strikes me that would be a very good one; particularly since the porter and Mrs. Heston heard voices in the lounge here, at the same time I did, and the porter found Mr. Milburn dead very shortly afterward. So if you are intimating, my dear Captain, that I was this clever murderer, you must reason that I jumped out of my window, swung on the back platform as it dashed past, committed the crime, and then perhaps crawled over the top of the car, reentering my stateroom through the ventilator—and all during the time I was talking to the porter at my door."

"You think you're very smart," sneered the enraged Captain. "This cocksure alibi of yours won't look so tight when we find your confederate. Do you know what I'm going to do with you? Lock you up!"

Aitken seemed mildly surprised. "Indeed? On what charge?"

"We'll find a charge. Obstructing justice, for one thing. There'll be no bail, either—we'll see to that until you change your mind about not wanting to talk."

Inspector Laval, regarding Berthier somberly, seemed to shake his head, ever so slightly. But the Captain, if he observed the gesture, did not heed it. "I think you had better have one of your men take him to headquarters, Inspector," he snapped.

"An ancient and accepted procedure," approved Aitken, smiling. "I had not hoped to be so promptly honored."

He turned at the door. "Will you grant me the privilege of a few minutes' conversation with Mr. Milburn's secretary? There are affairs of the estate to be considered, you know."

"Yes," said Berthier shortly. "And afterwards she can confer with you in jail."

All the excursionists of the Dorothea with the exception of Bob Aitken found themselves unexpectedly at liberty when noonday came.

Captain Berthier imposed upon them the stipulation that they must remain in Montreal until further notice for appearance at the coroner's inquest and for other possible questioning. Berthier also specified that all must remain at the same hotel—with the exception of Detective Moode and the porter—and intimated none too delicately that an attempt on the part of anyone to leave the city without permission would result in summary arrest. In other words, they were all under surveillance. Wilks the porter was to remain in charge of the Dorothea.

Such conditions, however, were to be considered far from harsh when compared with further detention in a hot railroad car, however private. There was a general packing of bags in a spirit almost light-hearted while Bob Aitken and the secretary of the late Mr. Milburn conferred in the dining room.

"It's this way," explained the lawyer for the second time. "I am technically under arrest, but nothing can come of it, save for the temporary unpleasantness—I am absolutely sure of that."

"But why, Bob, why?" exclaimed the perturbed girl. "It seems so grossly unjust. What have you done to deserve such treatment? How on earth can they connect you with this terrible thing—you, of all people—the only decent man of the whole miserable outfit!"

Bob smiled and patted her hand gratefully. "It is a sort of grudge arrest, dear. The fact that some one seemed to have summoned the porter from my stateroom just at the time Mr. Milburn was killed may look suspicious; but the real reason for punishing me is that I decline to tell them of Mr. Milburn's private affairs, matters which he discussed with me when indicating his last wishes."

"Do you really think," she inquired earnestly, "that Mr. Milburn killed himself?"

"I have reason for believing that he did, naturally—his frame of mind during our last talk, for instance—but they are not conclusive reasons. On the other hand it seems hard to believe that anyone could have killed Mr. Milburn and got away between the time the porter knocked at my door and the time he found Mr. Milburn's body."

Helen shivered. "Do you think Wilks really heard someone talking to Mr. Milburn?"

"I can't be sure, myself, but Mrs. Heston backs him up in it."

Helen made a wry face. "That woman!" she commented.

"She says she was awake when the train was leaving St. John; that she heard Wilks talking to me and also heard somebody's voice in the lounge, just as Wilks tells it. It sounds pretty straight to me. And yet—"

"Then it must have been some person," said Helen nervously, "who jumped off the train—it was going slow, wasn't it?"

"But within the space of three minutes or less! To converse with a man, to shoot him down without causing him to raise an outcry, to escape from a moving train—it sounds incredible!"

"But how, with such evidence, can they possibly think you had anything to do with it?"

"The suggestion is," he said with a laugh, "that I had a confederate; that I knew the crime was to be committed just as, supposedly, I summoned the porter to let it be seen that I was safely asleep in my stateroom, thus preparing an excellent alibi for myself and also establishing the fact that nobody in the car could have killed Mr. Milburn. The only thing they lack," he ended in amusement, "is my motive. They think I am suppressing that. Therefore I am to be jailed and, I suppose, put through a lovely third degree."

She gripped his hand. "Bob! they won't dare abuse you, will they?"

"I think not. I happen to be a lawyer. And they know it. I intend to keep silent on the subject of Mr. Milburn's affairs until I am legally—and legitimately—forced to talk."

"You cannot tell—even me?"

"Not even you, dear, for the present. Things may look even blacker for me than they do now, but you'll trust me—won't you?"

She squeezed his hand impulsively. "All the way!" she declared. "I'm going to stay right here in Montreal, as long as you need me."

"Oh, no, you must not. There's no need of that, Helen. It may take weeks—months."

"I don't care. I'll get some kind of an old job and camp right here."

"You'll get nothing of the sort. You're in the employ of the estate of J. Proctor Milburn. Somebody's got to look out for things, and these idiots are going to keep me tied hand and foot, evidently. The first thing I want you to do is to notify the law firm of Dalbey & Pitts of my detention. You know them; St. James street."

"Yes, we wrote them a letter once, didn't we?" She looked at him compassionately. "Oh, Bob, it's awful of them to treat you this way!"

"It's all right," he said with a grin. "I'm losing nothing by it—and don't ask me to explain that, either. It's all in the game of being the legal slave of a deceased millionaire."

There was a rapping at the forward door of the dining room, and Sergeant Detective Thwaite entered.

"Sorry, sir, I'm to take you to headquarters," asserted Thwaite, adding with a grin: "The Inspector says you can continue your 'conference' there."

Thwaite was a powerful, heavily built chap of bright blue eye, granite jaw and not unpleasant demeanor.

"You're not going to be mean to him, are you?" entreated Helen.

"Us? Oh, no, lady," returned Thwaite cheerfully. "He's one of these gentlemanly prisoners, and we always try to show that kind how well-born we are at headquarters."

Helen kissed Bob Aitken goodbye. It was the first time that happened, but a mutual genuineness in its consummation seemed to promise that it would not be the last.

A tapping, this time at the rear door of the dining room, interrupted them. It was Lotus Decker, who

Bob Aitken's Silence Sends Him to Jail as the Investigation Centers in a Letter He Sent

As Helen kissed Bob good-bye, Lotus Decker appeared at the curtains at one end of the room. "Now, what do you want?" Growled Sergeant Thwaite. But his twinkling eyes belied his gruffness

pushed her way in promptly on hearing Sergeant Thwaite say something like "Who is it?"

"Good Agnes Miss Gracious!" exclaimed Lotus, "What have I busted into? I didn't know you were shooting a movie in here."

"Now, what do you want?" growled Thwaite, but his twinkling eyes belied his gruffness.

Lotus measured him swiftly. She stepped up to him confidentially and looked up into his face with big-eyed innocence. "I want to see this gentleman, Mr. Aitken, on legal business," she advised the Sergeant sweetly but unconvincingly. "The Major or Captain or whatever he is back there said I couldn't, but he's gone now and the nice Inspector man said I could. Who's boss around this dump anyhow, the Colonel or the Inspector?"

"Don't ask me to take sides, lady," objected Thwaite, grinning. "Where does this bird get all his 'conference' privileges with pretty girls, anyway? I think I'll try going to jail, too, myself, and maybe I'll have some luck with the beauty chorus, too."

"Oh, Lieutenant," cried Lotus, smearing it on, "you're so kind and brave and strong. Won't you let me say a couple little bitsy words to poor Mr. Aitken?"

Thwaite apprised her amusedly. "Who told you I was a lieutenant?" he demanded.

"Nobody, sir. I could just tell by your fierce masculine bearing. You don't even need a uniform."

"You're spoofing the majesty of the law, little one. But listen. I'm stepping out to smoke half a cigarette. When I get back I want this 'conference' business over, and this gentleman is going with me to headquarters."

"What makes you be so sweet!" Lotus murmured after him, and Thwaite went out with reddening ears.

Helen turned Aitken over to her. "I yield the directors' room to you, Miss Decker," she said smilingly, and to Bob: "I'll attend to that matter for you, at once. And I'll see you later. Bye! And don't be downhearted."

Lotus, when they were alone, went swiftly serious.

"What is it, Achey?" she begged, clutching his coat lapels. "What are these fools doing? Not arresting you? They don't think you had anything to do with it—do they?"

"I think not," said Bob. "They're merely trying to extort a little information out of me, that's all."

"What information?" asked Lotus, paling. "Not what I told you—not about my brother? I haven't got you in trouble, have I?"

"Oh, no, no. Nothing of the sort. You didn't tell them about him, did you?"

"Not a word. They didn't ask, of course, and I did as you said. I didn't volunteer anything. Oh, Achey, do you think—"

"I think you're silly to worry about it. There's nothing to connect your brother with this business."

"But he was—he was due to be in Montreal last night." Her voice dropped. "I called up the hotel where he always stops here, the Strathcona, and they said he had a reservation for last night but he hadn't shown up to claim it. You see, he really had planned to be here. Gosh, I'm worried!"

"Does your brother own a Glickenswerfer typewriter —one of the old-fashioned kind?"

Lotus shook her head wonderingly. "No, not any kind. He can't even use a typewriter. Why didn't I think of that! He dictates all his letters to a public stenographer at whatever hotel he's stopping."

"Well, there you are. The Inspector told me our crank letter was typed on that special kind of machine. You just forget all this business about your brother."

"Gee, you're comforting. But I'm so worried about you. Isn't there something I can do? Want me to go to jail with you—keep you comp'ny? I'll do it. I'll vamp this blue-eyed mountain range that's waiting outside and make him take me, too!"

"You're a great kid," declared Bob, patting her on the shoulder. "But I'll be all right. You just come to see me and bring me all the news. By-by."

And Lotus kissed him, too, just as Sergeant Detective Thwaite shouldered back in.

"This is the most affectionate murder case," grumbled Thwaite, "that I ever looked in on. Come on, Maurice Chevalier!"

"Can't I go along, too?" wheedled Lotus. "As far as headquarters! I look so nice with a big, strong, handsome detective alongside me."

"Yes, you can not," said Thwaite grimly, peering out of the window. "What do you think this is, a picnic? There's the Inspector outside, now. He'd bust me to a constable if he saw me making a social tea out of an arrest."

"I think he's mean," pouted Lotus. "I'll get even with the hungry-faced nut!"

On the platform outside Sergeant Montigny, making use of the porter's steps and a magnifying glass, was carefully examining the car windows, one at a time. Inspector Laval, Moode and another detective were making a similar but more general inspection. Captain Berthier had been summoned to the telephone for a long-distance call from Quebec.

"Thwaite," Laval accosted him. "You stay here and let Ansley go with this gentleman to headquarters. I want to talk to you."

"Yes, sir," said Thwaite, relinquishing his charge to the other detective.

Laval's eyes followed Aitken and his captor thoughtfully as they went out of the station. He took Thwaite
aside.

"You checked up these letters and telegrams which
we permitted the people on this car to send out, did you
not?"

"Yes, sir, Lennox and I. We copied the telegrams and
made a memorandum of the person to whom each letter
was sent, and the person by whom sent. I believe those
were the instructions."

"Yes. Did Aitken have any mail or telegrams going
out?"

"Yes, sir. One letter. Long manila envelope, pretty
bulky. He gave it to the porter to post for him, and we
took charge of it. It was sealed with sealing wax; opened
at the end—clasp but no glue on the flap."

"To whom was it addressed?

Thwaite referred to his notes. "Dalbey & Pitts. St.
James street. It's a law firm. The letter had been addressed on the typewriter to 'Robert Aitken, Present.'
This was scratched out and it was readdressed in ink to
Dalbey & Pitts, with a note down in the corner, 'Please
deposit for safe keeping.— R. A.' There was also another
line on it: 'Not to be opened until September 18.'"

"Hm! Dalbey & Pitts are probably his correspon-
dents in Montreal. I want you to find out, unobtru-
sively, Thwaite, what his business is with them. Do you
think you are equal to it?"

"I'll do my best, Chief. These K. C.'s are rather
hoity-toity, you know."

"On second thought," added Laval, "I'll' interview
Dalbey myself. I know him of old. Very pompous, as
you say. You may set a man to learn for us, meanwhile,
whether this firm makes use of safe deposit vaults at
any of the banks, or whether they are equipped with

vaults at their own offices. Probably they have their own vaults."

"You'd like to get hold of this letter of Aitken's, eh?"

"I should, very much. He is concealing something of importance from us. Come inside, Thwaite. Doctor Phillips just telephoned that he is coming back to the car. He has something for us. They have finished the preliminary autopsy."

Doctor Phillips arrived ten minutes later and found the police officers conversing earnestly in the lounge, Berthier having returned to the car.

The medico-legal expert tendered to Inspector Laval an envelope containing a small leaden pellet, about the size of a twenty-two bullet. It was corset-shaped but flattened at the point and otherwise slightly marred.

"You gentlemen were right in surmising," said the doctor, "that Mr. Milburn was killed with a Nebley-Stott air pistol. This is the bullet we extracted from the brain. We estimated, after certain preliminary tests with one of the pistols, that the bullet was fired from a distance of approximately five feet."

"How do you get that?" demanded Captain Berthier.

"Merely by ascertaining the penetrative force of bullets fired from these air pistols, and checking by such other data as we already possess, as to the resistive power of the skull at the temple, for instance. If Mr. Milburn had shot himself, the penetrative force of the bullet would have been much greater. Moreover, it would have traveled an upward or at least a horizontal course upon entering the cranium. The bullet which killed Mr. Milburn traveled downward. The shot was fired, I should say, by a man who stood at or near that door where the curtains are. The angle of penetration indicates, I should say, that a fairly tall man shot Mr. Milburn, probably a six-footer."

"Well, suicide is out," snapped Berthier. "That's certain. I'll have to commend you, Doctor, on your ballistics."

"We may have more deductions for you," said the doctor with modesty, "if you give us time. By examining the barrel of the pistol you found on the floor here, and checking by the microscopic abrasions on this bullet, we may establish still more definitely that that was the weapon used. Its barrel will contain tool marks left by such machining processes as turning, drilling and reaming, and corresponding abrasions will be found upon the bullet, even though it had been further damaged by passing through so coarse an abrasive as bone."

Laval stepped off the distance from the chair in which Milburn's body had been found, to the portieres of the door.

"Five feet, four inches," supplied Sergeant Montigny, who had taped it; "that is the exact distance from the chair to the curtains."

Laval stepped past the portieres. "Then a person standing behind the curtains, outside the door," he observed, "would have had the barrel of his leveled pistol approximately five feet from Mr. Milburn's head." He came inside the curtains. "Whereas if he had stood here in the lounge and leveled his pistol it would have been fully three feet nearer Milburn—approximately two feet, four inches."

"He was not that close," said Doctor Phillips firmly. "I will stake my reputation on it."

"And a justly celebrated reputation it is," agreed Laval suavely. "I am inclined, Doctor Phillips, to concur with you. Unless Mr. Milburn were asleep at the time he was shot, he would not have suffered an assailant to stand deliberately at his side and level even an air pistol at him."

"And he was not asleep," put in Captain Berthier testily. "There were voices in here. And the man who fired the pistol could not have stood outside the door in the passageway without being in plain view of the porter, Wilks, and perhaps of Aitken. The Heston woman also says she heard the killer talking. What's the answer? Wilks and the Heston woman lying—in league with the killer?"

"Scarcely that," mused Laval. "If they were, why should they deliberately take pains to awaken Aitken and other possible witnesses as well, by pounding on the door of the stateroom? Why should they ring bells, to run the further risk of arousing everybody? Can we conceive, on the other hand, of Aitken being in the plot with the negro porter and Mrs. Heston? Assuredly not. I think they speak the truth."

"Then we can believe one of two things," asserted Berthier. "Either Doctor Phillips is wrong about the pistol having been fired at a distance of five feet, or Detective Moode, here, is right in his theory."

"What was that, sir?" asked Moode stupidly—he seemed dazed by the mental intricacies of the discussion.

"Your suggestion that the murderer was a lunatic, or a fanatic, who first killed his man, then stood here and talked about it, after having rung the bell for the porter."

"Oh!" said Moode. "Yes, sir, I'd forgot that."

"But our witnesses," interposed Laval, "heard two voices; a rather high-pitched voice like that of Mr. Milburn, and another, deeper voice."

"Oh, they could have been mistaken about that— hearing a voice through the curtains," argued Berthier, plainly exasperated by the contradictions of the case. He was not used to being contradicted.

"Well, gentlemen, my job is in the laboratory," remarked Doctor Phillips. "Shall I take along the pistol you found on the floor? Shall I examine the barrel microscopically?"

"If you like," said Laval, "though there seems to be no doubt whatever about the weapon used."

He turned to Montigny as the doctor departed:

"What's new with you, Pierre? Anything this morning?"

Montigny looked about hesitantly. "Why, I interviewed the conductor of the train, Inspector. He thinks he knows the gentleman who left the yellow and white Pullman receipt on the back platform."

"Yes?" said Laval and Berthier in the same breath.

"Yes. He accepted a cash fare, Rutland to Montreal, from a passenger who was trying to get a berth, but had to be satisfied with a seat. The conductor promised to fix him up later, if possible, and at Rouses Point two other passengers got off, so that a berth came available. But when conductor went back to notify the man that he could accommodate him, last night at midnight, the chap was nowhere to be found—he had left the train. There were other cash fares paid for from Rutland to Montreal, but the conductor particularly remembered this man because he had gone the extra trouble to get him berth which the man was not present to accept. It strikes me as being quite possible, Inspector, that this individual got off the train at Rouses Point, walked back to the last car, this one, boarded the rear platform and rode there until the train reached the next stop, St. Johns—"

"And killed Mr. Milburn the train pulled put!" exclaimed Moode with his air of surprising discovery.

Montigny smiled dubiously. "That we do not know. He had forty-six minutes, if he rode the observation platform in this manner, to plot the crime, to see what was going on in the car here, while he himself was unobserved. The conductor describes him as a tall man, about six feet, noticeably nervous, who spoke in a decidedly bass voice."

*A Tiny Drop of Sealing-Wax Occupies the
Attention of Sgt. Montigny at Police
Headquarters
In Montreal*

"*Here you see Milburn's sealing-wax*," *announced Montigny,
displaying the oddly glowing stick and several melted specimens of it in the path of the ultra-violet rays.*

6

"Tall, nervous basso!" murmured Laval. "That is at least a partial description, and it may prove helpful. Anything from St. Johns, Captain Berthier? Any suspicious characters?"

Berthier made a gesture of exasperation. "Nothing," he snapped. "Nothing but some day coach passengers the immigration inspectors took off for their usual questioning."

"I thought this was an all-Pullman train."

"Normally it is. But on account of the delay and mix-up due to the wreck they attached a day coach at Rutland. It is possible that this passenger the conductor referred to got off the train at Rouses Point—we may be able to check up on that—or perhaps he merely stepped up into the baggage car to see about his luggage, and rode the rest of the way into Montreal on the day coach. At any rate he did not get off at St. Johns, as far as our men there have learned. No stranger or suspicious character has left St. Johns on a train since last night at one-thirty, or by automobile, either. If your nervous basso got off there after killing Mr. Milburn he is still there, and we'll get him. It's a small place to hide in."

There was an almost mischievous light in Montigny's eyes as he observed:

"If our tall gentleman killed Mr. Milburn, I scarcely think he rode into Montreal on the day coach. He would have had to be fleet of foot to drop off the back platform, then outrace the train to the extent of catching the day coach at the forward end."

Berthier glanced up quickly, grunted, and chewed at his cigar.

"A clever operative," vouched Laval, "if he did all the things he seems to have done, in the space of time allotted to him."

"'Seems to have done,' Inspector, yes," replied Montigny with emphasis. "If, in the first place, he killed Mr. Milburn with the air pistol, he must have had intimate knowledge of the properties of that weapon—something that Captain Berthier and I, for instance, did not have, for you alone were familiar with that kind of gun. It is scarcely likely, I mean, that a murderous assailant plotting a crime of this character would pick up an apparently harmless target pistol he found lying around, and use it to commit murder."

"He might have thought it was an automatic," contended Berthier. "It looks enough like one."

"Or, if he was a passenger on the train," put in Moode, breaking his accustomed deferential silence, "he could have known about the target practice. At the stops we made, passengers were curious about this car. Some of 'em walked down the station platform at Rutland, I remember, to look us over. We were tied up there, four hours at Rutland. Then, too, these pistols are pretty well known in New York. Sporting goods stores sell 'em."

"Granting, then," summed up Inspector Laval, "that he knew the pistol would kill a man, we may assume that the culprit spent forty-six minutes crouching on the back platform, awaiting his opportunity to use it. Mr. Milburn was engaged, part of that time, with Mr.

Aitken and his secretary. Moreover, the assailant knew he must choose a time when the train was moving slowly enough for him to make his escape. What better chance than when the train was leaving St. Johns? Perhaps Mr. Milburn was nodding in his chair. Reaching his arm through the broken window, the man on the platform unbolts the door, tiptoes in, shoots Mr. Milburn in the temple with the air pistol and then, in a lunatic spirit of bravado, rings for the porter, runs to the back platform and shouts through the broken window before he jumps off."

"But he has not yet had time, Inspector," purred Montigny, "to visit Mr. Aitken's stateroom, press the bell button and place incriminating bullets in Mr. Perry Laith's dressing gown."

"Both of those, Pierre, may be entirely unrelated incidents. The ring from the stateroom might indeed have been an accident—it's easy to roll over in one's sleep and bump an elbow against a bell button. As to the bullets in the dressing robe, most of the people present for target practice had been drinking—Laith himself may have put the ammunition in the pocket of his dressing gown and forgotten all about it."

"Assuming which," said Captain Berthier, "we have a fairly reasonable reconstruction of the crime. All I would add to it is the amendment that this lawyer, Aitken, had knowledge of what was taking place—he is undeniably withholding something of importance—and himself pressed the bell button in order to establish an alibi."

"But until we find at least the shadow of a motive," demurred Laval, "we must admit that we are merely holding him because he declines to answer questions. What else have you found, Pierre? Where are the clues you invariably nose out? What are you suppressing?"

Montigny smiled through the smoke of a black cigar.

"Only a spot of sealing wax," he said, producing an envelope from which he took out a small reddish-brown pellet which he displayed in the palm of his hand. "I found it on the carpet near the desk there."

Sergeant Thwaite, who had been listening with quiet interest to the discussion of matters somewhat unfamiliar to him, snickered aloud.

"Up to your old tricks, Pierre!" he chuckled. "Now what has a spot of sealing wax to do with a man getting shot?"

"How do I know?" countered Montigny placidly. "Perhaps it may solve the riddle."

"Don't forget, Thwaite," cautioned Inspector Laval, "that the footprints of a cat once led Pierre to the answer in a murder problem quite as exasperating as this one."

"As for me," said Captain Berthier, rising abruptly, "I am going to lead myself to a spot of lunch before I puzzle my brain any longer. Join me, gentlemen. I'll have to hurry, though—I've got to make a train to Quebec. No—let's see—not until 4 o'clock."

Detective Moode and Sergeant Thwaite could not accept his invitation, but Laval and Montigny did. Moode said he had to transfer his bags to a room somewhere and he would join them later at headquarters. Thwaite had already snatched a bite, he said, at the station lunch room.

The police officers abjured the subject of the crime until they had almost completed their meal. Berthier paid his respects heatedly and at length to the nuisance of rum-running and the necessity of co-operating with the American border patrol, the subject which was calling him to Quebec.

There followed a long pause during which Berthier was thoughtful and uncommunicative. Presently he demanded of Montigny:

"That spot of sealing wax, Sergeant—what are you trying to make of that?"

Montigny was deprecatory. "Oh, I don't know, Captain, that I shall be able to make anything of it. Sealing wax in itself is interesting to me. No two given kinds of it in the world seem precisely similar, chemically. It has long proved a stumbling block in criminology."

"Montigny," announced Inspector Laval, "is beginning to lecture. Set a time limit, Captain, or he will address you indefinitely; you will miss your train."

"I want to know," said Berthier. "Go on, Sergeant."

"A very short lecture," promised Montigny, "because I know precious little about it. As I was saying, despite the dissimilarity of two given kinds of sealing wax, it is virtually impossible for a chemist to trace, by analysis, the origin of a particular sample, even though he is provided with the original stick. It has been difficult, for instance, to fix the identity of seals in certain cases of robbery, and the like. I say 'has been,' because it is no longer difficult. The ultra-violet lamp—the kind we have at headquarters—has changed all that."

"Hm!" The Captain was skeptical. "How can the ultra-violet ray show differences in sealing wax?"

"It will, Captain, even when chemical analysis fails. Sealing wax, as you know, is mostly shellac combined with various mineral filling materials and a bit of coloring matter. If a stick of sealing wax is merely softened by heat, then the seal from it may retain the same chemical character as the parent stick, and a chemical analysis may show the sample and the stick to be the same wax. But—melt your wax, let the shellac in it catch on fire— that self-same moment the content of organic substance is diminished and the percentage of mineral substances increased. Your chemist is sunk. Thus, if five seals are dropped from one stick, the first sample being of

softened wax, the second of melted wax, the third of
wax that has been on fire, the fourth containing black
granules from burning, the fifth a bit worse charred—
then what have you? You have obtained from one stick
of wax, five seals of differing chemical composition.
Your chemist may use up the whole stick analyzing it,
destroying your evidence while he is at it, and in the
end he is stumped. He can never identify, by analysis,
the seal and the suspected stick."

"You're a bit of a chemist yourself," applauded Berthier.

"Merely rudiments of the thing, which I am repeating by rote like a parrot. Quite simple. I got it out of
a book. Now—examine these same five seals from the
same stick under ultra-violet light, and you have five
identical specimens. No change caused by the melting
or burning—the luminescent color peculiar to that particular kind of sealing wax is the same in the original
stick and in the five seals."

"You mean chemical change makes no difference in
the color, the appearance to the eye?"

"None whatever, under the actinic ray. But—compare these five seals with any other stick of sealing wax,
or samples from it, and you see an amazing difference.
Every stick has its particular color and luminescence. It
is due to the carrying content of luminescent materials
in the wax—there is a vast number of these materials in
nature, and only the ultra-violet ray may seek them out
for the human eye. I do not mean phosphorescent substances, which light up independently of the ultraviolet
ray—there are very few of these, mostly chemicals, for
example several sulphur and metal combinations. But
there are a very great number of substances that light
up, that is, become luminescent or fluorescent, only
when the ultra-violet rays, of short wave-length and
invisible to the eye, fall upon them. These substances

are contained, in varying degree, in different sealing waxes. Thus the lamp tells us what chemical analysis will fail to disclose."

"But the connection?" fretted Berthier. "Get to that. What can this spot of wax on the floor of Milburn's car have to do with our crime?"

"I do not know." Montigny smiled sagely. "I promised no startling disclosures. I was merely discoursing upon the interesting phenomena of sealing wax. So may little sermons lurk in stones and things. Suppose a robber opened a sealed package, filched part of its contents, then resealed it neatly with his own brand of sealing wax? Would he fool us? To the naked eye the seal would appear not to have been tampered with. Under the ultra-violet rays the effect would be as comical as that of a yellow wig on a red-headed man."

"Interesting," said Captain Berthier, rising, "but unprofitable. I can see no point of contact with our murder case."

"The envelope containing documents which lawyer Aitken dispatched to Dalbey & Pitts was sealed with wax."

"Yes? Granting it was?"

"There was a stick of sealing wax in Milburn's desk—it is in my pocket now. The ultra-violet eye will tell us that the spot on the floor, the seal on the envelope, the stick in Milburn's desk, are identical—or maybe not."

"Well?"

"We shall know whether Milburn—or Milburn's wax—sealed the envelope."

"Or Milburn's lawyer or Milburn's secretary sealed it with Milburn's wax," scoffed Berthier. "You are a glutton for details, Montigny, but I am afraid this will lead you nowhere."

"Or perhaps—somewhere." Montigny shrugged.

There was a momentary twinkle in Laval's brooding eyes as they left the restaurant.

"Montigny," the Inspector observed, "nearly always has something up his sleeve. He is an incurable showman, Captain. You'll have to watch him."

At detective headquarters Montigny closeted himself in his sanctum of the ultra-violet lamp, while Inspector Laval telephoned for an appointment with the Honorable Seumas Dalbey, K. C., of Dalbey & Pitts. Mr. Dalbey's dignified secretary permitted Laval to speak to the dignified chief clerk, and the latter advised him after a suitable period of chastening delay that Mr. Dalbey was presently engaged but intended during the afternoon to pay a visit to headquarters for the purpose of conferring with a client of the firm, one Mr. Robert Aitken, and at the time of this visit he would be pleased to ascertain the wishes of Inspector Laval.

Laval smiled bleakly, murmuring, "Typical!"

Sergeant Montigny invited the Inspector into the small laboratory where the lamp of the quartz burner, fitted with a filter almost black, shed eerie rays beyond the solar spectrum.

"Here you see Milburn's sealing wax," announced Montigny, displaying the oddly glowing stick and several melted specimens of it in the path of the rays. "And here—the spot of wax I found on the floor. It was not the same wax."

The samples fluoresced in markedly different colors.

"But all we know," said Laval, "is that somebody, some time—no doubt recently, for it is a bright, fresh spot of wax—sealed something at Milburn's desk with a stick of sealing wax which was not the stick you found in Milburn's desk."

"*Hélas,* that is all, Inspector."

"There was not a second stick of sealing wax in the car?"

"There was, Inspector, in the desk of Miss Eastwick, the secretary—but it is gone!"

"Ah! So?"

"We looked everywhere. It was not to be found. It was not in the car—unless somebody had it in his pocket."

They returned to Laval's office.

"Perhaps you attach too much importance to the spot of wax, Pierre."

Montigny grimaced. "Perhaps, Inspector. But it is the unexplained little details that pester me most."

"I am more interested," said Laval reflectively, "in the unexplained detail of the killer's call for the porter."

"Yes. Strange, the bell-ringing in this most diverting murder! We must look for an oddly defiant and reckless culprit."

"A six-foot, nervous basso who had something to gain by the murder of Milburn—and was not at all nervous, apparently, when he did his work. We have not as yet uncovered a shred of a motive."

Montigny stroked his black mustachios and withheld comment. "Tonight," he said, "I should like to spend on that car."

"It sometimes helps—your procedure of sleeping at the scene of the crime."

"I should like to live there, Inspector, until our puzzle is answered."

"But there are no lights on the car, detached from the train as it is."

"Yes, Inspector; what they call batteries 'floating on the line.' They need them on private cars which are so frequently detached. I wish an electrician to look them over, however; they seem weak. When we have the time, Inspector, I should like to re-enact the crime in accordance with our theory of an intruder on the back platform."

"As you like, Pierre. Go back to the car. Meanwhile I have some questions to ask the obstinate Mr. Aitken."

Captain Berthier joined Laval in the re-examination of Bob Aitken, as did Sergeant Thwaite. The latter brought in the information that Dalbey & Pitts were equipped with their own fireproof vaults at their offices.

Aitken was polite and unruffled as a constable ushered him into the Inspector's office. He seemed little impressed by his detention. He answered questions and cross-questions promptly and lucidly, with the exception of those bearing on his last conference with Milburn.

"Last night when the train arrived at Montreal," stated Laval, "you sent the porter out to post a letter addressed to Dalbey & Pitts, St. James street."

"I had permission to do so. I trust it was mailed."

"It was. We did not know so much about this case then as we do now, or we should have intercepted it."

"Thank you," murmured Aitken, "for not knowing."

"It was a manila envelope, flap and clasp at the end, which had been addressed to you with the written instruction, 'Not to be opened until September 18.'"

"Correct, Inspector."

"Probably having no envelope at hand large enough in which to enclose it, you scratched out your name and readdressed it, to Dalbey & Pitts, with the added instruction that it was to be deposited for safe keeping."

"Correct again, Inspector."

"The envelope was sealed with a stick of sealing wax from a drawer of Mr. Milburn's desk."

A flicker of surprise lighted Aitken's face, but he said nothing.

"What, Mr. Aitken, did that envelope contain?"

"I decline to answer, Inspector."

"We shall require you to answer, on the grounds that you are obstructing justice by not doing so."

"I am not obstructing justice, Inspector, I assure you."

"Then why do you withhold information concerning your talk with Mr. Milburn immediately prior to his death?"

"For reasons intimately affecting the relations of Mr. Milburn and myself as client and counsel. I think no court can compel me to betray a confidence of my dead employer. I shall have nothing to say, in that respect, until the 18th of September."

"Then you will spend a month in jail."

"I am prepared to do so."

Laval ordered him back to his cell.

When the weighty and pompous King's Counsel, the Honorable Mr. Seumas Dalbey, appeared at Laval's office shortly afterward, he likewise was firm, and indignantly so. Mr. Dalbey's head was bald and nobly domed, and there was a fringe of thin, curly hair at the nape of his neck.

"I think, sir," he blustered, "that this is an infamous outrage, an incredible shame, a grievous insult to the Canadian and American bar, an uncalled-for reflection upon the rectitude of a profession, sir, that has always been found arrayed upon the side of justice."

"Your client Mr. Aitken is not arrayed upon the side of justice. He is deliberately withholding information which would throw light upon the murder of his employer."

"You have no right to that assumption, sir."

"Answer this question, if you will, Mr. Dalbey: Did or did not the packet of documents sent to you by Mr. Aitken contain copies of the will of Mr. Milburn?"

The King's Counsel permitted himself a look of mild surprise. "Will? Why, the last will and testament of Mr. Milburn is in the hands of his solicitors, sir, in New York. They so advised me by telephone this morning."

Laval did not betray his eager interest.

"A will recently made?"

"About a month ago, sir."

"What does it contain? Do you know the names of the chief beneficiaries?"

"I do, sir. Mind you, I am not required to tell you this, sir, until the will is filed for probate; but I will tell you, in strict confidence. The bulk of Mr. Milburn's estate was left to his wife—or ex-wife, according to the courts' interpretation—and his two sons, Herbert and J. Proctor Milburn, Junior."

"And Miss Dorothea Dustin—was she named in the will?"

"She was, sir. There is a bequest of one hundred thousand dollars for 'my friend'—as he put it—'Dorothea Dustin.'"

No hint of his elation disturbed the tan, lean-muscled face of Inspector Laval. He inquired: "Was Mr. Aitken named in the will?"

"He was. As executor and administrator."

"Not as a beneficiary?"

"No."

"Nor any of the other persons mentioned in the newspapers this morning as having been passengers on Mr. Milburn's car?"

"None of them, sir. No one but Dorothea Dustin."

"I wish you to surrender to me, Mr. Dalbey, the letter sent to your firm by Mr. Aitken for safe keeping.

"I decline to do that, sir."

"Do you also decline to give me any information concerning it that you may have?"

"I do, sir, absolutely."

Laval pursed his lips in thought.

The telephone rang. He would not have accepted the message had he not been told that it was Sergeant Montigny on the line.

"I am at the station, sir," said Montigny. "I have discovered something of interest in the car."

"What, Pierre?"

"Twelve hundred dollars in Canadian bank notes, hidden in a corner of the porter's linen closet, under a pile of bedding."

"Ah! His private banking place, eh?"

"They are new notes, of the same series as currency we found upon the person of Mr. Milburn this morning. He had procured this Canadian money in New York, for use on this trip. The bills I have found are of numbers immediately following the numbers of the notes we found on Mr. Milburn. Shall I bring this porter in?"

"Yes, bring him in," said Laval.

When first he had been questioned by police officers on the private car of his late employer, Homer Wilks, cook and porter of the Dorothea, had not seemed more frightened or ill at ease than the average individual of his race would have been expected to be. His summary removal to headquarters in custody of a grim and taciturn detective, however, was something else. Wilks was thoroughly unnerved when he faced his inquisitors in the Inspector's office.

At first he denied all knowledge of the money Montigny had found secreted in the linen closet. Montigny explained to the Inspector that the bank notes had not been in that hiding place when he first searched the car—and Montigny as a searcher of premises was without peer. Hence the assumption was that the money had been placed there since morning.

"Somebody must've put it there to get me in trouble," iterated Wilks, over and over.

"You are lying," thundered Captain Berthier in his most savage tone. "You stole the money. You found Mr. Milburn asleep in his chair. You picked up a target pistol and shot him—"

"No, Chief!" shrieked Wilks.

"You shot him so you could steal the money from his pocket. Then you rang the bell to 'call yourself' to the lounge. You went to Mr. Aitken's stateroom—"

"No, Chief! Ain't none o' that a fact—"

"You rang the bell from the stateroom, too. You put bullets in the pocket of the dressing gown hanging there—"

"I swear it, Chief, I swear it!" moaned Wilks. "I'll tell you the truth, I'll tell you the truth! Mr. Milburn give me the money!"

"Now I know you stole it!" shouted Captain Berthier. "'Gave' you twelve hundred dollars for a tip, eh?"

"It's what he did, Chief, or I hope the Lawd may strike me dead!"

"When did he give you all this money? Why? Was he drunk? Crazy?"

"No, suh, Chief. He wasn't at all. He give it to me for promising to do something for him, and made me swear not to say a word about it to anybody, no time, no matter what happened. And that's why I didn't say nothing about it, Chief, when you was asking me questions this morning."

"What was it you did for him?"

Wilks rolled his eyes fearfully. "I guess I got to tell you, now, or you'll hang me," he muttered.

"You bet we'll hang you. We're going to hang you anyhow. Spit it out!"

"I didn't do nothing but mail a letter for him, suh."

Berthier swelled with anger. "When you're trying to save your neck," he roared, "why don't you tell a good lie?"

"It's the truth, Chief! That's all I done for him. Mailed a letter. He told me not to say nothing about it to nobody, and he'd give me the swellest tip I ever had in my life. So he takes out his pocketbook and gives me mos' all the money in it. He says to me, 'Here, Wilks, I've intended to do something for you, anyhow. You've been a faithful boy!' Seems like to me now, Chief, he knew he was gonna die, and he give me that like a sort of something in his will."

Berthier and Laval exchanged swift glances.

"Where did you post this letter?" inquired Laval, in a tone more reassuring.

"St. Johns, Chief. He give it to me after we'd left Rouses Point. I remember because he asked me what was the next town we'd stop at, and I told him St. Johns."

"What kind of letter was it?"

"Big envelope, boss. Heavy. Had a lot of stamps on it."

"What was the address on it? Did you notice?"

Wilks paused in agitation. "I don't like to get nobody in trouble, Chief," he faltered.

"Answer my question," snapped Laval.

"Well, suh, that was the funny part about it. The letter was going, seems like, to Mr. Robert Aitken, but it couldn't a-been our Mr. Aitken, because he was right there on the car, and he wasn't going off to no India—"

"India?" growled Berthier. "What are you talking about?"

"Yes, suh, that's right. The letter was going to India, Cal—Calcutta, yes, suh, that was it. Care the American Express Company."

Berthier was thoroughly enraged. He leaped up and strode to the chair where the trembling negro was sitting. "Don't think we can't check up on a crazy lie like that," shouted the Captain. "Come through with the truth, you fool!"

"It's the truth," vowed Wilks hoarsely.

"Did Mr. Aitken know of the letter?" asked Laval.

"No, suh. He was the one particular I wasn't to tell—I mean Mr. Milburn told me to tell nobody, specially, on the car."

"Was there any return address on the envelope? Mr. Milburn's name?"

"I don't know, suh. I didn't notice. I was in a awful hurry."

Laval took Montigny aside and instructed him to get in touch with the post-office at St Johns. "Find out whether there is any record or any recollection of this letter. If the negro has told us the truth, the letter would come direct to Montreal for forwarding on the first mail steamer. We may be able to intercept it."

Montigny pursued these inquiries while Laval and Berthier inflicted more fruitless pounding on Wilks. He clung tenaciously to his story. In the end he was lodged in a cell.

"I am inclined to credit his story," Laval told Berthier.

"Why?" demanded the Captain irritably.

"Simply because it is too bizarre for Wilks to have manufactured. Surely he would tell a simpler story than that, one nearer to his type of mentality, if he had stolen the money—or killed Milburn."

"No, he didn't kill Milburn," grumbled Berthier. "The Heston woman clears him of that—Aitken, too.

She heard somebody talking to Milburn—while the porter was waking Aitken. Besides, wouldn't have had the
nerve. But I'm not so sure he didn't steal the money.
Milburn might have given him ten dollars, twenty—a
hundred would have been a magnificent tip, but twelve
hundred!"

"If Milburn really gave it to him," said Laval thoughtfully, "it would strengthen the suggestion of this man
Aitken that Milburn committed—or at least contemplated—suicide."

"How do you mean, Inspector?"

"I mean this. It is Milburn's last night on earth, and
he knows it. He wants to do something for this porter,
a faithful servant. He has made a will but perhaps had
forgotten Wilks. He doesn't want the negro to know
what he is planning to do, so he gives him the money in
payment for a stated service, and silence."

"And what did he want to send to India, then, addressed to a man who was on the car with him?"

Laval was pensive. "There we are in the dark. I think
I could come nearer to guessing the contents of the
envelope he turned over to Aitken, with the stipulation
that it was not to be opened for thirty days."

"And what the devil could that be?" demanded Berthier
testily.

"It could be," said Laval with emphasis, "a new
will—a new will omitting the name of one Dorothea
Dustin as beneficiary."

Berthier stared at him for a moment, and said nothing. "By Jove!" he exploded. "We are floundering near
to a motive in this beastly case, at that! But why, if it
was a will, should he want his lawyer to hold it up for
thirty days? And what could he want to send to India,
addressed to the same lawyer? Was Aitken, do you suppose, planning to go to India?"

Aitken's Letter to India and the $1200 Found in the Pullman Porter's Linen Closet Add to Further Mystery

Bob gave Helen the chair and perched on the edge of the desk himself. But she elected to come nearer to him, very close, in fact, and put her arms about his neck and kissed him

7

Laval shrugged. "We might ask the gentleman—not that he would tell us."

"I don't get it," fumed Berthier. "It sounds crazy."

The discussion was interrupted by the return of Montigny, who did not appear happy. "No luck, Inspector," he reported glumly. "No record of such a letter at St. Johns—there would be no record of it, of course, if it were not registered, but I mean they can't tell us. They had an unusually busy day today, crowd of tourists there, rush of mail for a small force, one of the clerks taken ill with ptomaine poisoning, too. Nobody remembered the letter to Calcutta, and if it was posted at all it must have been handled by the fellow who was taken sick, and he's too sick to ask about it. They say if the letter went through it would be in Montreal now. But nobody remembers it here—nobody would. Big batch of mail for Calcutta forwarded on a mail boat today."

Laval considered that unemotionally. "Well, let us keep on the track of it as best we may. We can cable Scotland Yard. Unless the British authorities are able to help us I am afraid we shall be a long time tracing it."

"We'll make this clam Aitken talk before we can catch any fairytale letter to India," growled Berthier. "There's the bird that knows everything we're trying to find out. We've got to loosen his tongue."

"Detective Moode is outside, Inspector," said Montigny. "He wants to know whether he can do anything to help us."

Laval made a small grimace. "That stupid fellow again? I think I shall send him to New York, to get rid of him. What do you say, Captain? He might be useful looking up a few small details for us there. Later I can send someone to check up on him."

Captain Berthier grinned. "Suits me, Inspector. He's only in the way here."

Laval directed an attendant to show him in.

There seemed to be something on Moode's mind besides his derby, which he removed awkwardly only after he had greeted each person in the office, in turn.

"I was down to the car, Inspector," he said, a little shamefacedly. "I thought I would look around some and see if there was anything we missed. But the flatfeet there wouldn't let me come near it."

"The constables on guard?" said Laval, suppressing a smile. "Well, why didn't you telephone here?"

"Oh, it didn't matter, I just thought I'd like to help if I could," returned Moode, with an effort at lightness which could not, however, keep resentment out of his tone. "They said they didn't care whose private detective I was, I couldn't get on that car without an official pass."

"Well, well, I shall write you one if you wish," promised the Inspector. "But there is something else I think you might do for us, Mr. Moode. There are a good many details at the New York end of this affair that require attention, and, being a former member of the New York police force, you should be able to get the best of co-operation for us."

He outlined some of the things he wished Moode to do.

"Sure," said the detective cheerfully. "I'd be glad to go back for you. When you want me to leave? Tonight?"

"The sooner the better," admitted Laval. "There's the New York Express at eight-thirty or the Limited at nine. Both get to New York at the same time, I believe, six-twenty-three in the morning. The Limited is a little faster and may be crowded, but I think you could get a reservation on either train now, if you'd hurry."

"Then it's what I'll do," decided Moode. "And if I need any help in New York I'll holler. Can I use your phone, Inspector?"

They waited resignedly while he sprawled over Laval's desk and barked into the telephone. He made a reservation on the earlier train, the Express. The Limited was sold out.

Moode paused on his way to the door. "I had a talk with some of the people at the hotel, Inspector," he said in connection with his adieux. "The Dustin woman, that Heston pair, Miss Decker and Miss Eastwick. They was all wanting to know when you gonna leave 'em go."

"As soon as ever we can," declared Laval. "I have a feeling that we are going to get to the bottom of this business before long."

"Anything new come up, Inspector?"

Laval told him about the money that had been found in the porter's linen closet.

"Made a sweet haul, didn't he?" Moode grinned in a fashion that aroused the Inspector's impatience. "I didn't think that bird would have the nerve to rob the dead. But it looks like that's what he done, don't it, Inspector?"

"Was the suggestion at any time advanced," asked Laval, "that Aitken intended going to India?"

"Nah, Inspector—poppycock!" replied Moode scornfully. "Mr. Milburn might have got the porter to mail a letter to India, but Wilks probably made that up about it being addressed to Aitken—any old kind of a smoke screen, you know, long as he was in trouble. Holding him, ain't you, Inspector?"

"Yes," said Laval curtly. "Thank you, Mr. Moode."

Moode departed as awkwardly as he had arrived, promising the Inspector that he need not worry any longer about the New York end of things, now.

"No wonder Milburn lost his life," grunted Berthier when the detective had gone, "with a moron like that for a bodyguard!"

"Ah well," proposed Laval, "now that the private detective is temporarily eliminated, let us get back to the private lawyer."

He sent for Aitken.

"There's a lady wants to see him, too, sir," said the attendant. "They told her to ask your permission. Her name is Miss Eastwick."

"Is that so? Very well. Tell her she may see him when I am through with him."

"Pretty thick, that pair," observed Captain Berthier as they waited. "All they do is 'confer.' What do you make of them?"

"Why, it is natural that they should have common interests. There is no one else just now to look after Milburn's affairs. His son Herbert is hurrying east from Denver. The wife, or former wife, and the other son are traveling in Sweden. We shall have to give the secretary a free hand, I suppose, while we are holding Aitken."

The late Mr. Milburn's personal counsel was still pleasantly courteous and undisturbed when he was shown in again.

"Yes, Inspector?" he said gravely.

"Sit down." Laval went directly to the point. "Have you any knowledge, Mr. Aitken, of a letter addressed to you in care of the American Express Company, Calcutta, India, which was posted last night from the train, by Mr. Milburn's orders?"

Aitken straightened in genuine surprise. "Calcutta, India! Assuredly not, Inspector. Why should I receive mail in Calcutta, India? I have never been there and never expect to go there."

Laval reviewed the incident of the hidden hank notes and the assertions of Wilks the porter.

Aitken sat pondering. He shook his head. "I cannot help you in this matter, Inspector. Not that I don't want to, but I haven't the vaguest suspicion of an idea what such an act on Mr. Milburn's part could mean."

"Did Mr. Milburn at any time leave the suggestion with you that he intended to 'remember' Wilks—in his will?"

"Why . . . No."

"You seem to hesitate, Mr. Aitken. Why?"

"I was merely considering, Inspector, the likelihood that Mr. Milburn might in fact have given the money to Wilks—as a last gift, you know. He liked the negro. Wilks had been a faithful and intelligent servant."

"In other words," put in Captain Berthier belligerently, "you are working around again to your cooked-up theory of 'suicide.' It won't stand, Aitken, I'll tell you that. We are prepared to prove in court that the shot which killed Milburn was fired at a distance of five feet or more. You'd better cut out this cagy beating about the bush and tell the truth, son. It's going to go harder with you if you don't."

"I am sorry," said Aitken, "that I am unable to give you further information. . . . Is that all, Inspector?"

The Inspector studied him with somnolent eyes. "Yes," he said shortly. "That is all. There is a person waiting to see you, Mr. Milburn's secretary, I think. The constable will show you to a room where you may talk with her."

"Thank you, Inspector. You are very kind. My cell block has an unpleasant odor of disinfectants."

The Inspector smiled when the door closed behind his caller. "Nice chap," observed Laval. "He may be guilty, but I like him. And now, Montigny, you are free to return to your private car, with electricians, chemists, palmists and any other specialists who may be able to help you. I hope you will be able to discover something more. I am becoming just a bit muddled over this case."

"Muddled!" snorted Captain Berthier. "If Montigny finds out anything else to complicate this mess I'll be loony as a bat." The Captain rose. "Well, I've got to leave it with you, Inspector, for the rest of the day and most of tomorrow. I've got to run for that four o'clock train to Quebec. I don't have to say that I know you will carry on till I get back."

Laval assured him that he would and told him good-bye.

Bob Aitken met Helen in the small, bare office which Laval referred to as his "conference room." Favored prisoners were permitted on occasion to talk to callers there. It contained no furniture save a small desk and a small straight chair.

Bob gave Helen the chair and perched on the edge of the desk himself. But she elected to come nearer to him, very close, in fact, and put her arms about his neck and kissed him.

"There!" she said with an effort at levity. "I shouldn't do that. It's a bad habit for an efficient secretary to have."

"But when the receptive executive," rallied Bob, "is in jail—"

"Bob! I've done everything you told me to do. I came to see you about something else, something that may be urgent. The Decker girl wanted to come herself, but she was afraid—thought they wouldn't let her see you, perhaps, or would suspect something."

"The Decker girl? Suspect what?"

"I don't understand the message. She seems all cut up about it—frightened to death. She said I was to tell you about it, and ask you what she should do."

"About what?" pressed Bob.

"Her brother is in town. She saw him on the street this afternoon. She said he acted awfully strangely when she caught up with him—he warned her to go away and not let herself be seen with him, and to tell nobody she had seen him. But she said she just had to get word to you, and ask you what to do."

"Not so loud—whisper!" Aitken looked around speculatively. There was no person nearer than the constable outside the door, but Bob thought suddenly of dictographs. There was no place in the bare room, he concluded, that could harbor one.

No place but the ordinary brass lighting fixture on the wall, and Aitken did not think of that.

There was a microphone behind it, and Inspector Laval and a uniformed stenographer were listening quietly through headsets, in his office.

Bob told himself there was nothing to fear from listeners, but something about the hollow, resonant acoustical properties of the uncarpeted visitors' room made him cautious. He beckoned Helen to the single barred window, where a cacophony of sounds rose from the street below. He resumed in a tone she could hardly hear:

"This is safer. Tell the Decker girl I said to sit tight and say nothing."

"Yes, Bob. But why all the mystery and secrecy about her brother? Hasn't he a right to be in Montreal?"

"I can't tell you now, dear. It's too long a story, and they'll be sending to tell us the time's up, before long. It's all right. There's nothing to worry about. The Decker girl is alarmed over a trifle. Listen, dear." He took a leather key container from his pocket. "While you are here I want to give you my keys, some of Mr. Milburn's, too. One, in particular, is a key to a mail drawer at the general post-office in New York—the one on Eighth avenue, you know. It's a box Mr. Milburn and I used occasionally. There may be something in it, though I don't particularly expect anything."

"And you want me to take care of the key?"

"Yes. They probably will permit you to go back to New York very soon, if you wish. I think you ought to go, Helen. Mr. Dalbey says the people of my firm are on their ears about a lot of things you or I could set straight for them. Somebody ought to see young Herbert Milburn, too, when he gets in from Denver; somebody, I mean, who was close to his father. The funeral, I understand, is to be day after tomorrow—that's Friday, isn't it?"

"All right, Bob. I'll go back if they'll let me—and if you want me to. But after I've done all I can there I'll return to Montreal, whether you want me to or not. I've got to be here near you."

He asked her what she knew of the letter Wilks professed to have posted, and she declared she knew nothing about it.

He was outlining briefly some of the matters that would require attention in New York, when their whispered conversation was interrupted by a rapping at the door. Bob kissed her quickly.

"Time's up," said the constable, sticking his head in.

Learning that Laval was in his office, Helen went to him at once to ask his permission to go to New York. The Inspector listened gravely to her reasons for wishing to go, and decided:

"Very well, if you will give us your agreement in writing to return when you are needed and to waive extradition in the event we find it necessary to force you to return."

"You will not have to force me to return," protested Helen sweetly, and the Inspector believed her.

"If you are going tonight," suggested Laval, "you may get reservations on the Express, at eight-thirty. Shall I have them made for you?"

"You are so kind, Inspector.

The kind inspector had his reasons. When he, personally, had made reservations for her on the eight-thirty Express and had told her goodbye, he summoned Sergeant Detective Thwaite.

"I want Detective Lennox," he said after explaining, "to shadow this young woman to New York, to keep an eye on her activities there. Later I may send you, too, to assist this man Moode at the New York end. For the present I need you here. I want you to find Miss Lotus Decker's brother."

Thwaite looked perturbed. "It is hard to believe that little girl is mixed up in this mess," he declared.

"It's hard to believe anything just now. The Decker girl, like our friend Aitken, is withholding facts. Get them out of her, by whatever methods you choose."

"Yes, sir, I'll do my best." Thwaite hesitated. "If you want her followed, though, I suggest you put Ansley or somebody else on that part of it. She knows me too well, you see."

"Very well. Ansley, then, for the shadowing."

In accordance with this program, while Detective
Lennox boarded the eight-thirty train on which Moode,
the private sleuth, and Helen Eastwick had made their
reservations for New York, Sergeant Detective Bill
Thwaite was escorting Lotus Decker to the talkies. That
was one pleasant way of getting into her confidence.

He had called upon her at the hotel in his official
capacity, telling her that he just wanted to have a talk
with her. And since there didn't seem to be any highly
comfortable place where they could confer in private, he
had suggested that they go to the pictures and get a bite
to eat afterward.

"Good," said Lotus fervently. "You've got the nicest
police force in this man's town I ever went up against—
not, of course, that I've ever gone up against one before.
I've just been yearning," she added expressively, "for
some big, manly, blue-eyed shoulder to weep on. I'm
depressed to death, Mr. Thwaite."

"You're nothing but a kid," said Thwaite sympathetically. "It's a shame you had to get caught in this mix-
up."

"It's just half-past awful! It goes to show a girl ought
to mind her mommer—sometimes."

Lotus, rather than the detective, did the pumping
as they sallied forth for a glimpse of Montreal's lesser
night life.

"What do you think?" she asked him anxiously. "Who
do they think killed poor Mr. Milburn? They don't really believe Mr. Aitken had anything to do with it, do
they?"

"He had more to do with it than he's willing to tell
us," asserted Thwaite. "How about the others—Miss
Dustin and Laith; George Heston and his wife—how are
they taking it? Have you heard them express any opinion?"

Helen and Moode Go to New York; Lotus to the Movies and Sergeant Montigny to the Scene of the Crime

Montigny Sprang to the Rear Platform, Followed by Sims, the Electrician. "What is it?" He Shouted. "Murder!" Replied the Constable. "Another one of this outfit. The Inspector is calling you!"

"No. Dot's been in her room giving a correct imitation of a nervous breakdown all afternoon. The doctor said she had to be kept awfully quiet, and I was a little girl scout elected to keep her that way. Imagine! Gee, I was exhausted when you came around to play the good Samaritan."

"Have much trouble with her?"

"Did I! She's terribly cut up, Mr. Thwaite. She really was crazy about J. P. Milburn—even if they did have a knock-down and drag-out scrap last night."

"Yes. I heard something about that. What were they fussing about?"

"Oh, I don't know. Everything and nothing. All I know is that it was hot and heavy enough to make Dot lock herself in her stateroom and not say a word to anybody. When I asked her about it afterwards she was right in the middle of a couple hysterics, and wouldn't tell me."

"Does she know," asked Thwaite, eyeing Lotus shrewdly, "that Mr. Milburn—listen, I shouldn't tell you this; it's official stuff and if it goes any further it'll get us both in trouble. Can you keep a secret?"

"Can I! Why, the Sphinx is my blood-uncle. Just try me. If I tell it to a soul I hope you'll choke me."

"All right. Does Miss Dustin know Mr. Milburn left her one hundred thousand dollars in his will?"

Lotus stopped in her tracks and registered superlative amazement.

"Quit your kidding! He didn't."

"Remember, it's graveyard. It comes through his lawyers in New York. It's not supposed to be made public until the will is officially filed."

"I can't believe it. Why, Dot told me several times that Mr. Milburn said it wouldn't do any good for him to try to remember her handsomely in his will, because his wife and sons were sure to contest it—claim 'undue influence' and everything else."

"Then she doesn't expect it?"

"She's certainly always told me that she never expected anything. She said the only thing she would ever get out of J. P.—or would ever want—would be what he gave her when he was alive. She said she just didn't like to think about dead people's money."

"Hm! How long have you been with Miss Dustin and her friends—when did you get acquainted with them?"

Lotus told him how she had run away from home virtually, to break into the show world of Broadway; how, after repeated rounds of the agencies she had met George Heston, his wife, and through them Dorothea Dustin, who had taken a liking to her and helped to get her into the Hilarities.

"Hm; took you around everywhere with her, didn't she? Took you to parties, showed you off?"

"Why, how do you mean, Mr. Thwaite?"

"Listen, Gypsy—that's what they call you, isn't it?— don't you know this hard-boiled Broadway star wasn't doing that for pure friendliness—don't you know she was using you for a purpose?"

"What purpose?" demanded Lotus petulantly. "What makes you talk like this to me?"

"I'm talking to you like your Uncle Gizeh, the Sphinx. Don't let it go any further. I'm telling you this Dustin woman is not your friend. She's a bad egg, a grafter, the people she's been lined up with are crooks. And she was just using you to parade around as an innocent little friend of hers, of a fine old Baltimore family—just to show what decent, nice people she could go with. I'm telling you this for your own good, Gypsy. I like you a lot."

"Thanks for the buggy-ride. But you don't have to use the whip on me. You don't have to tell me what a crook I am."

"I'm not. I'm telling you what a crook you aren't. Your parents didn't want you to be a show girl, did they?"

"My parent. Father isn't living." Lotus gulped hard.

"Just your mother?"

"I've got a big brother. Big is right, too. He's two feet higher'n I am, and he's got a voice like a bull."

"What does he do?" asked Thwaite casually.

"Travels. For a seed house. Can you imagine! He's a big jonquil and canary food man, from Baltimore."

"Yeah? See him much?"

"Sure. He makes New York pretty often. He's out somewhere around Chicago, now." Lotus' lip trembled. "Got an awfully big territory—you have to go a long way to sell a lot of seeds. They make 'em so little, you know."

"It's a fact!"

Thwaite said nothing more on the subject, for the present. In fact he avoided entirely the topic of Milburn's death during the remainder of the evening, for he took Lotus to Gondolfi's after the picture show, and they danced. Detective Ansley, meanwhile, was outside cursing roundly at the unequal justice that decreed he should play this hangdog role while another beefy front-office man went skylarking with a pretty show girl.

Still another detective concerned with the Milburn case was improving his evening hours, meanwhile, in pleasant feminine company.

This was Detective Moode, who, strolling through the all-Pullman New York Express, encountered Helen Eastwick.

"Hey, Miss Helen!" exclaimed Moode. "I didn't know you was aboard. How'd they happen to let you go?"

"Oh, I have influence in high places," said Helen sagely. "Won't you sit down, Mr. Moode?"

The porter had not begun to make down the berths until the American customs and immigration inspectors had come through on their usual mission of investigation and delay at the border. They had held up the train for quite a time as was frequently the case, at Rouses Point, the first American town. Helen, wearily awaiting the opportunity to go to bed, was glad to have Moode to talk to her.

She explained to him why Inspector Laval had let her go.

"Well, listen," said Moode, lowering his voice as he glanced over his shoulder, "don't think they trust you so easy. Those guys don't trust nobody. There's a Montreal bull on the train following you right now, or I'm a Chinaman!"

"What's that! Are you sure, Mr. Moode?"

"A detective from Montreal, on this car. I'm almost sure he's a guy I saw around headquarters there. He's back in the smoker now—he knows there's no chance for you to get away."

"How perfectly delightful and thrilling," murmured Helen. "I've never had a detective shadow me before. I do hope you're not mistaken, Mr. Moode."

"Want to know how to shake him?"

"How—if I wanted to?"

"Get off the train when it stops at Hundred and Twenty-fift' street—make like you're going all the way to Grand Central, see, but drop off at Hundred Twenty-fift' instead." Moode chuckled. "I'd just like to see this Canadian hick stewin' around when he finds he's lost you!" He turned. "There he is now, three seats back."

Helen laughed. "I see, but I don't want to. I think it's too gorgeous for words to have a real live detective

following me. I'm glad you told me. I'll be a perfect
saint. I won't even smoke a cigarette."

They talked for a time about the Milburn case.
Moode, whatever had been his earlier convictions, declared for present company that he thought it was a
dirty shame they were holding Bob Aitken.

"Why, he's no guiltier than you or me," grumbled
Moode disgustedly. "But it's just the way those smart
Canuck cops do business—just because he won't tell
them all his business and Mr. Milburn's, too, they think
they'll sweat it out of 'im."

"Of course it's ridiculous," agreed Helen. "Haven't
they any clues at all—any idea who really was guilty?"

Moode grunted. "Outside job. That's a cinch. Some
slick bird, too, if you ask me. He's a thousand miles
away, by now. And I'll bet that Frog with the black
whiskers—what's his name, Montigny?—is still snoopin'
around with a magnifying glass lookin' for clues."

Detective Moode was right in his surmise concerning Sergeant Detective Pierre Montigny's renewal of his
search for incriminating minutiae.

Montigny had revisited the private car Dorothea late
in the afternoon, but had waited in vain for the electrician who had promised advice concerning the replace-
ment of the batteries. All the shops were closed and it
was difficult to get another man, but Montigny presently cornered one who was at home for his evening meal,
and who agreed to come to the car at eight o'clock.

The electrician, whose name was Sims, that tested
the batteries and pronounced them officially weak.

"Anything else you wanted me to check over for you,
Inspector?"

"The annunciator," said Montigny. "Set it right. It has
been disconnected in some way; and the porter is in jail."

Sims opened the annunciator box and viewed it critically. "Slick outfit, all right," he asserted. "All different-colored wires to make it easier to trace trouble if a bell didn't ring."

"Mm! Yes, I see."

"But your trouble's not here in the box. It's disconnected at the transformer. In a closet around somewhere, I suppose."

Sims found the transformer and plugged it in. He tried several buttons and the porter's bell gave forth a loud and distinct jangling.

Sims cleared off the calls and gave the car an admiring general inspection. "Must be terrible," he murmured, "to have more money than you can spend."

Dot Dustin's magnificent radio in the lounge—it had been Milburn's gift to her—engaged the electrician particularly, for his shop sold radios.

"Swell set," he vouchsafed switching it on. "AC electric. Lights up, all right, but not enough current with those weak batteries. Usually hooked in with the train circuit. Maybe when you get new batteries it will play for you, Sergeant."

"It will not play for me," said Montigny grimly. "I got enough radio at home. My boy keeps it going day and night. Besides, there will be other things to do here."

There were, at once.

One of the constables outside rapped sharply with his baton on the side of the car, and called the Sergeant's name.

Montigny sprang to the platform, shouting, "What is it?"

"Murder!" bellowed the constable. "Another one of this outfit. Inspector's calling you."

Montigny raced for the telephone.

"You, Pierre? Come at once to the Strathcona Hotel. Another killing on our hands."

"Who, Inspector?" rasped Montigny.

"Heston. George Heston. They've just found him strangled to death in his room."

At fifteen minutes to nine o'clock Wednesday night the girl at the telephone exchange of the Strathcona Hotel had received and recorded a call from Room 912, the room occupied by George Heston and his wife.

Heston had not used the telephone frequently and the operator on duty was not familiar with his voice. But she had assumed that it was he. It was a man with a deep bass voice, and all he had said was:

"Send up a boy, please."

The page had gone up to Room 912 approximately three minute later. He had knocked at the door and, receiving no response, he had tried the knob and found the door unlocked.

Entering the room he had faced a terrifying sight. George Heston lay dead on the floor, his staring eyes and swollen tongue protruding from his head. He had been choked to death, and in the opinion of the house physician had expired only a few minutes before the discovery of his body.

There was no evidence of a struggle. Apparently a far more powerful man than Heston, who was underweight and weakened by dissipation, had throttled him before he could make an outcry. The bruises on the throat indicated that the assailant had attacked him from the front. There was no clue of any description.

Heston's wife and Perry Laith had been in Dorothea Dustin's room on the seventh floor, they said, chatting with her and trying to cheer her up. The fast-traveling

news of Heston's murder had thrown Dot anew into
paroxysms of hysteria. Her doctor said it was imperative that she be kept quiet, and it seemed useless for the
officers to question her. The physician administered
bromides, however, and Dot presently became calm
enough to give the little information she had. She cor-
roborated the statements of Mrs. Heston and Perry
Laith, but beyond that she knew nothing.

The Strathcona Hotel did not employ floor clerks,
and no one was found who could testify to seeing any
person enter or leave Heston's room. Occupants of the
room across the hall had heard nothing out of the ordinary.

Clara Heston had left her husband at eight o'clock,
Perry Laith having urged her to come with him and
keep Dot Dustin company. Heston had said he had a
headache and intended to retire early. The two elevator
operators were confident that no passenger had entered
or left either car at the ninth floor for the period of
fifteen or twenty minutes prior to the discovery of the
body. They had remarked this fact because there had
been so many calls from the eighth and tenth floors,
both of which been reserved for delegates attending a
convention at the Strathcona and the elevators were
crowded with these men. When inquiry was made from
the rostrum of the convention hall no delegate could
testify usefully to having been stranger on these floors,
for they were all strangers to each other. Some wore
badges and others did not.

Moode Is Bound for New York and Bob Is Still in Jail When the Second Murder Is Committed

There was an expression of pained soberness on Thwaite's face as he ushered Lotus into Laval's office. The girl seemed speechless with apprehension. "Take that chair, Miss Decker," said Laval, not unkindly

8

Clara Heston, unlike the Dustin girl, did not lose control of herself. On the contrary she was preternaturally calm, though showing the evidences of great strain. She had lost her previous manner of acting a role, for the second nearer tragedy had shocked her into naturalness.

The officers interviewed her in the room adjoining the one where Heston's body lay.

"It is simply too terrible to believe!" she kept repeating to Laval and Montigny in an awe-stricken voice. "George did not have an enemy in the world—not an enemy in the world."

"Who was the last person, to your knowledge, who talked to him?" asked Laval.

"Why—" Clara hesitated, "he was alone in his room most of the afternoon; I went to do some shopping. I don't recall anybody particularly who talked to him. We saw the others of our party in the dining room downstairs at lunch time. We didn't go down for dinner. George said he felt badly and we had dinner served in the room, about six o'clock. Mr. Moode was around early in the afternoon to talk to all of us, but I don't know of anybody else. Inspector, I'm scared! It looks like the work of a madman!"

Clara buried her face in her hands and her body shook with sobs, though she could not cry.

Laval was sympathetic, but he continued to question her until he had satisfied himself that she knew nothing that could lend the remotest explanation to the crime.

Montigny and an assistant, examining every square foot of surface area in the room where Heston had been killed, could find absolutely nothing. Montigny had been hopeful of finger-prints on the door-knobs or the telephone receiver, but he was disappointed.

"Wiped clean," he muttered. "This killer knows the business, Inspector."

"And he is confident—worse than that, foolhardy—like the slayer of Milburn."

"It is the same man, Inspector."

"You are convinced of that, Pierre?"

Montigny nodded slowly. "I feel that it is so. In both cases a big man, whose fingers could span two octaves on the piano—or the windpipe! In both cases, seemingly, a man with a deep bass voice, who insists on using it for the benefit of witnesses when he has completed his crime."

"And a man, I should say," added Laval, "who was well known to George Heston, perhaps even friendly. The attack was from the front, yet there were people in the room across the hall who heard no outcry. He must have been talking inoffensively with Heston before he attacked him."

"It is curious," murmured Montigny. "Very, very curious. No trace of a motive."

"The obvious guess would be that he knew something about the other crime—that it was dangerous to the killer for Heston to continue living."

"Heston, you thought, was not too drunk last night?"

"He thought he needed make-up this morning, to heighten the illusion. He seems to have gone to bed in a state of exaggerated inebriety last night—even requiring someone to help him into his berth—yet the others could give us no history of Heston as a drunkard! I daresay he had knowledge of what was going to happen to J. P. Milburn, and went to considerable pains to provide himself with an alibi."

"But if Heston had been a party to the plot, or had guilty knowledge of it, would he have joined with his wife, as he evidently did, in a palpable scheme to blackmail Milburn?"

"Why not, Pierre? An added proof of his innocence. If he planned—to bleed Milburn in an extortion conspiracy, he would not wish to have him killed during the night, would he? Naturally not. His threats to kill Milburn 'in the way it would hurt' was likewise a gesture of innocence, rather than guilt. Public threateners do not kill, as a rule."

"And his wife—do you suppose she was in on the murder plot, too?"

"Personally I do not think so. But if she was," added Laval significantly, "she may be—next!"

Montigny stroked his mustache. "If Heston was a party to the killing of Milburn, Inspector, then it seems to follow that the actual killer was someone on the car—and all out evidence points the other way."

"Not necessarily someone on the car, Pierre. Heston might have had knowledge of a plan to board the car at Rouses Point or St. Johns—an outsider who had inside information."

"But the killing was so neatly timed, Inspector; the bell-ringing alibi so smoothly worked. The use of the air pistol as a weapon—the distance from which Milburn was shot—everything seems to argue against the intruder from the back platform. And yet—" Montigny paused thoughtfully. "At least we are sure of one thing, Inspector—if the slayer of Milburn killed Heston also, then it was not the lawyer Aitken and it was not the porter Wilks. Both are in jail."

Laval shrugged. "I have not suspected either—of actually committing murder. Of withholding and disguising the truth? Yes. Of Aitken as an accessory? Perhaps. But I am going to release the negro tomorrow and let him return to the car—your car, I had better say. He may be of some use waiting on you."

"And the lawyer?"

"I am continuing to hold Aitken, largely because Berthier desires it. But the Captain seems to have bequeathed us the entire case, now."

Montigny grinned ruefully. "If the case is ours, we have done little to deserve it—at least I have done nothing."

"You have done well, Pierre. And you are just beginning. No man so careless of his safety as this murderer can escape us long."

Montigny smiled grimly. "I think myself that he will use his bass voice once too often. He seems to be making sport of us. Evidently after telephoning to the operator from Heston's room he stepped down to the eighth door, mingled with the convention delegates there and escaped unobserved."

"Or walked down the service stairs. At any rate, the point is, he escaped. And we can't dispute that point."

They questioned Perry Laith, but entirely without result. The former dancer was obviously stunned and frightened by the inexplicable death of his friend Heston, for he said they had been intimate for years. Heston's acquaintances in New York, he asserted, had been none but law-abiding theatrical people, and there was no person in the world known to Laith who had a serious grievance against Heston.

"It's got me shaky, Inspector," declared Laith, visibly trembling. "It looks like a maniac running loose who has got it in for all of us. That crank who wrote that letter—" Laith stared in affright, as though awed by the thought.

"If such a crank killed Milburn, said Laval quietly, "with the idea that he was ridding the world of a menace, why should he also wish to destroy George Heston?"

"I don't know, sir," faltered Laith. "Unless—"

"Unless what?"

"Unless he felt that poor George had been responsible for making these girls acquainted with Mr. Milburn—like Dot and Lotus."

Laval considered the point without great interest. "Rather farfetched assumption, I am afraid. Do you know anybody in New York, Mr. Laith, who owns a Glickenswerfer typewriter?"

"What kind is that, sir?" asked Laith blankly.

Laval eyed him narrowly. "If you do not know, it does not matter. That will be all for tonight, Mr. Laith."

As Laval and Montigny were leaving the hotel they encountered Sergeant Detective Thwaite and the fair young person he had been so pleasantly investigating. Thwaite turned beet-red upon thus unexpectedly meeting his superior, but Laval's peremptory news swiftly swept away all other concerns. Laval took him aside and questioned him regarding his meagre findings.

"Bring the girl to headquarters," ordered the Inspector. "I can talk to her more freely there."

At his office Laval found a message from Detective Moode, who had telephoned from Bonaventure Station just before his train left at eight-thirty. He had wanted to ask somebody to do him a favor. Instead of stopping at a hotel, Moode had engaged an inexpensive room at a boarding house, and in his hurry to get off he had forgotten to lock the door. He believed he had left the key in the lock. Would Inspector Laval send somebody around to lock up for him? He was afraid somebody might steal his other pair of pants.

"That clown!" muttered Laval, passing the memorandum to Montigny, who read and pocketed it. "He thinks I have nothing more important to do than to safeguard his extra pants."

"I shall perform the service for him if you like," volunteered Montigny, grinning.

"Very well. I am ready now for the Decker girl."

There was an expression of pained soberness on Thwaite's face as he ushered Lotus in. The girl seemed speechless with apprehension. Every vestige of color had left her face, and her sloe-black eyes contrasted almost painfully with the pallor of her cheeks.

"Take that chair, Miss Decker," said Laval, not unkindly. "I do not wish to frighten you with the things I am going to ask you, but I want you to tell me the truth, and nothing but the truth."

"Yes, sir," said Lotus, almost inaudibly.

"Where is your brother?" demanded Laval abruptly.

Lotus cast a despairing glance at Thwaite, at Montigny, and looked pleadingly again at Laval.

"You mean my brother—Warren?" she evaded desperately.

"Yes."

"Why. he was in Chi-Chicago—"

"The truth, Miss Decker," said Laval sternly. "He is in Montreal. Why did he try to avoid you when you met him on the street? Why did he ask you to say nothing to anybody about having seen him in Montreal?"

"Oh, oh, oh!" cried Lotus, and gave vent to a sudden fury of tears. "You can't trust anybody, you can't trust anybody! That lying, double-crossing Eastwick woman—"

"Miss Eastwick told us nothing," said Laval sharply. "What makes you think she did!"

"Then Mr. Aitken—surely it wasn't Mr. Aitken?" sobbed Lotus,

"What leads you to think Mr. Aitken told us?"

Lotus opened her lips to speak and halted as though stricken by a terrifying thought. "Have they—have you—has my brother been arrested?" she moaned.

"I am asking the questions," Laval rebuked her. "Now tell me everything about it, Miss Decker. And don't deviate from the truth, for what we know may contradict you."

Lotus made ineffectual dabs at her tear-swollen eyes and told him everything that she had confided to Bob Aitken on the train. "I wasn't really concealing anything, Inspector," she pleaded. "I intended to tell you if you should ask me about it, but not just to bring up suspicions against my brother that might not have anything to them, really."

"Your brother threatened to make trouble, did he—for you or Mr. Milburn?"

"For me and—Mr. Milburn both," faltered Lotus. "He said I was under age, and I didn't have any right going on this trip without my mother's consent, thought I hadn't given her a chance to forbid it, and that Mr. Milburn could be prosecuted for 'impairing the morals of a minor,' he called it."

"Did he go to Mr. Milburn with these complaints?"

"No, sir. He couldn't get to him. Mr. Milburn wouldn't talk to anybody he didn't know, or who wouldn't state his business beforehand. So that made Warren madder, and he told me if I went on this trip he was going to make trouble."

"And you think—he did?"

"Oh, no, no, no, Inspector," the girl cried frantically. "My brother wouldn't—he couldn't—he couldn't possibly do anything like—like what has happened!"

"Do you know what a Glickenswerfer typewriter is like?" Laval went on relentlessly.

"I know what you're asking that question for," sobbed Lotus, "and it isn't so—he didn't write that letter—he didn't, I tell you!"

"What letter?"

"You know the letter I mean, Inspector—the one that threatened Mr. Milburn."

"Oh, you knew all about that, too, did you?"

"Yes, sir, we all knew. Mr. Milburn told Dot. He seemed to think it was a great joke."

"Your brother did not own such a typewriter?"

"He didn't own any kind, sir. He couldn't use one. I gave him a portable for a Christmas present and he pecked on it a while and said he'd have to pass it on to somebody else, because he would never have time to practice enough to learn to use it, and all the letters and reports he wrote, anyway, he would have done for him by public stenographers."

"Hm! Describe your brother, Miss Decker."

Lotus did so, hesitantly. "Why, he's tall, Inspector, he's six feet. He's got brown hair, not as dark as mine, and brown eyes."

"Is he nervous?" put in Laval, with a glance at Montigny.

"Why, yes, sir, I suppose you'd say he was," admitted Lotus with increasing uneasiness. "Rather high-strung."

"What kind of speaking voice has he—a shrill voice, would you say?"

"No, sir. A deep voice; not at all high."

"Is he inclined to be religious?"

Lotus shook her head wonderingly. "Why, no, sir. He goes to church once in a while with mother, but he has never joined. But he's a good man, Inspector," she added with fresh tears, "and kind to everyone. He never did anyone any harm in all his life. He couldn't have had anything to do with this—these terrible things."

"Hm! Very well, Miss Decker, if that is so I want you to help us find your brother. If you see him or hear from him I want you to persuade him to come to me at once."

"Then you haven't," questioned Lotus with ill-concealed relief, "that is, he hasn't—been arrested?"

"No. But he will be, Miss Decker. He is in Montreal and he can not possibly get out. Every road, every train, is watched. It will be only a matter of time. That is why it will be best for him, and for all concerned, if he causes us as little trouble as possible. Now you may go back to your hotel."

Sergeant Thwaite spoke to Laval privately, clearing his throat. "If you have no objection, Inspector, I think I'd better see her to the hotel. She may need—you know—protection. We can't tell what's going to happen next in this bloody business."

Laval studied him shrewdly. "Then you had better do that," he said with twinkling eyes. "And when you have the leisure you may tell me more of what you learned from her this evening."

"Yes, sir," said Thwaite sheepishly. "But you've heard it all. She's made a clean breast of everything."

A caller awaited Laval in the outer office, an inspector of the immigration service named Lemaire.

"The Senior Inspector thought I ought to come and tell you about this, late as it is, sir," said Lemaire. "I am afraid we rather balled things up for you today—very early this morning, I mean—down at St. Johns."

"Yes. In what way?"

"Why, we just had a chance to talk it over when I saw the Senior Inspector here tonight. It looks like we helped a chap to escape—a fellow the provincial police were looking for, at St. Johns."

"What's that!" barked Laval.

"Why, I'll tell you how it was, Inspector. You see, there were two of us, Inspector Cartwright and myself, working that train this fellow Milburn's car was attached to. Well, as a rule I get off at St. Johns to see to the deportation of immigrants who are not allowed to enter, and Cartwright goes on to Montreal. I did this last night; we had a bunch to deport on the first train back across the border. Well, I checked up the slips and deportation orders Cartwright had turned over to me, and there was one fellow there in the bunch at the station that I didn't have a deportation order for—"

"And you deported him!" cut in Laval. "Is that what you did?"

The inspector grinned foolishly. "Yes, sir, I'm afraid that's what I did. He said his name was Beckwith, and he was going to Montreal to get a job, and the other inspector had put him off with the rest, because he didn't have the required sum of money on him, in cash, to insure him against becoming a public charge."

"Yes?"

"Well, I figured I'd lost or misplaced the deportation order somehow in the rush, and the fellow didn't raise much kick against being deported, so the safest thing for me to do was to go on and ship him out with the rest."

"And you did, eh—escorted this fugitive to Rouses Point, with a guard of honor?"

"Yes, sir," said the immigration man with a wry grin.

"While the provincial police were looking all over St. Johns for him!"

"He might have been the man, Inspector. I'm quite afraid he was.'

"Was he a tall man?"

"Yes, sir. Six feet, I'd say, and he'd weigh about a hundred and eighty-five."

"Did he appear nervous?"

"Well, yes, sir, rather fidgety."

"And he spoke in a high, piping sort of voice?"

"No, sir." The inspector brightened. "He did not. He had a deep, rumbling sort of voice. That was the first thing you noticed about him."

"My, my!" said Laval—it was his favorite expletive. "And at Rouses Point he could have caught a morning train into Montreal, told another inspector that he was a traveling salesman going to Canada for a few days, and passed in without the slightest difficulty."

"Yes, sir, he could have done that," admitted the immigration inspector. "That is, if he knew the ropes."

"He knew the ropes," muttered Laval. "He knew the ropes!"

Had Helen Eastwick elected to leave the Express at One Hundred and Twenty-fifth street upon its arrival Thursday morning she would not have been so free of surveillance as Moode had playfully suggested.

When the train drew into this station at twelve minutes after six, Detective Barstow of the New York force was waiting on the platform. No one of Helen's description having left the train, Barstow swung aboard as it departed, and made his way with the help of a Pullman conductor to the space occupied by Detective Lennox, who was dressing.

"We had a ring from Montreal," explained Barstow. "They thought you might need help. You needn't worry about this frail of yours. I'm to take her off your hands."

"I'm glad enough to hear that," said Lennox with relief. "I'm going to have my hands full enough, with all the things the Chief gave me to do here."

"Another murder in Montreal last night, eh?" observed Barstow, tapping a newspaper he had. "Did you hear about it before you left?"

"No!" exclaimed Lennox. "Who?"

Barstow told him, and gave him the newspaper. Lennox scanned it eagerly.

"Say, I just missed that one, didn't I? It must have happened ten or fifteen minutes after we left. Well, I'll be blowed!"

The train pulled into Grand Central Station and Barstow left him.

Helen Eastwick, for all her pronouncement of the thrill it might have given her, was not a little relieved to find that the man Moode had pointed out as her shadower did not seem even slightly interested in her, now that they were in New York. It was Detective Barstow instead who followed her and Moode—for they took the same taxi—to 1440 Broadway, where Moode's agency had its offices, and thence to an apartment house on West End avenue in the Seventies, where Helen lived. Detective Lennox of Montreal, meanwhile, had breakfasted and put in a long-distance call for Inspector Laval. He wanted to be sure he was doing right in relinquishing his quarry to the Nev York operative.

"Yes, it's quite all right," Laval told him. "I asked their help because I thought you would have too much to do. You are not to depend on a certain private detective of our acquaintance. They haven't much confidence in him there—he was on the force at one time but resigned by unanimous consent. His record is all right except that he is regarded as somewhat stupid."

"He's thick enough with this Miss—the secretary," remarked Lennox, and told his superior of their apparent friendliness on the train.

"Hm! Perhaps they are plotting together to solve the mystery. I hope so. And I hope you uncover something, Lennox."

He discussed the Heston case briefly, and added further instructions. Lennox reflected ruefully that he had nothing to do, now, but get in touch with detective headquarters, search Milburn's residence in New York, interview his lawyers, check up on the movements of Warren Decker, look up the antecedents of the Hestons, Dot Dustin and Perry Laith. and get back to Montreal in a hurry with something useful.

His first move obviously was to make contact with headquarters, and accordingly he spent an hour closeted then with Inspector McEniry, a broad, big-fisted, hard-eyed policeman of the old school.

Moode, he was told, had already been there. The private detective and bodyguard of the late Mr. Milburn had presented himself, McEniry said, as a sort of official representative of Inspector Laval of Montreal, whereas Laval had made it clear privately to the New York police that he had sent Moode there principally to get rid of him.

"So I passed the buck," said McEniry with a grin, "on to Baltimore. I sent him down there to look into the Decker situation. I'm sorry I did, now, though. If it's possible to ball things up that boob will do it. Gad, I never saw such slues of detectives, working on one case. Milburn's son has hired a couple, and yesterday the insurance investigators washed in on us."

"Insurance?" queried Lennox.

"Sure. The man's policies ran up four, five, six hundred thousand dollars. No drop in the bucket. And some of them were taken out during the past year. That's what the insurance boys are het up about, mainly."

"Anything wrong with them, you mean?"

"No, I don't mean that exactly, Lennox. But the situation is this. Most of them had the double indemnity for accidental death. All of them, of course, had the suicide clause."

"Suicide?" repeated Lennox. "Are the insurance people working on that theory?"

"Well, they'd like to prove it. The standard life insurance policy is void, as you know, if the bozo commits suicide within one year of its issuance. Some of Milburn's insurance, as I told you, was taken out within the past year—before this illness of his showed up. Now, if Milburn committed suicide the companies pay nothing—not a red cent—on those policies. But if he was murdered then it would be classed as 'accidental death'—and the insurance lads would pay twice the face value of such policies. Do you wonder they are standing on their ears?"

"But how could anybody have the face to call it 'suicide'," protested Lennox, "with this second killing last night?"

McEniry smiled grimly. "You'll have to show a connection between the crimes—a whole lot more definite connection than just some bird with a big voice calling down on the telephone."

"What do you think, Inspector?"

"Think? How can I think, five or six hundred miles away like this? It's you boys who've got to do the heavy beanwork. I'm going to help you all I can, of course, at this end. What do you want me to do next?"

"These insurance policies," said Lennox, "who were the beneficiaries?"

"Milburn's sons, so far. Something new may turn up. The insurance folks act cagy—they know something we don't know. We've gone through Milburn's boxes at the bank, but we haven't searched his offices and his house yet, the Manhattan place or the one on Long Island, either. I believe he made over the summer place to his wife. Moode wanted to do these things today, but I sent him about his business and waited for you. We've got the houses under guard, of course; his offices, too. His lawyers seem willing to help all they can, though they're red-headed over you chaps locking up one of the firm. Tell me the low-down on this fellow Aitken. What have you got on him?"

Lennox told him all the lowdown he knew about Aitken and the Inspector grunted reflectively. "Well, thirty days is a long time to wait for important information. But I guess you're doing all you can to twist the facts from him."

They agreed that an examination of all records at Milburn's offices was the first step indicated, and this would take most of the afternoon.

"I suggest you get in touch with Milburn's lawyers," said McEniry. "We ought to have their help. This Miss Eastwick would be useful, too. I'll call them up and make a date for you."

Mr. Colton, of Donwood, Colton & Donwood, said he could see Mr. Lennox at two o'clock, and that he would try to have Miss Eastwick present at the same time.

The remainder of the morning Lennox spent looking up the employers of Warren Decker. There were seventy-seven firms of seedsmen having headquarters in New York, but by canvassing the better-known establishments first Lennox registered success on his ninth telephone call. Graves & Company of Baltimore employed Warren Decker as a salesman, traveling out of New York, and the sales manager, Mr. Landers, volunteered readily enough the information that Decker was in Chicago, Minneapolis or thereabouts. His weekly report had come in from Chicago several days before, and he would not be heard from again until next week.

Lennox followed this up with a personal call on Mr. Landers, a brisk gentleman who received everybody with the practiced courtesy of the well-met salesman. Having accepted Lennox at first as a mere out-of-town friend of Decker's who was looking him up, Landers presently found his suspicions aroused by searching questions. Lennox saw the time had arrived to disclose his identity.

"Montreal!" exclaimed the manager. "Say, I've been wondering about that. Is the Milburn murder case—this Decker girl! Is that the point? Is she kin to our Decker?"

"Brother," said Lennox.

"And is he mixed up in it—suspected—"

"Oh, no, nothing of that sort. We're merely trying to find him it order to check up on the girl, don't you see? What kind of chap is he? Tell me what you know about him."

The sales manager gave Decker an excellent name. He said Lotus' brother was the ablest and most successful salesman in the firm's employ, an indefatigable worker, a "live wire who sizzled all the time," sober, industrious, steady, reliable; had never been in trouble to their knowledge.

"But," said Landers, "of course that may not mean anything. A lot of fellows lead double lives."

"Right," agreed Lennox, thanking him. "Sometimes the smugger the crookeder."

The Milburn-Heston murder case, reflected Lennox as he ate his lunch, was not clearing up so rapidly at the New York end as he might have wished.

At two o'clock Lennox was ensconced in a luxurious leather armchair in the waiting room of the firm of Donwood, Colton & Donwood. These swell lawyers made you wait, all right, but they took pains to see that you were comfortable as possible while you tarried. The waiting room, thought Lennox, was furnished like a millionaire's club in the movies. In breeze-inviting windows overlooked the bay from the nineteenth story of an office building.

Lennox was tracing the course of tireless ferries to and from the Jersey shore, and ruminating perplexedly on the Milburn mystery, when Helen Eastwick came in. The detective heard her give her name to the sedate and gray-haired office boy.

Lennox turned and she recognized him, smiling. He arose to introduce himself.

"I already know you," said Held with a laugh. "I saw you on the train. You see I'm getting to be a detective myself."

"You are," acknowledged Lennox, "and so is Mr. Moode."

Helen chuckled. "Mr. Moode? Where is he? I haven't seen him since I dropped him out of a taxi cab this morning."

Lennox told her Moode had been sent on an assignment out of town. "And what's new with you?" he questioned. "What have you discovered in New York?"

She shook her head. "Nothing, I am afraid. I've been at Mr. Milburn's offices all morning with a lawyer and an auditor. Mr. Colton said you wanted to go over records there, but unless you are luckier than we were this morning I'm afraid there'll be nothing repay you for the trouble."

The aged office boy came presently to conduct them to the inner most legal lair where Mr. Colton held sway.

Their conference with that weighty gentleman was brief. He reflected principally the shocked attitude of this firm on the subject of the detention of Mr. Robert Aitken, which situation, he had reason to hope, would be remedied by a summary recourse to Canadian justice.

He replied gravely to all questions asked by Detective Lennox, with the exception of those bearing on the possible nature of the matter or matters which Robert Aitken seemed to be suppressing.

"There I can give you no information," said Mr. Colton firmly. "I would not if I could. If, in the relation of counsel, Mr. Aitken accepted confidences from Mr. Milburn which he is not yet free to divulge, I think it presumptuous and utterly unjust for any police authority anywhere to seek to bulldoze and third-degree him into betrayal."

Lennox made inward comments on this sonorous flow of words, but merely thanked the lawyer in parting.

"We're obliged to you for your co-operation, Mr. Colton. If we learn anything of interest in going over Mr. Milburn's records I'll let you know."

But Lennox learned nothing. He spent the remainder of the afternoon at the Milburn suite in a neighboring office building, examining such matters as Miss Eastwick, an accountant, and a representative of the law firm regarded as significant.

9

Mr. Milburn's affairs were in apple-pie order, said the accountant. While he had retired from all active business of his directorships in important enterprises, Mr. Milburn had maintained a complete and efficient office establishment and all his interests were cared for with the precision and accuracy of corporation conduct.

"In other words, if he had intended to depart this life on five minutes' notice," summed up the auditor, "he could not have made better provision for every detail that might arise afterwards."

"Except," suggested Lennox, "the arrest of his lawyer. It seems to me he might have foreseen trouble when he bound Aitken to keep something secret from the police for thirty days."

"Oh, Mr. Aitken is not worried," said Helen Eastwick, with a trace of pride in her tone. "I talked to him yesterday in—at headquarters. He really seems to be enjoying it."

"Well, I'm not," the detective informed her. "I suppose the next thing in order will be to ransack Mr. Milburn's town house. Perhaps you will help me in that tomorrow, Miss Eastwick. I won't ask you to do anything more tonight. I know you're tired."

"I'm utterly exhausted—but keyed up with excitement. I didn't sleep half a wink last night and I'm afraid I won't tonight, either. But I'm certainly going to go home and try."

Helen kept her promise and was in bed well before nine o'clock. She had the small apartment to herself, for the business woman who shared it with her was away on vacation. They occupied the parlor floor of one of the thousands of New York's private dwellings which during the post-war housing shortage had been renovated and remodeled into compact quarters for apartment dwellers. There were two bedrooms, a kitchenette and a breakfast room in the rear of the apartment, and a large living room comprised the front.

Helen tumbled into bed and fell promptly, despite her previous qualms, into a profound sleep. She had rested miserably for two successive nights, and on the third an overpowering fatigue asserted itself.

She did not know what it was that awakened her in the middle of the night. She sat up in bed, instantly alert, as though a warning voice had spoken into her ear. A voice indeed had spoken in her sub-consciousness, a hollow and terrifying voice that had repeated the death message, horribly simple, of George Heston's murderer:

"Send up a boy, please!"

Helen listened acutely. She could hear nothing but the far-away, detached, mechanical, unconcerned sounds of traffic which drifted into this normally quiet street. The apartment itself was so oddly still that she could hear the tick of her wristwatch on the bedside table.

But there came from the living room presently just the suggestion of catlike motion, a minute creaking of an occasional floorboard—sounds, indeed, which any room might make without human agency—the swish of

While Detective Moode Scours New York for New Clues, Helen Eastwick Has a Very Narrow Escape

Helen felt a vague nausea of terror—when she advanced one foot determinedly in the direction of the light switch she withdrew it and listened. There was a presence in the room a curtain at an open window, perhaps a questing mouse, the contracting of old timbers.

But Helen was depressingly conscious of unseen intrusion. She was obsessed with an impulse to scream, to turn on the lights against the sentient and sinister blackness. But something warned her against this course, perhaps the fear of her own self-ridicule for being silly.

She slipped resolutely from her bed and padded barefoot to the door that opened into the living room.

The three front windows were outlined faintly against the reflected light of distant street lamps. A curtain at an open window was indeed gently in motion, and she felt the draft.

"Who is there?" she called, in a strained, curious voice that she meant to be fearless and commanding.

There was no sound; only the half-heard wraithlike disturbance of the curtain. The room save for the faintly illumined area near the windows was lost in stolid gloom.

Helen felt a vague nausea of terror—unreasoning fright, she told herself, for it was only her idiotic imagination. But when she advanced one foot determinedly in the direction of the light-switch on the other side of the room, she withdrew it suddenly and listened, with painfully suspended breath.

There was a presence in the room, a noise faint and palpitant, the unforgettable sound of someone breathing in the dark, quite near. Helen felt her throat constricting, her limbs powerless.

Then a form bulked vaguely against the window light and a voice, deep, menacing, blood-chilling, intoned:

"Scream you, and I'll kill you!"

Helen screamed.

All went red and reeling. And black.

Sergeant Detective Pierre Montigny enjoyed sleeping at the scene of a murder. It was a custom to which the portly Madame Montigny objected bitterly, maintaining that the nature of his work kept him away from the family roof quite sufficiently without the self-imposed absence involved in such unholy out-sleeping.

Madame Montigny had even prompted their small son of eight, Jean-Baptiste, to beg his papa not to do such things, and there were few sacrifices which Montigny would not make for Jean-Baptiste. But in this matter of murder case procedure he was adamant. If there were women in the case who also slept at the scene of the crime, said Montigny with twinkling eyes, it might be different; Madame Montigny might have grounds for objection. But you seldom found dormant ladies around a place where there had been a murder.

This was notably true of the private car Dorothea, which on the night of the murder of George Heston began to house Montigny regularly. There were no other candidates of either sex to bargain for the doubtful privilege of spending a humid night in a railroad car that was hot enough in motion with the fans running briskly, and anticipatory of Hades itself on an August night under railroad sheds. The fans, energized only by the weak batteries supplanting the train's dynamo, made two or three lethargic whirls per minute. Montigny cut them off, and economized on lights, too. The heat did not bother him; he was too intensely interested in what he was doing.

It was past two o'clock, but Montigny did not give a thought to sleep. Instead, he sat in the dimly lighted observation lounge where Milburn had met his death, and consumed a long black cigar while considering the crowded events of the past twenty-four hours.

The seemingly unprovoked and brutal murder of George Heston had stirred Montigny even more than had the death of Milburn. It seemed wanton, this killing of the inoffensive theatrical agent. It seemed thrown in for good measure by a fiend who merely wished to demonstrate his prowess; an egocentric criminal who fancied himself invincible.

What could have been his purpose in boldly telephoning for a witness to find the body, just as the slayer of Milburn had boldly summoned the porter? Only one purpose, Montigny told himself—a sop to the killer's vanity. In the room across the hall from Heston's there had been hotel guests who might have heard a cry for help, or the sounds of a struggle. The floor below and the floor above were swarming with convention delegates on their way down for the evening session. But these facts had not deterred the killer; rather he had found safety in numbers, had made his escape in the confusion of crowded halls and elevators.

The fact that Heston had made no audible outcry argued one of two premises—either that Heston had been asleep and had been taken unaware by his assailant; or that the killer was known, supposedly friendly to his victim, and had entered the room without alarming Heston.

Small shreds to depend on; these and the deep bass voice. Montigny stirred uneasily in his chair. There had been few major crimes in his long experience—he had served eighteen years as criminal investigator—that had seemed to be so stripped of clues, so bereft of motive, as the killing of Heston. Either his fellow passengers on the tragic excursion of the Dorothea were not telling all they knew, or the murderer was a man of excessive cunning. There was no such thing as a crime, Montigny told himself tartly, in which some tiny discrepancy of fact or circumstance or human planning would not be left to betray eventually the perpetrator.

Somewhere on this car, the great wealth of whose owner, no doubt, had provoked both brutal killings, Montigny proposed to find the key to the riddle. It was there. His innermost conviction hooted all thought that it was not.

The hour was late and the light insufficient for further useful examination now, however. Tomorrow the electrician would provide new batteries and thereafter Montigny would not want for illumination. The annunciator was already working. Tomorrow with Laval's permission he would attempt a reconstruction of the crime.

Montigny put out the lights and went to bed, grinning, in Stateroom B. He had risen in the world. At last he was sleeping in the private car of a millionaire.

He slept well, too, but was early astir, searching the car again from platform to platform. Inspector Laval, whom he telephoned after breakfast, agreed to join him on the Dorothea at ten o'clock.

Sergeant Thwaite as well as the Inspector appeared at that hour, with Homer Wilks in his custody. The porter was overjoyed at the news that he was to be permitted to remain on the private car, under guard, instead of in jail. He was by no means cleared of suspicion, however, he was given to understand, and the bank notes found in his linen closet were not to be considered his until his story had better corroboration.

Robert Aitken also was awarded a temporary outing for purposes of Montigny's test. He arrived under escort of Detective Ansley. He still seemed undismayed by his detention.

Montigny had desired the presence likewise of Mrs. George Heston and Detective Moode, but the fact of

Heston's death obviated the widow's presence and Moode was in New York.

The Inspector told Montigny of his telephone conversation with Detective Lennox. "Well, we are certain of one thing, Inspector," observed Montigny ruefully.

"What, Pierre?"

"It was not Miss Eastwick who killed Heston."

"She seldom speaks in a bass voice," said Laval dryly.

"And she was a passenger on a train which left at eight-thirty last night, whereas the murderer telephoned from Heston's room at eight-forty-five."

"We are equally sure," supplemented Laval, not without sarcasm, "that Detective Lennox did not commit the crime. Now what of this test, Pierre, this reconstruction?"

"It is my suggestion, Inspector, that we try to re-enact the crime; Aitken in his stateroom, Wilks in the galley. Detective Ansley in the upper berth occupied by Mrs. Heston. The porter has made down the berths, just as they were night before last. I shall be the killer. It is too bad that Captain Berthier cannot be with us—he would make an elegant corpse."

"He is still out of town," said Laval with forced severity. "He has asked us to proceed with the case."

"Very well, Inspector. Now I propose to set my watch at two minutes past one o'clock—the time the train left St. Johns Tuesday night. I propose to enter from the back platform, to re-enact the murder, to ring the bells as the calls were registered on the annunciator. Let us see whether it would have been a physical possibility for the culprit to have done all the things he seems to have done."

"It should be tried on a moving train, Pierre," objected Laval. "We cannot determine, for instance, whether certain voices in the lounge could be heard elsewhere under conditions as they existed, unless we duplicate those conditions."

"True, Inspector. Then we can try it later upon a train in motion. Let us call this the rehearsal."

Montigny accordingly took his place upon the back platform, set his watch at two minutes past one, and tried the locked door, which had been fitted with new knobs to replace the others held as exhibits. He reached through the broken glass with his left arm, tried the inside knob, then felt for the thumb bolt. For the space of two minutes it resisted all his efforts, but he presently sprang the bolt and entered the car.

With Laval watching him interestedly he went through the pantomime of creeping swiftly across the floor, picked up an imaginary air pistol from Milburn's desk, crept through the curtains and took aim at the chair where Milburn had sat. Then he hurried down the corridor, opened, softly enough, the unlocked door of Stateroom B, went through the motion of putting bullets in the pocket of a dressing robe hanging there, and rang the bell at the window near Aitken's berth. Then he hastened back to the lounge and pushed the button on the desk.

Wilks the porter came to answer the bells as promptly as he said he had done on the night of the murder. As he knocked at Aitken's door, however, he called out somewhat indignantly:

"You didn't do it right, Cap'n! You rung the dining room bell. Ain't nobody rung the dining room bell night befo' las'."

"What's that?" exclaimed Montigny angrily, emerging from the lounge, where he had begun to talk in a borrowed bass voice. "What's the matter with you? Why do you interrupt me, you fool! We are trying to do this on schedule time. Now we have it all to do over."

"Yes, sir, Cap'n," persisted Wilks, "that's all right, but ain't like it happened. You jus' rung the dining room bell. Ain't nobody rung the dining room bell night befo' las'."

"You are insane!" accused Montigny hotly. "I did nothing of the sort."

"Jes' you come, look at the 'nunciator, then, boss," challenged Wilks. "It don't say the lounge. It says the dining room and Stateroom B."

Laval, Montigny and Thwaite hurried forward in the car with Wilks leading the way.

Precisely as he had said, the annunciator indicated no call from the lounge, but one from the dining room and one from Aitken's compartment.

"Let us ring them again," ordered Laval impatiently. "Never mind the pantomime, Pierre. Let us solve this bell puzzle. I shall stand here to watch."

Montigny hastened to the lounge and pressed the desk button again.

"It shows Stateroom B," called out Laval. "Now try the stateroom."

The button in Stateroom B registered a call from the dining room.

Laval himself stepped to the nearby dining room and tried the bell on the center fixed table. It rang up on the annunciator a call from the lounge.

"Send for your electrician, Pierre," said Laval peremptorily. "We must trace the wiring."

"He is here now, Inspector. He has been changing the batteries."

Sims, the electrician, confronted with the odd behavior of the annunciator, scratched his head.

"Now that's funny," he declared. "Somebody's been playing monkey-shines, that's sure."

He opened the annunciator box and carefully inspected the terminals.

"Red," he murmured. "Yellow. Now let's see."

He stepped back to Stateroom B and thence to the lounge.

"Sure, I thought so!" he called out triumphantly. "Somebody's switched these terminals in the box." He hurried to rejoin the officers who were examining the annunciator. "See?" He used his screw-driver for a ferrule. "This red wire here is supposed to go to the lounge—but it has been switched to the Stateroom B terminal in the annunciator."

A murmured exclamation escaped Laval. "You can trace the colored wires at the other end, of course?"

"Sure. Yes, sir. The way it's hooked up now, if you ring from the lounge you ring up a call from Stateroom B. And the dining room wire, the green one, has been shifted over to the lounge terminal."

"So that ringing from the dining room registers a call from the lounge!"

"Yes, sir, that's it. Then there's one more wire he changed—whoever the bird was. He took the yellow wire off the Stateroom B terminal and hooked it to the dining room post. See?"

Laval, a bit confused, made him repeat it.

"The devil," muttered Montigny. "And we did not guess it!"

"Well, we didn't have a chance to guess it, sir," said the electrician placatingly. "I was getting ready to test every button in the car last night, when you got called away on this other murder case. I tried two or three, you remember, but they happened to be connections that hadn't been tampered with."

Laval peered into the annunciator box again. "It seems, Montigny," he observed quietly, "that one peculiarity of our murder is explained—Mr. Aitken the lawyer did not necessarily ring for the porter at all, night before last."

Montigny Discovers the
Killer's Plan to Create
a Complete Alibi
By Changing
the Wiring
in the Bell
Annunciator.

Precisely as the Porter Had Said,
the Annunciator Indicated No
Call from the Lounge but One from the Din-
ing-Room and One from Aitken's Compartment. *"Nom du diable!"* Muttered Montigny. *"And we did not guess it!"*

"No, sir." Montigny had trouble curbing his excitement. "But somebody went further still, and rang from the dining room—before or after pressing the button in the lounge!"

"And why should he do that?" Laval said it with a meaning glance. "Why, particularly, if he were a stranger who had been crouching on the back platform?"

Montigny shrugged. "It was no stranger, Inspector," he replied in a low voice. "It was one of the passengers on this car!"

Laval turned to the electrician. "Switching the wires in this annunciator—would you call that a very difficult job?"

"No, sir, not at all. Anybody could do it in two minutes—anybody that ever tinkered with a bell system, and I suppose every kid has, some time or other. No trouble to get in this box, you see. The face swings on hinges, and you can see plain enough where every wire goes, once you look inside."

The Inspector sent for Robert Aitken. "Let us see what he thinks of the altered situation," he proposed.

Aitken, who had been waiting patiently in the rear of the car, came forward with his usual cheerfulness. Inspector Laval explained the discovery to him.

"Hm! That looks bad," commented the lawyer with apparent concern.

"Looks bad for whom?"

"Why, I mean it appears, Inspector, that somebody who was on this car might really have plotted to kill Mr. Milburn."

"Ah! You admit that much, do you? I am inclined to agree with you, Mr. Aitken. It 'looks bad'—for you."

Aitken seemed genuinely astonished. "For me, Inspector? Why?"

"Simply because this simple shift of the wiring," said Laval, "made it possible for the man who killed Mr. Milburn to press a button in the lounge and summon the porter to your stateroom, where you were found 'sound asleep.'"

"Indeed?" said Aitken quickly. "And why should I—or anyone else—go to that pains, when it would be necessary to go back to the dining room to ring up an apparent call from the lounge—which seems to be what happened?"

"You had a friend," said Laval curtly, "in the dining room."

Aitken stared at him. "Why, you don't mean for a minute to insinuate—"

"I insinuate nothing," said Laval bluntly. "I know that you and Miss Eastwick have been very close in this affair—like that." He illustrated with two fingers held close together. "And very close-lipped, as well. I know that both of you have conspired to protect the brother of this girl Lotus Decker—a man who made threats against Mr. Milburn and who is now, to our knowledge, hiding in Montreal."

"I had never heard of this man, Inspector," interrupted Aitken, "previously to the night Mr. Milburn was killed."

"I know that Miss Eastwick had access," continued Laval steadily, "to the small safe in the lounge where Mr. Milburn kept papers of value—I know that she alone knew the combination. I know that you have been successful in concealing these documents from us. Your lawyers are trying to enforce a court hearing for the purpose of getting you released. And I am prepared to go into court, let me tell you, with evidence sufficient to hold you."

The lawyer was smiling faintly. "To some people that may sound very logical, Inspector," he acknowledged. "Do you mind if I smoke?"

The Inspector ordered Aitken back to Stateroom B.

"We shall resume the test, Pierre," he said, "with certain changes. We may do away, I think, with the assumption that the man who climbed on the back platform came further forward than the door of the lounge. He did not have to—he had help. It is unthinkable that a stranger, an outsider, could have rung up both calls, or could have tampered with the annunciator."

"It follows also, then, that someone in the car was responsible for the bullets in Laith's dressing gown?"

"That, too, is possible, but it is the annunciator trick that I am interested in now. The killer—or the killer and a confederate—summoned the porter by pressing two buttons; one in the lounge, which rang up a call from Aitken's room, and one in the dining room, which registered a ring from the lounge. Just why it was planned that way we do not know. But we do know that Aitken was ostentatiously waked up for a witness. And the girl, his friendly assistant, could have pushed the button in the dining room which registered the necessary call from the lounge."

Montigny shook his head, much puzzled. "I do not see it, Inspector. The porter, summoned so that he may hear voices in the lounge just before discovering Milburn's body, finds Mr. Aitken seemingly asleep in his stateroom. But why should anyone wish to have the porter hear the voices? Why call the porter at all?"

"Simple enough, Pierre. It cleared every passenger in the car—as the schemers thought—of the appearance of guilt. It made it look like an 'outside job' in its entirety. Not the porter alone was to testify to hearing the voices, but Aitken also was to be rung in as a witness. It so happened that still another person, Mrs. Heston, was awake in her berth and listening. But I believe there was only one voice—the porter and Mrs. Heston may have thought they heard two, but it is easy enough for one person to fake his tones so that, muffled by the curtains of the lounge door, for instance, it would sound as though two were talking."

"Then Milburn—"

"Was already dead, I think, when the bells were rung for the porter."

"Ah!" Montigny looked at him shrewdly and admiringly. "I had become convinced of the same thing, Inspector. It is inconceivable that the killer could hold a conversation with his victim after summoning the porter, then stand off five meet and calmly take aim with his pistol. Milburn would have offered at least a mild objection. This trickery with the annunciator explains much. It proves beyond a doubt that there was inside co-operation in this business." He paused to fish out a cigar. "But, Inspector—" he added reflectively.

"What, Pierre?"

"Why," said Montigny, puffing rapidly, "should so clever a manipulator have left us so bald-faced a clue as the altered annunciator? Why should he not have been clever enough to devote two minutes to restoring the wires to their proper places?"

"He did not have the chance; that is why. He was afraid to risk detection. We took Aitken into custody before he could get to it. Probably he did not think, moreover, that the car would be occupied afterward, and the change in wiring discovered. He did not bargain, Pierre, with your quaint custom of camping at the scene of the crime."

"I thank you, Inspector, for the compliment. Shall I resume the show now?"

"Please."

Montigny this time went through his continuity with greater dispatch. He re-enacted the slaying. Then he pressed the button on Milburn's desk and Laval rang from the dining room. As the porter approached State-room B, Montigny was heard talking, not ineffectively, in two voices. He found that by swift work he could escape from the car before the porter, pausing for the time he estimated it took to arouse Aitken, could reach the lounge.

"That was the only way, Pierre," concluded Laval, "that it could have happened—with the aid of a con-federate inside the car. Your reconstruction has been exceedingly helpful."

"And our star suspect, Inspector, our tall, nervous basso who is a brother of Miss Lotus Decker—no word of him as yet?"

"Not as yet. But I expect developments. Thwaite learned the girl's nickname, which is 'Gypsy.' I am to-day advertising in the 'personal' columns of the newspa-pers that 'Gypsy' is urgently desirous of communicating with 'W' on a matter of life or death. She suggests a roadhouse out beyond Mount Royal for a meeting place. Something may come of it. I do not know."

"Hm! There was motive in that quarter, Inspector."

"Yes. He looked upon Milburn perhaps as the betray-er of his sister, as the arrogant man of wealth who lured giddy girls to their ruin If he killed Milburn he should have done it across the line—he would go free in New York for such a service."

"But not in Quebec, Inspector."

"Not in Quebec," said Laval grimly.

"And Heston, as Perry Laith suggested, might have been marked for the same punishment because as theatrical agent he introduced these girls to Milburn."

"Perhaps," said Laval unemotionally.

"But I cannot—I seem to be catechizing you, Inspector, but I am merely thinking aloud."

"Don't stop, Pierre."

"I cannot yet, I was going to say, fit Aitken and the Eastwick girl into the conspiracy."

"I cannot either. But there is enough concealment in this case to hide a dozen motives that we will unearth eventually. We know beyond a doubt that Aitken and the girl are withholding facts—facts so important that Aitken is willing to arouse serious suspicion against himself to remain in jail for thirty days—"

"Thirty days?" put in Montigny. "Why thirty days?"

"Perhaps to give an accomplice time to escape. Doubtless something still more important than that."

"The envelope he sent to Dalbey & Pitts—is there no way, Inspector, that we can get possession of it?"

"I wish I knew a way," confessed the Inspector. "It was a mistake to permit these people to send out uncensored mail when the train reached Montreal. We should have intercepted it. Use your cunning, Montigny. How shall we retrieve it?

Montigny smoked and pondered.

"Thinking of what, Pierre?"

"Of many things, Inspector. Of ships and shoes—but principally of sealing wax. I should like to get a look at the sealing wax on Aitken's letter. Perhaps he and the Honorable Mr. Dalbey would consent to that. I should not ask them to open it."

"But what good would that do us?"

"I was thinking, Inspector, of the great American game of bluff. Suppose we were to go to Aitken and persuade him that the seal on the envelope had been broken—the contents were perhaps disturbed and the envelope resealed?

"Yes? Would he believe us?"

"We could try. I could invite him and his very honorable Mr. Dalbey to inspect the seal of the envelope under our ultra-violet lamp—without suggesting that they open it."

"Yes—and then what?"

"I should present a stick of sealing wax which is not the one we found in Milburn's desk. I should melt a bit of it, for comparison. I should say, 'See here! This is the sealing wax which Mr. Milburn used—compare it under the light with the seal on your packet of documents.' Anyone with eyes, Inspector, would see that they were totally different kinds of sealing wax. Then I should say: 'Mr. Aitken, Mr. Dalbey, it is as we informed you—that seal has been broken, restored with a different sealing wax!' Would or would not Aitken and Dalbey be intrigued into opening the packet of their own free will?"

An Interesting Test of the Ultra-Violet Ray Upon Sealing Wax; Laval's Surprise When the Letter Was Opened

Aitken and Mr. Dalbey Emerged from the Adjoining Room. "There has been trickery and theft!" Burst Out Dalbey. "We have opened the envelope; you can see for yourself!" There Was Nothing In It But a Thick Sheaf of Blank Papers.

10

"I do not know, Pierre," said Laval. "But it may be worth the attempt. Other methods have failed. Doubtless they would refuse to let us see the contents of the envelope, even if they opened it."

"But it would give at least, Inspector, an opportunity to examine the seal on that envelope."

"To what purpose?"

"To the purpose that I might learn definitely whether or not Milburn himself sealed that envelope—with his own sealing wax. The spot of fresh wax I found on the floor near Milburn's desk is still bothering me—like a gnat that I cannot slap."

"Very well. Let us try."

Bob Aitken at first seemed mildly amused when they broached the subject to him. But when Montigny explained the effect of ultra-violet rays upon the appearance of various kinds of sealing wax, and asserted he could prove that the seal had been tampered with, Aitken began to listen with increasing soberness.

"We do not suggest that you open the packet at all, or divulge its contents," said Montigny. "It need not leave Mr. Dalbey's hands. I merely ask that you look at it under the quartz-mercury burner."

"And why are you doing this magnanimous service," inquired Aitken, "for a suspected felon?"

"Because," said Montigny significantly, "we are convinced there has been trickery in this car."

"Obliging of you to see that," complimented Aitken. "It might even be possible to convince you—eventually—that someone deliberately changed the wires of the annunciator in order to incriminate me."

"It might. Do you consent to our little experiment with the sealing wax?"

"Yes," said Aitken, "provided there is to be no tom-foolery. Provided Mr. Dalbey at all times is to retain possession of the envelope. Is that understood, Inspector?"

"Agreed," asserted Laval. "Then let us call at once upon Dalbey & Pitts."

The Honorable Mr. Seumas Dalbey, K. C., whom they were able to interview without waiting more than twenty minutes, seemed perturbed and astonished by this suggestion coming from Aitken.

"How pseudo-scientific," he commented, "our systems of alleged police protection are getting to be. Ultra-violet beams, indeed! I take no stock in it, Mr. Aitken. It is humbuggery. I advise you to waste no time on it. But still . . . If it is your wish that we look at the letter under the silly lamp, Mr. Aitken—"

"I am, as they say in the States," observed Aitken smilingly, "from Missouri. If Sergeant Montigny can show me something of interest, he shall have the opportunity."

"Very well, very well," puffed Mr. Dalbey. "Let us go and have it over."

Fifteen minutes later Sergeant Montigny proudly conducted his visitors into the ultra-violet laboratory, as he called it, at headquarters. He first cited his

authorities on the subject, the records of the Illuminat-
ing Engineering Society of America, the criminal super-
visor of the police department of Munich, the official
chemist of the city of Amsterdam, and an array of others
that impressed even Mr. Dalbey.

"Ah, then, perhaps you may be well advised," admitted the King's Counsel. "It is interesting, quite. Now,
after so weighty an introduction, perhaps you will show
us the effect of the rays."

"Presently," promised the suave Montigny, darkening
the room and turning on the mercury lamp. "While the
burner is heating I shall melt some of this wax from the
stick we found in Mr. Milburn's desk. I shall display
three specimens—softened wax, melted wax, and wax
that has been set afire. So—"

The man would produce a rabbit shortly from Mr.
Dalbey's waistcoat pocket, thought Aitken. He had
never encountered a detective whose patter he found so
entertaining.

"Sealing wax to the naked eye is red or brown, or
reddish brown," went on Montigny. "There are one hundred and twenty-six varieties of brown, which I shall
show you presently on my color charts. They range down
the alphabet from alizarin brown to zinc brown. There
are one hundred and forty-four shades of red, varying
from acid magenta and Adrianople to Xylidin—"

"Yes, yes, let us waive that, for the sake of dispatch,"
proposed Mr. Dalbey, who was growing increasingly
curious. "What of the ultra-violet rays?"

"I was getting to that," said Montigny with dignity,
and added several hundred words on the subject of
chemical change caused by the ignition of shellac, the
luminescence and fluorescence, or the contrary, or
organic and inorganic material.

"If I should examine, for instance, your teeth," he advised Mr. Dalbey, "under the ultra-violet light I could detect the true ones from those possibly false. Bones, ivory—the composition, one might say, of certain human skulls—would light up beautifully under the rays, but a false tooth—never. It would not be one particle luminescent. It would appear black."

"Yes, Pierre, I think the burner is warm enough now," said Laval discreetly.

"Pardon the delay," begged Montigny. "It is necessary for the reason that the quartz burner must be well heated before it will begin to emit ultra-violet rays. Now, Mr. Dalbey, if you will hold your mysterious packet tightly in both hands, so that no one may snatch it from you, and pass it under the filter—"

Dalbey did so with a grunt of amusement.

"The devil!" shouted Montigny, after his first glimpse of the wax seal. "You need no comparisons. You can see for yourself."

They crowded about the oddly glowing mass on the envelope which Mr. Dalbey exposed to the filtered light.

"Yes! By Jove! Odd!" exclaimed Mr. Dalbey. "One can see distinctly wax of two colors!"

"One upon the other!" murmured Aitken in astonishment.

"Right!" said Montigny triumphantly. "Your packet was sealed with wax of one kind, broken open, resealed with another."

No one was more astonished than Montigny that this had proved to be the case. His bluff had turned into a genuine demonstration.

He had at hand genuine samples of the sealing wax he had taken from Milburn's desk in the car, and these he placed under the light for contrast. "Milburn's sealing wax," he pointed out with ill-concealed excitement, "is identical, you may see, with the original seal on the envelope. The wax of the second application is totally different. Your packet, Mr. Aitken, has already been opened—by you or by someone else. That is all I proposed to show you."

Aitken stood glaring at the object held in Mr. Dalbey's hands. The barrister's fingernails glowed oddly under the light.

"I believe you are right, Sergeant," said Aitken slowly. "Someone has broken into that envelope. I cannot conceive of such a thing happening. I cannot imagine when it happened, unless the letter was intercepted in the mails. There was no other opportunity. Mr. Milburn gave it to me night before last. He suggested that for safe keeping I put it in his small safe in the lounge of the car, until we arrive in Montreal."

"What is in it?" asked Inspector Laval softly.

"That I cannot tell you, sir."

"You mean that you will not tell me?"

"I cannot. Strictly speaking, I do not know."

"And only one person knew the combination of that safe—your friend Miss Eastwick!"

"May I have a few minutes of privacy with Mr. Dalbey?" requested Aitken, in somewhat uncertain tone.

"Certainly," agreed Laval.

In the Inspector's office, Montigny paced back and forth nervously. He stopped abruptly.

"That spot of wax from the floor near the desk, Inspector," he declared, "came from the same stick that resealed that envelope! Now what do you make of that?"

"That Aitken himself resealed it," responded Laval promptly.

Before they could discuss it further Bob Aitken and Mr. Dalbey emerged from the small adjoining room.

Dalbey looked gravely concerned. Aitken was pale, a trifle agitated.

"There has been trickery and theft!" burst out Mr. Dalbey. "We opened the envelope. You can see for yourself!"

He drew out its contents.

There was nothing in it but a thick sheaf of folded papers, entirely blank.

When Helen Eastwick returned to consciousness the room was still in darkness and utter silence prevailed.

She stirred, started in affright, threw out an arm protectively and struck the facing of the door near which she had fallen. Her head throbbed miserably, and the insistent pain took precedence over her fear. Slowly the familiar aspect of the three dim windows brought her back to recognition of her surroundings. She wondered vaguely whether it had not been simply a harrowing dream.

Then she rose in a recurrent impulse of fright and made her way swiftly through the dark to the remembered location of the wall switch. She blinked painfully in the sudden light. She felt of her head. No blood, she found with quick relief, but her fingers encountered an acutely sensitive bruise and swelling.

It had not been a dream, she realized, shivering. There had been that terrifying form in the dark, too brutally real; that sepulchral voice that had threatened her with death. He had struck her down or she had fainted. The latter was more probable, she reflected, for she retained a vague feeling that the man had been on the other side of the room when she lost consciousness. She had fainted and struck her head against the sharp edge of the door frame. That was more probable; at least it was more comforting than the thought that she had been attacked.

She looked at the clock on the mantel. It was half-past three. How long she had lain unconscious on the floor she had no means of reckoning.

The intruder had left testimony of a hasty search. The drawer of the small library table had been over-turned on the floor and its contents scattered. A small secretary in a corner had been treated similarly.

Helen snapped on the lights in the rear. The burglar had left his traces here as well. Evidently he had conducted a swift but systematic search in every place where he might expect to find—

What? What, thought Helen in a cold terror, could she be suspected of having, that would provoke a ghastly visitation of this kind?

She thought suddenly of the handbag containing her small purse. It was gone. She had left it on her dressing table as usual. There was nothing in it of considerable value—five or six dollars in change, and—her keys!

Helen remembered them with swift dismay. Not only her keys, but Mr. Milburn's keys—among them the one with which Bob Aitken had specifically entrusted her, the key to the private drawer at the post-office. What a fool she had been not to go there at once! But after all, Bob had not seemed to think it very likely that there would be anything of importance in the box.

She would remedy that, without delay. She would go to the central post-office in the morning and ask for the contents of the drawer. Surely they would be reasonable.

Stung by resentment and chagrin, she went to the telephone to call the police. But what good would that do? More excitement, more interminable investigation with no result, except that they would diagnose the case as one of burglary. More reporters and publicity. And her people in Connecticut would be frightened to death.

Not the police, she decided with faint resolution. She thought of Detective Lennox. He had given her the name of his hotel and urged her to call him at any time if she needed him. Nice, sensible fellow, Mr. Lennox. Not bad looking either; tall, blond, gray-eyed. Detectives were nice, a lot of them, thought Helen a little incoherently.

She called Detective Lennox and that gentleman, wide-awake and cheerful at once, promised to be on hand as soon as a taxi could whisk him there.

Helen bathed her head and swallowed an aspirin tablet and dressed. No use to try for further sleep this dreadful night. It was morning now, anyway. And she had to get down to the post-office soon as anybody would be stirring there. She could not tell Detective Lennox about that, though. Odd, how she was co-operating with the police in one phase of her loyalties, and dodging them in another. What had been happening in Montreal? She longed to get hold of the morning papers and see. If they would quit persecuting poor Bob Aitken, let him go, she could call him at once on the telephone and ask him what to do. She longed for a bit of capable masculine direction.

Detective Lennox came, and she felt ever so clandestine and mystery-novelish, admitting a minion of the law in this manner and at this hour. She had brewed some coffee in an electric percolator and he took a cup gratefully.

He made a rapid survey of the premises. The door was securely locked at the ground floor entrance. The stoop leading to the "parlor" floor of this old type of dwelling had been removed and a vestibule entrance created leading to the former basement floor. Helen's apartment was on the parlor floor. The windows were too high for access without a ladder. The intruder evidently had come in through the back door, which they found unlocked. It opened into a small back yard separated by a high board fence from the areaway of a big apartment house adjoining in the rear.

The living room entrance to Helen's apartment was equipped with a jimmy-proof lock, but the kitchen entrance was not. Here the door had an ordinary lock and the key had not been in it—any skeleton key would have unlocked it.

"He got in through the rear," concluded Detective Lennox. "But that is not the important point, after all. The point is, what was he after?"

"I can't imagine," confessed Helen nervously. "Judging by the places he ransacked he must have been looking for—papers, would you say?"

"Yes—and what papers?"

"I wish you'd tell me. Do you think"—she said it a little tremblingly—"do you think this could have had anything to do with—Mr. Milburn?"

Lennox nodded decisively. "You bet it did. And I don't like the looks of it. Milburn and the Heston murder, too. This chap is overworking his deep voice—or somebody who read the lurid stuff in the papers has been making quick use of it. Did the voice sound at all familiar to you?"

"It sounded like nothing on earth," said Helen with a shiver. "It scared me speechless. I never fainted before in my life, but I had been dreaming about that very kind of thing, and—goodness, here in the dark! Have I got any gray hairs, Mr. Lennox?"

He laughed. "You haven't. You've got a lot of nerve. Any other woman would be in bed with hysterics. I don't believe you even screamed."

She told him, hesitantly, about the loss of her keys.

"Keys to what?" he asked quickly.

"To Mr. Milburn's desks and things at the office— another desk at his house—and, oh, yes, a small steel filing-cabinet he had at home, too. It's fireproof and strong as a safe. Mr. Milburn kept private records there. And we were to go through them today, weren't we?"

"Yes," said Lennox, getting up abruptly. "I'm glad you told me. I've got to dash around there at once. That house is under guard, but I'll give you any odds this same prowler has been there, too." He almost added that her house was being watched, too, for a shadower was still on the job, but he refrained from telling her. "I'll ask the policeman on the beat to hang around in front pretty close," he promised. "I don't think you have any-thing to fear, though."

"Oh, I'm not afraid now," declared Helen cheerfully. "It's daylight, and everything looks absurdly safe and normal. What time do you want me down at Mr. Mil-burn's house? I ought to go downtown—"

"No hurry. Say nine-thirty or ten. That will do. We'll probably be at it all day."

Helen was on hand at the central post-office long before anybody in sufficient authority had arrived there. She did not even know, she recalled with dismay, the number of the drawer in question or the name in which it was listed—whether Bob Aitken's, Mr. Milburn's or the name of one of the many enterprises in which Mr. Milburn was interested.

The clerk looked at her curiously when she explained this. She was shunted from one official to another and finally referred to the third assistant postmaster, who was engaged. She waited anxiously, read the morning papers. Absolutely nothing new in Montreal—the police had evidence, as usual, that would "lead them to an early arrest." No publicity had been given as yet to the detention of Robert Aitken.

She telephoned Detective Lennox that she would be late.

"That's all right," he said and added casually: "By the way, I think our friend has been here, as I expected."

"What! Last night?"

"Yes. I don't know that anything's missing, but somebody has been looking for something. The steel cabinet you spoke of—I found it unlocked. Did you by any chance have among those keys a key to the front door here?"

"I don't know," said Helen excitedly. "It's possible. Mr. Aitken gave me a number to take care of."

"Well, come along when you can."

The third assistant postmaster received Helen presently but could give her no encouragement.

"Even if you could give me the number of the box and the name under which it is listed," he said, "I could not surrender the contents to you until you were properly identified. I suppose that should be very easy," he added, regarding her keenly, "if you were the late J. P. Milburn's secretary."

"But there is no time to lose," entreated Helen. "The key has been stolen. It might take an hour for me to get somebody to identify me—and even now the thief may be going into that box and taking everything out of it."

"But how can I help?" demanded the official querulously. "I don't even know the number of the box."

"You could look up the listings to see whether Mr. Milburn or Mr. Aitken—"

"That is being done."

The dismaying report came in very soon—no listing under either name.

"Heavens, what shall I do?" implored Helen.

"Get in touch with Mr. Aitken in Montreal and ask him the number of the box—that is all you can do."

"And that will take hours!"

It could not be helped. The third assistant postmaster promised her that all mail addressed to Mr. Milburn, Mr. Aitken or herself would be held for safe keeping, meanwhile, and not deposited in any box or drawer. But that was small comfort.

She would have to tell Inspector Laval about it. There was no other remedy. The Montreal police certainly would not permit a prisoner to be summoned to the telephone for a long-distance call. Inspector Laval might take the message and relay it to Bob, but that was the best that could be done, manifestly.

Helen hurried to the gray stone mansion in the East Sixties which had been the town house of J. P. Milburn. A policeman on the stoop took her name and rang the doorbell. A ponderous gate of decorative iron grille work protected the front entrance, and contained a staunch tumblered lock. The basement windows were barred. All other windows were equipped with heavy board shutters, for the house had been closed for the remainder of summer. If any intruder had entered this house last night he had done so with a key. The place was under surveillance, but, as Detective Lennox presently explained, the watcher had been rather cocksure and had strolled off for a time.

Helen at once told Lennox about the circumstances of the private mail drawer and her visit to the post-office. She begged him to do something about it, quickly.

"Oh, we'll fix that," Lennox assured her. "I have a call in for Montreal now. I'll tell the Inspector about it and he will ask Aitken for the box number. I suggest you race back to the post-office and call me from there, to save time. I'll call headquarters and McEniry will send someone over to identify you. But I don't think you need worry I don't think our thief stole your keys for that purpose—what he wanted was the keys to this house. Run get your mail—and hurry back."

"I'll hurry!" promised Helen with a gasp.

The telephone was ringing even then for the detective's long-distance call.

He spoke to Laval about the lost post-office key at once, and there was a pause while Laval ordered Bob Aitken brought to his office.

"Hm! Peculiar, wasn't it?" commented the Inspector whom Lennox had retailed the news of the burglar's visit to Helen. "A man watching the house from across the street, and he saw nothing of this?"

"Nothing," said Lennox. "No lights were turned on in the house until three-thirty, which is about the time the girl called me."

"Ask McEniry to detail two men to look after that lady," ordered Laval. "She's smooth. She's more than that. She's cunning."

Lennox was frankly surprised. "You mean you think it sounds fishy—about the burglary?"

"Very fishy, Lennox. There are developments at this end, incidentally, that I cannot discuss with you over the phone. What else have you? Tell me only the things that are urgent."

"Yes, sir," said Lennox briskly. "I am talking from the house, you understand. . . . I hurried over this morning after hearing from the girl about the loss of her keys. One was a key to a fireproof steel filing-cabinet here. When I arrived I found the cabinet open—unlocked. The men had no key and hesitated to break it."

"Yes?"

"I can't tell you whether anything is missing, though there seems to have been a search. But I can tell you what I found. Another policy—Continental Guaranty & Fidelity—straight life. One hundred thousand dollars."

"Ah! And the beneficiary?" returned Laval quickly.

"May I call names?"

"I think so, Lennox."

"Miss Dorothea Dustin."

The wire was silent save for the electric buzzing.

Then: "Date of issuance?" asked Laval quickly.

"Last January."

"Double indemnity?"

"Yes, sir, for accidental death. And the suicide clause, as usual."

"Hm! That puts a— Wait a minute. Here's Aitken now."

There was an interval that seemed somewhat lengthy to the waiting detective. The truth came to him fully, while he pondered, that Dorothea Dustin had profited handsomely by Milburn's death. A legacy of one hundred thousand dollars in Milburn's will—a doubled indemnity, now, of two hundred thousand dollars, because Milburn had been murdered. No wonder she had gone into hysterics!

Laval was back on the wire. "Here's the number, Lennox: Drawer sixteen seventy-eight B—B as in bulldoze. Get it?"

Lennox repeated it.

"Now, anything else, Lennox? I am up to my eyes."

"Yes, sir, one thing else," said Lennox hurriedly. "I found a typewriter—a peculiar little dinky typewriter—hidden away on the top shelf of a closet in Mr. Milburn's study. It's one of those—what do you call them, Glick—"

"Glickenswerfer?"

"Yes, sir, that's it. This machine has been around here for years, so one of the servants tells me. Milburn bought it for one of his secretaries at a time when he had considerable correspondence in French and German. You can change the typewheels, you know, to write in any language—"

"Yes, I know," interrupted Laval. "Bring it to Montreal when you come—and come tonight. And bring the girl with you. What else have you to do?"

Lennox told him.

"What is Moode doing? Has he accomplished anything?"

"He called up McEniry from Baltimore this morning. He has managed to discover in twenty-four hours what I learned yesterday in fifteen minutes—the name of the firm Decker travels for. That's all."

"Bright boy, that!" observed Laval. "Very well, Lennox, you've done good work. I shall expect you in the morning."

Lennox called up detective headquarters at once, and Inspector McEniry told him there would be no difficulty about Miss Eastwick's identification.

But Helen did not require it.

When she had talked to Lennox on the telephone and had hurried to the locality of Post-office Drawer 1678-B, she observed through the mail glass pane in the door of the box that it was totally empty.

Inspector Laval detained Bob Aitken for questioning when he had finished his long-distance conversation to New York with Lennox.

"Something more you and Miss Eastwick were concealing from me, eh?" charged the Inspector grimly. "You sent her back to New York to get something out

Helen Eastwick, Regaining
Consciousness, Reaches
the Post Office Too Late—
Milburn's Mail Box Is
Empty!

Helen Hurried to the
Gray Stone Mansion
in the East Sixties
Which Had Been the Town
House of the Late J. P. Milburn.
A Policeman on the Stoop Took
Her Name and Address.

of that post-office box, didn't you? So she loses the key
and thinks up this cock-and-bull story about the 'attack'
on her in her apartment to explain the loss. Is that it?"

"There was nothing in the post-office box that I
knew of, Inspector," replied Aitken evenly. "And you
may disabuse your mind of any vagrant theory that Miss
Eastwick told an untruth about the burglary."

"I happen to know that it cannot be true, Mr. Aitken."
The Inspector's tone was acid. "For your information,
Miss Eastwick has been under constant surveillance since
she left Montreal, and still is. A member of the New
York detective force was stationed across the street from
the house where she lives. He observed no one enter the
house. The lights were not on in Miss Eastwick's apartment until three-thirty, when she telephoned for help.
Meanwhile, the intruder was supposed to be making a
thorough search of her premises—in the dark."

"The burglar may have used a flashlight, Inspector."

"And the story of the man with the hollow voice
threatening her," went on Laval, ignoring Bob's suggestion, "sounds to me like a deliberate attempt to mislead
us, to make us believe that the guilty man in this double
murder has left Montreal, is at large in New York."

"Inspector, will you tell me, please," questioned Aitken wearily, "what conceivable motive Miss Eastwick
could have—or I could have—for wishing to do harm
to J. P. Milburn? He had been exceedingly kind to both
of us. We both stood to lose, not profit, by his death."

"You have been at great pains, Mr. Aitken, to conceal
your motive. I do not know what it was, but I propose
to find out. It will be explained by the true and original
contents of that envelope which you posted on the night
of your arrival in Montreal to Dalbey & Pitts."

"Just what do you mean, Inspector?"

"I mean that someone acting in your interests, or you
yourself, opened that envelope, extracted the original

document or documents, replaced that with blank paper, resealed it with a different kind of sealing wax, and waited confidently for the time when we should force your counsel, by process of law, to surrender the packet. That is what I mean."

"But, Inspector, why should we so willingly have permitted you to examine the seal under your trick light, if we had tampered with it?"

"Because it gave you an excuse for surrendering it. Because you wanted to surrender it, knowing that the discovery of a supposed 'theft' would throw suspicion on others."

Aitken was thoughtfully silent. His eyes met the somber and penetrating gaze of Laval.

"Inspector," he said slowly, "do you want me to tell you what that envelope originally contained?"

"I do."

"Then I shall tell you. Please bear witness to the fact that I am not in a legal sense 'divulging' its contents. I am merely going to tell you what, physically, the envelope contained. May I say this to you in absolute confidence, Inspector?"

"You may."

"It contained the last will and testament of J. Proctor Milburn."

Laval's eyes grew piercing. "The last will? More recent than the one your firm has in its possession in New York?"

"Yes, Inspector. It was drawn up four days ago in New York. I drew it up. No one but Mr. Milburn and myself, to my knowledge, was aware that it existed. I even typed it myself. The witnesses did not know that it was a will. They merely witnessed Mr. Milburn's signature, when he was signing a number of other papers."

Laval studied him skeptically. "Then why did you not tell us this before?"

Still Clinging to the
Suicide Theory,
Aitken Is Again
Questioned by
Inspector Laval

"I should not tell you now, Inspector, but for the fact that the will has been stolen. And I do not know where the duplicate copies are—unless they are on their way to Calcutta."

"To Calcutta! Do you expect me to believe that Milburn would do so asinine a thing? Or did you expect—" the Inspector's tone changed—"to go to Calcutta when you had made your escape, to reclaim the copies there?"

Aitken shrugged. "It sounds fantastic, Inspector. Mr. Milburn was not in a normal mental state—few men would be, who were planning suicide. I am not surprised that you are suspicious. I have felt no resentment toward you for the course you have taken in respect to me. But I have been, and still am, in duty bound to respect Mr. Milburn's last confidences—"

"What," demanded Laval, "were the provisions of this new will?"

"I cannot tell you. To answer that question would be to betray the confidence of which I speak."

"You told me yesterday," countered Laval swiftly, "that you did not know."

"I told you that, 'strictly speaking.' I did not know. I meant that while I knew the contents of the will I did not know the contents of a message which Mr. Milburn included in the envelope."

"A message?"

"Yes, Inspector. He sealed two envelopes, enclosing a note with each. He gave one to me, explicitly instructing me that it was not to be opened for thirty days. He retained the other and did not tell me what he intended doing with it. At his suggestion I left the envelope he had given me in the small safe in the lounge of his car. Someone got hold of it and stole the contents."

"When did you again get possession of it?"

"After the death of Mr. Milburn."

"Did you know how to open the safe?"

"I got the combination from Miss Eastwick, and asked her, in the interests of a secrecy which I felt doubly bound to observe, in view of Mr. Milburn's death, to say nothing about it."

"You asked her to say nothing about it, even to the police?"

"I did."

"Why did you do that?"

"Because I knew, Inspector, that you would consider it your duty, confidence or no confidence, to find out at once what the envelope contained."

"I still consider it my duty, Mr. Aitken. And I think you are telling me an involved and fanciful lie."

"Thank you, Inspector. I accept that as a professional, rather than a personal, aspersion."

Laval ignored that.

"In this new will," he demanded, "were you named as a beneficiary?"

"I decline to answer, Inspector."

"Was Dorothea Dustin named as a beneficiary?"

"I decline to answer that also."

"Are you aware," went on the Inspector doggedly, "that Dorothea Dustin is named as beneficiary in a one hundred thousand dollars life insurance policy issued last January?"

"I am."

"Why have you not told us so before?" snapped Laval angrily.

"I was not asked."

"Must you be asked specifically about every individual item that might lead to the arrest of the man who killed Mr. Milburn?"

"I still do not believe," asserted Aitken in a matter-of-fact tone, "that any man killed Mr. Milburn."

Laval stood up with abrupt impatience. "Are you aware, Mr. Aitken, that your persistent prattling about 'suicide' makes things look worse for you?"

"Whether it does or not, Inspector, I had ample reason to believe that Mr. Milburn in fact intended to end his life. I may have more difficulty in establishing that fact now than I would have had—but never mind that. Your theory of the intruder on the platform of Mr. Milburn's car is a very pretty one. But such an intruder, Inspector, had he wanted to kill Mr. Milburn, would have done it with a weapon certain and deadly—not with an unfamiliar target pistol."

"And did Mr. Milburn know," suggested Laval, "that the target pistol was capable of killing a man?"

"He did. He so warned us while we were at target practice. He said a bullet from the air gun had the destructive force of a bullet from a twenty-two rifle—that we must be careful."

"Hm! The death of Mr. Heston, I assume, you also attribute to suicide? He knew that his hands possessed strength capable of choking himself to death, so he acted upon the coy impulse?"

Aitken leaned forward intently. "Had it occurred to you, Inspector, in the course of your puzzle-solving peregrinations, that the murder of George Heston might have been camouflage?"

"What do you mean?" queried Laval sharply.

"That it might have been a murder deliberately and cruelly staged for the purpose of making the suicide of J. P. Milburn appear definitely as a murder?"

Laval stared at him. "Absurd!"

"The life insurance—the policy issued last January?"

"Yes?"

"If J. P. Milburn were murdered in August what would his beneficiary get? Two hundred thousand dollars—double the principal sum. If J. P. Milburn committed suicide in August, what would the beneficiary get?"

"Nothing!" exclaimed the Inspector softly. "The policy would be void in case of suicide within one year."

"Very well," said Aitken, smiling.

"What are you getting at?" asked Laval sharply. "Whom are you accusing?"

"Nobody. The Dustin baggage cajoled him into 'protecting' her, as she called it, with this policy. She was afraid that if 'anything happened' to Milburn, any provision of his will in her favor might be knocked out in the courts. And it would have been, I am satisfied. If ever there was 'undue influence'—"

"'Would have been?'" interrupted Laval shrewdly. "Do you mean would have been under the old will, but not under the new? Did the new will neglect to mention Miss Dorothea Dustin?"

Aitken smiled. "You cannot corner me there, Inspector. I decline to answer."

Laval seemed lost in thought. "Assuming for the moment," he said after reflection, "that Milburn actually killed himself, and that the murder of Heston was committed, as you hint, by one of the Dustin gang—who could have killed George Heston?"

"Really, you ask too much, Inspector, if you're depending on me to guess it. I know nothing of the killing except what I read in the newspapers. I know merely that someone possessing or simulating a deep bass voice telephoned from Heston's room night before last at eight-forty-five, and that evidently he was the murderer. I know that of the four other men who came with Milburn on the private car, two were in jail—the negro porter and myself. I know that Perry Laith has an alibi—the papers said that he was in Dorothea Dustin's room in company with Mrs. Heston. There remains only the detective Moode. Do you suspect him?"

Laval smiled disparagingly. "Moode was on an eighty-thirty train bound for New York. He was observed on that train not only by Miss Eastwick, who talked with him at length, but also by one of my detectives. Now what?"

Aitken shrugged. "Then we are all innocent, pure and happy."

"There is one loophole in Laith's alibi. I don't mind telling you because it cannot go further than your cell."

"Yes, Inspector? Thanks for the confidence."

"Mrs. Heston left the Dustin woman's bedroom for the period, she thinks, of five or six minutes, about half-past eight on the night of the murder. She did not recall the incident when first we questioned her. She had gone into the bathroom or the adjoining room—it was quite of two—to mix some medicine. When she returned Laith was in the bedroom as she had left him, with Dorothea Dustin. The Dustin woman swears Laith did not leave her. But there was a period of five or six minutes during which he might, with the Dustin woman's consent and connivance—"

"And he says?"

"That he did not leave Miss Dustin's bedside. But a hotel employee, one of the bellmen, 'thinks' he saw a man of Laith's description, about half-past eight o'clock, in the corridor on the seventh floor."

The lawyer pondered, "Frail evidence, of course, but much can happen in five or six minutes. Still, if you are asking me, I should not care to commit myself."

"I am not asking you," said Laval curtly. "I am telling you."

"And you are not, Inspector," suggested Aitken suavely, "building up a hypothetical case merely to encourage me into, er—further confidences?"

"You flatter yourself. There is one other matter I wish to mention to you, and then I am through. The so-called 'warning' letter which Mr. Milburn received had been typed, we found, on a distinctive sort of typewriter —a Glickenswerfer—the printing is easily identified."

"Yes?"

"Do you know that Mr. Milburn himself possessed such a typewriter—that it was hidden on a closet shelf in Mr. Milburn's study at his home in New York?"

"Why, no, Inspector. That is interesting. I had never heard him speak of it—not that he would, of course."

"What does the circumstance suggest to you?"

"Why, I hardly know, Inspector. Very few persons had access to Mr. Milburn's study—myself occasionally, Miss Eastwick—"

"Do you know what it suggests to me?"

"I should like to know."

"It suggests to me," said Laval deliberately, "that Miss Helen Eastwick typed that letter of warning to Mr. Milburn, at your suggestion."

Aitken was amused. "I should be interested in knowing, Inspector, why we should have done anything so sophomoric. In a sort of, er—comic valentine spirit, would you say?"

"As a means of diverting suspicion—to a supposed crank or fanatic who might have killed Milburn."

"Really, Inspector!" Aitken lighted a cigarette and blew a reflective cloud. He knitted his brows. Laval watched him coldly. "Would you like for me to suggest a theory, Inspector, as to the authorship of that letter?"

"Yes, Go ahead."

"I think Mr. Milburn wrote it—to himself."

"Yes?" The Inspector's tone was richly sarcastic. "And why?"

"Who knows? To make it appear, perhaps, that his suicide was homicide!"

Laval, with an uncomfortable feeling that he was being ridiculed, sent Aitken back to his cell.

There had been a telephone interruption, too. It was Captain Berthier of the Provincial Police. Berthier was not in Quebec at all. He was in New York, on the way home from Washington. He had missed his men in Quebec, he explained rather lengthily, or rather had been turned back by a telegram delivered to him on the train, advising that these individuals already had departed for Montreal and New York. They were two supposedly important officials of the American Department of Justice. Berthier's superiors, for some reason deeming the matter an urgent one, had ordered him to double back on the next southbound train and go after them. He had missed them in Montreal but had caught them at Rouses Point and continued on to Washington with them.

Laval listened to all this impatiently. He had things more pressing to concern him.

"But I understand," concluded Berthier, with a certain pompous irony, "that you have been carrying on handsomely during my absence with the Milburn-Heston case. The papers say you expect to make an arrest 'almost momentarily'."

"We do," said Laval shortly. "Today."

"You've got the right man in jail now," asserted Berthier more soberly. "I picked him from the start. Well, I'll be back with you in the morning and we'll see what we can do."

Laval's jaw tightened as he replaced the receiver. "We" had a lot more seeing to do yet.

Sergeant Thwaite came in to make a personal report and to receive detailed instructions. He had paid a call on Sergeant Montigny at Bonaventure Station to see if he could be of help, he said, and had found Montigny puttering around as usual examining his private car with a fine-tooth comb and a magnifying glass.

"He found two holes, size of a pin-head, in a window screen in the lounge, Chief," chuckled Thwaite. "I had to laugh. Then he found a couple more in the window screen of the stateroom this Aitken had—the one Montigny's sleeping in now. 'Well, sir,' I says, 'Montigny, now you got it! This fellow that killed Milburn changed himself into a gnat, but he had to have him a one-way hole coming and going, didn't he! He crawled in one hole,' I says, 'shot Milburn, and then crawled out the other one.'"

Thwaite's hearty guffaw shook the papers on the desk, and Laval could not suppress a smile. "He shows me these holes," Thwaite continued hilariously, "and he says to me—the nut!—he says, 'Thwaite, on one pair of these apertures I observe brown whiskers, on the other, none. Now what do you make of that?'"

"Pierre overlooks nothing," murmured Laval. "Now listen carefully, Thwaite. This is important, highly important; the most delicate assignment, perhaps, you have ever had. You know about this personal advertisement concerning 'Gypsy' and 'W'?"

"Yes, sir," said Thwaite, his face suddenly lengthening.

"You seem to have been rather successful in, er— gaining the confidence of this Decker girl."

"Yes, sir," said Thwaite, cautiously.

"It is rather a new role for you. I have never used you before in investigations of, er—a social character. But the other night when I saw you with this amiable young person whom you had been, er—investigating. I concluded that you were rather good at it."

"Yes, sir," said Thwaite, turning a shiny pink.

"You know, of course, Dominique's, the roadhouse I mentioned in our decoy advertisement. By the way, Thwaite, have you talked to Miss Decker recently? Has she by any chance noticed the small 'personals' in the newspaper?"

"No, sir," declared Thwaite, shifting in his chair. "That is, I'm pretty sure she hasn't, sir. In fact, I talked to her on the phone this morning—a few minutes ago—"

"Oh, you did! Now, that is what I call a persevering investigator, Thwaite. And she said nothing about seeing anything unusual in the papers?"

"No, sir. She was just—crying."

"Crying?"

"Yes, sir. You see, she's worried, I guess, about this brother of hers."

"So am I. Frightfully worried, Thwaite. I think he is still in Montreal. I am quite apprehensive that he will get away without paying us a call. And he owes us a call, don't you think?"

"Chief," said the Sergeant with shy bluntness, "I don't think that fellow had a thing to do with it. I swear I don't!"

"You don't? And why, Thwaite, are you so positive?"

"I don't know whether this Decker was anywhere near the car, Chief, when Milburn was killed. But whether he was or not, I can't see anybody climbing on the back platform, breaking in, having a conversation with Milburn, and shooting him, of all things, with a target pistol. Can you, Chief?"

"It sounds improbable. Thwaite. But it is not impossible. It is no less plausible than many another strange case that we have had. We must presuppose, of course, an acquaintance between Milburn and such an intruder. Milburn was not alarmed when he saw him—did not call for help. We must assume also some connection between Decker, if he was this man, and Aitken—perhaps also the Eastwick girl—both of whom may have had something to do with the annunciator shifting and the ringing of the porter's bell. We know, of a certainty, that Aitken and Miss Eastwick both have sought to shield Warren Decker. We know that he is or has been in Montreal, under very suspicious circumstances, while the people of his firm believe he is out West around Chicago or Minneapolis. Mr. Decker has much to explain to us. I want him."

"Yes, sir," said Thwaite, obediently.

"I want you to take the Decker girl this afternoon to Dominique's. Stay there as long as you like, as long as you may. Go back again this evening with her, and again tomorrow and tomorrow evening, if you can do so without arousing her suspicion. Take her sightseeing, but wind up at Dominique's. Give her opportunity to be alone there—have yourself called to the telephone or something—so that her brother, if he has taken the bait, may see her."

"I don't like to do this, Chief, but if you say so—"

"Ansley and another man will take care of Decker, if he shows up. You need not appear to have anything to do with the arrest. I merely want you to get the girl to Dominique's."

"All right. Chief, if it's my job it's my job."

"You will have, of course, the use of a car on an expense account. Good luck, Thwaite."

Sergeant Thwaite felt like a destroyer of young corn and a persecutor of widows and orphans, as he went about his afternoon's assignment. Lotus Decker was pathetically glad to see him, and childishly gleeful when he told her he was going to take her for an automobile ride.

"It's not the kind of ride the gangsters take you for in New York, is it?" she asked him in mock concern.

"I wouldn't bump you off, Cutie," asserted Thwaite, beaming at her; "You're the one bright spot in this beastly case. I'm supposed to take you out and pump you, see what you know—see?" He winked. "So I'm going to take you out to a place where you can eat cherries off the cocktails and we can dance. It's a nice place called Dominique's, out beyond Mount Royal Park. Want to go?"

"Mercy me! Does a duck like duck soup? Maybe not! But lead me to it!"

Lotus snuggled up close to Thwaite in the shiny sedan, and he took his good time about getting out to Dominique's. He took her for a rubberneck tour of the city, but cathedrals, ancient landmarks and public buildings were points of less interest to her than was Sergeant Bill Thwaite of the Montreal detective bureau.

"Mind you, this is strictly business," Thwaite reminded her. "Some of these days I hope to be shed of this blooming murder case and follow this up on purely personal lines."

"You can't get too personal with me, Mister," asserted Lotus. "If there's anything I like better than a nice detective it's a nice detective named Bill."

"You think I'm nice? I'm not, lady. I'm double-crossing you right now. I'm snooping around trying to get friendly with you so you'll loosen up and tell me all you know."

"All I know is I'm having a grand time, honey."

Both of them were. Thwaite all but forgot the fell purpose of his afternoon. Nothing happened for so long a time that he began to feel sure that nothing would, that Inspector Laval's advertising scheme would come to naught.

But after they had had tea and a cocktail and had danced and chatted happily—Lotus seemed to have forgotten all her woes—for an hour or more, Thwaite was brought back to his unsavory aim by a telephone call. It was Laval.

"Just to give you an opportunity to get away," explained the Inspector. "Any results as yet?"

"No, sir, not a thing happened." The Inspector would not have been pleased if he could have seen the satisfaction written on the sergeant's face.

"Ansley and Porter there?"

"Yes, sir, they're on the job."

"Very well. It is a waiting game, Thwaite. Nothing may come of it, but it is worth the effort."

"Yes, sir," said Thwaite gloomily.

"I suggest that you stay away from your table for a considerable time, now, in order to give this man an opportunity, if he is there—"

"Yes, sir, I understand."

Thwaite strolled out upon the deep veranda of Dominique's rather pretentious establishment, and glanced through the French windows across the dining room. He noted with a start of surprise that Lotus was not at their table.

He loitered about uneasily for a few minutes, smoked a cigarette, peered into the dining room again. Still no Lotus.

Then he saw her—at the other end of the veranda. She was talking, hurriedly furtively, with a stranger—a tall, quick-eyed, rather restless chap, Thwaite observed, in the brief moment he was visible. He had a rolled newspaper in his hand and was pointing with it. He saw Thwaite. He said something which caused Lotus to turn sharply, too, and the expression on her face was an unforgettable picture to Thwaite.

The stranger fled. He took the veranda steps at one bound and skirted the corner of the building. He leaped into a waiting taxicab—but Detective Ansley leaped after him.

"Headquarters," rapped Ansley, flashing his badge on the scared driver.

Thwaite and Lotus Decker saw them drive off. The pale face of the captured man seemed to have lost its hunted look; it bore an aspect of something approaching relief as he called out to Lotus:

"Don't worry, kid. It'll be all right!"

The girl came up to Thwaite, her features distorted by hatred.

"All right, you've got him," she hissed, "you dirty, double-crossing snake in the grass! I hope you're proud of it."

"Listen, little one," Thwaite began helplessly.

"Don't ask me to listen to you, you cheap hick snooper! You lying, sneaking booster, you second-rate pickpocket with a badge!"

Thwaite waited with parted lips for her stream of epithets to cease. She called him many names that he could understand and many quaint others that must have meant something on Broadway but registered with Thwaite only as things obviously not complimentary.

"Listen, girlie," he managed to entreat finally, "don't blame it all on me. I had nothing to do with that arrest."

"You didn't! You lying, simple-headed dope! You didn't know about that foxy want-ad in the papers, huh? Gee, how I hate myself for telling a sneaking cannon that anybody ever called me 'Gypsy!'"

With that she broke down and began uncontrollably to cry.

Patrons of the place attracted by their verbal conflict had drifted near, and resentful looks were directed at Thwaite. Evidently the big brute had done something terrible to this little girl. Things like that did happen at Dominique's.

"Listen, come on, Lotus," begged Thwaite, increasingly uncomfortable. "Let me take you back to the hotel. I want to talk to you."

"I wouldn't ride a foot with you, you miserable, cheating dog!" sobbed Lotus. "I might have known better than to trust a crooked flat-foot."

A pompous interloper shouldered up.

"What seems to be the trouble here?" he demanded officiously. "What's the matter with this little girl, you?"

"Mind your business," muttered Thwaite warningly.

"What have you done to this little girl? What is she crying about?"

"Get out of this and keep out," growled Thwaite. "This is my affair."

"I'll make it my affair, sir, if you get impudent with me," declared the impromptu Galahad, conscious of much moral and physical support at hand if he needed it. "I'll call a constable!"

Thwaite suddenly flashed his badge and snarled at the gathered spectators:

"Now clear out, all of you! Move on. Speed it. Come on, Miss Decker. If you won't come of your own accord I'll have to make you come."

"You just dare!" she wailed defiantly.

"I'll ask you again," he said grimly. "Are you coming or not?"

"I won't, I won't, I won't!" squealed Lotus.

Then Thwaite acted.

He gathered his one hundred and five pounds of disputant into his arms and carried her bodily away from the place and plumped her into the front seat of his car.

"There, by gravy!" he panted. "One advantage in being a cop—if your wife won't mind you you can give her a ride to the hoosegow!"

"Your wife!" retorted Lotus with tear-stained sarcasm. "Where do you get that stuff? Why, I wouldn't look at you twice if you washed your neck once in a while, even! You—you—"

"Here, here!" barked Thwaite, grabbing her by the wrist as he stepped on the starter. "I've had enough of this. I'm boss around here and you might as well know it."

"Why, of all the nerve—"

"You cut it, and cut it quick! Get down to earth. You call me another name and I'll pull your hair and bite your ear off!"

Lotus laughed into his blazing blue eyes. She couldn't help it. It was nice to be manhandled this way.

"You want to keep your head, if you expect to help that brother of yours," Thwaite went on, less severely. "He's all right. He didn't do it—he didn't have anything

Still Camped at the Scene
of the Crime, Sergeant
Montigny Makes Further
Headway With New Clues

Then Thwaite Acted! He Gathered His One Hundred and Five Pounds of Disputant Into His Arms and Carried Her Bodily Away From the Place and Plumped Her Into the Front Seat of His Car.

to do with knocking off Milburn. I've got sense enough to see that."

"He didn't, he didn't!" cried Lotus.

"He's been a fool to hide out like this. He has only made it look worse for him."

Thwaite put on speed.

"He wanted to—to give himself up," faltered Lotus, "but he was afraid. He didn't do a thing wrong. But he was on the platform of that car—he told me he was—and he was afraid he couldn't prove he wasn't the man who—who—"

"He was on the platform?" snapped Thwaite. "When? The night Milburn was killed?"

"Yes," said Lotus tremblingly.

"And he didn't do it?"

"No, he didn't, he didn't!" quavered Lotus. "But he saw it all—he saw Milburn killed!"

"Well, now, this is getting thick!" muttered Thwaite as he worked his way through traffic. "Is that all he told you? Didn't he give you any details?"

"He couldn't. That's all he had time to tell me, when I was talking to him back there. I asked him to tell me the truth, if he was the one who did it. And he swore he wasn't. He just said he saw the shot fired—he didn't see who did it. But he said it was going hard with him if you caught him. You ask him. He'll tell you the truth now. He's sick of this dodging."

"All right now, sweetie. I was joking about taking you to headquarters. The Inspector doesn't want you—unless you want to talk to him. I'll take you back to the hotel, and you lie down and take it easy for a while. I'll let you know how things come out, after we've talked to your brother."

"No! I don't want to go to the hotel. I want to go with you—to some place I can be of some use. I'm all right now, Bill. I'm sorry I cussed you out. I see how everything was. You're right. It's the best thing for Warren to come clean with everything. You'd have caught him sooner or later."

At headquarters Laval was preparing with rare satisfaction to receive his long-awaited but unexpected guest. He had sent for Montigny to be present when he questioned Warren Decker. Lotus was told she would have to wait outside until she was needed.

Laval took time to commend Sergeant Thwaite privately.

"Good work!" he said warmly. "I promised a certain party we would have an arrest today, and thanks to you the promise has been kept."

"You haven't got your man, sir," declared Thwaite soberly. "But I think you've got an A-1 witness." He told the Inspector what Lotus had said.

At Sergeant Montigny's request Warren Decker was not merely fingerprinted by the bureau of identification, but was palm-printed as well. It developed that he wore a number eight shoe, his height was six feet one, his weight one hundred and eighty-six pounds. No Bertillon measurements were needed to determine the bass timbre of his voice.

Montigny, conferring with Laval before the examination of the prisoner was started, displayed his photographs and developed records on the knobs he had removed from the rear door of Milburn's private car.

"This is the man," said Montigny confidently, "who tried the outside and inside knobs. You can see it plainly, Inspector—better than finger-prints because the lines are bolder. You can see that he tried the outside knob with his right hand, the inside knob with his left."

"How do you get that, Pierre?"

"In the right hand the so-called head line and life line are closely conjoined at the side of the hand. In the left, you see, these lines do not join at all, but are fully a quarter of an inch apart. There's a significance to that, a palmist would tell you."

"What, Pierre?"

Montigny shrugged. "I put little store by it, Inspector. Science maintains that the various irregularities and flexion-folds of the hands are purely accidental and mean nothing at all, save that they mark the points where the skin of the palm is tacked down, so to speak, to the deep layer of the dermis, to permit the thick skin to be created when the fist is doubled. Yet I have checked many palms in the identification bureau, and it seems to me that the lines do mean something—in denoting character, I mean, not in foretelling the future."

"What would these mean?"

"The distance between the life line and the head line in the left hand, Inspector, would be taken by a chiromancer to mean that the owner of this hand was inclined by Nature to be radical, rather than conservative and conformative to custom. Many murderers have that peculiarity—they lack self-control, they fly off the handle; they have not been able to live rationally, to conduct their lives in accordance with the dictates of their head—the life line and the head line are far apart. But in the right hand of Decker—"

"The lines do meet, are closely interwoven," said Laval, smiling faintly.

"Indicating, supposedly, since in palmistry the left hand is 'what you are,' the right 'what you make of yourself,' that Mr. Decker succeeded in controlling these impulses. He has lived rationally, though his impulse is to live emotionally. He controls himself, but since he is markedly neurotic and knows it, that effort to keep himself in check has been a miserable, lifelong job."

"Ah, yes, you said he was nervous. Now, just where is that displayed, Pierre?"

The Inspector's tone was ironical, but there was no mistaking his interest.

"In the scores of tiny, criss-cross lines running here, there, and everywhere in Mr. Decker's palm. Look at your own hand, Inspector. It is hard, sallow, smooth, almost without lines save the three main ones. You haven't a nerve in your body. This gentleman is a prey to nerves."

Laval shook his head in mock sadness. "Montigny, you missed your calling. You should be on the stage. As a magician, a clairvoyant and fortune-teller, you would be unexcelled. . . . But I admit one thing—it was Mr. Decker's palm that tried the doorknob of the private car. Let us talk to him."

Warren Decker was a person of mobile and sensitive features. His eyes were soft, worried brown, his face prematurely lined with wrinkles. His complexion was pale and he flushed quickly when annoyed or excited. His voice was a deep, rich bass, pleasant in ordinary speaking tones but capable of harsh gruffness.

He said he was twenty-eight years old and that he had traveled for the firm of Graves & Company for six years. He admitted at once the accuracy of most of the information the police had about him.

"Yes, sir, I'm supposed to be out around Chicago or Milwaukee," he said.

"Then what are you doing in Montreal?" asked Laval.

"I came here," he replied quietly, but in a voice that tremble faintly, "to protect my sister."

"You felt that she needed help, that she was in danger?"

"Yes." He paid his respects bitterly to Milburn and his associates. "My sister is only a kid, Inspector," he said huskily. "She had no business with a gang like that. Milburn had no more conscience than a rattlesnake, and the people who rode him to his death were worse."

12

"You seem convinced," said Laval drily, "that Mr. Milburn was a gentleman well worth killing."

"Good riddance," said Decker unfeelingly. "I didn't kill him—I would not have done that—but I'm not sorry that it happened. I didn't do it," he repeated angrily, "and you'll have a hard time proving that I did."

"You had threatened Mr. Milburn, had you not?"

"No, I never talked to him, or about him, either, to anybody except my sister."

"You called him on the telephone."

"I tried to. They wouldn't let me speak to him, once they learned who I was. They pretended he was of town. I tried to get my sister to break away from these jackals who were trying to drag her with them. She wouldn't listen to me. She said I was narrow and old-fashioned, silly to talk like that. Her mother was worried sick when she went to New York in the first place. I tried to keep an eye on her, to get her connected somehow with decent people—there are decent people connected with the stage—but she fell in with the worst scum afloat."

"You did not want her to go on this trip."

"I forbade her to go. I tried every means of persuasion I could think of, and then I forbade her. I threatened her."

"With what?"

"I threatened to make trouble for her and for Milburn, too, if she I insisted on going. Her mother knew nothing about it and I did not tell her, because I didn't want her to be anxious. But Lotus is not of age—she's only seventeen—and I told her there was a way to stop her by law if she would not listen to reason."

Decker had worked himself into a frenzy of hatred and resentment.

The Inspector waited until he was quieter. Then:

"So you killed George Heston, too?"

Decker retorted with a bitter laugh: "I did not kill either of the dogs. The evening George Heston was murdered I spent in a tavern on St. Catherine street—from seven o'clock until eleven. You can leave that out, Inspector. The waiter there will remember me. So will the man who sat at the same table with me. I did not speak to him for an hour, but then we got talkative. We drank six bottles of ale apiece. His name is Jones and he's a little Cockney who told me he was a clerk at the Ritz. Later he got confidential and told me the truth—he was a waiter at the Ritz. He was out on a postman's holiday, but he was letting somebody else wait on him, for a change. Go get him, if you don't believe me. William Jones."

"That shall be done," promised Laval. "Tell me when you got on the rear platform of Mr. Milburn's car."

"At St. Johns. I don't know just what time it was. Somewhere around one o'clock."

"What were you there for?"

"To see what was happening. To find out what I could. To see whether it was necessary for me to force my way in and get my sister out of that crowd of libertines."

"Why did you not do this sooner? You were on the same train all the way from Rutland, were you not?"

Warren Decker, the Sole
Witness of the Crime,
Tells His Story to
a Skeptical
Audience

". . . I had one foot over the railing
of the platform, and was getting
ready to get off, when something made me
take another look inside the car. I saw Mil-
burn slump in his chair and I knew that someone had killed him."

"All the way from New York, for that matter. There was some mix-up on account of a wreck, a lot of switching and delay. A mixed train was made up at Rutland. I had the chance to go back to Milburn's car, yes; but I did not want to, before dark. I did not want my sister to see me. I did not want to cause trouble publicly unless I had to. I intended to take charge of her when we got to Montreal, anyhow. And the first chance I had after dark—the first stop we made was Rouses Point—I walked to the rear alongside the train to see what was happening on Milburn's car."

"And what was happening?"

"I could not see into the car. I decided the next time the train stopped I would climb up on the back platform—I did not have time at Rouses Point—so I did that at St. Johns, the next stop. The car was last on the train, away down the track, so nobody saw me."

"And what did you discover this time?"

"Nothing, at first. Everything was quiet. There was nobody in the back end of the car but Milburn, and he was sitting in a chair the left side of the car, as I looked in. He seemed to be dozing."

"And what did you do?"

"I started to get down off the platform so I could hurry back to my car. I decided that if everything was all that quiet I wouldn't bother about raising any row with Milburn until the next morning in Montreal. I had one foot over the railing of the platform and getting ready to get off, when something made me take another look in the car. I was looking through the left window as you look forward in the car—the window had been broken, so I could see everything plainly. I saw the curtains of the door move, over by Milburn. And then somebody poked an automatic pistol through curtains, leveled at Milburn's head. The train had just started off with a lurch and I could hear two or three porters calling 'All aboard!' I think I shouted to warn Milburn, but it was too late. I didn't hear a report or see a flash at all, but I saw Milburn slump in his chair, and I knew somebody had killed him."

"You gave no alarm?"

"I tried to get in, Inspector. I tried the door and it would not open from the outside. I reached my arm in through the broken window and tried the inside knob. Nothing doing. I could not find the latch that was keeping the door locked."

"So you did what?"

"I jumped off the train, and nearly broke a leg doing it."

"Why did you do that, why did you run away, when you knew a man had been murdered?"

"Who wouldn't do it?" retorted Decker. "Why should I stay there, be caught on the back platform of the car— get mixed up in a murder case—perhaps be accused of murder?"

"You are," said Laval succinctly, "accused of murder."

"But I didn't do it," cried Decker hoarsely. "I swear I didn't! I swear I could not get into the car."

"Hm! You did not wait to see whether the person who killed Milburn came into the car?"

"No, sir, I didn't wait for anything."

"Did you see the arm, or the hand that held the pistol—was it a man's arm or a woman's arm?"

"I could not tell which it was, Inspector."

"You did not see a man's coat sleeve or cuff."

"Yes, I saw a cuff—it could have been either a man's or a woman's. It was a blue sleeve with a white cuff—the sleeve and cuff of a bath robe or dressing gown, I figured, a blue one trimmed in white."

Montigny explored his pocket for a cigar. His eyes met Laval's significantly.

"Are you absolutely certain of this, Decker?" asked Laval sharply. "Can you take oath it was a blue sleeve with a white cuff?"

"Yes, sir. I am absolutely sure of it."

"And you are sure it was an automatic pistol this person aimed at Milburn?"

"I felt sure of it at the time. But since then, of course, I've read in the papers about the target pistols that looked like automatics."

"Did you not, as a fact," demanded Laval coldly, "know all about those target pistols—about the target practice they had been having in the car?"

"No, sir. I did not."

"Hm! What did you do when you jumped off the train at St. Johns?"

"Why, I walked back to the station, Inspector. Nobody had seen me. evidently, and I was glad of that, for I knew an awful row was going to be raised when they found Milburn dead, and if anybody should have seen me hopping off that car I would have been as good as hanged."

"What did you do at the station?"

"Why, there was a bunch of people there—ten or eleven, I'd say—in charge of a uniformed immigration inspector. I knew the idea—they had been taken off the train and were going to be deported back to Rouses Point. I had friend once who was going to Montreal to take a job, and they did him that way—classed him as 'alien contract labor' because there was a lot of unemployment in Quebec and they were enforcing the immigration laws to the letter. I thought of that when I saw the inspector and those people. I hung around for a bit while the inspector was going over his papers—I knew there were two inspectors and the other one had stayed on the train—so I went up to this inspector pretty soon and told him the other one had put me off the train. He couldn't find me on his list, of course—I gave him a phony name—but he decided the safest thing to do was to go on and deport me with the rest."

"So you got a free ride, under escort, to Rouses Point?"

"Yes, sir. On the next train." Decker, for the first time, smiled faintly. "It was just luck, Inspector. I suppose you'd have had the bracelets on me long before, if it hadn't been for that."

"What did you do with your grips? You did not leave them on the train."

"In the baggage car, Inspector. I had checked them through. I caught the first northbound train out of Rouses Point and came to Montreal and claimed them."

"You had no trouble getting by the inspectors?"

"No, sir. There was another pair of them, and this time I was not an 'immigrant' but a harmless traveling salesman."

"You seem very proud of your cleverness," observed Laval tartly. "You were extremely anxious to get into Montreal, weren't you? Why? For the purpose of killing George Heston?"

"No. I didn't want to kill anybody, Inspector. But I knew my sister needed me more than ever, when there had been a murder on that car. I was afraid she might get mixed up in it somehow—and you did detain her, you wouldn't let her go back to New York."

There was a pause and Montigny took advantage of it.

"May I ask him a question, Inspector? . . . When you came up from New York on this train, Mr. Decker, you rode in a Pullman, of course?"

"Yes, sir."

"You had a through Pullman ticket to Montreal—a lower berth or a seat?"

"Good riddance," Said Decker, Unfeelingly. "I didn't kill him —I would not have done that— but I'm not sorry that it happened!"

"No, sir. The train was crowded, and I could only get a chair, as far as Rutland. The conductor said he might be able to fix me up later."

"And did he? Did he sell you a lower berth from Rutland into Montreal?"

"No, sir," said Decker positively. "What he sold me was a seat from Rutland to Rouses Point."

Montigny delved into an envelope and extracted the Pullman cash fare receipt he had found on the platform of Milburn's car.

"You are mistaken, Mr. Decker," insisted the Sergeant. "I have your receipt here. You dropped it, unfortunately, on the platform of Mr. Milburn's car. It is punched for the correct date and amount and filled in with the plain inscription, 'Rutland to Montreal.'"

Decker looked at it thoughtfully and shook his head. "Somebody else dropped it, then. That isn't mine. As a matter of fact"—he reached into his inside pocket—"I've got mine right here. I saved it, force of habit, don't you see, for my expense account? The company requires it."

Laval and Montigny inspected the neatly folded slip which he drew from his pocketbook. Decker was right. It was a cash fare receipt from Rutland to Rouses Point.

Laval tapped it reflectively. He pressed a button on his desk. "I am holding you, Decker, for further examination," he said.

When Decker had gone the Inspector and the Sergeant sat for a time in silence.

"It seems to me, Inspector," said Montigny presently, "that the young man may be right—and the other one I found on the platform had been planted there!"

"I don't agree with you, Pierre," declared Laval. "The second Pullman receipt does not mean necessarily that he speaks the truth. If it were a 'plant,' as you suggest, my guess would be that Decker planted it—he produced the other receipt with suspicious readiness."

Montigny nodded slowly. "Left it as a blind. I see what you mean."

"What would be easier than for Decker to pick up a receipt discarded by someone else, with the very purpose of leaving it on the back platform—knowing that, if he were ever accused of having dropped the receipt there, he could clear himself in a measure by producing his own?"

"The fellow," agreed Montigny, "would be capable of even so involved a plan as that, I admit. And yet . . . why should he wish to leave on the car platform any indication whatever that he had been there—he or anybody else? Particularly when he intended to tell us, if apprehended, that the murder was committed, not by an outsider, but by one of the passengers on the car?"

Laval permitted himself a gesture of resignation. "We are at sea, Montigny," he acknowledged "We are floundering. We cannot know what to believe."

"Then the white and blue dressing gown of Perry Laith," added Montigny, as though thinking aloud. "How could this chap who had never been on the car know of the existence, even of this garment?"

"He could have seen it through the windows of Aitken's stateroom, when it was hanging in there," said Laval. "But I acknowledge that is unlikely, extremely unlikely. It is virtually impossible to see anything through the fine-meshed and smoke-blackened screens of a Pullman, unless it is something very close to the window. But then—"

"Decker's sister," interrupted Montigny. "He saw her, had occasion to talk to her. She might have told him of Laith's dressing-gown—the bullets in its pocket."

"Laith!" said Laval meditatively. "There is one worth watching. It is unpleasant to fill our jail with suspects we cannot convict. But I ought to lock him up."

"At large, it is always possible, he may be more useful; he may make a false step."

"We could prove a beautiful motive there, could we not?"

"Perfect—the known friend, confidant, grafting partner of Milburn's mistress, the lady who receives three hundred thousand dollars as a dying gift of Milburn. But one thing we cannot prove against him, Inspector—opportunity!"

Laval frowned. "Exactly. We cannot prove that, in Milburn's murder, against a single individual on the car. Three witnesses—a lawyer, a porter, the wife of the second man murdered—all tell us they heard the voice of the killer, directly preceding the discovery of the murder. There remains, by the simple process of elimination, only one living person who could have killed Milburn and escaped by way of the rear platform—and that is Warren Decker!"

"And he, I predict," said Sergeant Montigny placidly, "did not kill Milburn."

Laval turned on him impatiently. "He must have killed Milburn. We have no choice but to believe it. He admits his presence on the platform, his motive, his animosity. You will have to give me better reasons for not believing it, Montigny, than the Pullman receipt and the dressing gown."

"I have a strong conviction, Inspector," said Montigny slowly, "that the man who killed Milburn is also the man who killed George Heston. And I am convinced that this man Decker's alibi is a perfect one—I am sure we shall find that his drinking partner Jones and the waiter at the St. Catherine street tavern will bear him out."

"Thwaite shall see to that at once," promised Laval, and he sent for the Sergeant, who had been waiting none too patiently in the outer room with Lotus Decker.

Thwaite heard his instructions and hurried off with promise of immediate results.

Inspector Laval questioned Lotus Decker briefly.

She asserted tearfully that she had never seen or heard of Perry Laith's white and blue dressing gown, and consequently would never have mentioned it to her brother Warren if she had had the chance—which she did not have, she declared, for she had exchanged only a few hurried words with him at their two meetings.

Laval sent her back to her hotel.

"Aitken is right," he observed to Sergeant Montigny; "that one is of better stripe than the others with whom she associated. Heigh-ho!" he slumped in his chair and arched his ten finger-tips pensively. "Where do we go, as the Americans say, from here?"

Montigny puffed vigorously at his cigar. "Perhaps tomorrow," he observed through the blue haze, "when Captain Berthier returns to help us, all will be quickly unraveled."

"He so indicated," said Laval dryly. "I shall not hold my breath, however, until he solves the mystery. He still sticks to Aitken."

"And Aitken could not have done it. He could not have killed Milburn, and assuredly he could not while languishing in jail, have paid an ectoplasmic visit to George Heston and killed that gentleman."

"No," agreed Laval unwillingly. "I had thought of him mainly as an accessory. I had hoped to find some trace of a connection between Aitken and Decker—but I

Warren Decker's Failure to
Identify the Slayer Puts Him
In a Suspicious Light In Spite
of His Pullman
Ticket Alibi.

There Was a Long-Distance Telephone Call
for Laval Just at That Juncture, But It Was
Not from New York. It Was from One of
Capt. Berthier's Men at St. Johns. "Perhaps," Said Laval, "that Eastwick girl didn't
lie after all—about the postoffice box and
the stolen key."

confess there seems no present hope. Lennox and Moode and the New York police department have not been able to establish the fact that Aitken and Decker even knew each other—or that Aitken was acquainted with the Decker girl, for that matter, prior to this trip on the private car."

"I should say, Inspector, there is no more to be gained from Aitken save the contents of the will which he claims Milburn entrusted to him. Our steamer bearing the mail for India—when does it reach Liverpool?"

"Day after tomorrow," replied Laval. "Scotland Yard has promised full co-operation. I have been in touch with the ship and have tried to get quicker action, but it is impossible to have the seals of the mail bags broken until arrival at Liverpool. However, I am afraid that Milburn's supposed documents dispatched to India— even if they exist—will not help us. If they prove to be copies of Milburn's will, I do not see even then how they can have a bearing on the solution of these murders."

"Aitken still contends that his employer killed himself?"

"Yes, and probably not without reason. I think the man is convinced that Milburn intended to end his life. I think it quite reasonable to suppose that Milburn might indeed have had that intention."

"But failed to carry it out? That is my belief, too, Inspector. He was murdered before he could become a suicide."

"And the murderer in so doing," added Laval, "presented two hundred thousand dollars indemnity to Dorothea Dustin in place of—nothing! Astonishingly simple motive there, Pierre, if we could only pin it to a personality. There is every indication of a carefully plotted and skillfully executed crime so skillfully done, Pierre, that it seems no one could have done it—except Decker."

"And he would have had grave difficulty, Inspector. In order to fulfill our conditions, he must have had fore-knowledge of the deadliness of the air pistols, he must have unbolted noiselessly the door of the car, which I found no easy task; he must have found Milburn nodding in his chair—or held a conversation with him, as you wish—he must have stepped off a distance of five feet, which would have put him beyond the curtains of the door and therefore in sight of the porter knocking at Aitken's door. Or he must have killed Milburn—this is the other theory—summoned the porter, and talked, for some unexplained reason, in two voices. And he must have gone as far as the dining room to ring a bell, and to Aitken's stateroom to put bullets in the pockets of the dressing gown. To complete his test of extraordinary agility, he must have made his exit through the back door and escaped from a train which must, by that time, have been moving considerably!"

Laval grinned perplexedly. "True, true, Pierre. And all of it argues indisputably a confederate in the car. Mr. Decker could not, in his wildest feats of dexterity, have gone to the other end of the car to tamper with the annunciator. Then who did—who was the confederate?"

"I have canvassed the possibilities, Inspector." Montigny took out some notes he had scribbled. "I think we may eliminate the women. We must find someone, in the first place, who changed the annunciator wiring. That is not a woman's trick. Women seem to have no talent for the intricacies of wiring and the mysteries of electricity. I have known women lawyers, women doctors, women elevator boys, but no women electricians. Am I sound, Inspector?"

"You are sound, Pierre."

"A woman would have been afraid of getting shocked fooling with live wires; whereas a man would be likelier to know that an annunciator system requires only two to six volts of power and therefore is harmless."

"Agreed, Montigny. A man committed the trickery with the bell system. What man?"

13

"We have five who were on the car. Aitken, whose possible culpability we have discussed extensively; Wilks
the porter, Moode the detective and bodyguard; Perry
Laith, the particular friend of Dot Dustin, and George
Heston, who paid for something or other with his life."

"Any of them," said Laval, gloomily, "could have
changed the wire terminals. This gets us nowhere."

"I was going to say, Inspector," replied Montigny
suavely, "that the most likely suspects are those against
whom we have a bit of evidence. There are two—Aitken and the negro porter. Aitken, we may say, profited somewhat by the shift in wiring. The change made
it possible for the murderer, summoning the porter
by pressing a lounge button, to ring up a call on the
annunciator from Aitken's stateroom—and this, of
course, made it possible for Aitken to be aroused by the
porter just at the time when both of them could hear the
voice or voices in the lounge. It seemed to give Aitken
a complete alibi."

"I don't know," said Laval, a shade irritably. "We
might as logically take things the other way around—
someone else might have profited more than Aitken by
the change in wiring. Someone might even have made
the shift to incriminate Aitken."

"And that," conceded Montigny promptly, "is well to consider. Viewed from one angle, it would have been folly for Aitken to leave this damaging evidence against himself, when he could just as easily have summoned the porter by pressing the button in his stateroom, without any tampering with bell system. So suppose, for the moment, we eliminate Aitken?"

"All right. Consider him out of it."

"We come next to the porter. The negro Wilks had had long experience on Pullman cars. Bells were his principal concern in life. He knew annunciators—this one, by the way, is not a standard Pullman annunciator; it is a special type ordered by the architect for Milburn's private car. It is simpler than the usual kind—easier to get into."

"Very well. The porter could have changed the annunciator easily. So could anybody else, unfortunately."

"But the porter had a motive, a reward. Twelve hundred dollars, a fortune in his eyes. A change in the bell system gave him the excuse of awakening Aitken—of having Aitken as a witness to the voice or voices in the lounge—which, in turn, established a beautiful alibi for Wilks."

Laval considered that. "Specious," he conceded. "But much above, I am afraid, Brother Wilks' mentality. Also, he bears too emphatically the appearance of innocence. No Machiavelli, that black fellow. He might be capable, yes, of stealing twelve hundred dollars from the dead form of Milburn, though I doubt it greatly. But not this careful and cunning pre-arrangement, this preparation of an alibi. No, Montigny. Not Wilks."

Montigny smiled, almost happily. "I was sure you would say that, Inspector. I wanted you to say it, for that is my opinion, too. We eliminate Wilks, then, as the inside confederate. There remain Perry Laith, George

Heston and Moode the detective. Mr. Moode, so far as we know, is merely a dumb animal, a blundering body-guard—but no one, in this inquiry, can be placed above suspicion."

"Except Heston," specified Laval. "He was murdered."

"But he might have been murdered, Inspector," put in Montigny quickly, "because he was the confederate—because he knew too much."

"That, of course, has occurred to me," said Laval, "but it is only another might-have-been. He is eliminated by death, at least, from our present list of possible living suspects. That does not mean, of course, that he was not the confederate. It is conceivable that he pretended drunkenness so that his wife would permit him to take the lower berth which gave him the opportunity to play the necessary tricks."

"But excusing him now on the ground of his decease," went on Montigny, "we have left only Detective Moode and Perry Laith to suspect. We exclude Moode because we know nothing against him but his stupidity. We are more attracted by Mr. Laith because we know of a possible motive, a plausible collaboration, a great gain that might accrue to Laith by the death of his friend Dot Dustin's good provider. We know that Laith and Milburn disliked each other, that Laith figured in the last quarrel Milburn had with his mistress. And we know last but not least"—Montigny paused to give his words emphasis—"that of all our little group of serious parasites, Laith is the only man who had the opportunity to kill George Heston!"

Laval eyed him keenly and nodded. "All of which makes it appear," he remarked, "that we are arguing in favor of two confederates—Perry Laith and George Heston in league—while a third person killed Milburn. Really, Pierre, we are going too fast. Neither Heston nor

Laith could have killed Milburn, without the knowledge and subsequent perjury of the negro Wilks and Mrs. Heston, who would have seen anybody who came out of the lounge through the corridor leading forward into the car. And if that pair lied, we are saddled with four confederates."

Montigny chuckled. "That would be four. I could add even a possible fifth—provided we agree that Decker did not come in and kill Milburn. For if he did not, and if a person from the inside actually did shoot Milburn, wearing Perry Laith's dressing gown, why then we are forced to the assumption that it was a stranger who had hidden in the car, perhaps, who shot Milburn and made his escape by way of the back platform."

"And vanished into thin air at St. Johns!" Laval rose abruptly and strode the length of the room. "Absurd, absurd, it is all absurd, Montigny! Warren Decker killed Milburn, and that is all there is to it. He had a confederate—and we must find out who that was. Perry Laith is the most likely. The man has a bad record."

"Anything new about him from New York?"

"Yes, a little. Laith has never been accused of a crime, but he was questioned, and privately suspected, in connection with the Coringham jewel robbery—you member the case? The rich Mrs. Coringham enjoyed playing around with 'bohemians.' Laith was one of her playboys, was present at the party at which she was robbed. Nothing definite against him, but McEniry says he is unquestionably a crook."

"Shall you take him in, Inspector?"

"Not as yet. He cannot get away. I've two men on him. There should be another report from Lennox, by the way. I have ordered him back, the Eastwick girl with him, and Moode, too. I think they have done all they can at that end."

There was a long-distance telephone call for Laval just at that juncture, but it was not from New York. It was one of Captain Berthier's associates of the Provincial Police, at St. Johns.

He was calling, he said, in reference to the letter to Calcutta which was supposed to have been posted by the porter Wilks on the night of Tuesday, August eighteenth.

"It was mailed, Inspector," said Laval's informant. "We have been able to trace it."

"Yes? That is helpful."

"But it was not forwarded as addressed. It went back to New York."

"Back to New York!" exclaimed Laval. "Why?"

"Insufficient postage—or rather, the wrong kind of postage, sir. It had American stamps on it. I'll tell you how it happened, and why we haven't been able to get on the track of it before this. One of the postal clerks here was taken sick day before yesterday, Wednesday, that was, with ptomaine poisoning, and they thought he was going to die."

"Well, did he?"

"No, sir. He's getting over it, and he was just able to talk today, for the first time. He remembered the envelope. He handled it. Ordinarily they might pass a letter on through that had an American stamp on it instead of a Canadian one; but this one took a lot of postage, and there has been such a rush of tourists around here lately, and so many people mailing picture postcards with American stamps on them, that the post-office people got tired of it and issued an order to simply stamp 're-turn to sender' on all mail matter that had incorrect postage."

"And they returned this letter to New York?"

"Yes, sir, to the box number on the envelope."

"And the clerk made no record of the box number?"

"No, sir. That isn't customary."

Laval thanked him. He replaced the receiver. He passed a hand wearily over his brow.

"Perhaps," he observed, "the Eastwick girl didn't lie after all about the post-office box and the stolen key!"

The funeral of J. P. Milburn was delayed until Friday afternoon, August twenty-first, awaiting the arrival of his young son, Herbert, who had hastened across country from Denver by air express.

Helen Eastwick felt in a wretched state, but she considered it her duty to attend the services and to do all else that she could to comfort Milburn's boy, an earnest and likable youth of twenty-two who had been deeply affected by the tragedy.

She returned to the house with him after the last rites at the cemetery. She had urged him to try not to give further thought to the circumstances of his father's death, at least until he had had a night's rest. But he asked her interminable questions, eagerly and nervously, and she told him all she knew.

A uniformed policeman on the stoop of Milburn's town house had a message for her.

"You are to call Inspector McEniry at headquarters, Miss," he said, "at once. The Inspector says it's extremely urgent. There's a car waiting to take you down."

The policeman had not said please, but that breach of amenities did not disturb Helen. She hurried to the telephone.

"I want you here, pronto!" McEniry told her. "Young Mr. Milburn, too, if he feels equal to it. I think we have something of importance to him—I don't know yet. We're waiting on you. Make it snappy."

"I'm not," gasped Helen, "arrested, am I?"

The Inspector laughed. "No, we've got nothing on you yet, lady. We're calling you in on this mainly because you were Mr. Milburn's secretary, that's all."

Herbert Milburn accepted the chance with alacrity. He would work day and night if need be, he declared bitterly, to help the police find the man who killed his father.

They were whisked down Madison, Fourth and Lafayette—ignoring traffic lights with their officially tagged car—to Centre street. In the office of Inspector McEniry a group of men awaited them. With the Inspector were Detective Lennox of Montreal, a representative of Bob Aitken's law firm and Detective Moode, back, it seemed, from Baltimore. Moode's forehead was wrinkled in fixed puzzlement. He seemed beset by a legion of knotty problems.

McEniry indicated seats for his new callers.

He had on his desk before him a large and bulky manila envelope, its face much decorated with stamps and inscriptions. He turned it over speculatively and a red wax seal on the flap at the end of the envelope came into view.

He handed the unopened packet to Helen Eastwick.

"Know anything about this?" he queried crisply.

The first glance brought an exclamation of surprise from Helen. "Why, yes! That is—no. Mr. Aitken told me about it. I mean he told me that he had been questioned about it. How did it get here so quickly?"

It had been addressed to Robert Aitken in care of the American Express Company in Calcutta, India, and was postmarked St. Johns, Quebec, August nineteenth. It bore a further bold inscription: "Not to be opened until September 18." There were rubber-stamped legends, "Return to sender," and "Incorrect postage."

"It didn't go to India," said McEniry bluntly. "It had the wrong kind of stamps. Were you the one who was dumb enough to put American stamps on a letter mailed in Canada?"

"Thank you, no," said Helen sweetly but effectively. "I did not handle that letter. You will note that it was addressed by Mr. Milburn himself, with a pen. I understand the colored porter mailed it. I had no knowledge of it until Mr. Aitken told me, later."

"What did he tell you about it—later?"

"Why, I talked to him in—at headquarters in Montreal," faltered Helen. "He told me he had been questioned about such a letter which the porter on Mr. Milburn's car said he had mailed at St. Johns. He asked me whether I knew anything about it, and I told him that I did not. There was another envelope, of the same size, that I addressed to Mr. Aitken for Mr. Milburn, but I did that on the typewriter."

"On the typewriter, eh? When was that?"

"Why—" Helen hesitated. "Some time that evening—that awful night. But Mr. Milburn didn't tell me to address it to Calcutta, but just 'Mr. Robert Aitken, Present,' and to type on it, 'Not to be opened until September eighteenth.'

"Yes, we know all about that one," growled McEniry. "It's the one Aitken sent to his lawyer friends in Montreal, and they found out afterwards it didn't have anything in it but blank paper. All right, now." The Inspector tapped the envelope before him impatiently. "The question we've been discussing here is whether or not to open this. It's private mail and all that, and this gentleman from Mr. Aitken's law' firm advises against it. But Mr. Aitken is in jail in Montreal, suspected of murder or connection with it. And it's my opinion that if there's a chance of there being anything in this envelope that would throw light on the question of who killed Mr. Milburn, why, it's my duty to open it—thirty days or no thirty days. What do you think, Miss Eastwick?"

"Why—I hardly know," hesitated Helen.

"I'll leave it up to Mr. Milburn's son, then. What do you say?"

"May I ask how it came into your hands?" inquired Herbert Milburn dubiously.

"The postal authorities turned it over to us. Miss Eastwick, you see, had the key to this post-office box it was returned to—Drawer 1678-B—which was a private box Mr. Milburn and Mr. Aitken had for their own, er—purposes. But she lost the key—or it was stolen from her—last night, and today when she went to look in this box it was empty. Is that right, Miss Eastwick?"

"Why—yes, it was empty."

"Well, sir, none of us had sense enough to think of asking at the General Delivery window till Mr. Moode here"—he indicated the detective with an amused gesture—"got back from Baltimore today. It occurred to him that maybe there would be some mail for Mr. Milburn or Mr. Aitken, so he went and asked, at the central post-office. He didn't know about the box. Well, there wasn't any mail at the General Delivery window, but they referred to the third assistant postmaster, and that gentleman called me up and asked me what about it. He said there was some mail, addressed to that box, but he was holding it because Miss Eastwick had reported losing the key. So I sent a man over to identify Moode, and this is what we got. The post-office people couldn't trace the box number, because it was listed under a company name Miss Eastwick couldn't give them, but they went through every drawer in the outfit—there's a limited number, this size—until they found this letter addressed to Mr. Aitken. Now the question is, Mr. Milburn, what do you say? Do we open it, or turn it over to Mr. Aitken? I'll leave it up to you."

Herbert Milburn hesitated but a moment. "Open it," he decided.

Inspector McEniry did so.

He took from the envelope two separately folded documents in pale blue brief-backs. They bore on their backs the typed inscription: "Copy. Last Will and Testament of James Proctor Milburn."

"Aahh!" exclaimed McEniry with a long-drawn exhalation. "I say we found something!"

He directed his attention first, however, to a folded sheet of white stationery. He opened it and read it to himself, with rapidly moving lips, and then exclaimed, "Listen to this!"

He read aloud:

> Dear Aitken:
> This scheme may be a poor safeguard, but I trust nobody on the car. They are desperate and unprincipled crooks, the lot of them, and my hurried thought just now it to get these copies safely out of their reach. I shall mail them to you at a ridiculously distant address. In the event anything has happened to the original, now in your hands, these copies will come back unclaimed, in due course—I should think within thirty days.
>
> I have not told you why I asked your promise of a month's silence. Perhaps it may sound simple, childishly bitter, to you when you read this. But I am bitter. For thirty days this scheming woman will think that she has come into a fortune—and then she will find

there is not a penny for her. I myself, as you probably know, wrote the "crank" letter. Let them think I was murdered—the miserable parasites! Let them think it for a month.

But I did not want you to know, dear boy, that I purposed to end the whole sorry business tonight. I shall. Do not think of it as the act of a coward, but only as the feeble refuge of a tired and sick old man, your friend,

J. P. Milburn.

P. S.—I am going to get Wilks to mail this, and bribe him to say nothing. He's a good boy, and I'm going to give him a last tip that will stagger him.

There was an awkward silence, an exchange of questioning glances.

Herbert Milburn choked a sound in his throat that might have been a sob.

"Then," he said huskily, "poor dad killed himself— after all! They drove him to it!"

McEniry said "Hm!" in a voice tinged with skepticism. He passed the paper to young Milburn.

"Your father's handwriting, is it?"

The youth nodded, swallowed hard.

McEniry opened one of the blue-backed documents and skimmed through it. The other he gave to the lawyer from Aitken's firm, requesting:

"Look this over, please, sir. You have a copy of the will that preceded this one. and you know more about it than I do.

"It's a hell of a note!" muttered Detective Moode, adding hastily: "Oh, I beg pardon, Miss Eastwick."

Another Elusive Envelope Is Located, This Time the
Contents Are Real; a Final Will and—a Suicide
Note from the "Murdered" Man

"Sorry," said the New York Inspector to Helen
Eastwick. "You're going back to Montreal tonight. I had a talk with Inspector Laval a while
ago." Detective Maude Grinned.
"Guess I'm not such a bum detective after all, Inspector, even
if I ain't on the force any more."
He Glanced at Helen Significantly.

Helen did not mind. She was patting the trembling hand of Herbert Milburn.

"I mean it's devilish," amended Moode awkwardly, "the way those grafters hounded the poor old gentleman—and a nicer man never lived, I'll say that for him!"

The lawyer cleared his throat.

"There is only one essential difference," he announced presently, "between this will and the preceding one, now revoked, which we had in our possession, and a copy of which I have here now for comparison."

"What's the difference?" grunted McEniry. "Trim off the legal embroidery, please, sir, and tell us briefly."

"The only difference," continued the attorney, "seems to be in Clause Eighteen. In the previous will Clause Eighteen provides a bequest of one hundred thousand dollars 'for my friend, Dorothea Dustin.'"

"And this will cuts her off," demanded McEniry quickly.

"It does. Clause Eighteen in the new will merely provides a bequest of ten thousand dollars for"—the lawyer paused as though it pained him—"for 'my friend, Robert Aitken.'"

There were two or three murmured exclamations from the listeners.

"Aitken!" growled Inspector McEniry. "How did he come in for a pick-up like that?"

"Who'd a-thought it!" murmured Detective Moode. "Didn't he leave me ten grand, too?"

The lawyer cleared his throat again.

"There are conditions stipulated. The first will, I should explain in justice to Mr. Aitken, made him executor and administrator of Mr. Milburn's estate, the emoluments of which appointment, I need not point out. would have been very considerable. The second will, which names Mr. Aitken as a beneficiary, does not name him as executor and administrator, our firm being substituted in that capacity; but it provides for Mr. Aitken the bequest of ten thousand dollars on the express stipulation that"—he read from the document—"that he observe strictly and to the letter the conditions imposed upon him as the sole possessor of this document, my last will and testament, not to divulge the nature of its contents, in full or in part, for the period of thirty days next succeeding the date of my decease.'"

"Oho!" interpreted McEniry. "Then he paid Aitken ten thousand bucks to keep his mouth shut for thirty days! Well, I wouldn't mind staying in jail myself for three hundred and thirty-three dollars a day!"

"I am sure," said Helen Eastwick, in low, incisive tones, "that Mr. Aitken would not have betrayed this confidence of Mr. Milburn's if he had not been paid a cent for it."

"Hm! I'm not so sure," grunted the Inspector. "I'm not so sure he didn't do his bit to 'speed the parting guest,' if you ask me. It looks funny! He was the only man who knew just what Mr. Milburn intended to do— and it looks like somebody who knew a lot of secrets stepped in and did it for him!"

"There is no justification," flared Helen, "for a remark like that."

"There's not, eh?" McEniry looked at her belligerently. "What's your big interest in this chap Aitken?"

"The 'big interest' that anybody would have," retorted Helen, "who knows Mr. Aitken as I know him. They haven't the slightest grounds on which to hold him, now that you have intercepted and read his mail. He at least did his best to keep his promise, but you have cleared him now—absolutely."

"He seems to have an ironbound alibi," supported Lennox, who admired Helen's spunk. "I mean as far as Mr. Milburn is concerned."

"Sure, two people besides Aitken heard somebody talking to Mr. Milburn before they, er—found the body," put in Detective Moode, and glance at young Milburn with a guilty knowledge of having talked too much.

For Herbert Milburn, his face the color of a sheet, had risen steadily and felt for the back of his chair.

"If you don't mind, gentlemen," he said almost inaudibly, "I'm going home. I'm pretty much done in with all of this."

"Sure, that's the thing for you to do," boomed the Inspector with hearty friendliness. He got up and put an enormous arm about the youth's shoulders. "You go home and rest up, old man. There's no help for things that are past and gone, is there? We can't make it any better by grieving, can we, boy? You come in to see me whenever you can, and if there's ever anything you need in my line, you just call me."

"Thank you," said Herbert Milburn. "Thanks to all of you gentlemen. And you, Miss Eastwick—"

He leaned against the facing of the door and sobbed aloud.

"I'm going with him," Helen impulsively.

"No, not so fast!" warned Inspector McEniry. "You stay here. He'll be all right."

Young Milburn left the room without turning his face to them again,

"Sorry," said the Inspector to Helen Eastwick. "You're to go back to Montreal tonight. I had a talk with Inspector Laval a while ago. He wants all three of you back. I've got to call him now, and tell him the news. Good work, you boys have done on this trip. That was a good hunch you had calling for the mail, Moode."

He glanced at Helen significantly. "We might not have thought of it in time."

Moode grinned. "Guess I'm not such a bum detective after all, Inspector," he said, "even if I ain't on the force any more!"

Jean-Baptiste Pierre Le Moyne Montigny, eight-year-old son and heir of the French-Canadian crook-catching house of that name, was vastly inveigled by the elegance of his papa's (temporary, it is true) private car.

Madame Montigny, whose reputation for thrift extended into many a mart of retail trade, had sought to reduce her husband's expenses by sending Jean-Baptiste to Bonaventure Station on Thursday with luncheon for his papa.

Madame Montigny's motive, were she perfectly candid, was not unmixed with stirrings of curiosity. She wanted Jean-Baptiste's opinion of this magnificent car of a millionaire in which the peculiar exigencies of the detecting business had landed her husband. Nor was she poorly entertained by the glowing account which poured from the lips of Jean-Baptiste when he returned home from his errand Thursday afternoon.

The chairs of the lounge had been magnifique in their softness, the carpets underfoot had yielded like velvety moss to his tread, the upholstery of the three staterooms had been a dream of opulence, but the crowning glory of it all, in Jean-Baptiste's opinion, was—the radio, oo, mamma, the radio!

14

Montigny had permitted him to switch on the non-singing radio, and Jean-Baptiste had been bitterly disappointed that it gave forth no melody. Jean-Baptiste had a small set all his own, a set of sorts, limited of range and raucous of tone, yet still a radio and his pride. It had been the gift of a dealer whom Montigny had helped in the small matter of apprehending a burglar. But it was not a millionaire's radio, and now Jean-Baptiste was spoiled. He wanted, above all conceivable desires just now, to hear the indescribably marvelous set on the Dorothea.

"It is in a most grand cabinet, mama, more wonderful than any to be seen in the magazine pictures. It has tubes, tubes, unbelievable—rows of tubes, so beautiful! And they light up!"

Madame Montigny shrugged. "Still—if it does not make the music—what good?"

"It will play," cried Jean-Baptiste ecstatically. "I know that it will play. Papa is wrong. He says it is the batteries. But it is not the batteries, because the electrician this morning has put new batteries in the car. And still it lights up but will not play."

"Do not annoy your father," counseled Madame Montigny. "He does not wish to be worried with you and with music when he is busy at work. I shall not send you again with luncheon tomorrow if you distress your father."

"But he will not be distressed," pleaded Jean-Baptiste. "He also wishes the radio to play—and I have told him that I am certain I know how to make it so."

"And what did your father say to that, young know-it-all?"

"He said to me to get out, that the electrician knew his business and the electrician had said the reason that it would not play."

"So? You see! You are, well enough, annoying your father!"

"No, mama. I wish only to try one thing, please, please! You remember when once our radio would not play music, and the tubes were lighted up just the same, and everything seemed to be all right, and we could not for the world find out why it would not play, and then we saw that a mouse had gnawed at the wires to the loud speaker! You remember?"

"I remember some happening of the kind."

"Well, that is what I am sure is the matter with the millionaire's radio—it is perhaps the loud speaker! And tomorrow when I go to take my papa his luncheon, can I not, please, take also my little loud speaker—just to try?"

Madame Montigny shrugged again. "Try it!" she challenged. "Your papa will box perhaps your ears. Then do not come crying to me."

Accordingly it transpired that on Friday at noon when Jean-Baptiste appeared again at the private car with a totally unneeded luncheon, he carried also, swathed in newspapers, the small loud speaker of his radio set.

"See, papa?" announced Jean-Baptiste, in a stage manner not unlike that of his elder. "I have brought just the thing to make the wonderful radio play."

Montigny was vexed. "You think this is what—a play-house! Out with you. Go home."

"Please, papa, just let me try it!"

"It might, suh, sho-nuff," suggested Wilks the porter. "It might be that. I caint see any reason we don't got some music."

"All right, try it," snapped Montigny. "But hurry. I have no time to waste."

The handsome cabinet radio in the lounge of the Dorothea had a built-in speaker, but Wilks, who was fairly familiar with the set, found a circular hole in the back through which the two terminals which served the speaker mechanism were visible. It was a matter of seconds to unhook two wires and substitute Jean-Baptiste's loud speaker. Wilks snapped on the switch.

There was an instant hum, which grew into promising static.

Wilks twirled the dial slowly, stopped at a growing disturbance. Music flooded the room—music from Toronto!

"There, there, you see! I told you!" cried Jean-Baptiste in ecstasy. "And oh, how beautifully it plays!"

Montigny conceded a mild and dignified show of interest.

"Very well, now," he said. "It plays. Not much better than your own, though. I hope you are satisfied. Take the loud speaker now, and go. I am very busy."

"I will go, papa," said Jean-Baptiste with shining eyes. "But I leave you the loud speaker so that you may have music tonight. You will be otherwise lonesome!"

Montigny patted his shoulder. "Very well. You are a good, unselfish boy. Now run along."

Montigny switched off the instrument and gave it no further thought. There was much to occupy his attention during an afternoon climaxed by the arrest and examination of Warren Decker, an event followed at dark by more important tidings from New York.

It was well past ten o'clock Friday night when Montigny, after a late dinner with Laval, returned to Bonaventure Station. He had discussed at length with the Inspector the closely crowding developments of the day.

Wilks the porter was a free man, but they would not tell him so as yet. He had not lied about the letter he had posted for his employer. The money he had hidden in the liner closet, fearful of its discovery on his person, had been in truth a gift from Milburn, a legacy, in effect, from a grateful employer.

And Aitken had been truthful at least in his assertion that Milburn had contemplated suicide. There was no element of guilt, necessarily, in the lawyer's stubborn refusal to talk, to divulge the contents of the envelope Milburn had given him. Not only would he have violated a professional confidence in doing so, he would also have forfeited a handsome bequest made to him on the explicit condition of his silence. Ten thousand dollars was not bad, for a month in jail.

And yet . . . There was a fishy whiff about that business. What had become of the original contents of Aitken's envelope—his copy of the will if he or his legal associates had not removed it? Who else could have had the opportunity to tamper with the packet? Who indeed knew anything about it, with the exception of Aitken? Had someone entered the small safe in the lounge on the night of the murder—opened the envelope and stolen its contents?

That spot of wax on the carpet—the same wax that had resealed the broken packet. Not Milburn's sealing wax. Whose, then? Obviously the missing stick from the desk of the secretary, Miss Eastwick. Who could have used it for that purpose, afterwards throwing it away?

Who, but Aitken!

Who had played tricks with the annunciator wires, the net effect of which had been—well, there was more to explain, there. The purpose of that shift, from Aitken's standpoint, was not wholly clear.

Aitken's motive? Well, ten thousand dollars, before Milburn could change his mind. Not enough there, though. Something more.

Who alone, knew of the contents of the new will—who had drawn it, four days or so before the murder? Aitken.

Still . . . Montigny checked his racing thoughts and smiled ruefully. Still, all this brought them no nearer to the actual killer. Aitken's hand had not ended the life of Milburn. The same line of reasoning applied to Perry Laith, who might have had similar motives; who might have learned of Milburn's intentions by eavesdropping at the curtains of the lounge door way.

But who could prove that Laith—or anybody else in the car—had been the slayer?

It couldn't be done, sighed Montigny, in the present state of their knowledge.

He entered the car through the front platform. There were lights in the lounge but few elsewhere, for Wilks was following orders to husband the current.

As he walked through the car Montigny heard voices in the lounge. He stopped, puzzled, to listen. What the devil! He hurried on.

There was no one in the lounge but Wilks the porter, who was toying with the radio.

Montigny leaped across the room, grabbed Wilks by the shoulders and shook him, yelling and laughing.

"Wilks! I have got it! I have found it! It is explained! I have the secret at last!"

Wilks, rolling his eyes fearfully, sought to back away from the piercing gaze and bristling mustachios of Montigny.

"Y-Yes, suh, boss! What you found?" trembled Wilks.

"The radio! Blockheads, all of us! The radio—that was what you heard when you heard 'voices' the other night— the night Milburn was killed—you heard the radio!"

Wilks stared at him, white-eyed, with dropped jaw.

"Naw, suh, boss! Couldn't a-been. How come the radio gonna play—'less there's somebody in here to play it! Ain't no dead man played a radio!"

Montigny paused in dismay.

"When you came in and found Mr. Milburn—think, now!—was the radio off, completely off?"

Wilks nodded vigorously. "Positively, boss! Offer'n it ever had been. It was dead. Not a peep out of it. This was the stillest place I ever hope to keep away from, outside a graveyard—'cept for the noise the train was making."

"You are sure the radio had not just died down—the station signing off, or something?"

"Naw, suh. Fact is, I thought it might have been the radio. I went over close and listened. I was scared, boss!"

"Go back to your galley," ordered Montigny peremptorily. "Stay there until you are called."

Montigny spoke to the constable on guard outside. "Sims, the electrician we had—do you know where to find him?"

"Yes, sir. He doesn't live far from here."

"Get him. Telephone him. Get him out of bed, if need be. Tell him I want him here—at once."

Montigny returned to the lounge with a feverish light of triumph in his eyes. And yet he was profoundly

Pursuing His Investigation of the Empty
Pullman, Sgt. Montigny
Hears the Murderer's
Voice in the
Next Room

"Sacre Bleu," Shouted Montigny, In the War-
path Tone of an Indian. "I have got it! I have
found it! I have the secret at last!" He Leaped
Across the Room, Grabbed Wilks by the
Shoulders and Shook Him.

puzzled. He stood before the radio cabinet in deep thought. He snapped on the switch. He manipulated the dial, past cacophonies of jazz and symphony and skits and sketches and speeches. A magnificent set. Even Miami and Havana came in with fine clarity—on an August night.

The sergeant retreated into the front of the car, again approached through the corridor to the lounge. In a tone slightly louder than conversational, an announcer was saying something that Montigny could not quite understand. It sounded startlingly like someone in the lounge.

"That was the method!" muttered Montigny. "And we never dreamed of it. What dubs policemen can be. But how did he work it? Perhaps Sims can tell me."

Montigny improved his interim of waiting by getting out his flashlight and magnifying glass and again going over the windows on the righthand side of the car going forward. It was on this side that the three staterooms were located. He dwelt again on the two pinhead-size holes he had found in the screen of the lounge—nearest the radio, he observed now with deep satisfaction. From the edges of these apertures, which were only slightly larger than the mesh of the fine screen, Montigny had already removed certain fine scrapings of material which under the glass seemed to be brown silk thread— the brown "whiskers" he had mentioned jokingly to Thwaite. He examined the corresponding holes in the screen of Aitken's stateroom.

He had again resorted to his fingerprint outfit and was busy with it when Sims arrived.

"Well, well, Captain!" said the cheerful electrician. "And what's the ticket tonight? Not having more trouble with your bells or your lights?"

"The radio," said Montigny, and told him all about it.

"Well, pinch me for a dead one!" exclaimed Sims. "A fine radio-ician I turn out to be! Any simp should have known it was a dead speaker, not the batteries."

"And you were not, unfortunately, 'any simp.' Now tell me this." Montigny outlined a hypothetical case. "Suppose I am at the other end of the car, or half-way, sitting on the same side of the car as the radio, the right side looking forward. The radio is going. Rudy Vallee is singing tenderly, and I am jealous. My wife is crazy about him. She will go surely to the bughouse if I do not stop him. How do I stop him? Without leaving my seat—without going near the radio? Tell me!"

Sims looked at him with an inquiring grin. "It can't be done, Captain!"

"Oh, yes, my dear Sims, it can be done. It was done. Tell me now! It's your business. You've got to know. Think!"

Sims thought. "You want to stop the radio and not go near this room? Let's see. It's an AC set. You don't mean kill the current—cut off the main switch—put out the lights on the car, too?"

"Oh, no, no, no! Simply silence the radio—not hurt it: Leave it so the tubes light up—but the speaker will not speak. And do nothing to attract anybody's attention."

Sims thought again. "Let me see! You might have a string tied to the radio switch, and running to where you are sitting. Then you could yank off the radio—but people might see the string."

"And the string might not come off the switch after you pulled it. No, not that Sims. You must silence the speaker, and leave nothing to show for it. Let me show you something."

He indicated to Sims the two tiny holes in the lounge screen and the similar holes in the screen of Stateroom B.

"I got you, Captain!" shouted Sims. "I got you spotted. You're gonna have plenty of time to fix this up in advance, are you?"

"Oh, a reasonable time. People may be watching, though. They must not see me preparing."

"Hm! All right. You get a coil of fine insulated wire, the finest made—magneto or magnet wire they call it. You go outside and while nobody is looking stick a wire, or two wires, better, through the screen of the lounge near the radio. See?"

"Yes," said Montigny intensely.

"You walk alongside the car to the window where you're gonna be sitting and stick the other ends of the wires in that screen. See?"

"Yes?"

"When you get the chance you slip back of that radio. There's a round hole and you can see the speaker terminals through it. You can hook the ends of these two fine wires to the terminal posts—just lightly, so you can pull 'em off with a little jerk. Your wires run along the floor in a corner to the window, so nobody ever notices them."

"Yes?"

"All right, you're set. When Rudy begins to sing you're sitting up at the window where the other two ends of the wires are. You poke these ends into your light socket there, hitting both contacts. Blooey!"

"What happens?"

"Rudy shuts up! Sudden. You shoot a hundred and ten volts into the speaker mechanism. Short hell out of it. Then you pull in your wires or drop 'em out the window—nobody ever knows."

"And do you hurt the set?"

"Maybe so, maybe not. A very short contact would just burn out the speaker coils, which would act like a fuse. Chances are you wouldn't hurt the set and any new speaker would play it."

"Sims," said Montigny proudly, "you are a fine detective. Now show me these speaker terminals you are talking about."

Montigny's magnifying glass disclosed more tiny scrapings of brown silk on the terminal posts where the wires had been pulled away.

"Sure, that's just what happened," said Sims.

Montigny thanked him jubilantly and sent him away.

The sergeant spent a long time in Stateroom B, searching. He had searched many a place, but never in all his career had he ransacked a room more thoroughly. He paused at intervals to look at his watch. At one o'clock sharp he turned on the radio. It was still dialed for the Chicago station. A man spoke, a somewhat nasal-voiced station announcer. Then a network announcer—a basso, if ever there was one. He was giving, he said, the aviation weather report, in cooperation with the United States Weather Bureau. It was broadcast every night at this time, he said. It was twelve o'clock in Chicago, Central time. One o'clock in Montreal—three minutes after, to be exact.

"Fiendish!" said Montigny aloud. "The ingenuity of it! And that's why he killed Milburn at one o'clock!"

The perspiration streamed from his face. He paused for a drink of water from the cooler in a corner of the stateroom, which Wilks kept iced for him. The water trickled abominably slowly. Always did, on trains, some-how.

"The devil," hissed Montigny. "Everywhere else I have looked!"

He bared his arm with a jerk, clambered up and thrust it into the cooler. He drew it out dripping. Gripped in his hand there was a sodden coil of fine wire, insulated in brown silk.

Montigny heard a shout outside, the constable's baton beating on the side of the car. He hurried out.

"What is it now?" he exclaimed impatiently.

"Hell's popping again, Sergeant!" boomed the constable. "They've killed somebody else!"

A plain clothes man was with him, panting for breath.

"Inspector sent me—car waiting," cried the detective. "Wants you over at Notre Dame Hospital—quick!"

"Who this time?" demanded Montigny, hurrying to join the newcomer.

"Dot Dustin—they say she's dying!"

The constable had got it wrong, Montigny's companion explained to him as they sped through the silent streets to Notre Dame Hospital. It was not another killing. Dorothea Dustin had been fatally hurt, but it had been an accident. She had tried to escape in an automobile—she and Perry Laith. The car, doing seventy miles with two detectives in pursuit, had gone off an embankment.

"And the Dustin girl is dying, eh?"

"That's what the doctors say. The Inspector has been trying to get her to talk, but they shot her so full of dope on account of the pain she's in, she keeps coming to and passing out again, and even when she can talk she's delirious. The Inspector wanted you with him—he always does when there's anything important stirring."

"Where is Laith? In the same hospital?"

"Yes, and he can't talk, either, or won't—says all he knows is the Dustin girl tipped him off that you had dug up some important evidence that made it look bad for the pair of them, and were going to slam both of them in jail right off. We asked him what evidence he meant, and he said he didn't know, the Dustin girl hadn't told him definitely."

"Eh, bien," murmured Montigny. "At the present mortality rate we shall soon have no one left to suspect!"

Laval met him in the corridor outside the last room Dot Dustin was to occupy. A nurse preceded them in to see if the doctor thought they might enter. The doctor came out. with pursed lips.

"She's going, Inspector, fast," he said. "She can't last half an hour. Too bad she's in this shape—she might tell you something."

Laval gestured to Montigny to enter, and followed him, closing the door softly.

Dot Dustin, with red-golden hair and lovely features tautened now by suffering, lay unconscious on the bed. She stirred, and a grimace of agony curled her lip, baring her perfect, almost translucent teeth. The long eyelashes that had lain calmly closed like those of a sleeping doll quivered, flashed open over terrified eyes.

"Oh, God!" she moaned. "Gimme the needle, Doc. Pass me out! Don't let me suffer like a broken-backed dog!"

Her agonized gaze found Laval's dark eyes, brooding in pity, for Laval at the core of his heart was very soft.

She wept in self-pity and trailed off into hysterical laughter.

She ended in a paroxysm of grief and pain so racking that it left her spent and collapsed, insensible.

The Inspector looked at Montigny and shook his head mournfully. "It's no use, Pierre! I've had twenty minutes of this. It's about all I can stand of human agony. The doctor must end it for the poor little wretch. He has held back the needle in hope that I might hear something—but I haven't the heart, Pierre, to keep it up."

"Milburn and Heston!" said Montigny coldly. "They suffered, too, Inspector. This woman killed them—she and her crony!"

"You have something new?" asked Laval quickly.

"Yes. Something very new, Inspector. Tonight I have found the proof that a person in that car—not Decker or anyone from the outside—killed Milburn—"

"Shhh!"

Dot Dustin stirred again. Her voice rambled in delirium:

"What do you mean, three hundred grand? You can't do it, I tell you! You can't bump him off and get away with it. It isn't worth the risk—you can't, I tell you! All right, you fool, but I'm out of it, get that? I'll split the gate with you if you pull it—but I don t know a thing about it, see? C'mon, boys! 'Nother little drink won't do you any good. . . . Whoopee! Le's make whoopee! That'aboy, Perry."

She burst again into hysterical song and laughter, and again her broken body was twisted in anguish until she lost consciousness.

"She mentioned Laith," muttered Laval.

"But she is rambling," said Montigny. "She was talking to Milburn, too. Everything is jumbled. Too bad. I wish we could get her to talk rationally, but I'm afraid you're right, Inspector. It's hopeless."

They were loth to leave, however. It was tantalizing. In her next breath the dying girl might give them the admission needed. They waited until she should return once more to consciousness, tacitly agreeing they would desist, after that.

Dot stirred again, moaned, spoke inaudibly, then wandered again in delirium. They were incoherent, gasping snatches now. The listening men were startled when she said suddenly:

Dot Dustin's Last Words
Identify Bob Aitken as
the Slayer; Police Plan to
Reenact the Crime

Dot Dustin, a Wrack of Red-
Golden Hair and Lovely Fea-
tures Tautened Now by Suf-
fering, Lay Unconscious on
the Bed. She Stirred, and a Grimace of
Agony Curled Her Lip, Baring Her
Perfect, Almost Translucent Teeth. The Inspector Looked at
Montigny and Shook His Head Mournfully. "It's no use, Pierre.
I haven't the heart to keep it up."

"The law? You're not afraid of the law, eh? Yeah, you've had enough to do with it—I know all about that! . . . Well, listen. Leave me out. Do you hear! Leave me out. Don't let me know, for God's sake, when you do it! . . . George—you and George— Oh, God, I can't go through with it, I—"

She lay back in terrible tension, a constricted gurgling in her throat. The watching men could endure it no longer—the end was at hand. They hurried out into the corridor and the doctor, waiting there with a nerve-stricken nurse, went in without a word to them and closed the door.

But Dot was past hypos and listening detectives, now.

There was no sound from the room, and when the doctor presently came out they saw that he had covered her with a sheet.

"She's gone, Inspector," said the doctor without emotion. "I don't know how she lasted as long as she did. The other fellow was luckier. Would you like to talk to him?"

They went to Laith's room. Sergeant Detective Thwaite and others had already interviewed him, and he was weak and spent with pain. His head was swathed with bandages and his right arm was in splints.

"She's dead?" he muttered listlessly when they told him. "I'm sorry. I guess it's just one of those things!"

"She talked of you," said Laval, "just before she died."

"She did?" Laith moved his head slightly and groaned. "What did she say about me?"

"She told us about the scheme to kill Milburn," went on Laval steadily, "for the three hundred thousand dollars she would get out of it. She said you killed him."

Perry Laith fainted.

The doctor begged off for him, admonishing: "No more for tonight, Inspector. The chap is suffering pretty

severely from shock. If you want to get something out
of him you'd better wait until tomorrow—give him half
a chance."

"Very well," said Laval, and they left the hospital.

Montigny told him, as they drove away, of his dis-
coveries in the car.

"All roads converge," said Laval, thoughtfully, "at
Aitken's door. I am a bit surprised, Pierre. I am also a
bit ashamed. The radio! How gullible we have been. I
have never had one of the things in my house—and this
is what I get for it!"

"But I have had one in my house, going forever," replied Montigny. "I have walked in the front door with
the absolute conviction that a stranger was talking in
my living room—and found it a radio announcer. Yet I
never thought of it, either, Inspector. If Wilks, when he
found Milburn's body, had also found the radio going,
why, then—"

"But the game was not to have it going; to stop it at
precisely the right moment. Diabolically simple, Pierre.
He killed Milburn a few minutes after one, because he
knew that every night at that hour, without fail, there
would be five or ten minutes of talking on the radio
from Chicago. He had previously changed the annunciator terminals, and during the long delay of the train
at Rutland he had plenty of time to fix the small wires
to the radio. He shot Milburn at one o'clock, turned
on the radio, pressed the buttons to call the porter as a
witness. A witness to two things—the voice of the killer,
supposedly, in the lounge; and the fact that Aitken himself was innocently 'asleep' in his stateroom. He had
planted the yellow Pullman receipt on the back platform
as further evidence of an outside job—he could have
picked it up on the train during the afternoon. And just
as the porter came to answer his call, he thrust the ends

of his wires into his socket, silencing the voice. Damnably ingenious! It would take a lawyer to think of it."

The car stopped at Laval's home, but they kept their seats and continued talking.

"And the Dustin woman," added Laval, "though she died before she could confess, virtually said it was Aitken. He 'knew all about the law,' was not afraid of it, had had 'enough to do with it.'"

"It dovetails," mumbled Mon tigny, lighting a cigar. "A very pretty murder. The insurance money, of course, will not be paid to the Dustin girl's estate—we have proved conspiracy. But there are loose ends, Inspector, that annoy me. If the lawyer killed Milburn in this manner, which he well may have done, who killed George Heston—and why?"

"A thug he hired to do it. Why? Heston was in on it. 'You and George,' the Dustin girl kept saying."

"And why," added Montigny, as though musing aloud, "did the second killer telephone recklessly, in a big bass voice, to let it be known he had killed Heston?"

"Because the big bass voice at the radio announcer had been heard at the time of Milburn's death—the game was to make it appear that the same man killed both of them."

"And the deep voice of the burglar who threatened the Eastwick girl with death—what of that, Inspector?"

"A likely invention," scoffed Laval, "to throw more dust in our eyes. There might have been a burglar, but the girl lied about the voice. She is hand-in-glove with Aitken."

"And the Decker chap, who says he saw the killing—you no longer suspect him, Inspector?"

Laval did not reply so readily to that. "There have been many cases in our experience, Pierre" he said presently, "in which a witness to a crime has run away, fearing he would be suspected—and has been suspected. I am inclined to think, in the light of your new findings, that this is one of those cases."

"Then if Decker spoke the truth, which I think he did, it was Aitken, wearing Perry Laith's dressing gown, who shot Milburn. But why did Aitken return the robe to his stateroom—and leave bullets in its pocket?"

"To puzzle us. Like the bark of the chicken in the conundrum—to make it harder. Suppose, too, that his other plans had gone wrong, that someone had seen him in the dimly lighted corridor of the car—would it not add to his safety to be mistaken for Perry Laith? The door of his stateroom had been left unlocked for the convenience of other men in the car. Could he not claim, if ever he was accused, that Laith or somebody had planted the robe there to incriminate him?"

Montigny smoked. "I am keeping you up all hours, Inspector," he apologized, "but the puzzle gnaws at my brain. Ono or two other points and I desist. Why, if Aitken killed his employer, must he throw suspicion on himself by withholding from us the fact of the new will?"

A long pause preceded Laval's answer. "He destroyed it, of course. That was part of his agreement with Dorothea Dustin—it would have cost them one hundred thousand dollars if the new will came to light."

"But why the blank paper in the supposed packet of documents? Did he destroy, as he thought, all copies of the will, or was he afraid others would show up later?"

"Probably that. He opened the envelope, discovered that Milburn had held out two copies of the will. He hoped they would turn up safely, later, but meanwhile he must bluff us. He must make it appear, too, that he had been robbed by conspirators on the car. All was planned to add to his safety if accused—even his harping on 'suicide,' which he knew we would take seriously. Don't you see that it all works out to make him appear as the innocent victim, rather than the arch crook himself?"

"Yes, Inspector," agreed Montigny hesitantly. "You explain much. You clarify it beautifully. You clear up every point except the sealing wax."

Laval snorted. "The sealing wax! Are we coming back to that, Pierre?"

"It seems trivial," said Montigny softly, "yet we do not want one single small discrepancy to creep into our perfect case, do we, Inspector?"

"All right. Out with it."

"The envelope which Aitken posted to Dalbey & Pitts in Montreal was sealed—but not resealed—with the sealing wax we found in Milburn's desk."

"It was not. We learned that."

"A spot from the stick with which it was resealed dropped on the floor near the desk."

"Well?"

"The resealing, in other words, was done at that desk on the night of the murder."

"True. The envelope was posted the same night."

15

"Then if it was Aitken who removed the contents, substituting blank paper, what did he do with the original contents? He did not leave the car—he sent nothing out but the sealed packet—"

"Somebody else," interrupted Laval, "made away with the documents for him—and I think it was the clever and able Miss Eastwick."

"And the stick of wax?"

"She took that, too. Or he threw it away."

Montigny nodded slowly. "I should like to have track-walkers tomorrow, at St. Johns, Lacadie, Brousseau and Ranelagh—the points the train passed before stopping at St. Lambert. I should like to offer twenty dollars reward for a certain 'small red or brown object' that might be picked up along the railroad track."

Laval laughed. "Ye gods, your thoroughness! And if you get it—what will you have?"

"Warm wax may leave, Inspector, not only fingerprints, but congealed fingerprints, which days and nights or weather and constant handling would not destroy."

Laval grew sober. "And that would clinch our case, Montigny," he exclaimed. "You are right. You are always right! . . . And I am going to bed. You are returning, I suppose, to the station?"

"Yea," said Montigny, bidding him good night. "But I have, before dawn," he added, as the detective who was driving started the motor, "just one more room to search."

The week-end following the Tuesday night on which J. Proctor Milburn had met his death saw a regathering in Montreal of all individuals who had taken part in the inquiry.

Moode, Lennox, and Helen Eastwick arrived on an early train from New York, and with them was Captain Berthier of the Provincial Police, who informed them that he also had been on the same train with them Wednesday night when they departed from Montreal, though he had been closeted in a drawing room most of the time conferring with the officials from Washington.

"Didn't notice any delay at Rouses Point, did you?" he asked Lennox with a wink.

Lennox had, but Berthier would say no more on the subject. Berthier liked to be mysterious.

There was an early conference in Laval's office, at which all old and new points of discussion were threshed out thoroughly, and Lennox made report in detail of his New York accomplishments.

"Well, it turned out as I said it would, from the start," declared Captain Berthier, with a self-satisfied air. "My advice to you is to lock up the Eastwick girl, too. She's dangerous running around—if it hadn't been for Moode, here, she would have got possession of those copies of Milburn's will and we would still be in the dark on that point."

"She is under surveillance," said Laval. "She will not get away. I am uncertain as yet whether she was actually implicated in the crime. She has done what Aitken told her to do, no doubt, not knowing the full significance of her acts."

"I think you're wrong about that New York affair of the burglar, Inspector," asserted Detective Lennox. "I was there a few minutes afterwards and I'm certain the girl had had a terrible scare. She was hurt, too, though that might have happened when she fell and hit her head against a corner."

"Oh, it's possible there was a prowler around," conceded Captain Berthier generously. "He got her pocketbook, which is just what a thief would nick. And I suppose she imagined the rest. Still, I wouldn't trust her far, Inspector. She has been too thick with this fellow Aitken to suit me."

"She will do no harm," said Laval calmly. "She asked permission to see Aitken this morning, which I refused. She seemed to think, curiously enough, that the discovery of the will copies in New York had cleared Aitken completely. She was quite astonished when I told her otherwise."

"Well, what remains to be done?" asked Berthier, in a summing-up tone. "It appears to me you have a complete case to turn over to the Prosecutor, as to the murder of Milburn."

Laval toyed with a letter knife. "And as to Heston?"

"Well, we haven't got anything much there, have we? Still, I think the man will confess, implicate his confederate. These birds all hate to go to the gallows alone. It wasn't the Decker chap that did Heston in—that's certain, isn't it?"

"Absolutely. His alibi is unassailable. Two waiters at the tavern and also the man Jones, who was with him, bear him out. And I am inclined to accept his story of what happened while he was on the back platform of

Milburn's car. I am inclined to let him go—under bond, of course, to assure his appearance when we need him."

"Good!" applauded Sergeant Detective Thwaite. "I knew you'd do that, Inspector. I never for a minute believed that fellow did it."

"I shall do nothing, however," added Laval, "until Montigny has finished a certain supplementary investigation he had in hand. He wants to have tonight another 'reconstruction' of the murder of Milburn—tonight at one o'clock—under conditions as nearly a possible identical with the actual conditions of the crime."

"On the car?" queried Berthier, a bit annoyed.

"On the car. And this time attached to a moving train as it pulls out of St. Johns. There is a freight leaving St. Johns at that hour which will hook us on for the purpose."

"Say!" objected Captain Berthier. "Isn't that carrying things a bit too far—keeping up everybody half the night, for nothing?"

"It will be an interesting experiment, and probably useful, Captain. For instance, we shall be able to demonstrate exactly to what extent the voice over the radio would be deceptive, with the noise of the moving train to interfere. Mrs. Heston, unfortunately, is not here—I permitted her to go back to New York, of course, with the body of her husband. But we shall have Wilks as a witness, and there are other details which Montigny wishes to study. I am afraid that trickster may have something up his sleeve."

"Well. I'll be with you, promised Berthier, "though I can't quite see the sense of it. Got to run along now. There's an ocean of work waiting for me at the office.

Sergeant Montigny, it had been noted, was present at the conference for only a part of its duration. He had been summoned out for a telephone call and afterwards had been busy for a considerable time in the room where he kept his mercury light with the quartz burner. When he returned to Laval's office the conference had dispersed. With an odd glint in his eye he departed for Bonaventure Station and the private car Dorothea. He questioned a great many people about the station, including a number of customs inspectors.

Sergeant Detective Bill Thwaite, upon departing from Laval's office, had made his way resolutely to a telephone booth and had conversed with a certain party at the Hotel Strathcona.

A certain bull-necked dick, he reflected humorously as he regarded his broad visage in the mirror of the washroom at headquarters, was certainly getting to be a ladies' man these days.

Lotus Decker was waiting to be taken to luncheon. Sergeant Thwaite felt that he had expended a lot of time and energy upon the winning of her confidence, and the effect of that valuable preparation must not be wasted. It was, in fact, imperative that he keep on interviewing her, for he might get a lot more information out of her yet.

He had warned her that he had good news for her, and her face was wistfully eager when she met him. He declined to tell her what it was, however, until they had ordered luncheon. He said she needed a good strong feed before she heard anything, and that was true, for the death of Dorothea Dustin, of which she had learned upon first awakening, had appalled and depressed her.

"She might not have been a good woman," said Lotus, her eyes bright with tears, "but she was good to me when I needed a friend."

"You're a loyal little cuss," approved Thwaite. "But your confidence was misplaced in that one. You got in with the wrong sort of crowd, honey, and it wasn't your fault. You're as decent a little thoroughbred as ever a big-footed sergeant of detectives asked to marry him—"

"You shut up, Bill Thwaite, and tell me what the good news is you promised me. I need it, Lordie knows I need it!"

"All right, it's about your brother. They're going to turn him loose!"

Lotus almost bounced from her chair with joy, and she did lean forthwith over the table, much to the astonishment of many diners and the rubicund dismay of Bill Thwaite, and kiss him—smack!

"I knew it, I knew it!" chortled Lotus. "I knew you were going to get him free for me!"

"I didn't do it," protested Thwaite with a dry grin. "Inspector Laval and Montigny did it." He glanced around self-consciously.

"I'm sorry if I disgraced you," said Lotus contritely. "I couldn't help it. Now tell me the rest."

Thwaite told her all of the rest that he thought she ought to know, which was much more than Inspector Laval would have sanctioned but Thwaite was irresponsible now.

"Anyhow, they're going to hang on to him for a few days as a material witness, and after that he may have to rake up a good stiff bond, but that can be arranged, all right. And you can go home, the Inspector says, any time you want to."

"I won't go home," pouted Lotus. "I don't want to go home. I won't be sent home like this!"

"Who's sending you home?"

"You are—talking about it."

"Well, will you—would you like to—" stumbled Thwaite, wholly crimson, "that is, could you stay on, maybe, as Mrs. Bill Thwaite!"

"Oh, that's different," said Lotus mischievously. "There's a long waiting list ahead of you. You'd have to ask my mama, or my big brother. You see I'm just a chee-ild. But I guess they wouldn't mind having a real live detective in the family—after all this we need one!"

"All right," said Thwaite, his blue eyes bright with glee. "I'll take care of your brother's permission. I've got him where I want him. If he says no I'll put him under the jail!"

He informed her that she had a date with him that evening to ride to St. Johns on the private car, returning between one and two o'clock. That suited her admirably.

"Who's going?" she wanted to know. "The whole bunch?"

"All but Laith; he's too banged up. And Aitken. He stays in jail. I'm afraid things look pretty black for that chap."

"Oh, I can't believe it, Bill. It's out of all reason."

"A lot of fellows fool you," Thwaite reminded her. "A lot of fellows think the only thing wrong about breaking the law is getting caught. And this slick bird didn't count on getting caught."

"I'm so sorry for poor Helen Eastwick—she's terribly in love with Bob. She was all broken up this morning. She could hardly talk to me. Is she going, too, tonight?"

"Yep. And that remind me. I've got to go over to the hospital pretty soon. The Inspector's got to put Laith through the mill, to see what he can be made to tell."

The determined and necessarily unpleasant grilling of Laith that afternoon, however, was to yield no results.

Laith broke down from weakness and sheer nervous collapse, after two hours of it, and he was in no condition to be questioned further.

He swore he had told the truth, completely and in every detail, that he knew nothing whatsoever of any

plot to murder J. Proctor Milburn, that he did not believe Dot Dustin could have been capable of being a
party to it.

Laval at length desisted. Laith was docketed as a
prisoner with orders for his removal to jail when his
condition permitted.

"I don't know what Miss Dustin 'confessed' to you,
Inspector," he declared, "but if it concerned me it was
wholly untrue. It seems to me that you rely for my conviction upon dreadfully frail evidence."

The Inspector, however, was hopeful of more definite
things from his lieutenant, Montigny.

Montigny could be blandly secretive, and he was so
today. He did not as a rule confide important suspicions
to Inspector Laval until he had been at long pains to
substantiate them. But Laval knew the look in his eye
which meant that Montigny, in his own cherished way,
was preparing to spring something.

On the twenty-seven-mile trip to St. Johns that night,
where the Dorothea was to be side-tracked until the
departure of the northbound one o'clock freight, Montigny advanced nothing new in his conversation with
the Inspector and Captain Berthier. He talked about the
weather.

"Atmospheric conditions," he reported with satisfaction, "are almost identical with the conditions pre-
vailing last Tuesday night. I learned that from McGill
Observatory."

The porter, at Montigny's suggestion, had made
down all berths in the car as they had been arranged on
the night of the murder. Captain Berthier, he suggested, could take the place of Mrs. Heston, in the upper
berth across from the section which had been occupied
by Moode and Perry Laith. Detective Ansley impersonated Laith—they might as well have a complete cast of

characters, Montigny pointed out—Detective Porter
was to occupy the lower berth where the unfortunate
George Heston had slept, and Sergeant Thwaite should
go into Stateroom A, which had been occupied by Dorothea Dustin.

Detective Moode was sulky. Like Captain Berthier,
he thought it was all a lot of foolishness, though he
did not say it in so many words. He had complained to
everybody who would listen to him that on his return
to his boarding house in Montreal he had found that a
sneak thief had gone into his room and stolen, as he had
jocularly feared before he left, his extra pair of pants.

"Montigny went over and locked your room, as soon
as he had the chance," said Thwaite sharply, for he was
getting tired of it.

"Were they the same pants you wore last Tuesday
night, Mr. Moode?" asked Montigny slyly.

"Yeah. But that don't help me any."

At half-past twelve o'clock, as they waited at St.
Johns, Montigny began the re-enactment of the crime.
He seemed to savor his role as master of ceremonies.

"We know," he reminded his audience, "that at half-
past twelve Mr. Milburn was conferring with Robert
Aitken in the lounge. Mr. Moode heard them talking
in here at that hour, and Aitken admits he continued
in conference with Mr. Milburn until twelve-forty. All
right. That conference, we will say, is now in progress. The train has crossed the border, is approaching
St. Johns. Mr. Milburn has previously called upon you,
Miss Eastwick, to open the small wall-safe for him, having forgotten the combination. In the safe, no doubt,
were the copies of the last will and testament which
Aitken had prepared for him."

"Mr. Milburn also had asked me," declared Helen Eastwick, in a voice taut with strain, "to address a large manila envelope to Mr. Aitken, and to type upon it, 'Not to be opened until September eighteenth.' I did so."

"Very well, we must hurry," cautioned Montigny, glancing at his watch. "If we don't we shall be behind schedule. Mr. Milburn, then, sealed something in the envelope which he gave to Aitken." Montigny spoke swiftly now, for the private car was already in process of being switched to position behind the caboose of the freight train. "He sealed the envelope," continued Montigny, "with the stick of sealing wax which we found in this desk. He had previously entrusted to the porter another envelope, addressed to Mr. Aitken care the American Express Company, in Calcutta, India. And this envelope Wilks, without the knowledge of anyone else, posted at St. Johns. Is that right. Wilks?"

"Yes, suh," said the porter apprehensively. "That's right."

"Very well," said Montigny grimly. "It is nearly one. We are ready for the killing. Everybody to his post."

Only Laval remained at Montigny's side.

"The killer," whispered Montigny, "stood here at the doorway, behind the curtains. Milburn was asleep, or nodding."

He fired one of the air pistols.

"Anybody hear a shot?" he shouted.

Several answering calls asserted the negative.

Montigny swiftly made his way to the wall-safe in the lounge, fumbled with its dial, allowed the time that would have been necessary for the culprit to remove something from it—to open and reseal an envelope. Then he switched on the radio—it was already carefully dialed for Chicago. The freight train had started with a jerk. Montigny hurried back to the dining room and pressed a button.

"Hear me, Miss Eastwick?" he called.

"Only your voice—now!"

Montigny hurried to the lounge, pressed another button there, and disappeared into Aitken's stateroom before the porter had emerged from the galley at the front of the car.

At two minutes after one a nasal-voiced station announcer called his letters from Chicago, and the deeper-voiced New York announcer launched into the aviation weather report.

"That's what I heard!" cried Wilks as he applied at the door of Stateroom B.

The voices in the lounge suddenly were silenced. Montigny had thrust the ends of two wires into an electric light socket.

"All right," said Montigny. "Now discover the body, and return to this door as you did Tuesday night."

They went back together to reenact the awakening of Moode. Then Montigny called the others to the dining room.

"Are you satisfied, Captain?" he asked Berthier. "Could you hear, as Mrs. Heston said she did, the bells, Wilks knocking at the door of the stateroom, the voices in the lounge?"

"Perfectly," declared Berthier. "That's the way it was done, all right. I could hear the voices, but not what they said. They sounded very natural. But how did you get on to it? Tell us that, Montigny. It was a splendid piece of work!"

Montigny paused and looked about him keenly.

"I will tell you," he said, "and you will laugh. It was a trick of palmistry."

"I told you that you would laugh," asserted Montigny solemnly. "I must find the right kind of palm before I can show you what I mean—one in which the life line and the head line are far apart—really, this must occur in both hands. Let me see your palms. Captain Berthier."

Berthier extended them with a humorous growl.

"Not the right kind," declared Montigny. "Yours, Sergeant Thwaite. . . . Wrong again. . . . Let me see yours, Miss Eastwick. . . . Decidedly wrong! . . . How about yours, Mr. Moode?"

Moode extended his left hand grudgingly.

"Your right, too, please," requested Montigny politely.

Quicker than the astonished eyes of all in the car were the deft hands of Montigny.

He had snapped a pair of gleaming manacles on the wrists of Moode, the private detective.

With the bellow of an enraged bull, Moode struck at Montigny, hammer-wise, his ironed fists clenched, and Moode sprang through the doorway that led to the front of the car.

Thwaite, recovering, was first to leap after him. Lotus Decker screamed.

Moode, reaching the vestibule of the car, open where it coupled to the caboose of the freight train, stepped the gap there, found the iron ladder of the caboose, in a trice was on its top, and off across the train. He had hesitated a moment, considering a desperate leap, but the speed of the train was too great.

Thwaite followed, and behind him clambered Porter and Lennox. They raced after Moode, across the lurching roofs of the freight cars.

Moode, seeing the hopelessness of flight, turned to make a stand. Reaching his hip pocket despite his manacles, he drew a pistol and laid it carefully at his feet. Lying at full length he grasped his weapon, took careful aim, resting his elbows to steady himself, and fired at Thwaite. The detective dropped with a pierced left arm.

Moode had taken him by surprise. Thwaite had not believed the pursued man was armed.

Porter and Lennox also had fallen flat. The conductor of the freight was signaling the engineer frantically
to stop. The train was slowing down.

Thwaite took deliberate aim at the spot where the
last flash had appeared, and shot Moode through the
neck. The tracks at this point were on a slight embankment, and the wounded man rolled off the car and free
of the train as it ground to a stop.

They found the huge body crumpled and inert. Moode
was severely wounded, they could see, and the fall from
the train evidently had injured him, too.

It was a voluble group that besieged Montigny in the
room adjoining that where Moode lay, attended by the
vigilant doctor. Lotus and Helen Eastwick were not admitted; they had been sent back, protesting, to the car.

"It was the only way, Inspector." Montigny lighted
his inevitable cigar. "My evidence was slight. I had to
surprise him—to force him to betray himself."

"You think Moode was in on it—that he helped kill
Milburn?" demanded Captain Berthier, perhaps the
most astonished man of all.

"He did not 'help'—he killed Milburn—alone. He
also killed George Heston."

"Oh, come, now!" admonished Berthier irritably.
"Don't expect us to believe the impossible. He was not
in Montreal when Heston was killed."

"He killed Heston," said Montigny steadily, "and
you, Captain Berthier, helped him get away."

"Unwittingly of course," amended Montigny. "I
learned of it only today, from something you had
said to Detective Lennox. You doubled back from an

The Reenactment of the Crime Proves
Too Much for One of
the Detectives and
the Killer
Is Caught

They Found the Huge Body Crumpled and Inert Beside the Tracks.
Moode Was Severely Wounded, They All Could See, and the Fall
From the Train Evidently Had Injured Him, Too.

uncompleted trip to Quebec last Wednesday night. Your train got in too late to catch the eight-thirty Express, on which your important Washington officials had reservations for New York. Is that right?"

"Yes," said Berthier, glowering.

"You knew you would arrive too late to make that train. But you could—and did—catch the nine o'clock Limited. And you had wired ahead from up the line to have the Express held up at Rouses Point, to await the arrival there of the Limited."

"Yes, I did that," exclaimed the choleric Captain. "I had a right to—official business. But what the devil has that got to do with it?"

"Moode learned of your order. He heard of it at Bonaventure Station Wednesday night. It gave him an idea. Some of the customs men had talked about it, they admitted to me today. They said you wouldn't have had the nerve to hold up a train in Montreal, but at the border it was different—the railroads are used to delays there. So Moode placed his grips on the eight-thirty Express, gave his ticket to the porter, and said he was going up to the baggage car to see about something. He telephoned Inspector Laval from Bonaventure Station— we traced the call. He walked to the Strathcona Hotel, three blocks away, strangled George Heston, the man who 'knew too much,' telephoned down in his assumed bass voice—and thus established the time of the murder, to fix his alibi. Then he stepped over to Windsor Station, only one block away, boarded the nine o'clock Limited, rode a smoker to Rouses Point and changed, unnoticed, to the waiting Express, as you did."

"Good God!" exclaimed the staggered Captain. "And nobody ever thought of it!"

"He took a long chance at that," observed Detective Lennox. "If anybody had seen him—"

"He was a desperate man," said Montigny. "An infernally clever man, too, with a mask of stupidity for his protection. Thursday night, when the New York police thought he was in Baltimore, he broke in Miss Eastwick's apartment, to steal her keys and to look for the missing copies of Milburn's will. Luckily for her she fainted and hurt herself, or we might have had a third murder to solve."

"And how," demanded Laval, "did you convince yourself that he killed Milburn?"

Montigny smiled. "His extra pair of pants, Inspector. It was I who stole them when I searched his room a second time last night. The first time I had found nothing. This time, in one of the cuffs of these trousers—a spot of melted sealing wax that had fallen there, adhered to the fabric, when he resealed Aitken's envelope last Tuesday night. It was identical with the spot of sealing wax on the floor near Milburn's desk."

"You did not find the stick?"

"No, Inspector, but I did not need it. The dust on the window ledge of Moode's berth—on the same side of the car as Aitken's stateroom—showed the place where the wires to the radio had passed. He had drawn the wires under the screen. He had punched two holes in Aitken's screen, had hidden the coil of wire in Aitken's stateroom. He was not sure that his radio alibi would work, perhaps. He took too deliberate pains to cover his tracks in case it didn't. The annunciator trick had a double purpose—it woke up an extra witness for the 'voices' in the lounge, and it seemed, in a manner, to incriminate Aitken. Even the dressing gown of Perry Laith, I am satisfied, he thought was Aitken's, because it hung in Aitken's state-room."

"The documents he stole from Aitken, I suppose, he destroyed."

"Yes, but we do not need them. We have the copies. The hundred thousand dollar insurance policy, of course, is useless to anyone. Dorothea Dustin's heirs, if any, cannot profit by it. We have proved conspiracy between the Dustin woman and Moode, to murder J. P. Milburn for the doubled money the policy would bring, and for the additional bequest that would have been hers if the last will was suppressed. You heard her last night, Inspector—the three hundred 'grand' was to be split between her and the man who 'knew all about the law,' the killer. Detective Moode. Heston figured in on it somehow. I have been hoping that Moode himself could tell us about that."

Laval had another question on his lips, but the door to the adjoining room opened and the doctor beckoned, cautioning them to silence.

"He is mumbling something, Inspector," said the doctor. "He seems in great pain, but I think his mind is clear."

The wounded man's eyes were filmy, but there was a light of recognition in them as they rested on Laval.

"Moode," the Inspector told him, "you can't get over this. The doctor says you are going to die. I want you to tell me the truth. Did you kill Milburn—with the knowledge of Dorothea Dustin?"

Moode's features twisted into a grimace of agony. He swallowed painfully. But he answered, in a guttural whisper:

"Yes. I talked her into the scheme. I was on to the new will—he had cut her off—talking about killing himself. That meant she wouldn't have got one buck."

"And Heston? You killed him, too?"

Moode rested as though to gather strength for the effort. His thick lip curled. "Yes, damn him—"

A gurgle ended the sentence. Moode's head fell back with a jerk. His eyes stared starkly at the ceiling.

"He is dead," said the doctor.

COACHWHIP PUBLICATIONS
COACHWHIPBOOKS.COM

COACHWHIP PUBLICATIONS

CoachwhipBooks.com

**VULTURES
IN THE SKY**
A HUGH RENNERT MYSTERY

Todd Downing

COACHWHIP PUBLICATIONS
CoachwhipBooks.com

I'll Hate Myself in the Morning

Murder on the Left Bank

Elliot Paul

COACHWHIP PUBLICATIONS
CoachwhipBooks.com

NARROW
GAUGE TO
MURDER

Carolyn Thomas

COACHWHIP PUBLICATIONS
CoachwhipBooks.com

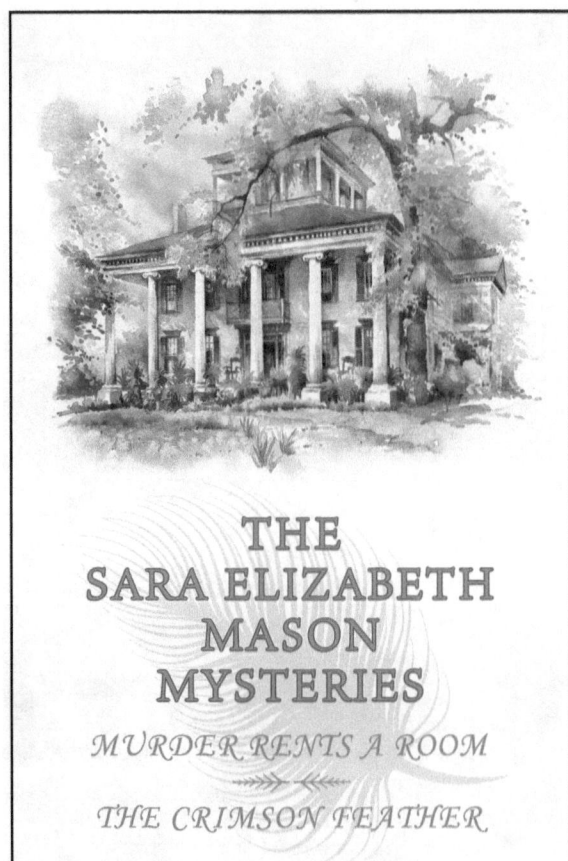

THE
SARA ELIZABETH
MASON
MYSTERIES

MURDER RENTS A ROOM

⋙ ⋘

THE CRIMSON FEATHER

COACHWHIP PUBLICATIONS

CoachwhipBooks.com